*To Thelma
with best
Avalon Weston
Nov. 2016*

A Midwife Abroad

by

Avalon Weston

Published in 2013 by FeedARead.com Publishing – Arts Council funded

Copyright © The author as named on the book cover.

First Edition

The author has asserted their moral right under the Copyright, Designs and Patents Act, 1988, to be identified as the author of this work.

All Rights reserved. No part of this publication may be reproduced, copied, stored in a retrieval system, or transmitted, in any form or by any means, without the prior written consent of the copyright holder, nor be otherwise circulated in any form of binding or cover other than that in which it is published and without a similar condition being imposed on the subsequent purchaser.

A CIP catalogue record for this title is available from the British Library.

A MIDWIFE ABROAD

Contents

Prologue: Somewhere in Sub Saharan Africa
Chapter One: The Raid
Chapter Two: Night Calls
Chapter Three: Comings and Goings
Chapter Four: The Dreamtime or Cloud Cuckoo Land
Chapter Five: The Adventure
Chapter Six: The Dawning
Chapter Seven: Sunday Lunch
Chapter Eight: What happened next.
Chapter Nine: Communications
Chapter Ten: Each to their own
Chapter Eleven: Confrontations
Chapter Twelve: An Ending
Chapter Thirteen: Home Sweet Home
Chapter Fourteen: Another Ending

Cover: J Russell
Based on image by Brendon Crème/Caters

A Midwife Abroad

PROLOGUE

Africa: Gamma, a village on the edge of the Kalahari Desert

The watcher saw the car winding along the track through the camp, over the dry sand and between the rows of wooden houses. It crawled, both flashers winking. Exceptionally all he could hear was the sound of the birds. Every bar and Cuca shop was shut. Every speaker system was turned off. As the cortege reached the grave he heard the powerful raw sound of the women's voices rise through the silence, singing their hymns to the dead child.

He saw the family get out of the car. The grandmother walked to the graveside and bending over handed the small bundle to the man standing shoulder deep in the hole in the sand. The man took the child and laid her on the grave floor. He took the other things the family gave and placed them on the little bundle. The other two men then reversed their shovels and pointed the handles towards him. He grasped them and was pulled up out of the grave.

As the three men shovelled, the singing swelled, many of the crowd joining their voices with those of the women's choir. The men piled sand up until a mound was visible and then added thorn bushes to deter curious animals.

When the grave looked satisfactory to all, the singing stopped and the crowd melted away. The watcher from his vantage point on the water tower recorded the picture in his mind in order to relate it later to his masters. There had been so many people, just to bury a baby. He was uneasy. He was unsure that this time all had gone according to plan. He climbed down and slipped away.

CHAPTER ONE

The Raid

England: Rymouth, a county town in the West Country

"All Right people – in we go."

The crack of the breaking glass was different from the crackle of the ice on the ridges of the frozen cart track they had just left. The freezing fog had been an unexpected complication but now they'd finally found the right field it was working in their favour. Getting through the hedge and fence had been simple. The building too, was surprisingly unprotected. The five invaders expected to find cats and dogs and maybe mice and rats. All the cages however were empty. They were puzzled. Clearly there had been animals here. The long corridor was lined with empty cages but none showed signs of recent habitation. All were scrubbed clean and smelt of disinfectant.

They moved through the building and at the end found a more secure looking section, with newer looking fittings. The leader levered the door open with a crowbar.

The blast of heat hit them in the face. Before them they saw a familiar sight. This was definitely a laboratory. Here were cages and benches, glass tanks and freezers, expensive looking digital machinery and rows of bottles of chemicals on shelves but frustratingly almost no animals.

They hadn't expected to find monkeys. Certainly not the two elderly chimpanzees who admittedly did seem pleased to see them, but who apparently had no intention of being liberated, even when their cage doors were opened.

The raiders held a quick conference.

'There's supposed to be something here. This was a Number One priority site. That's what London said.' It was Jemal who spoke, 'and all we've found is a laptop and two chimps.'

The leader made his decision.

'We'll just have to trash it. Let's get the pictures and do it'

So that was what they did. Using the crowbars they cracked and destroyed each and every glass tank. They bent and broke every cage. They opened the freezers, ripped their plugs off and sprayed the insides with aerosols of red paint. They smashed every glass jar and bottle and threw the complicated, delicate looking machines down hard onto the floor. The only other living inhabitants they found inside the laboratory beside the chimpanzees were insects of various kinds. Given that they had discovered nothing else to liberate, these were freed as their glass vivariums were smashed. Even those who freed them were aware that their liberated lifespan wasn't going to be long, having been released from a tropical tank into a freezing English January night.

Within twenty minutes the destruction was complete. They took their photographs, both of the damage and the chimps. The five stood back and inspected their work. Their blitzkrieg was total. The only thing they had kept safe was the laptop found hidden in a drawer and it was now in Jemal's backpack.

There were alarmed whimpering noises from the cages in the corner. The two old chimpanzees had not liked the destruction and were cowering in the furthest corner of their cages. Both had greying fur. One, obviously a very old lady, had her hands over her head as if in an attempt to shut out what was happening around her. Their distress was heartrendingly apparent.

The smallest of the invaders seeing a pile of bananas and apples on a shelf stripped off her black glove and peeling the banana held it out. The old chimpanzee recognised the gesture, came forward, took the offering and settled herself next to its maker. Sal stroked the animal's head and put her arm round its shoulders. The old lady reciprocated, putting hers firmly round the young woman's waist.

'What are we going to do with them?'
'We can't take them with us'
'There is no where to send them.'

They had come prepared to free caged rats and mice and rescue dogs and cats but not chimpanzees the size and weight of ten year old children.

'They'll have to stay.'
'But we've just buggered up the heating system. Look, she's cold.'

It was true the old lady was beginning to shiver.

'We'll have to call the fuzz ourselves. We can't leave them to freeze.'

Looks were exchanged. It was a consensus.

'Right, agreed. But now, that means we've really got to move. We can't hang about.'

They looked around again. There was a bale of straw in the corner and white lab coats behind the door. Sal took off her black anorak and held it out towards the elderly chimpanzee. The animal seemed to know exactly what to do and like a small child in nursery school put one arm after the other carefully into the sleeves. Her wannabe liberators were not to know that the two animals' previous employment had been in a circus menagerie and they had been well trained to ape their betters.

'You can't give it that.'

'Its OK I got it from Oxfam. No one can trace it to me.'

The police arrived a further twenty minutes later, summoned by an anonymous phone call from a nearby phone box. They found the two animals, covered in straw, one wearing a black coat, both cowering in the middle of a scene, clearly the outcome of major vandalism. Their first impressions were that the apes were the cause, but the red paint, the logo and the systematic nature of the destruction made the two men who'd arrived in the panda car change their minds. They called in the incident and asked for backup. Then looking at the scene considered their options.

'They'll need to get a vet and the RSPCA. We're not going in there with those creatures loose.'

'Who called it in? Can we talk to him?'

'Guy wouldn't give his name. Said he heard breaking glass when he stopped for a slash. Probably scared we'll breathalyse him if we see him tonight.'

'Well we'll have to stay here till the cavalry arrives. First time I've had to be a Zoo keeper!'

Settling themselves in the car, outside the front door with the broken glass panel, they waited for reinforcements.

*

A few miles away the invaders had reached base. The post-mortem began. The group sat around a glowing red stove, fuelled partly with the socks they had worn over their shoes, their balaclavas and anything else felt likely to bear a physical traceable connection with the lab. The leader was sanding the blades of the bolt-cutters they'd used to cut through the fence. No marks were going to be traceable back to this particular pair.

'Well, will someone tell me what we've just done and why?' The speaker was Logo, logistics organiser for the group who had been on at least a dozen raids.

'Where were the animals? Why was our intelligence crap?' said Vix, a newer younger recruit to the cause, who drove the van.

'Like I said, London said it was a No. 1 priority site. No one told me exactly why, but they were insistent,' answered Jemal, whose responsibility was information.

The leader, a veteran of the previous generation, with twenty years of such activities behind him, took up the argument.

'That place has changed hands recently hasn't it? Are we just out of date? Or is something going on? Used to be something different. It was hit a few years ago. Then it used to supply beagles to labs. When they went in, they found, on top of everything else it was filthy. This time is was spotless, smelt like a hospital.'

'Not that clean,' said Sal showing the red insect bite mark on her hand that she'd been scratching, 'Those chimps had fleas.'

'None of this helps,' said Vix. 'What counts is what is we are going to do about THEM. We should have brought them with us.'

'You know we couldn't. Calling the fuzz was the best we could do.'

'But how did they get there? Where have they come from?'

'That's anybody's guess. They're valuable, especially since they're protected now and can't be imported. And there is no other animal as good for AIDS research. And anyone who has them, menageries and photographers can make a good bit by selling them to the labs. Nobody wants holiday snaps of themselves and a chimp these days.'

'Cats and dogs are bad enough, but chimps...' said Sal.

Logo interrupted her.

'Aren't we having a little philosophical problem here? Aren't all animals equal or do you find some more equal than others?'

His tone wasn't entirely kind. This sort of discussion arose whenever the group moved their focus away from a particular target and into the theoretical basis for their actions.

'There's an answer to that. You know there is. That's what that lot in the Great Ape Project are about. They want apes to stop being

property and have rights – "Life, Liberty and Freedom from torture." '
It was Vix who spoke.

'That's what I'm saying.' replied Logo. 'Getting sentimental about how human gorillas are doesn't help all those rats in labs being fed shampoo.'

Sal re-entered the battle.

'But if we get human rights extended to apes then we've broken the barrier which makes humans special. We've started by moving the goalposts. And anyway,' she went on, 'it was so amazing to be close to that old lady chimp. You could feel her thinking. I do want to free every caged rat in the universe but the thought of anyone using those two old chimps for experiments – and that was what they must have been doing. That was a lab. Makes me so angry...'

'Some more equal than others eh?'

'Like I said. It's where we're at. They are what we've got to sort out today. The rest of the world tomorrow. What are we going to do about them?'

It was another half an hour of to and fro argument, before they came up with a plan all were happy with.

Publicity seemed their only weapon. After some thought, they decided to avail themselves of the services of a place that "Offered support services to local community groups."

'They've got good computers, graphics, and scanners and everything. We can write all our stuff there, include the photos and send it out as a press release to the local papers and all the national charities and then we can put it on the net. Then there will be such a fuss someone will find a proper home for those chimps.'

'Won't they check what we're doing?'

'Naw, they're careful not to. When they just had typewriters we used to do the Hunt Sab stuff there for years and photocopy there. They're on our side but have to stay neutral to keep their grant. We'll go there tomorrow. Then we can take everything to London and post it there.'

'Will that do it? Will somewhere rescue them?'

'Sure it will. Think of those Americans. They're setting up a sanctuary for all the space chimps. Think of the number they've got to find room for. We've only got to persuade someone to take in two.'

It was the moment to adjourn but the young woman called Sal, stood up. Standing, she felt she could look down at the others while she made her announcement.

'Look I'm sorry, that was my last outing for a while. I'm stopping. I'm pregnant.'

She paused but continued in a rush before anyone else could jump in. 'I know, I know. There are too many people. Our species is dominating the planet.'

'You said it.'

'Well I'm sorry, but I want a baby. So we're moving on and we'll have to stay away from all this. I'll have to register with clinics and hospitals and such.'

Her audience didn't congratulate. The atmosphere was odd. An outsider observing might have suggested that jealousy was the emotion floating in the air.

'We're going now,' said Vix. He rose as well and stood behind the young woman. The other three looked surprised, but it seemed to settle the matter. There was no more criticism, implicit or explicit.

'Bye then.'

'Bye.'

And that was it. The two of them left the circle of firelight and set off on foot back to their own place, holding hands.

CHAPTER TWO

Night calls

England: Rymouth, A county town in the West Country

The phone rang. The midwife sighed. She was on call and it was Saturday night. She'd been about to go to bed. She picked up the instrument.

'Sister Larriot. It is you covering for Hatherley Common isn't it?'

'Yes, 'Fraid so – what've you got for me?'

'It's a Mr Vix. He says his wife is pregnant and now very ill and you've seen her.'

'Vix... I don't remember the name. Let's have the details.'

'Well... Sister I'm afraid it's the phone box in Hatherley Lane. The address is the common.'

'Oh no. Not the travellers?'

It was nothing personal. Annie Larriot rather enjoyed having New Age travellers on her patch. It added contrast to an otherwise prosperous area. But it was mid January and she firmly believed traveller camps were best experienced on balmy June evenings.

'He says he'll wait for you at the phone box. He's in a real state. Do you want me to get the police to go with you?'

Was it genuine concern for her welfare, out alone at night, she pondered, or merely another manifestation of West-country anti-traveller paranoia?

'Vix...Vix. I don't remember him. What's the wife's name?'

'He said she's called Sal.'

She remembered. 'Vix 'n Sal.' They'd been young, very young: him, short and fierce and trying unsuccessfully to look polite and cooperative. Tangled red dreadlocks and large boots were her main memory. The girl was even smaller, with short spiky black hair, ear and nose rings and clear blue eyes. She had been too thin. They had come to see her at the health centre having managed, just, to get past the receptionist. They'd booked for antenatal care. That had been a month ago. She'd only be about twenty weeks now.

The voice in her ear spoke again.

'Sister do you want me to get the police?'

'It's alright Josh, I remember them now. But what's the problem. She's not due yet.'

'He won't say. He just says she's very ill and he wants the midwife. And he hasn't got a GP.'

She remembered. She was still working on that one. None of the local doctors were keen to have travellers on their list. Usually she'd solved the problem by the time the baby was due. Her thoughts coalesced. It was no good. She was going to have to go out.

'OK I'm on my way. I'll call you if I need an ambulance.'

The drive to her destination took about a quarter of an hour. It was cold and crisp, but thankfully, there was a moon.

In the lane ahead Annie could see the bright sanctuary of the phone box. There were three silhouettes in the beam of light. The small man she recognised as Vix. Beside him was a dog and just visible behind them a very tall man, apparently wearing a turban. She wound the window down and opened her mouth. The small man didn't wait.

'Come on, come on, where the f… have you been?'

She looked at him, thought about shutting the window, locking the door and phoning for the police. The dog whimpered. The huge turbaned figure in the background spoke.

'Cool it Vix,' and to her, 'It's alright really. He's just worried. She is ill. I'm Jemal. My Mum does your job,' he added 'in London, - Ealing.'

She looked at the small angry young man again. He was just plain scared. This, she thought, is what gets me into trouble with my managers. The rules were clear. Shut doors and windows and call for help. She reached for her midwife bag, climbed out, locked the door and turned to the two men.

'Right now, tell me slowly. What's the problem?'

By the time they reached the van, about quarter of a mile down a track off the frosty lane the picture hadn't become much clearer. The tall Sikh had done most of the talking, clearly trying to reassure her. His accent was Trowbridge with a touch of Tottenham.

'My mum hates going out at night. I used to go with her sometimes. There're some funny people out there.'

Annie managed not to laugh.

The van was like one of the many she saw every summer at the Festivals. It had a stove chimney sticking out of the roof and a golden sun painted on the outside, which tonight was glittering in the moonlight. The inside was wonderfully warm and mostly blue, with silver stars and a yellow moon painted on the ceiling. There were hanging swathes of tie dye gauze floating dangerously near a candle lantern. On a shelf bed which took up a third of the floor space, underneath an old and faded banner which read "Dig deep for the Duke," lay Sal.

'Minimal postcoital bleed' was the common phrase used in summary of such visits. This was clearly not the case here. The girl was flushed and restless. She was talking and not making sense. Annie touched her forehead. About 103 she thought, 39C. Not good. She couldn't stay here. She spoke to the two men.

'She needs hospital – why didn't you call an ambulance?'

'She could talk half an hour ago and she said to get you.'

Annie left the van and called it in. Soon the stretchered Sal was being hustled over the frozen ground into an ambulance. Vix followed. Annie turned around before she climbed into the ambulance and looked at the scene she was leaving. This wasn't a usual traveller's site. There were no other vans, no other dogs and apparently no other people. She looked for the second man she'd seen. Jemal was it? The one wearing a turban. He was nowhere about, neither was the dog.

As she balanced on the narrow bench opposite Sal, Annie heard the paramedic calling in.

'Query overdose. Traveller female. Arrival time –about twenty minutes.'

She didn't think so, but who knew. It wouldn't account for the fever anyway. Vix heard too and raised his head, seemed about to object, then looked at Sal and relapsed into silence.

The girl continued feverish and delirious on the journey and her breathing became laboured. As Annie and the paramedic put and oxygen mask over her face Vix again looked as if he was about to protest, but was calmed by Annie.

'It will help her. It's just oxygen.'

He sat back in his corner looking simultaneously both frightened and frightening. The journey was fast. Within fifteen minutes the little procession was pushing its way through the swinging double doors of the Casualty Department of the city hospital.

As Annie completed her handover report to the night charge nurse her phone went off again. Answering the call she was put through to a sleepless mother of an equally sleepless fourteen day old baby. It was ten minutes before the mother was sufficiently reassured to ring off, and then only on the promise of a visit within the hour.

Glancing back to the cubicle where Sal lay, she saw her surrounded by white coats and blue uniforms. She caught the charge nurse's eye.

'It's OK. You go. We've got all you can tell us. As they say – "Be careful out there!"'

She found the ambulance men and persuaded them to drop her, on their way back to base, at her car, still parked where she'd left it, by the phone box in Hatherley Lane. As she left she took one last look back. Her view of Sal was obscured by Vix and the charge nurse who were engaged in fierce conversation.

The call of the bleep was imperative. Squashed companionably in the front of the ambulance with the two paramedics she remembered why she didn't mind being called out at night. There was the closeness and warmth of a busy team doing a useful job. However much you might disagree with the views, opinions or politics of your companions – about the place of travellers in the universal scheme of things, for instance, the fact remained that the structure of the medical world ensured the job got done. Everyone went home feeling comfortably pleased they'd done their bit towards saving the world. It was never the same during the day, she thought. Then the rules did just the opposite – tried their best to strangle any attempt at individual cooperative human action.

'Careful dear, your chip is showing,' said sensible Annie to herself.

As the phone box appeared in front of them a tall gangly figure emerged from inside it. He had clearly been sheltering from the January frost. He came towards them. She could sense the alarm of her companions in the ambulance. He really did look rather strange.

'No really it's OK. He's a friend of theirs. Probably waiting for news.'

'We'll see you into your car Sister, if you don't mind.'

'He really is OK. His mother is a midwife in London.'

As if he'd heard the conversation Jemal stayed back until she was safely in her car. Then she lowered the window and called him. He came over.

'How is she?'

'We don't know yet, but she's in the best place. I've got another call now, but thanks for your help earlier. Listen, any idea what was wrong? If she has taken anything you do need to tell me you know. It's the only way we can help her.'

'No, not them, not now. Really not.'

'Any other ideas?'

He was bending down talking to her through the window. There was a moment of uncertainty in his eye.

'No, none,' he said, barely hesitating.

Annie didn't believe him but could see that he wasn't going to tell her anything else.

'Well Goodbye Jemal and thanks.'

She drove off and an hour later was home and in bed.

*

The remainder of the night was quiet, but sleep was not easy. Her thoughts were with the scene in the van. She really didn't think the girl would have taken anything she shouldn't. She was so thrilled to be pregnant. The girl's happiness and determination to be a good mother had, as it did more and more often these days, set her thinking about her own circumstance. Every time anyone said the words 'biological clock' or 'tick tock' she refused to react, but, as she said to herself, at thirty five one can't really be unaware. I'm going to have to think seriously about this soon, was her final thought before sleep finally came.

*

As she drove towards the hospital the following morning Annie reminded herself of the advantages of working in the community. It meant, as far as she was concerned that she didn't have to spend much time in the hospital that employed her. Giving the night report and handing over the 'on call' phone was one of those moments of compulsory attendance. But as hospitals go, she thought, this one really wasn't bad. It had been kind to her over the years. She had known several worse.

All hospitals are more than the sum of their buildings. This one was an oddity because as well as being the area general hospital, it also housed the medical training units for the local Navy and Marine base. In addition, the nearby dockyard serviced the nation's nuclear submarines. This meant that as national military commitments came and went so did the hospital personnel. There was a regular influx of young fit sailors and marines, either as patients or as trainees.

As we get older, thought Annie, most wards are more like geriatric units and are not the jolly places where we used to work. She recalled her friend Elaine's comment, referring to the presence of the military. 'They lighten our lives and improve the wallpaper no end.'

To a midwife, whose concern was exclusively with women between 16 and 50 this was, in theory, of little relevance, but in fact the military presence was all pervasive. Any national alert would produce an increase of uniforms around the corridors. Those who followed these things would comment on regimental changes and the least knowledgeable would note that increased density of uniform meant, to quote Annie's colleague again, 'There's a flap on or an admiral is having his piles done.'

Today as Annie entered the gates she could see things were quiet. Not a uniform in sight at 8.00 hours. She made her way round the back of the main building and through a couple of long corridors to the office of Mrs Elizabeth Galoow (acting assistant midwifery manager) and current Authority in Annie's professional life. The manager took the report and read it. Minimal detail and essential facts only were included.

"Never write more than you need. They can't get you on what isn't down in black and white."

That advice had been given to Annie by the first midwife she'd ever worked with. Why did she feel it was going to be good advice for today? Authority looked up.

'She died about three this morning. Overdose they think. They had a lot of trouble with the partner.' She paused.

Annie with years of experience of saying the wrong thing in such circumstances maintained her silence.

'Did you have any trouble?'

'Not really. He was just scared for her. He had a friend with him who helped.'

More silence. Annie remained determined not to elaborate. Authority looked at Annie in an unsatisfied sort of way. Annie knew what she was thinking. She doesn't trust me. I make her uneasy. She's wondering what I did last night and why my reactions are different from everyone else's. She's worried about what she doesn't know.

'Well the police will want a statement. They've said they'll see you here in my office on Monday morning. We'll get someone from the legal office to be with you.'

'Thank you,' was all Annie said.

Not kindness, nor support, she thought. Just making sure I don't drop the Trust in it somehow. Protecting themselves. Oh dear, how did I get so cynical?

Years of doing what seemed the right thing at the time and then being hauled over the coals afterwards for the most incomprehensible of corporate reasons had made her a very wary woman.

'Well have a good sleep then. See you tomorrow.'

Annie left. The civilities were unconvincing to both sides. It was time to go home.

An hour later she had spoken to Elaine the old friend who worked in Casualty.

'Ah yes, the traveller girl. She was one of yours wasn't she? I thought you'd ring.'

'What happened?'

'Well to be honest no one really knows. It was so quick. That high fever! We gave her antipyretics and antibiotics – then suddenly she was in multisystem failure. They tried everything, but she just wouldn't pick up. No one has a clue what she had. I have to say, that the fever didn't make it seem like an OD. But who knows. There'll be a death meeting, so they'll get to the bottom of it.'

'You know I saw her first three weeks ago – and I did take the bloods, They'll still be in the lab somewhere. Could you tell the team. They could get extra investigations done on them if they need to.'

'Sure, I'll tell Martin Shaw, he's the reg. Might be useful actually. Everyone's worried. Don't want an epidemic on our hands.'

The conversation puzzled her. There had to be more. Had she missed something? Maybe it was a good time to visit a friend of her sister's who happened to live not far from Hatherley Common.

'Not wise, don't do it, stay out of it,' she advised herself.

She rarely took her own advice and so Sunday afternoon saw her setting out plus jar of homemade jam to spend the afternoon ostensibly helping friend of sister to pick and freeze her brussels sprouts.

As the car turned onto the main road to the west of the city, walking along the pavement in front of her she saw a short stocky red-haired familiar figure. Even from her car, at that distance she could see

17

the tension and anger in his back view. Don't do it – she advised herself. She braked and pulled up beside him.

'Hello. I'm so very sorry about Sal.'

He looked at her uncomprehendingly. She saw there were tears on his face. Then she realised his problem. She wasn't wearing her uniform – so he didn't know her.

'I'm Annie, the midwife, I heard the news this morning. Look can I give you a lift?'

She saw recognition appear.

'You left her,' he said.

'I had another call. I'm sorry I just had to go.'

'They said she'd taken something. We wouldn't, not now. We wanted our baby so much.'

Though a sunny January afternoon, it was still bitterly cold and another ten miles to the phone box where she'd picked him up the night before. He'd obviously been up all night, had no money or he'd have been on the bus and he'd just lost his little world. He was bitterly miserable not aggressive. She decided not to be intimidated by the locks, tattoos and ironmongery.

'If you want I'll give you a lift to Hatherley Lane.'

She opened the car door. He seemed suddenly to deflate and dumped himself in her front seat.

'Have you had anything to eat?' she asked.

'Forgot to take any bread, didn't I.'

She drove, wondering what to say. He just sat there, staring straight ahead, hands gripping his knees. She could see a blue tattoo of a dolphin disappearing up his sleeve.

She was still wondering when the phone box came into view.

'Have you any idea what made her ill?' she asked. 'The police are going to talk to me tomorrow morning. Is there anything I should say?'

She halted by the phone box and he opened the door and got out.

'Just tell 'em we don't do drugs,' he said and set off down the lane.

She watched the matted red hair, torn black leather jacket, and battered combat trousers recede into the distance. Beyond him she could just see part of the roof of the van in its discreet woodland hideaway.

She drove another quarter of a mile to her afternoon appointment in a house backing onto Hatherley Common.

Rosina Laxton, her host, had a sister who was a good friend of Annie's own sister. She and Annie had been thrown together when both their sisters had emigrated to Australia at the same time twelve years earlier. They continued to meet about twice a year to discuss that nebulous time in the future when they'd make their own odyssey down under.

As the years passed it had become clear that the two women had very little in common financially, socially or politically but somehow the acquaintance continued. Friends of both wondered at it. Annie's father's view, which when he was alive, he had frequently offered was that each saw the other as their personal window into another cage in the monkey house.

If that was true it didn't seem such a bad thing to Annie. Any attempt, by anyone on this planet to understand how one's neighbour ticked had to be a good thing.

Rosina's half acre garden opened directly onto the Common. From her gate you looked out across rough grass and scrubby trees until on the other side you could see other houses, gardens and the church steeple. Known locally as the Piece, this patch of common land had last summer been transformed by an impromptu Traveller's Free Festival involving 200 vehicles, their inhabitants and, if local accounts were to be believed, more dogs than people, all, both dogs and people in receipt of their own social security payments.

Local inhabitants had been apoplectic with rage. Their targets were, firstly the police, for not protecting them from invasion, secondly, the travellers themselves for existing outside the system, thirdly, the press for their contribution to the chaos and finally social services for aiding and abetting in matters of toilets and water standpipes.

As the anger became more focussed, with the truly daunting organisational skill of the English middle classes, they set up the 'Piece Preservation Society', privately known to it's members as 'Travellers Watch.' It was now probably the most well informed organization in the West country, not excluding the police, as to local traveller movements.

To do the group justice they had no political agenda. They had one simple objective – to prevent the Piece ever again becoming a camping ground for itinerants. Local inhabitants and therefore members of the group included retired army officers, civil servants, social workers, estate agents and farmers. When their combined skills were pooled, their intelligence gathering and networking capacity was formidable.

The English man or woman in defence of his or her castle finds it easy to make bedfellows with those they might not normally consider allies.

With modern communications all traveller movements in the area were logged and plotted by the retired Brigadier who was the group coordinator. Rosina was the group secretary and it was this aspect of her life Annie was interested in, on this cold Sunday afternoon, rather than the harvesting and freezing of brussels sprouts she found herself engaged in.

Eventually she broached the topic of travellers. The monitoring group was one of those unsecret secrets. Nobody admitted to more than a community preservation society. However everyone involved knew exactly from what they were preserving their society. Once before Annie had come to Rosina for intelligence – when a family vanished and the baby had needed treatment. She'd been spot on then.

'No, no settlers at the moment. Everyone's tucked up somewhere for the winter and none of them on our patch!'

Annie told the story of her call out, preserving all the proper anonymities.

'Well we didn't know anything about them.'

The tense of her remark made Annie a little uneasy.

'We've mainly been worried about break-ins lately.'

They carried their baskets indoors to a kitchen Annie could only dream about. Sitting at a big white wood scrubbed table they began preparing the sprouts for freezing. Conversation moved on to local topics. A planning victory against a new factory which had been redesignated as a research facility was the monitoring group's latest triumph.

'That's where the most recent break in was. But it's all been kept very hush hush. I'm not sure what they are doing there but whatever it is from our point of view it means no large workforce, no lorries and mostly no more traffic round the Piece.'

Such blatant nimbyism rather took Annie's breath away.

'Met the new director at a party. Charming man. Good head of hair. Quite made my heart flutter. Which reminds me, found yourself a man yet? He might do you.'

Annie ignored the remark and the two women turned to discussing Australia and their respective sisters' lives. They both lived in Sydney, but Annie's sister was married to a sociology professor and taught English to 'New Australians'. She lived in inner city Chippendale, while Rosina's sister was married to the director of a computer company and lived on the north shore.

'She really doesn't have time to work what with all the travelling and entertaining she has to do for her husband,' said Rosina.

Nevertheless and notwithstanding the chasms of political and social philosophy that lay between them, at the end of the afternoon there on the kitchen table in front of Annie and Rosina were 30 lbs of cleaned and labelled sprouts in 1lb bags, ready for the freezer.

'How on earth are you going to eat all these?' asked Annie.

'Didn't I say? We've been doing most of these for the WI. Food parcels for the elderly. Actually I can't stand sprouts – but they do freeze well and there's not much else in January is there?'

Oops! thought Annie my self–righteousness is showing again. Defending one's patch with an information network that the Israelis would have envied wasn't incompatible with ensuring the local elderly had a decent diet.

*

The police interview the following day was routine. The man from the Trust sat in, taking notes. Annie produced her official diary entries and related the story of Sal's admission. Everything was very low key. When pressed as to why she made no very serious attempt to get further details of name or next of kin, she cited her years of experience of working with 'marginal groups' and her belief that as the couple began to trust her she would get more reliable information.

'It seemed more important to keep in contact at this stage. If they'd felt threatened they'd have upped and offed and she was pregnant. I didn't want to lose them.'

The man from the trust nodded ponderously. Annie wasn't asked and saw no need to mention she'd seen Vix the previous afternoon. The whole encounter was over by eleven o'clock.

By two in the afternoon it became clear that Vix wasn't going to attend his interview with the social worker about arranging Sal's funeral and giving permission for a post mortem.

By five o'clock the police had checked the Hatherley Lane site to find no trace of a camp, legal or otherwise. In the clearing under the trees they found little on the frozen ground to indicate anyone had ever camped there.

It all left an unsatisfactory unfinished feeling. As far as anyone could ascertain at the moment no crime had been committed, yet in the mortuary there lay the body of a young woman and her unborn child. No cause of death was known, yet she had died in one of the best equipped casualty units in the country. She was without name, address or relatives.

*

A week passed. Preliminary pathology results produced no further evidence of cause of death, medical or illegal. No one else got ill. No epidemic raised its head. The sense of crisis faded. The police added Vix to the list of people they would like to interview, but they didn't pursue his whereabouts with any great energy.

The hospital put the case on the back burner, to be considered when all appropriate test results had come in, at the next Maternal Mortality meeting.

In defence of both the police and the Health Service, it has to be said that had it been the pregnant Sal who was missing, while Vix lay dead, much energy would have been expended looking for her and it would have been successful. In England once a woman announces her pregnancy she ceases to be a private individual and becomes a public responsibility. If necessary at public expense, she will be fed, clothed, protected and supported. All medicines will be supplied to her free of charge.

What had pleased the Hospital Trust's publicity officer was that the death wasn't even yesterday's news. She'd prevented so much as a mention of the incident appearing in the local paper. In her favour, that week more immediate local matters dominated the press pages. Someone had placed an explosive device in the rubbish bin adjacent to the university biology laboratory which had broken a considerable amount of plate glass. Much space had been devoted to the rumour that the new research facility near Hatherley Common used chimpanzees in experiments. Local papers received pictures, which they had published, which purported to be of the exploited animals. However, most column inches were devoted to the current thaw and its resultant bonus for local plumbers. Flood stories were the main news for the two weeks after Sal's death.

One evening Annie caught the end of the local news. She had followed the chimp story in the paper. It had become so persistent that the director of the establishment had gone on local television to deny there were any animals at all on his premises and invited the cameras to see his shiny new laboratories. Annie watched, wondering if the man doing the talking was the one who had caused Melanie's recent heart palpitations. It seemed likely. She would have found that leonine mane of hair and that impeccable suit quite irresistible. Not my style, thought Annie.

CHAPTER THREE

Comings and Goings

Outerbourne: A Health Centre in the West Country

Leaving parties are an integral element in the English National Health Service. Annie considered the phenomenon as she drove towards Outerborne clinic. There seemed these days to be one every week. Funnily enough 'welcome' parties were rather rarer. Typical, one might celebrate endings, departing – wishing it was you, but not beginnings, new starts or new ideas.

'Party' implies some sort of festivity. It's not an adjective that could easily be applied to the social gatherings prevalent in local clinics. However they did provide a variation from day to day routine and allowed everyone to contribute their 'bit'. Women were expected to produce home-made cakes and quiches and sausage rolls. Men were expected to provide the excitement and drama. A health centre with a good supply of male staff, chiropodists, physiotherapists as well as male doctors always managed jollier events. The men did produce food. Though, it has to be said, thought Annie, I've never yet come across a man who produced a good home cooked quiche unless he got his wife to do it.

The greater number of female doctors in the clinics was shaking this patriarchal structure. A new model had yet to emerge which would allow such occasions to be enjoyable. A sociologist would have had a great time analysing the class, gender relations and stereotyping of roles demonstrated by clinic life in the health service.

Current practice was socially unsatisfactory, but in these days of time famine and decline in cooking skills, it seemed the best most clinics could come up with. The person with overall responsibility for the spread would, on the day, inventory her supplies, raid the petty cash and make a quick trip to the local supermarket or if indicated by the status of the leaver, Marks and Spencer, and plug the gaps in provisioning.

It was an invitation to one of these happenings which led to Annie's analysis of the nature of clinic celebrations. It was some three weeks after Sal's death and though she still had questions, it had been made clear to her that she had completed her duties and the matter was out of her hands and none of her business.

She turned her mind back to the present. Today's retiree was the clerk in one of the clinics on Annie's patch. She had served as a medical clerk for over 40 years, most recently in this new purpose built rural clinic. She hadn't quite been in at the beginning of the National Health Service, but there wasn't much in it. She was a socialist through and through, born in Barnsley, reared on Union politics and unsure herself how she had come to end her working life in True Blue rural Outerbourne.

She frequently voiced her view, that with minimal provocation she would man the barricades to defend the principles of the NHS and incidentally the public library service. She ferociously defended the principle of free care at the point of delivery for all those whose files passed over her desk. Recent attempts at privatisation had not impressed her. These days however her opportunities to foment revolution were limited. She could be guaranteed to thwart, in any way she could, the comfort and convenience of visiting consultants to her clinics particularly those who were known to have a large private practice. Her attempts to abolish the class system and enforce equal access for all were currently directed to ensuring that the reserved parking space for the consultant was always occupied whenever he was expected.

The nurses and midwives running the clinics would equally deviously, attempt to ensure the space was vacant. They didn't want an irritable, late consultant and a clinic full of annoyed patients. This undeclared war had been going on for the last five years since Maisie had been exiled to Outerborne. Her previous post in the central clinic had given her some creative opportunities to better the lot of the less equal, but her current post had offered little chance to raise the red flag and had thus reduced her to harassing passing fat cats. Between Maisie and the other staff members there was no common ground. As a result both she and the rest of the staff were eagerly anticipating her retirement and all had put considerable effort into the spread provided.

Various managers who had been responsible for Maisie over the years were invited, as was the deputy chairperson of the trust and appropriate local dignitaries. Annie parked her car, noting with amusement the empty space. Obviously the consultant expected to make the presentation hadn't arrived yet.

To everyone's surprise the event was unexpectedly lively. Attendance was high. It was hard to discern whether those attending who genuinely wished Maisie well, were outnumbered by those who came to ensure, so to speak, she was really in her coffin and definitely retiring.

The local press attended. Pictures were taken of Maisie receiving her cheque and her rose bushes. Those who worked at Outerbourne kept on finding themselves saying – 'and who is that then?'

Annie sat on the sidelines holding glass and plate, enjoying the game with the district nurse from a neighbouring clinic. It wasn't so much that they needed to participate, they just had to be seen. It would have been their absence that would have been commented upon.

'That's Mr Roborough isn't it? I thought he was a Professor now. What's he doing here?' asked Annie's companion.

'Oh didn't you know. Maisie was clerk to his clinic when they set up the open access family planning - years ago now. I was just a student then and had a placement there. They're both still in the Clifton Labour Party. I've always thought that being a socialist from the best part of town had its appeal. You feel good about yourself and have nice rich people living around you and plenty of trees.'

'Really Annie. That's not fair. You can't tell me you're from a true socialist, worker family. Your father never went down the mines. I seem to remember he was clerk to the Water Board.'

'Oh sorry. But there's a certain smugness about those well born Hampstead type socialists that gets my goat. Take no notice of me.'

They sat back and continued to watch the meeting and greeting, the forming of new alliances, the gentle dropping of hints. Who spoke to whom and who ignored who, were real indications of how their own working lives might be managed in the next year. For all their limitations, these gatherings often were the place where new ideas and new initiatives began their existence. Real change might come from the, 'What if we did this and you did that' conversation.

It was while she was watching the proceedings that Annie became aware someone had sat down beside her and was about to start a conversation.

'Sister Larriot?'

Annie wasn't particularly surprised at being addressed by name. She did have it enscribed on a plastic badge pinned to her chest. The man who had spoken looked vaguely familiar.

'I've been hoping to bump into you. Yours was among the names given us by your Human Resources department. I believe you have been enquiring about leave of absence to work abroad?'

Annie was completely nonplussed. She intermittently had wondered about an adventure, particularly, every time she found herself hauled over the coals for what had seemed normal, commonsense behaviour at the time, but had somehow, obscurely upset Management. She had even, on one occasion, got as far as asking HR about their leave of absence scheme. At these times she recalled, with mild bitterness that her sister had done Voluntary Service Overseas on leaving school before university, but she herself had been turned down and gone straight into work. If she had gone abroad then, who knows where she'd be now.

'Can I introduce myself. I'm James Coniston-Brown.' The man was continued. 'We are new to the area. We've just opened premises on the estate. Our company specializes in medical equipment.'

Recognition dawned. This was Rosina's heart throb, the director of the new research place. Well OK, her taste was good. He looked better than on TV. Leonine golden hair and the usual towering 6ft2inches of the upper classes. Just a bit too Tory home counties for my taste though, thought Annie to herself. She heard him go on.

'We support a local charity working in the field, and to celebrate our move to the area and our cooperation with the Health Authority the Company would like to pay the full costs of a worker at our clinic in Bundu District for a year. We're looking for a mother and baby specialist, but someone who is an experienced community midwife. We wondered if you would be interested?'

'Me? But I've never really been seriously abroad, only to Europe and such. I've no tropical training.'

'That's partly the point. The charity tries to offer opportunities to UK citizens to broaden their experience. Your job here is kept for you, and all your benefits and we pay a volunteer's wage and a UK housing allowance. Meanwhile you take your skills to a place that would be unlikely to get professional staff if you didn't go.'

'Like Voluntary Service Overseas you mean?'

'Not unlike, but I think we pay better. We don't want our volunteers to be out of pocket!'

'But training for me?'

'Don't worry. We do all that in country. Give you the kit and get you the experience in a local hospital.'

'How many are you interviewing?'

'Well, we've been given names by your HR department. They spoke of your work with minority groups and the local itinerant community. You would I think suit us.'

'I've always felt for people who find themselves in a strange country or are at odds with the world.' said Annie. Unable to believe her ears she went on, 'Does that mean you are offering the job to me?'

'Well you need to come for a formal interview - say tomorrow, but subject to the usual medical if you want the job I think it's yours.'

The rest of the party became something of a blur. Try as she might to hold it down, her heart was leaping. A door somewhere had opened. There was, at last, change on the horizon. She had a chance to break the pattern or at least make a crack in it.

Something of reality came to her later as she sat up in bed and considered the offer. She couldn't really do it could she? And she wasn't entirely sure where Bundu District actually was. But the guy seemed to consider her suitable. HR had obviously had a hand in it. Was she that much of an irritant to management, that they'd be glad to see the back of her for a year? It seemed unlikely, but then who understood corporate ways?

Deep down she knew she was going to take it. It was what she had yearned for, but found no way of achieving. There had been her father to look after. By now she had felt she was past it and settled. She had missed the boat. Secure jobs couldn't just be abandoned. She hadn't the guts of a Gladys Aylward to just get up and go.

She didn't sleep at all well and woke at 4.30. The moment her eyes opened she knew that she so wanted that job. Absolutely. She saw it as her last chance of ever having anything happen to her in this life. She had to go. She was sure. She got up and started on her computer. By 8am she felt she was reasonably well informed about Bundu District, where it was and the sort of problems she might have to deal with.

On getting to work she found a message waiting for her to attend the HR dept at 10.00. The man with the leonine head wasn't there. There was no interview. It all seemed cut and dried.

'I gather you are coming to join the company,' said a round bespectacled man. 'Mr Coniston-Brown has let me know that we would need to make the arrangements. You'll be taking over from the current nurse.'

'So I will be able to meet her?' asked Annie.

'Well I'm afraid I don't know about that. The In Country Team will sort things out. I'm just Base Liaison. I'll arrange your flight and so on. They'll meet you there.'

The HR official with whom Annie was accustomed to battle about her payslip was in a very obliging mood. She produced a sheaf of forms which Annie assiduously read. Could she really could go away for a year and come back to her old job?

'Off course - that was what the scheme was for. It was designed by and for managers to go off and have their children.'

There really did seem no obstacles, so Annie signed. As she was leaving her Manager caught up with her.

'How I do admire you. Such a chance to be useful. I'd have expected nothing less of you. I gather you have a few days holiday owing. The Trust has made it up to two weeks to give you time to get organised and Occupational Health are expecting you for your inoculations and so on. You need to start your anti-malarials very soon if you're leaving in three weeks.'

Two and a half weeks later Annie held her own leaving party, in her own house. She had tried to keep her leave of absence a secret as far as possible. However, with a good many years in the same place there were still a substantial number of folk, let alone family, who were too close to her to be abandoned without explanation. There were enough people she cared about and who would have been hurt if she had just disappeared, to make for a pleasant gathering.

Her Australian nephew Max was present, being charming and trying not to look too gleeful at the prospect of taking up residence in Annie's house, in her absence. He was assuring her and anyone who would listen that he would sort out her email and pay all the bills and water the garden and do his washing up, though he was a little wistful at her lack of a dishwasher. He successfully enrolled all Annie's contemporaries as temporary 'aunts' and thus secured any domestic support he might need.

Rosina came with gifts, a Swiss army knife and a head torch and a Maglite. Annie was a bit embarrassed. Two torches and they didn't seem that relevant. Rosina was insistent.

'You'll be glad of these. Take my word for it.'

In months to come Annie was indeed to be so very glad of them. She had tried to thank Rosina for having a word on her behalf with the research director Mr Coniston-Brown. Her stumbling remarks had met a brick wall. She remained unsure whether Rosina really didn't know what she was talking about or wasn't prepared to admit intervening.

Present also were a few old, old friends who had started nursing with Annie years before, and like her, hadn't moved far. One was her friend Elaine from Casualty who had kept her in the picture about Sal and conversation turned in that direction.

'We never did get an answer to her you know. Ever so many tests were done. Your new boss, that guy, from the research place, even he had samples sent to him, but as no one else came down with anything, they've all stopped panicking. We never found out who she was though or saw her chap again. He never came back.'

Yet another story she'd never know the end of. One of the problems of being a midwife was that you bobbed into people's lives for this intense short time and then never saw them again, unless they had another baby which in this area they did rather regularly.

The spread in this house was not even Marks & Spencer, but homemade and heartfelt. When an awful lot had been consumed and it was nearly time to go Annie's largely female guests ganged up on her. They sent her upstairs to finish getting packed and promised faithfully to clear every dish and plate, see to the washing up and put it all away. Annie sensed Max's hand in this, but was grateful. The knowledge of the uncleared up party would have spilled over into her journey. She was determined to escape and start her new adventure with a clean slate.

A while later, she was leaning over the banisters and looking down at her living room. The table was clear, the vase of flowers back in the middle and all the good luck cards arranged around it. The fire was still alight and flickering on the walls. This was her Hobbit hole and she loved it. Was it mad to go on an adventure? She heard voices from the kitchen, from where she could also hear the clink of crockery and clunk of cupboard doors.

'Do you have any idea why she is doing this?'

'Well you know her. She's always had to be a bit different. If there is another opinion on anything she'll have it!'

'That's not fair. Well, it's true I agree, but that's just the way she is. She doesn't do it to be difficult.'

'Tell Management that.'

'A "Yes" woman she has never been. She does rather look for battles.'

'Don't forget, she never managed to get away, what with her mother disappearing and her father needing her. Her sister made it to Australia, she never did. Maybe that is what this is about.'

'You're probably right. But us stay-at-homes, our lives haven't been dull. We did all have some times didn't we though?'

'Do you remember when we had that callout to the fair? When the ghost train got stuck and that woman delivered at the top.'

'Yes, she was the only one who would go up and then those firemen came with their ladders and afterwards they gave us that ride back. Those firemen!'

'We had a great time at their Christmas party that year.'

'We were all younger then. Half her trouble is she'll get involved with any lame dog, so long as it's human, I mean. She has a heart of gold.'

'No argument. I hope they know how lucky they are in Bundu or where ever. We'll miss her.'

'Yes. A whole year with no one to raise objections at the midwives meetings and get us all going.'

'And who'll do our on calls for us at a moment's notice and never moan?'

'She is just one of those genuinely kind people but you do have to be her friend to know it.'

'I just wish, for her sake, she could be more comfortable and less of an oddball.'

Who says an eavesdropper never hears good about herself, thought Annie. What nice words. I couldn't ask for others. This recognition and understanding from her friends gave her a warm glow and some strange confidence. It wasn't difficult to find the courage to book the airport taxi after that.

The next time in her existence there seemed to be a moment to even pause, Annie was sitting in her seat on the plane looking out of the window. As she looked down, through a gap in the clouds, at the river below her she recognised a pattern from her school atlas.

That's the coast of Africa, it really is, and that's the Nile. And this is really happening to me, she thought. She remained stunned at the speed of her exodus (albeit temporarily) from the seemingly inalterable pattern of the midwife's life. It had never been a dull life, but it was routine. There were pregnancies. Babies were born. The cycle went on.

Ever since that brief conversation with the man at Maisie's leaving party, her existence had seemed to move as on oiled wheels on a railway track with no stations. Looking back, from her present seat on the plane, Annie recalled feeling like a goldfish opening and shutting her mouth. She had just been unable to stop the rolling juggernaut that seemed to be sweeping her in front of it. The song that continued to play in her head was Doris Day singing 'What ever will be, will be.'

Now anyway, at least she was in the juggernaut and on the road was her concluding thought before she dozed off again.

CHAPTER FOUR

The Dreamtime or Cloud Cuckoo Land

Letters from Annie Larriot to her sister, Julia, Max's mother, in Sydney, Australia

Letter One

To Mrs Julia McClaren
Sydney
NSW
Seat H18.
In the Plane
Above the World
In the clouds
In the sky
On the way to Africa

Dear Julia
I know the above is a bit childish, but I'm still so excited and as everyone else seems asleep I thought I'd write to you and update you. When I'm there I hope we'll have email but meanwhile back to the snail..

Getting off was very simple. I've left your Max in charge of my house and my car. He seems to be lining up all my friends to cook for him and do his laundry He's a charmer isn't he? I hope he can use a vacuum cleaner and keeps up with his studies.

The airport turned out to be easy. I was scared, I do admit. The weirdest thing was, I kept thinking I was seeing people I knew. I saw someone, I am sure, I'd last seen in Devon. He's not someone you can actually miss. He is a six foot Sikh in a turban, and I last saw him on a moonlit night at a phone box in a country lane. Then I thought I'd seen the guy who gave me this job, and I wondered if he'd come to see me off, but he didn't appear so it can't have been him. It was all just stress I suppose. First sign of psychosis, they say, recognising strangers. I know you've done this often, but if you think about it, nearly all my airport experience has been meeting you off the Sydney flight at Heathrow for the last fifteen odd years, so I'm enjoying my turn to be going somewhere.

I'm looking out of the window now and I can see the Nile below me, looking just as it does in an atlas.

I'm in the window seat, with two people between me and the gangway. I must admit I wasn't really sure of what the 'communication protocol' was when forced into such close proximity with one's neighbours, but they've both turned out to be really kind. I said 'hello' to the young man next to me, whose name is Mo and he took pity on me and sorted me out with the head phones and the TV screen.

The woman on the other side is older than me. It's her first big flight as well. She is going home after visiting her son in the UK. He is doing a masters degree and is a water engineer. When he's completed his course he will be promoted by his organisation to be a country manager of one of their projects. His mother's very proud, but a little sad because it could be any country in the world where the charity works. This would mean he would visit home and her and his family even less often.

It's fascinating what else I found out. I wondered how families kept in touch and I asked her about the post. Do you know, she just laughed at me and dug in her pocket and produced a mobile phone! Its a new one, a present from the son, but apparently, even before she had her own, every week she used to go down to the shop in her village and pay the shopkeeper to use the shop mobile and call him in the UK.

Mo must have been listening to us women talking, because he joined in. Apparently he can send money by phone to his mother and aunts in his village. And, if he knows there is a job coming up in the city or his company he can phone a friend and tell him. His cousin in New York sends him his old phone every time he gets an upgrade, but he says he gets better more modern ones, cheaper, in the capital now. He gives the ones his cousin sends to his aunties.

It turns out he works for a company that sells the mineral that they put in the phones. He showed us the pendant he wears round his neck on a leather thong. It's a dull black smooth round stone with a hole through it. It's called coltan and that's what makes the phones go. Capacitors I think he said. They mine it in the rivers just like you told me the Aus prospectors did in the 1890s when they were panning for gold.

This phone business is amazing. We just go on finding new things. And when I think that us midwives had practically to threaten to strike to get rid of our radios and get mobiles. And still there are quite a few places in Devon where we've no signal. However, apparently in remote African villages mothers ring their sons every week, even if they are in London. If you were a farmer and wanted to know the selling price of vegetables in the capital you simply ring your cousin.

It's all unnerved me a bit. I begin to realise how much I don't know.

I'm going to stop now. It looks as if breakfast is coming. Will update you later..........

Continued...

We've landed, but I'm not sure what's going on. I'm sitting in a big Landcruiser with vicious cold air conditioning waiting for the driver to come back with my luggage, and I think I've put my foot in it.

Anyway back to where we were.

I'll tell you what cheered me. It was standing at the door of that plane and feeling that wall of heat hit me. It really is hot in Africa. And anywhere that hot is OK with me. I began to feel warm through to my bones. I just love this heat. No need for woolly socks here!

There was a bus waiting for us at the bottom of those steps and it drove us to a building and inside there, you have no idea of the noise. You could see all the relatives behind the barrier. There was shouting and waving and everyone was on their mobile phone at the same time. Not like meeting you at Heathrow at all. I thought I saw the guy in the turban again. I tried to get near him and join his queue, but it was impossible and then I was whisked away.

I had watched a man being allowed through the exit gates by a very large uniform. It turned out he had my photo and a piece of paper with the company logo on it. He spoke perfect English and before I could do anything about it he picked up my suitcase and walked off. All I could do was follow him. And we got let straight through the gate, no queues.

And that's how I put my foot in it. Once we got to this car and I was in it, he asked for my passport and said he'd get it stamped. I wouldn't give it to him. I'd been told, by you among others, never to part with it. Anyway he gets out his mobile phone and dials, speaks to someone and gives it to me. There is this very superior voice on the other end, says she is Angela something or other and please will I trust the driver and give him my passport as he is only trying to save me a long hot wait in a queue. When I asked her who she was she was rather sharp and reeled off my name and job title and told me I was in a Toyota with the company logo on the side. I now feel a complete fool and am waiting for the man to come back with my luggage.

I think I can see my case coming...........so

To be continued.

Well it's a few days on now and I'm in my room. I will get on email but I seem to have offended someone and can't quite pull it off, so I'll continue the old-fashioned way.

When we got here it was clear I had already blotted my copy book and upset this woman. She turned out to be the Angela on the phone. I have to say she is about 5'10 " tall, thin and extremely elegant and very well made up. She made me feel short, shabby, not young and not thin.

They have arranged an induction programme for me. They say they anticipate me beginning at Becana, you know, the place where I'm actually going to be working, in about two weeks. It can't be soon enough for me. I'm not comfortable here and no one is friendly and I want to get on with the job.

A week later – sorry.

Tomorrow I leave for Becana and it will be a relief. I'm going to finish this now and walk to the post office and mail it myself. I don't trust that Angela to bother or do it right. I never did manage get anyone to sort out email for me.

love Annie

**

Letter Two

Becana Clinic
Bundu District

On the edge of Angola

Dear Julia

Well I'm here now and I've been here two weeks and it is the most EXTRAORDINARY place. Imagine an army camp built on sand. Everything here has sand underfoot. And there are no hills and not many big trees but quite a lot of shade from scrawny saplings a bit like hawthorn. It's all flat. This army camp is just that: rows and rows of wooden huts, graded by the status of who used to live here in the days before independence. There are eight abandoned swimming pools, also graded by status of user. It was built, by the then government to guard the border. Believe it or not, in the middle is a police station with a very British blue light above the door.

My clinic is amazing. It's a prefab like they had after the war in London, metal framed with built in windows and doors and cupboards. It's just put down on a concrete base on the sand. Most equipment is still there though it's all rather battered and tatty. We get fresh supplies of drugs and disposables delivered from town regularly. There are two people who work in the clinic and they seem glad to see me. There is a tiny bushman called Jason Petrus who, in theory only speaks his own click language and Africaans who is the caretaker and my co-nurse Inika, who is about my age and has assistant nurse training and some midwifery, but she's worked on a battlefield and knows what is what. She speaks English and her own language. She refuses as a matter of principle to speak Africaans, as it is the 'language of the oppressor.' You'd think we'd have communication difficulties, but we seem to work it out. They both have a real pride in the clinic and want it to stay open which is why they need me a registered nurse and midwife.

I suppose you are also wondering what I eat? Well, as I said I have moved into the little wooden house (an ex-army hut actually) of the previous nurse and have inherited everything including the contents of her frig/freezer and her vegetable rack. National dish here is millimeal porridge which is fundamentally unflavoured blancmange and I'm trying to like it. I don't think my predecessor did either as I have also inherited a large sack of lovely potatoes. The woman in the shop, (yes we have one that sells everything, like any village.) has already asked me to let her know when I want another one, so there is a source out there somewhere! The government here gives nurses a food allowance and so there is plenty of meat in the freezer, mince and steaks too, though I'm not sure what animal they are from, could be ostrich or some sort of venison. Old fashioned English housewife skills seem welcome here. The last nurse used to bake cakes and I've already been asked if I do. People have seen me sewing and knitting and are interested and want to be taught. I'm going to try to have regular Sunday lunches or teas at the clinic to get everyone meeting together. I don't know if it'll work or if it's what people want. It's a sort of counterculture against the bars and the alcohol shops, which are everywhere. No booze in the clinic but a good time can be had nevertheless is going to be the motto. Inika, brought up a Methodist, agrees.

That's all the fundamentals. Now I'll tell you my little triumph. Inika was determined to get me working, so the day after I arrived she'd arranged an antenatal clinic. Now I personally have always thought these regular checks are usually a waste of time unless you are doing something specific like checking for anaemia. In the UK they make the women feel better and a bit cared for, but I'm not sure what else they achieve. Well, here, you can be wrong. There were only five women to see, and I smiled and did the checks and introduced myself and Inika translated.

The last woman was very pregnant, but nobody knows their dates here, so you're just guessing. She had great big eyes and this was her third baby. Anyway I palpated her (you know felt her tummy) and it was clear to me that this baby was breech, feet first. Now this is not good. In Europe and Aus they nearly always have c-sections. I have delivered ONE the ordinary way and I'm lucky to have had the chance. We don't have an ambulance so I couldn't transfer her. She wouldn't go to our nearest hospital under her own steam. In the end I decided I'd ring the hospital when I could get through and get a plan made. Meanwhile I told Inika to tell the woman that if anything happened at any time, day or night, she was to fetch us.

Of course the inevitable did happen and two nights later Inika came to rush me to the clinic. She wasn't clear why, but when we got there, there was this woman, obviously in labour. I didn't recognise her at first. I'm still finding it difficult to tell one face from another. Inika just looked at me and said, 'It's her with the big eyes,' and I realised I was about to deliver my second breech baby in the middle of nowhere, with no paediatrician or any baby equipment.

Luckily I didn't have long to worry. Seconds later, just after I'd sent Inika to find some towels for the baby the woman's waters broke, all down my dress and we were in business. Both the baby and I knew the rules. I didn't pull and the baby didn't get stuck and came fairly quickly. When Inika got back with the towels most of the baby was there. It was a 'he' and by the time we'd rubbed him down he was yelling very satisfactorily. Inika then went outside the clinic, in the twilight, and let out this very loud sort of yodel. 'We always do it for a breech' she said, 'now everyone knows.' Mother and Baby are doing fine as is my reputation. But it was a bit of a rollercoaster ride.

This is an odd place though. There is loads of money here. That's partly because they are building the first tarmac road through this part of the continent, so we have a construction camp with men from all over Africa five miles up the road, thus all the bars and cafes. There is no kind of alcohol you can't get. I see bottles of Johnny Walker everywhere. But most people are eating millimeal porridge with a bit of veg or meat on top if they're lucky.

There is something else going on too. I can't put my finger on it.

An example; One of the important things in this sort of job is to know about trends. Part of my brief, I thought, was research. See how many of this and that you're treating compared to last year and so on. Make graphs and pie charts. There seems to be a positive conspiracy to prevent me doing that. The clinic records from past years have all vanished. Just before I arrived someone from the company came by and handed out new stationery and recordkeeping books and took all the old ones away. What do you think that's about? Maybe I'm being paranoid and they just wanted it all new for me.

We only have the Births Register still, because Inika keeps it at her house as it's now sort of unofficial because it goes from before independence. She's kept it up because it's a lovely old leather bound book and has so much history in it. We both take enormous pleasure in writing our deliveries in it, under the handwriting of those from years ago. Incidentally, it's the twin of the ones we still use at home, except that in this one they used to enter the date of the baptism as well. They seem to have mostly stopped doing that and when I asked Inika she was odd. 'They don't live so long' was all she said. Must follow that up. Can I remind you that we wouldn't have that lovely old register if we hadn't spread our health system along with colonialism – and no Aussie cracks, you were English born.

Anyway more next time. Oh yes. No email out here, or so they tell me, that's another thing I could get paranoid about! No mobile coverage either. So much for Mo's stories from the plane. We have a very dodgy landline, but very nice telephone engineers who mostly do turn up when called. They will post this letter for me in Bundu.

Love Annie

*

Letter Three

Becana camp

Dear Julia

The next instalment.
I've just reread this. It is a very watery letter, one way and another – even though it is officially from a desert!
The rains have started and my workload has tripled. I am really, really tired but flying. I can't explain how much I'm enjoying this. I feel like an eagle who has finally been allowed to stretch its wings. I can make things happen here and it does make a difference. It's magic. I get exhausted, scared, occasionally in over my head, but I just love it. I can just hear you making remarks about enjoying doom and disaster and nasty medical situations. But I'm afraid that is just me.
This place is full of children who are full of joy. One day I heard an amazing carry on. I followed the noise and found about 20 children on an old car wreck singing and making music, banging the wreck with sticks, using it as a giant drum. They were so carefree in such a bleak environment. Most don't get enough to eat and schooling is to say the least, intermittent. Anyway enclosed is the photo I took. I may not have email but I did bring my camera and that little printer your Max organised for me.

There IS something I don't understand going on though. I've begun to walk around the place a little more. As it is all straight lines, I shouldn't get lost but I do. You need landmarks to orientate yourself. But there are always children around though, who will see me back if I say 'clinic' to them. You get used to everyone knowing who you are even if you don't know them.

One walk last week I came across this huge container with 'Weston-Super-Mare' written on it down in the bottom corner. It's very securely chained and locked but you can see it is opened from time to time. I tried to make a joke to someone about there being less sand at Weston than here, even though Weston is by the sea. It's really upset people that I've seen the place and I've been rather firmly advised to do less walking as 'Its dangerous and you don't know who is about and there are animals.' That's rubbish - anything on four legs here is killed and eaten very quickly and that includes an elephant! I'll tell you that story another time.

My next campaign is an ambulance. It's mostly because of the children and the Malaria deaths, but we need one anyway.

The children with malaria would break your heart. I'm afraid you are just going to have to put up with medical stuff. I've got to talk to someone and here they just see it as routine. The rains come, the Malaria comes and children die. Not if I can help it! But I'm not sure how much I can.

What happens with Malaria round here is this. Spot on, ten days after the rain, in the morning, there is a queue outside the clinic of mothers holding small children with raging temperatures.

And the children - this morning for example I had three of them. The first two mothers were resigned, but the third was a young woman with a two year old in her arms. The child had a raging fever. The mother was totally hysterical. It was her first child.

What we do is take them to our back room and give the child a dose of liquid paracetamol to bring the fever down. When we've got that temperature down, perhaps an hour later, we give the anti-malarial. If we give both together the children usually vomit because the malaria causes brain irritation and the medicine is very bitter.

There is no telling if the anti-malarial will work. They'll come back for a check and another dose tomorrow but if any of them still has a fever then we have to send him or her to the hospital an hour away for the next line of treatment, which is intravenous, a quinine drip. And we'll have to find someone to give them a lift. If the family is among the poorer or one of the Bushman people it's difficult. So I need that ambulance.

How we're supposed to fight malaria is this. First you make sure everyone, but especially the children sleep under nets and secondly when anyone shows signs, you presume malaria and give the drugs. Then if the first line drugs don't work, you presume resistance and send them on. I don't have those instant test kits out here, which give you a diagnosis and I've not been taught how to use them. Oh and every six months I'm supposed to set up a huge cauldron of insecticide and get everyone to come and dip their nets. Inika says that doesn't work because it's like bringing your dirty washing out in public and nobody will come. She has a better scheme. She buys plastic bags in the market and anyone who comes with their net puts it in one of her bags and she pours the stuff on top. She did that just before the malaria season started and I arrived. I expect someone will criticize her for not being ecofriendly, using plastic bags. I'll just tell them to come and look at a child with malaria! I'm told though that there are going to be so many free nets soon that we'll be able to stop dipping. Then perhaps we can use the old ones to protect windows and doors. The beastly little beasts get in through any crack.

Whatever we do there are problems though. Nobody seems to have told the mosquitoes round here that they aren't supposed to be about at midday, let alone bite people. I watched one yesterday when I was sitting at my desk. It flew through a shaft of sunlight and settled on my bare arm. It didn't get me. I squished it dead, but I'm afraid there was a smear of blood on my arm which was a pity as it meant the mosquito had just got someone, even if it wasn't me.

There is exciting news. I'm having a visitor next week, to stay, to do a survey. Someone from a wildlife charity. It's partly to do with that dead elephant. I'll tell you about it next time. Now I must get this letter off.

I've evolved a new way of getting them posted. Of an evening I walk down to the road and get my letter taken by a passing tourist car. They all have to stop to negotiate our bend in the road and will often get out to buy a coke so if the passengers look friendly and speak English I chat to them and give them my letter.

Sorry about the medical stuff but someone has to listen.
love Annie

Letter Four

Becana Clinic

Dear Julia

    My visitor has arrived and she is such fun. She is very young, in her twenties and full of energy. She has some sort of Zoology degree and been commissioned to do a survey of the wildlife and write a report with a view to setting up an animal conservation programme and getting the locals to be the wardens. And she has a vehicle.
    I hadn't realised I was lonely. There is Inika but this is her home and she has a huge family here and though they try I'm not one of them. The new girl, who is called Joanna Smith is a stranger here too. Born in Africa, speaks English, but like your kids, has never seen snow. She is great company. We have lots of plans.
    I was whining rather about the swimming pools and the stagnant puddles of water and malaria and she said, 'Why don't you fill them in?' I said I'd been to the boss guy but he hadn't really taken any notice. She said, 'No I mean us. Direct action.' I have to say I thought she was a bit bats, but she was out all evening, wandering around talking to people.
    The next day, at lunchtime she came to the clinic and said would Inika and I come to talk to the women's choir. This is a Seventh Day Adventist choir and they are wonderful to hear. By the way, when I say 'choir' I mean African choir, not one of those stationary sets of standing bodies you get in the UK. These women move when they sing and dance as well if necessary. Their songs may be religious but are just as likely to be about social concerns. Anyway, when we got there it was by one of the swimming pools and the women asked me questions and Inika and Jo translated. I showed them the creeping things in the water.
    Then there was then a lot of chat I didn't understand and suddenly everyone produced spades and bowls and buckets and began to throw sand over the edge into the puddle at the bottom of this swimming pool. The older women at the back started singing and swaying and I grabbed a spade too, as did Inika. It didn't take long to sop up the water. We don't need that much sand in the bottom. Just

enough to absorb the water and any further rain. At 28C it will soon evaporate so the pool will be and stay dry and no insects can breed.

When we'd done the first one, the singing women sort of danced and processed to the next pool and we all followed. And we did it all again! By the time we had got to the third pool we had attracted the attention of the boss, but it turns out he has a wife, a mother and a two year old. After a bit more chat we had a work gang of men as well. The choir kept on singing, sometimes I recognised a hymn tune but according to Inika it was mostly special songs about what we were doing.

'Defeating the mosquito as we've already defeated our other enemies.' And about getting strong children for their country. We did seven of the eight pools. The eighth had a crack in the tiling and the water had drained away naturally, so we were saved the work. At the last one there was one long song and everyone, very pleased with themselves went home.

It was the most amazing afternoon. Just try and picture it ;The wooden huts, dirty yellowish grey sand under foot, some scrubby trees, Inika and I in our (very ill fitting) nurses uniforms, the women , perhaps 30 of them all in bright coloured African wraps and the usual myriads of roaming children. Tall thin Jo just keeping it all going. The swimming pools, just sit there in the sand as if dropped from a great height. They could have been taken lock stock and barrel from any British Municipality. They are just like the ones we used as children, in London, now however half full of sand! When the men came to join in, the women stood back and simply sang, but with such power and drive that none of those men were going to dare to stop until it was all done.

I'm sorry I didn't take any photos, but I wasn't expecting it all to happen and anyway I was too involved. I enclose one of a partly filled in pool. It does have enough sand in the bottom to prevent a puddle, honest! A bit dull I realise. Label it 'Achievement.'

That evening I asked Jo how she did it. 'Oh I just spoke to a few important grandmothers,' she said. 'They all fought in the war along side the men and if they want something they get it. All they needed was the info.' I think the moral of the above story is 'Don't mess with an African Grandmother.'

I sincerely hope it will make a difference but I sure feel better walking to the clinic everyday past dry partly filled sandpits instead of stagnant ceramic puddles full of breeding insects.

Her next project is called Social Mapping. It's new and trendy. They teach you how to do it on Developmental Courses. Basically you get everyone local to record all they know about the area on a huge map you all draw. It's a communal activity with tea and round here, sweets. Some one acts as the recorder, Jo in this case. Inika and Jason will interpret and will help. I have several rolls of wallpaper I found in a backroom, which given that our patch is a very long strip is very suitable for the map. I also have two new packets of felt tip pens and large bags of boiled sweets. That is apparently all we need. The idea is to involve people and record where everyone lives and what animals are seen and where the water is and so on. We start with the school children and the old people and hope everyone gets involved.

Meanwhile Jo has galvanised me about the ambulance. We've put together a plan which I think the Authorities in Katilo Hospital might go along with.

Will send this tonight. Jo is going into town and will mail it.

love from an energised
Annie

*

Letter Five

Becana camp

Dear Julia

The good news is now we've got the ambulance I can go with it to Katilo Hospital and they really do have email there!!!

And this is how we got it. Further investigation told us that Becana used to have one but Katilo said it was misused and beaten up out here and if we wanted one they would send one if we phoned. This isn't good enough. Well, we plotted and planned and put our ideas to Katilo. They just caved in and gave us our ambulance back.

Well, with the breech baby and the malaria children and the unreliability of the phone in the rains we had good ammunition but what clinched it, was me turning up on the back of a flatbed truck with an unconscious man with an airway in. The Health and Safety aspect of it finally persuaded them. There would have been an awful lot of explaining to do if a foreigner, a volunteer, had been killed by being thrown off an open lorry because there was no ambulance! One must use the tools one has! But with Jo's help I think we've got a management plan that will work after my year is up.

The problem is that possession of a vehicle is real power out here. The only other one in the camp is owned by the catholic priest. Whoever has the ambulance is subjected to huge pressure to use it for every conceivable purpose from carrying goats to wedding party transport and all sorts of things I don't want to know about. The answer seemed to be to divide the responsibility for it. We are going to keep it outside the police station, under the blue light where 'the people' can see it and the policeman is responsible for its safety. The only person who can authorise a journey is the nurse (me or Inika) and the driver keeps the keys and is responsible for its proper running and fuel and log book. And everyone accounts to Katilo once a month. I wonder if it will work. The important thing is I think ownership by the population. If it is seen as the Ambulance for the Sick and not X's private car, then if it is misused there will be complaints. We all only survive out here, courtesy of each other, so you don't want your neighbour's disapproval! It's a very rough and ready democracy, but it is one.

And now we've got it, this means we can do outreach at the villages along the strip, which I now know about thanks to Jo's map, (more about that later.) They need immunisations and babies weighing and generally finding out who is there and what is going on.

We've done the survey and the map is splendid. The one on the day was about 15' long and 33inches (a wallpaper roll!) wide. Some very odd things have come up. Among other things it turns out this place has an airfield capable of taking a small jet! It's left over from its army days and abandoned but the tarmac is still good. I've seen it. Now I know about it I send Jason down there to burn our disposable syringes and needles in an oil drum so they melt into a disgusting plastic mass and are unreuseable. Burning them near the clinic sends up a black plume of smoke and I get moaned at about the washing on the line! The HIV situation is pretty well under control here and most people who need the meds have them but the infection rate is still high and I don't want any syringes going astray and getting reused. I was horrified and started this when I saw syringe barrels as earrings on a young girl.

Anyway, back to the map. Every house anyone knew about is recorded and all water sources, the last births and deaths in each settlement. Animals seen. Geography, names and anything else anyone wanted put in - like the ghost everyone seems scared of. I'm making a smaller manageable copy in my boring solitary evenings and it will be photocopied lots and pinned up in the clinic, the church and the bars and everyone can comment. It's all pictures because not that many can read. I have to say that includes rather embarrassingly, our ambulance driver. He was well recommended to me and is a (very tall) respected Bushman which is important as they are the most deprived and poorly cared for group out here, but we still had to do the paper work and as I watched him realised he couldn't do the application form. So I filled it in to his dictation. He is called Jeff Soto. He can do numbers and used to drive for the Army in the Bushman Brigades, where literacy especially in English was positively discouraged in case people got ideas above their station. I haven't quite told Katilo yet that their new ambulance driver can't read.

    I thought I'd tell you a bit more about Jo, seeing she has become part of my life here and I suppose I feel a bit maternal towards her. She is a fourth generation South African of British descent, can speak Africaans, but thinks of English as her mother tongue. After giving her and her brother an idyllic home life, her parents got a divorce and she feels very rootless and I think bereft. As I said she is very well qualified in Zoology and has done this Community Development course. She has also got this Rainbow Nation guilt which I suppose one must have if brought up in luxury while most of the population around you was on the breadline and considered less than human. But, unlike me she is a true African. I saw a book once called "The white tribe of Africa." That's what she is. A member of yet another tribe to add to the list of those who live here in Becana. She doesn't live here though. She lives this nomadic and I think very dangerous life hurtling, up and down our new road in the truck with three or four men from the wildlife organisation. She comes to see me about three times a week. She has a boyfriend. He's called Ian Montgomery and I think that's serious. He got her this job. He works as a financial guy of some sort and has contacts. She like me is company sponsored as part of their public relations. She deals with conservation and the animals and I'm there for the inhabitants.

    What I get less and less sure about is why they do it. They aren't a charity they are a scientific company. They don't attempt to use our jobs for publicity. I see a man once a month when he delivers my anti-malarials and I give him a brief report of where I've spent the small charity budget I have for special cases. I sent a copy of our map back last time but I've had no interest or support.

Anyway, Jo: she has been an enormous help with the ambulance and the map. Empowered me, is I think the trendy phrase. But somehow she seems so fragile, not physically but mentally. She is pushing every boundary and living on the edge all the time. As far as I can see, she is at risk from a car accident, an animal encounter and any of the many passing diseases. I've given her a very serious chat about HIV and Malaria and TB and she did listen, but that's not really the core of it. It is so important to her to live 'with the people.' As I said, Rainbow Nation Guilt. I just don't know if she is tough enough.

We had a lovely Sunday lunch though, just she and I, talking English which is nice for me. We had a picnic by the only bit of open water near here, a pool about 10Km up the road. We sat and watched the birds and ate our food and chatted and then just as it was getting time to go home, the elephants came down to drink. We retreated discreetly but were able to sit and watch them from her truck for about half an hour. Amazing. These aren't Zoo elephants these are a wild herd, mothers and babies and teenagers, just splashing and drinking and playing. (Photo enclosed)

Less of a joy is Maria. She is a young girl, Inika's niece and she seems to have attached herself, or been attached to me as a helper. I have managed to persuade all and sundry that I do not need and will not have a servant but I seem to be stuck with her as a sort of apprentice. Inika is determined she shall train as a nurse, and to do this she must get her English up to scratch. She now comes to the clinic every day to help but I have managed to defend the privacy of my house - just. Nobody here believes one could possibly want to be alone. Me and Garbo both!

Re the email: The bad news is I don't have much time on the computer when I'm at Katilo and they don't have a scanner. So all you'll get is quick, but at least real time, greetings. The stories will still have to come by snail and plane.

You can send me emails though and they'll print them out and save them for me weekly. They won't print out photos though. The cartridges are too expensive, so we only do black and white.

    love
    Annie

Letter Six
Becana Camp

Dear Julia

It might amuse you to know that I actually did do my real job, just recently. Instead of just stitching up drunks and doling out antimalarials. I delivered a baby, admittedly in circumstances that would make my colleagues in the UK freak out. It was a Bushman baby 'Koisan' or 'Kwee' are the official names, but the people themselves seem happy with 'Bushman.' Anyway this woman is well known to Inika, and is rather special. She's a qualified schoolteacher. She always comes to Inika for her deliveries because traditionally Bushman babies have to be born outdoors under the sky and on the ground. The schoolteacher knows well she should have qualified help at delivery, but also still needs to abide by the tradition. There was no way Katilo Hospital, or the big Hospital at Bundu could deal with that. Inika, being Inika manages to sort this out and the babies are born in clean supervised conditions but on the sand in Becana clinic yard, under the sky. I was reminded of the bender deliveries in the hippie camps that cause so many administration headaches at home. The woman was fit and well nourished and it was her third baby so there was no cause for concern, except that it was 4am and cold, even in Africa. Inika's irritated remark while we waited for nature to take its course, that the only warm person here was the baby summed up all our thoughts. Anyway I delivered a little girl, with no problems. Her English name is 'Dawn' and her Koisan name a lot of clicks. It was fun to do what I'm supposed to do for a change. I don't deliver many babies. It tends to be support before or picking up the pieces after.

It's the annual vaccination days next month. Great excitement here. Even I get to go camping in the bush. Admittedly I had to pull rank, not something I often do, to get the chance. One of us has to stay in Becana and run the show from there and Inika was determined it was going to be me. I was equally determined that this was my chance to see more of the patch and camp under African stars. After some discussion during which I pointed out that she'd been out last year and would go next year she gave in with a fairly good grace. I will say that she never bears a grudge.

  Vaccination days are an extreme community event and effort. They are officially called National Immunisation Days but nobody here calls them that! All the hotels and businesses lend vehicles and staff and everyone is involved. I've never seen anything like it. I asked the lot who sponsor me if they'd lend a car. I thought they'd like their logo out there seen to be doing good. We all get our pictures in the paper and on the net. Apparently not. They pay for all the fuel used by the vehicles but don't want to be seen doing it. Jo was a bit odd about that. She'll be there with her conservation truck and her team. We intend to join forces and use the new map.

  The idea is to give polio and measles vaccine to all children aged under 14 on our patch. It's a combination of catch up on those missed and a general boost for the rest. It means we give one oral dose for polio and one injection for measles to each child over a year old, and that means hundreds of syringes, needles, cold boxes etc. for all the cars and lots of logistics if the teams are camping out. It's going to be very exciting.

  BUT It turns out there is even an agenda around immunisation. Nothing is simple. In our day immunisations were unequivocally good and you were neglectful if you didn't get your kids done. I've nagged many a mother to the clinic in my time. But do you remember Mum kicking up all that fuss about us having the oral polio vaccine not the injectable one, way back, years and years ago, when we were at school ? Well I've just worked out what that was all about. The injection is theoretically safer because it uses dead virus but in the 60s the Americans had a bad batch and some got polio cases, and Mum always being on the ball had her say, so we got British vaccine on sugar lumps while everyone else got an injection. The irony is that, as I said, the injection is in some ways safer. All these years later the argument is still going strong. For your info: it is as follows. Source, needless to say Jo.

  There are still two vaccines, one taken by mouth, the other an injection. The oral uses a live virus in its vaccine. Because it is oral (a drop on the tongue from a tiny bottle) it's simple to give and you don't need nurses to do it. This means it is easy to do mass vaccination campaigns on huge populations using non medical volunteers and so protect millions of children. It is a live vaccine though and for a few days after giving it the children shed the virus which somehow immunizes others around them, so it's always used when there is an outbreak. But if you don't keep up the campaigns, weird strains of the virus can develop especially among those that miss being vaccinated and then they get polio. It's caught through faeces (poo to you!) and remember we don't have main drainage and plumbing in bush villages! Also just occasionally, perhaps one in a million children gets polio from the vaccine and that can also spread if you don't keep up the vaccinations. The other vaccine, is a dead vaccine so you can't catch or spread polio with it but it doesn't give that protection to those around and a big BUT, it's an injection and mass vaccination campaigns just wouldn't be possible. There just aren't enough nurses in Africa. However if you are an African mother and your child dies of vaccine derived polio you aren't going to be any less angry than a European or American or Aus. mother are you?

    This argument is still going on. Here, there hasn't been a polio case for some years in this country, but apparently we keep up the mass campaigns with oral vaccine because our neighbour over the border isn't so organised and does regularly have cases. The international border in Bundu town is just a river and people regularly wade across just to come to work.

    I'm not sure what I think. I know that now in the UK we give a dead injectable vaccine, but then we haven't had polio for ages and ages and we don't want even one stray vaccine generated case or nobody would ever vaccinate their children ever again.

    We are just lucky that here in this district that we have the resources to give every child under 14 a booster injection for measles, but it would double the time and expense if we had to give two injections. I am old enough to remember people who had had polio. It was a summer disease and hundreds got it. Do you remember not being allowed to go swimming because Mum said we could catch it at swimming pools? Catching polio and being paralysed was one of my childhood nightmares. Do you remember those pictures on the news in the cinema of children in iron lungs for years? I just don't know what I think. I wish they'd sort out a vaccine of any sort for malaria though!

    Anyway I have my own sub agenda with the BCG vaccine for tuberculosis - TB and the babies. As I expect you know, (well you do now) with HIV around, there is a lot more TB . It's very easy for children to catch TB if they live under the same roof as someone who has it. Now our rules say we, nurses can vaccinate newborns. With the ones born in the camp, it's no problem, so long as they turn up. But with those born in the bush villages - which the map tells me is most of them, it's different. No newly delivered mother in her right mind is going to get herself on the back of a truck to the clinic unless she or the baby is ill. So I'm going to find them all and by the time I leave this country at least one yearfull of babies on my patch will be protected against TB. This means that in the bottom of my coldbox I will have, unofficially, a few doses of anti TB vaccine and the special tiny syringes we use and we'll have to do a few diversions to find the most remote settlements.

I'm sorry to use you rather as a diary, but a diary doesn't work for me and I know you'll say there is too much nasty medical detail in this letter. But I want to be talking to someone, even if I don't get a reply, though it's better now with the email every week, but with my letters going by airmail we're bound to be completely out of sync.

On that topic, diaries I mean, I've been reflecting rather on what happened before I left UK.

Did I ever tell you about that traveller girl, Sal, who died just before I left? We never found out what happened. Well since I've been here I have seen and treated a lot of Malaria and I do wonder whether there is any possibility that's what she had. After what I've seen here it ticks so many boxes and I doubt anyone would think of testing her. We just don't get it in UK unless you've come back from abroad - and she certainly hadn't. I'm writing to a friend who works in casualty and see if she thinks its worth suggesting to someone.

I've got two more stories for you before I finish this: the first about the elephant and the second the man with burns. Then next time it will be all about my adventures camping in the bush. Keep my letters and maybe when I go home I'll write a book about it all and make enough money to keep me in my old age!

The elephant! Don't kid yourself elephants are cuddly by the way! My most recent encounter frightened the living daylights out of me. It was Jeff's day off and someone needed a transfer to Bundu. Not totally urgently I admit, but I like a chance to drive and I only get that when Jeff is off. I also don't go a lot on showers and really wanted a bath and the Dutch nurses in Bundu have baths in their houses and when they see the ambulance they put out towels for me.

I got my comeupance though.

Inika and I were in the front of the ambulance, driving in the dark and watching quite literally the cat's (and other small creatures) eyes glittering as the lights picked them up, along our new bit of tarmac road, which is very smooth, with no dust and a great luxury. Then suddenly on the right I saw an elephant's head appear against the sand, walking away from us. Inika gasped and a moment later I realised what had happened and stopped the ambulance and sat there shaking. The elephant had walked in front of us perhaps ten feet ahead and we hadn't even seen it! It was dark grey, so was the tarmac. Had we hit it we would be strawberry jam. We have passed cars on the road that have hit elephants and both Inika and I have said,

'Must have been drunk. How can you NOT see an elephant!'

Well now we know. In the grey dark, against a grey tarmac road. I think I want yellow tarmac on my road like you get in children's playgrounds. And I'm not taking the ambulance out again after dark except in a real emergency.

Which leads me to the man with burns. It was both scary and funny. A very tall man, called Brown came and knocked on my little wooden house door one early evening, about twilight. He is the only Zimbabwean in the camp, and therefore he speaks English. He has also spent several nights in the police station for reasons I don't know about and Jeff the driver doesn't like him and told me to be careful of him. I respect Jeff's opinion on anything, so I was very dubious about being asked to go over to the far side of the camp because there had been an accident, but he said it was serious and urgent and the man was screaming with pain. I did remember my own scathing comment about characters in films who just go off and leave no message, so I left a note in the house saying where I was going and went with him.

By the time we got to the 'far side' which doesn't have electricity, it was almost dark. I had the maglite which Melanie gave me, in my pocket. By the way, that woman knows her stuff. I use it everyday and never go out after midday without it. You never know in this game when you'll be back.

Anyway, back to me standing outside yet another old wooden army hut, looking through an open door into complete darkness, with lots of tall men, behind me urging me on and some distressed crying from within. I took a deep breath and did go in and found this small old man (well about 40 but they look so old sometimes) rolling around and crying and clearly very very drunk. He was obviously conscious and I couldn't see any injury. Finally I got someone to tell me he had fallen into the fire, outside and they'd brought him into the house and gradually his screaming had got worse and worse. Well it's pitch dark inside and at least outside there was the moon and the open fire, so I made them carry him out onto the sand and I had a look. He had somehow rolled into the fire or fire had fallen on him. Eventually I managed to unwrap what they'd put round him and shine the torch on his burns, with everyone standing around and having a look and an opinion and most 'having drink taken' as they say. There also was a serious lack of women present which always makes me nervous. From what I could see, I think he'd been curled up asleep because he'd had his hands over his bits, but he had bad blisters on his hands and thighs and below his waist.

Well burns always look terrible unless you know what you are looking at, and the audience was very shocked and I think a little guilty as they'd just bundled him up into the hut and left him until his screaming got too loud to bear.

From my point of view the priority was to deal with the pain and stop him crying and howling. Now, you know your first aid. Put a burn under water and the pain stops. If someone had been sitting on a cloud that night watching me trying to make myself understood I'd have been given a celestial comedy award. What I wanted was a zinc bath full of cold water. I mimed washing and clothes scrubbing, said 'water' in every language I could think of and got nowhere. Finally I found a small pink plastic 'barbie' toy bath lying in the sand. I picked it up and I went bigger, bigger bigger with my hands. Meanwhile the old man was still rolling and screaming this sort of high pitched wail which was getting to us all.

Then a woman appeared. I think they'd brought her because of my scrubbing mime. I said it all again to her with expansive hand movements and I saw her understand. She disappeared into the dark and came back with the zinc bath I knew had been bound to be in there somewhere. With more effort I got it filled with cold water. Then I said to the guys 'In, in, in,' with appropriate gestures. They simply wouldn't lift our screaming sufferer into the water. They just didn't believe it was right and anyway, Bushman don't like water. They are desert people and regard it as something dangerous that drowns people and the old man was a Bushman. So here is all 5'1" of me trying to get this crowd of very tall men to do what I know is right, and they are sure isn't. I thought of those African grandmothers and the swimming pool and just stood my ground. 'Come on' says me and takes one leg of the wailing man. Something gets through and I get help and we lift him gently into the cold water. Its only a small bath and his legs are hanging over the edge . There is an immediate silence as the pain stops, and for a second I think, they think I've killed him, then he begins to sing. He is now a pain free singing drunk and everyone relaxes and I have time to think what to do next.

Meanwhile Brown, having disappeared when I could have used his English has suddenly reappeared with Jeff, who has the ambulance keys in his hands and I realise I am supposed to transfer the man to Bundu. It is also clear his friends intend to go along for the ride to see he has proper care and then no doubt continue their party in Bundu afterwards. Having looked at the burns, I know that though dramatic, they aren't that bad. No way, especially after the elephant, am I embarking on a night transfer let alone with an ambulance full of drunks. It's not easy to say NO though. In the end I just fold my arms and say, 'Fetch Inika, Fetch Inika.'

It's an annoyed Inika who turns up, having been brought to the most disreputable part of Becana thinking she had to rescue me. Between us we manage to convince the increasing crowd that what our man needs is to stay in that water till morning and then he is to be brought to the clinic where we can dress the burns in daylight. We agree to get him an injection and some medicine. We leave Jeff in charge of the patient, who is still intermittently singing. Inika intelligently takes the ambulance keys from Jeff, 'To hang them back in the clinic,' thus avoiding him being pressured into any unilateral action in our absence and she and I went and got the necessary supplies. We gave our patient a very large dose of antibiotics in a big syringe and a couple of codeine for any pain. He was very happy in the water, waving his arms and legs around, still completely drunk and incoherent.

The crowd suitably placated and the patient comfortable, the three of us were then able to retreat. As I looked back in the moonlight, silhouetted against the fire I could see the old man in his bath, looking like an upended giant turtle, still waving his arms and legs. I thought I recognised the hymn he was singing.

Jeff walked Inika and I home to our own front doors. Our usual 'end of day' remark to each other which we say every day when we close the clinic 'Manyana, another day.' (Inika was trained in Cuba) had a more than usual strength to it.

Given all that, you can understand my latest discovery! Team work actually works. You know that stupid children's cartoon with the animated guinea pig? They sing a song about it and they're right. It keeps on running through my head out here. Think what we (Me, Jo, Jason, Inika and Jeff) have achieved together that I couldn't possibly have done alone. I've always been too much of a loner. How's that for a confession from your bloody minded individualistic sister.

This isn't a bad life.

Next time all about the camping

love Annie

*

Letter Seven

Becana

Dear Julia
Firstly thank you for the posters, or Max really. But he wouldn't have done it if you hadn't nagged him! But he must have put a good bit of effort into their collection. What he sent, he had collected from all over the UK. I probably now have the largest collection of ethnically appropriate safe sex posters in Southern Africa. My favourite is one of a very sophisticated, well dressed couple dancing. It comes from Birmingham Health Authority! Anyway it's much admired here, and it's implication that the rich and clever take care and stay safe is good. And possibly if you take care you may get to be rich and successful! Here those who see themselves as successful seem to think nothing can touch them.

    The posters arrived very unconventionally, dropped off at my clinic by a huge beer lorry. Apparently the driver had seen the parcel in Bundu post office and told them he was passing the clinic and would deliver them. A fair exchange I felt for a course of anti-malarials. My Safe Sex poster display is amazing and attracts much discussion. There are local posters, but they are black and white and not on good paper. Their local themes are sound though. One slogan is

'Zero grazing' which I had to have explained to me. It means monogamy - eat grass only at home. Don't eat it elsewhere.

Another is very clear. It shows two girls, one pregnant girl outside her village hut and the other, thin, wearing a mortar board and accepting her high school diploma.

The RC priest raised his eyebrow at me last time he passed by but everyone else is very positive. As I think I've said before, in a society with limited literacy, pictures are so important. I've watched people looking at the display and discussing them and then asking Inika what it's about. She loves it and will give them a tour. I sort of think about cathedrals and churches in medieval England. The pictures and windows there were for teaching people before universal literacy.

We are all ready now for vaccination days next week. The amount of organisation involved is phenomenal. I am very impressed! Everyone seems to regard the days as some sort of holiday so I am too. I'm hoping to see some of the creatures I have yet to see. They are rare in Becana because anything remotely edible here is eaten! My wish list involves giraffe and ostrich and bush pig and if possible some of the birds I saw in the capital like the lovely crested hoopoes and the mouse birds with their long tails. I might even manage to sort out one sort of deer from another. I've got a book, but there are so many different kinds.

I promised you another elephant story, so here goes. You maynot be so pleased at this one. One evening sitting outside my little house I began to smell this wonderful cooking food smell. It's not something you get very often. People are often hungry here. Anyway I went to investigate. Wandering around Becana down the various alley ways, following the smell like a 'Bisto kid' almost everywhere I could see cooking fires lit, with pots on them. (They have a sort of junior witch's cauldron with three legs which they stand in the fire.) From them all this same smell was coming which was of a rich meat stew. Eventually I ended up outside Inika's and asked her what was going on and why every single person in Becana seemed to be having a good meal for a change. Her own pot was cooking outside her house.

'It's the elephant.' She said. The story she told me was this. Apparently about a couple of miles down the road a young elephant had been causing chaos in the maize fields. Once an individual elephant gets a taste for the maize, it is really difficult to move them on and they can easily destroy a family's food supply for a year. In exasperation, instead of getting in touch with Jo's conservation lot several owners hired these two not very bright young men to get rid of it. Either accidentally or deliberately they managed to kill it. Now this is illegal, so they then decided they had to bury it. A pretty futile project really! It's difficult enough to dig a grave in the sand deep enough for a human round here.

Meanwhile the bush telegraph had got going and people from all over descended with knives and bags to get a share of what was clearly free good bush meat. Eventually the police from our police station turned up and arrested the two young men who, by then, were trying to sell the meat to the assembled population. They theoretically took charge of the evidence. But you can't move a dead elephant, even a small one and they took the rather sensible view that they had the criminals and the very small elephant tusks and retreated leaving everyone else to collect their supper. At this point Inika invited me to supper and I sampled elephant meat. But what you get here is the meat on millimeal porridge, which is horrible. It's sort of solid cornflour blancmange and it spoils the rest - to my mind. I finally got Inika to agree I could have some raw meat for myself. She said she would sort it.

The next day Inika and I were invited to the police station to check the two young men who were fine and undamaged if a bit sorry for themselves. Then we were taken to a back room in the police station where there was a huge frig (which, incidentally, I strongly suspect was once the clinic frig when it was an army hospital). Inside the frig was a huge piece of meat. After negotiation I bought a chunk, about a pound of elephant meat. The policeman then looked me in the eye and asked me if I'd like a 'tooth.' I said no and thanked him, saying I just wanted to be able to say, when I went home that I had cooked elephant. It was only later that night, on reflection, I realised I had been offered illegal ivory (one of the tusks) by a policeman and only linguistic confusion had saved me from involvement in great complications, not the least with Jo, to whom I have not mentioned this.

The stew I have to say was delicious. Cooked like at home with carrots and onions and potatoes it did me the world of good. It tasted like a very, very, rich beef. I don't think this is a story I shall relate to the vegetarian contingent at home! BUT I do think I did the right thing. By cooking and eating it I was complicit so people didn't have to hide it from me but, even unknowingly by refusing the tusk, I showed I was only interested in the food aspect of this elephant! And whatever anyone says dead meat should be eaten, especially where there is a chronic shortage of first class protein in the diet, especially of the children.

Looking forward to my camping trip

Love, your well fed sister
Annie

*

CHAPTER FIVE

The Adventure

As Annie had told her Australian sister, Immunisation days were a great annual event locally and in fact, in many parts of Africa. Articles exist in academic journals which criticize them for their use of resources and disruption of the routine health service. It was said, a few years ago, that perhaps concentration on polio which is a disease few now get, was misplaced, but its recent re-emergence in some countries has revived enthusiasm for mass immunization.

It has become clear that if the campaign eases, the disease comes back.

The T shirt slogan 'Kick polio out of Africa' is still relevant. Some countries who are free of polio keep immunizations going, as their neighbours are yet to defeat the infection and no one wants it creeping over their border.

Smallpox may have been defeated but polio has become a more wily foe, so National Immunisation Days (NIDs) continue.

On the ground, they generate huge community participation and enthusiasm. Central Government pays for all the publicity and the much prized T shirts. There is always a poster of a local dignitary or politician giving the vaccine to his grandchild.

Annie had a very splendid one she displayed in the clinic foyer of the President giving the drops to a small child.

A successful NID depends on good local organisation. Bundu Region, within which was Becana, was very proud of its record and each year marshalled its resources to deliver the polio and measles vaccines to the children on its patch.

Becana camp came immediately under the direction of Katilo district hospital which was run by a very fierce Catholic nun, Sister Hildegard who never considered that less than 100% coverage was acceptable, thus nobody else did either. Every child who was supposed to be immunized had to be sought out and no exceptions were made. 'They are all God's children' was her much repeated saying.

The population around Becana wasn't that large but it was dispersed and a proportion of it was in small bush villages which were off the road, reachable only with very sturdy cars or 4x4 vehicles. The essence of an immunization day is that ALL the chosen population of children are protected against, most usually, measles and polio. Now a local district will have a limited number of ambulances, but Becana was near a National Park and had, in the area a good few Safari Lodges where tourists stay. All these lodges had minibuses and 4x4 cars with their individual logos on the sides.

Immunization is seen by almost all in this part of Africa as A Good Thing. As a result all the hotels and lodges were delighted to lend their cars and drivers and any extra staff and to be seen to do so. It was altruism, but neither did anyone want a measles or polio outbreak to frighten visitors away.

The construction company, Annie's employer, who was building the new road, added a vehicle or two to the pool, and loaned manpower in the form of a turbaned Sikh and three very handsome engineers from respectively Ethiopia, Nigeria and Sierra Leone, all of whom caused a fluttering in the hearts of the ladies seconded from the town offices of the two local banks whose job it was to keep the clerical work of the day up to scratch.

It was an adventure and a variation of daily routine for all concerned. To spend a night in the bush was also, a reminder, very precious to all who worked in the town, of where they or their parents had once come from. When she had heard people talking, it had reminded Annie of the attitude of American Irish or Dubliners to 'bog' Ireland. They were deeply relieved to have got away, but both curious about, and respectful of their roots and happy to go back to help, provided they absolutely knew it was just a visit and they could escape again at will to their new and modern lives.

There was the added benefit to all, that they knew they were doing good. There was, on Immunization Days, hovering over the district, an enormous cloud of self-satisfaction so tangible it was almost visible.

Annie's part of the patch was from Becana camp to the border, a 120km long thin strip of land. Inika was to stay in Becana and make sure all the villages within about 20km of the clinic were covered. Inika had most of the teams and most of the population under her control in the camp. She had come to realise that this was a promotion for her. If she could be seen to successfully organize these days, she would be well thought of in Bundu. It was her opportunity to prove she was worth sending to the capital for her long desired upgrade training to a full nursing qualification and thus she was reconciled to her lost camping trip into the bush. Annie too was happy. This was proper on the road, community stuff and dear to her heart. Sitting in a clinic all day was not her ideal way of working.

The morning of the NIDs dawned and in a very small corner of the nation, the Becana teams were ready to make their contribution to 'Kicking Polio out of Africa' and protecting their children against measles. The vehicles were loaded and assembled outside the clinic. Cold boxes were packed with ice and vaccines. Subsidiary boxes were packed with food and drink. Alcohol was officially, at least, banned. Cardboard boxes of syringes and needles all carefully enumerated and signed for were added. All the strangers who were coming to help arrived, mostly in a bus from town and were welcomed officially by Annie, dressed for the bush and Inika in full nurse's uniform, with white nurse's cap, an item of wear both she and Annie usually pretended didn't exist.

In attendance also was the man in charge of Becana camp, officially called 'the Administrator,' who had, eventually, been so supportive in the matter of filling in the swimming pools. Also present was the senior Policeman with braid and cap and holstered gun and the Catholic priest.

The Seventh Day Adventist Women's choir was there to start the day with song. The weather was unremarkably good, as expected. Not having to consider meteorological performance when planning a venture came unnaturally to the English born Annie and she was still getting amused smiles when she enquired about future weather prospects.

The Becana clinic team was assembled. Inika had her tables set up and her cold boxes ready. As the bus from Katilo unloaded, she greeted a number of the passengers as old friends and rapidly had them sitting at their tables, ready for the first customers, most of whom had already gathered, determined to watch the events of the day from the beginning.

The outreach teams were also ready. Annie's crew consisted of Jeff to drive, Inika's cousin Maria who it turned out had family near the border and a man seconded to them from the construction camp who was to be their recording clerk as he spoke and wrote English. He was needed because Annie didn't do anything else, Jeff could speak it but not write it and Maria spoke most local languages but as yet little English.

The ambulance held all that was needed to do the immunizations. Tucked away under the front seat Annie had added a copy of Jo's map. In tune with the holiday ambiance, she had also put in her camera and binoculars.

Jo too was ready, with her truck and her usual companions, the men from the conservation group. She had been rather silent lately and Annie was looking forward to finding the time to sit and talk to her. Her instincts told her there was boyfriend trouble.

The two womens' plan was that Annie and Jo's team should take the last 100km of the road to the border, one truck on each side, aiming to cover all the ground and find all the children. There were two big villages where the local health workers would have assembled most possible candidates. Then they would go and seek out the more elusive settlements, some at least of which were recorded on their map.

When both the outreach vehicles were ready and loaded, Annie was all for just driving off and getting on with things. This was obviously not going to be allowed. The day had to be launched with proper ceremony. The women's choir sang suitable songs. Everyone stood on the clinic steps watching, intent on giving the cars a proper send off.

Inika whispered to Annie.

'Maria will see you alright and she's part Bushman and a good cook. Can't have anything happening to you.'

Annie was touched. She seemed to have become a local responsibility.

As the Ambulance and the truck drove away Annie heard the women stop singing and the school bell start ringing. This was the signal that all was ready to begin and parents should bring their children to the clinic. She turned her face forward and looked at the road ahead.

'Well,' she said, 'I feel like a ship that's been well and truly launched. Is it always like that?'

'Every year,' said Jeff and he and Annie in the other front seat turned their eyes to   the road ahead.

Having left Becana, suddenly there were, other than the new grey tarmac beneath their wheels, no signs of humanity at all. There was just yellowish sand and small scrublike trees. In the distance Annie could see some sort of deer leaping across the landscape. That ought to be springbok, she thought.

Behind her in the back seat she could hear Maria and the new man getting acquainted. It never failed to amaze her that people's communication skills found it so easy to jump the language barrier. The chatter seemed to be in a mix of English, Dutch and Ovambo. Maria was making most of the running but the man with the turban seemed to be keeping his end up, largely by drawing cartoons of the animals they could see out of the windows in his notebook.

'A man with the turban,' repeated Annie to herself. Some thing was beginning to niggle at the back of her brain.

Their first stop was only half an hour down the road. It was a gentle quiet half hour with little more than the hum of the car engine and human murmuring as they drove.

They turned off the road and found themselves plunged into a turmoil, which initially anyway seemed chaotic.

This was Tundi, the next village along the road and the local health workers, both men, Jafeta and Togo, had been very busy. There were people everywhere, mostly holding small children. All the school children were also present. Every spare corner of shade was occupied by humans.

As the cars drove in Annie looked around her and realised that this place was completely different from Becana, which was still essentially the army camp it had been built as, with every dwelling in a straight line. Tundi was a 'proper African village' she thought to herself. There were round mud-walled houses with grass roofs, laid out in no particular order around a huge tree which provided some shade in the baking heat.

The cars drew to a halt at the village clinic and to Annie's amusement it too was made up of round hutlike buildings but these were metal and prefabricated, with a metal roof as well. Her amusement was noticed by Jo.

'Ah yes,' she said, 'Providing " tribally appropriate" buildings was part of the separate development plan of our previous masters. Recognising tribal differences and thus divisions was one way of ensuring compliance. It's called divide and rule!'

There was no time for Annie to pursue this comment as they were descended upon by anxious villagers and unloaded. Other than a 'This way Sister, we've been waiting for you,' Annie found herself ignored while a production line was set up. When everything was assembled she was led to the front where her place obviously was simply to give the injections.

As she felt she was technically at least, in charge and the only medically qualified person present she asked for a tour of the arrangements. This conversation also gave her an opportunity to ask for any babies under a year old who hadn't got a TB vaccine scar on their arm. Discussion among the listeners produced three suggestions and immediately someone was deputed to go off and enquire. Annie was amazed by the detailed organisation and knowledge of the local health workers. Though if it was my patch at home, she thought, I'd know too.

At Annie's table Maria was already opening boxes and laying out syringes. Jafeta had the vaccine in front of him in the ice and was ready to start filling the syringes. The turbaned Sikh from the construction camp whose presence was causing great interest among Tundi's inhabitants was being given his clip board, pen and instructions.

Annie looked at him. 'It couldn't be', she thought. 'You're falling into the "they all look alike" trap. For goodness sake how many Sikhs do you know?'

Someone else Annie didn't know was put in the line to take the used syringes and bin them for later burning. Finally, after the injection had been given, stood a young man with a pad and a purple inked stamp with which he marked the inside wrist of the children and gave them a sweet. The children carried by their parents, in the line for polio drops also got a stamp but no sweet. This reminded Annie of her last trip to a Devon music festival - no stamp, no entry though in this case it was no injection, no stamp and so no sweet.

Having last year completed a sociology evening class, she was still deciding whether it was ethnocentric or racist to be surprised at efficient African organisation when she slotted herself into place in the line and three solid hours of injections giving followed. Those from settlements furthest away were organised to the front of the queue so they could get home before the heat of the day.

It was hard work concentrating on keeping ahead of her production line while she injected the measles vaccine into fat arms and thin arms and lowdown young arms and eye level arms of the teenagers. She looked nowhere but at her pile of syringes and the arms in front of her. Around her she could hear everyone else talking in a tangled hum of incomprehensible languages and accents. Somewhere from the midst of this she kept hearing a voice and Annie felt her memory being jiggled again. She tried to pick this one voice out from the melee while she continued to give her injections. A phrase she'd used to someone to describe a particular accent slipped back into her mind. 'Tottenham with a touch of Trowbridge.' She was briefly back in a cold dark English country lane on a January night. She looked up and met the eye of the man doing the clerking. It was him. It really was. The turbaned Sikh looked back and nodded. From that same memory she dredged up his name, Jemal. Her questions multiplied but the production line of naked brown arms was relentless.

Half an hour later everything suddenly stopped.

'It's lunch time,' said Jeff. Exhausted she took the can of cola she was given and after checking the seal opened it and took a swig. Just occasionally, she thought, unlikely fluids tasted like the nectar of the Gods. This is one of them. Revived she looked around her. She had so many questions! But the man wasn't to be seen. She asked and was told he'd gone with Jo to help fetch some newborns in the conservator's truck so they could have their TB vaccine.

Lunch under the tree was millimeal and meat and cola, added to by Annie who had brought a cake for all and her own private supply of egg sandwiches. Try as she might she couldn't bring herself to like millimeal porridge. It was after all, just solid white blancmange with no flavouring and definitely no substitute for potatoes or even rice. She was so exhausted by the morning's work she simply sat and ate and responded briefly to the usual set of questions from a new set of colleagues.

'How old are you?'
'You don't ask a lady that!'
'Are you married?'
'NO.'
'Do you have children?'
'No.'

She knew she wasn't behaving as the 'new show in town' was supposed to, but as well as being seriously exhausted, her mind was buzzing with questions about the man she now recalled clearly as Vix and Sal's friend.

As lunch was being cleared away and the ambulance packed for the journey to the next village the truck returned. Jo and Jemal and one of the conservators got out with a young woman who held a baby in her arms. They brought her over to Annie.

Jo spoke.

'This is the only one we could find. Something has happened to the others.'

Annie concentrated on the mother and baby. He was a tiny scrap of a thing, perhaps two months old. Someone appeared who could translate the mother's language into Africaans. Jo did the Africaans into English bit. Practice had taught Annie that the way you had these complicated conversations was to look straight at the person you were talking to and speak, then even if they couldn't understand you, they could see your expression and they knew you were talking to them. If you could get them to reply direct to you, even with a double translation in between then the conversation worked.

This baby's name was George and he weighed 3.5kg on Annie's scales, which she hung from the car window. The mother's name was Ismia. When Annie asked her the father's name Ismia said in English 'Paterson and Paterson.' This was the name of the construction company building the road, Annie and almost everyone else's employer. Their male employees had made a substantial contribution to the number of local births and were usually very good at providing child support once responsibility was established, though establishing this might involve a visit to the Site Office by herself or the local priest.

The three way conversation allowed Annie to get permission for the immunisation. She then left Jo to talk to Ismia and see if they could offer her any other help. It turned out she was quite pleased with her life and George's father was good to her. He brought her clothes and food from the shop and a special mosquito net for her and George, which he said he had got from the miners. Much of her story was incomprehensible to Annie but her obvious satisfaction with her life left little for Annie to provide. Nevertheless fifteen minutes later the now quiet and fully immunised baby was feeding greedily from its mother while Annie sorted out a cocktail of vitamins for Mum and provided a 'New Baby Card' for George with his name and attendance recorded on it.

With this final injection, the session in Tundu was ended. The population stood back and watched the cars get ready to depart.

Ismia and George and Jo got into her truck with the rest of her crew and set off down the road. Jeff had the ambulance packed and ready for their next village stop. He opened the front door for Annie,

'No not his time, Maria. You are in the front. I'm going in the back with him.'

Maria looked a little miffed and considered Annie was trying to thwart her love life but Annie's motive was different. Having failed to corner Jemal during the morning she was determined to interrogate him now. They were barely on the road again before she started.

'It is you isn't it? What on earth are you doing here?'

'I got a job,' said Jemal, not meeting her eye.

'That's nonsense. Don't give me that. This is way beyond coincidence. I saw you before, last January at that phone box back in Devon, by the traveller camp. Now we meet months and months later in the same bit of sub saharan Africa. Chance. Give me a break. This is some thing to do with Sal isn't it?'

'So you do remember?'

'Of course I do.'

'But they sorted you out though didn't they. You got this job here.'

'What do you mean?'

'Well you're not there are you, back there, asking questions.'

Annie's thoughts went to the third person she'd seen that night.

'Have you seen Vix? How did he do?'

'He's dead. Killed. They said in a fight, but it wasn't like that.'

'I'm so sorry, but he was very angry the day after, when I saw him.'

'You haven't a clue have you? You just don't know what's going on.'

The two in the front seat could hear the acrimonious tone even if they couldn't work out the cause, but their next destination was only a further 10 km so before further explanations could be entered into, the two vehicles turned off the road and were greeted by a repeat performance of the morning.

This time however the local health workers were impatient having had their crowd waiting for several hours with the sun getting hotter all the time. Apparently the Becana cars were late. Had it been culturally appropriate, thought Annie, feeling the atmosphere, they would have been greeted by a mass rendering of 'Why are we waiting.' As it was, before she knew it Annie found herself back in the assembly line giving her injections, but her mind was full of whirling thoughts and questions.

Three hours later, just as abruptly as before, everything stopped and someone thrust a large mug of tea into Annie's hands. It was full of sugar and creamy rich milk. This isn't our UHT thought Annie, tasting it. The people at this end of the patch were, she knew, very proud of their cows and so she refused to think of brucellosis while she drank.

The cars were loaded and T shirts distributed while Annie made a short 'Thank you' speech for their skilled organisation. She incorporated into it her usual spiel about building strong young people to build a strong young country by making sure they don't get the childhood diseases which can be prevented.

And you know I actually believe all that, she thought to herself as she checked the reloading of the vaccines.

Meanwhile Jo was in consultation with Jeff about where they were going to camp that night. She had discussed with Annie before they set out which settlements they needed to visit to find all the new babies. There had been this area on the map called Kiara, near the border and the river, about which several people had said 'Well there are ghosts there now.' On the mapping day they hadn't been able to get more explanation except that those who spoke were scornful when Jo suggested there were white people in the bush.

'No, not Mesungu, ghosts, spirits,' had been the reply. 'And there are no animals or people now.'

The nearest settlement to the 'haunted' place was where they were headed now. Navigation in the bush remained a complete mystery to Annie. One bit of sand with scrubby bushes looked exactly the same as another to her. This meant her car had to follow closely behind Jo's and she felt she needed to sit in front with Jeff and watch their path, first along the tarmac and then through the bush as they plunged onto the sand.

She was however determined to continue her interrupted conversation with Jemal. He was equally determined to avoid such a confrontation so it simply didn't happen.

The car ahead of them signalled and turned left onto the sand, between the bushes and they followed. 'Well I wouldn't call this a track,' said Annie to herself. But the truck ahead seemed to know where it was going.

Evening was coming on and this made the finding of a campsite imperative. Without a secure camp they were very vulnerable to the big animals out here. Annie already knew what an annoyed elephant could do, but there were also, she'd been told, biggish cats like leopards and various wolfish animals that were to be feared. A fire needed to be lit. Her own concerns were that it was at dawn and dusk the malaria mosquitoes were active and she didn't want anyone to get bitten. For ten more minutes the truck drove on in front, on through the increasing gloom. It then stopped suddenly and Annie's ambulance followed suit. Maria, in the back looked out of the window and squealed in alarm and said something. Jeff, who was driving turned to Annie and said 'She says she can see the spirits.' It was true there were moving lights in the bush ahead, but they looked like hand held torches to Annie.

The truck ahead stopped and Jo and all her crew got out. As Annie and those in the ambulance behind watched, they saw the others surrounded by strange grey ghostlike creatures. Maria's wailing from the backseat had taken on a cadence that Annie recognised as prayer. That's a 'Hail Mary', she thought to herself.

In the twilight the creatures turned towards the ambulance. As they advanced it became clear that they were some form of human but they looked like walking skeletons. It was their bones that were visible to the watchers. The crescendo of fear in Maria's voice was reflected in the feelings both of Annie, and by the look of him, Jemal. Then suddenly Maria's voice stopped in midprayer and she opened the door with a jerk and shot out of the back seat and began to run towards the creatures shouting as she went. The shouts were indignant rather than scared. She stood in front of the leading spectre with her hands on her hips and berated him. The spectre in its turn looked a little daunted.

Jeff, the driver was laughing. 'It's her cousin,' he said.

The scary haunting had become a family reunion.

'But why,' asked Annie, trying to keep her mind on what seemed the relevant points and addressing no one in particular, 'are they painted like that?' For that is what, when the rest of the ghosts got nearer, she realised was the case. They had painted themselves with some sort of whitish grey mud. Her question was answered in impeccable English by one of the ghosts.

'It discourages visitors. We're miners and the mud comes from the river. We get covered in it anyway. This way, with a little decoration people leave us alone. It was my idea. Saw it in a movie. 'Crocodile Dundee.' We're like the black fellas in the bush. They are very superstitious round here.' He paused and held out his hand. 'I'm James, by the way, from Zimbabwe. We really didn't mean to terrify the medical services. Come and have supper and camp with us.'

Annie took the hand and shook it, and introduced herself. The others crowded round. Maria was engaged in a long discussion with at least three of the painted men. Annie looked at Jo.

'Did you know about this?'

'Not this, but I knew something was happening out here. We had to find out. The river was changing and people are moving and the animals dying or migrating. And remember what people said on our mapping day. I knew we had to come and look. The ambulance and the vaccination days was the perfect excuse. Everybody helps then and welcomes us.'

'Nice of you to tell me,' said an acidic and annoyed Annie. She turned aside to look at her new surroundings.

To say they were in the jungle would be overstating it. The nearest comparison Annie could think of was an under-resourced municipal park, but with sand underfoot. There were trees, true, but they weren't trees to write home about, more like undersized starved saplings, a bit like too many of the children round here, she thought.

Looking into the gloom she could see the outline of another industrial container, like the 'Weston-super-mare' one at Becana, but this one had a window cut into the side of it.

The focus of the camp though, was the fire with a selection of the universal, white plastic chairs set out round it. Annie looked at them with satisfaction. She had learnt, that in Africa you don't sit on the ground unless you really have to, as you never know what might creep up and bite you.

James and Jemal could be seen in earnest conversation near a small radio balanced on an upturned box. Straining her ears Annie caught a few words. They really were discussing cricket.

She realised she was watching two men seek common ground, just like at home, in the pub. There was though, an added fascination in watching a turbaned English-born Sikh and a black Zimbabwean, still painted to resemble an Australian bushman discussing in the Queen's English the latest cricket scores, while organising their supper on a fire in a fairly remote bit of the South West African bush.

It was a couple of hours later, sitting round the fire with full stomachs after some sort of venison stew, accompanied to Annie's delight, optionally with bread instead of millimeal porridge and a bottle of beer each that proper conversation began.

'So tell us, what's going on here, what are you mining and why?'

'And why is it so hush hush?'

'Well,' said James, 'this is good work. We get paid well, but it's not difficult. Really anyone could do it and we don't want anyone else doing it so we try to keep people away. That's what all the playacting is about.'

'But what are you mining? You're not starting a new goldrush are you?' said Annie

'No it's this blackstuff – look.'

He held out a small black lump . She took it in her hand. It was heavy and felt almost metallic. It reminded her of the iron pyrites she used to pick up on Dorset beaches back home in England when fossil hunting with her father. As she handed it to Jo another image flashed into her mind. She remembered the young man on the plane and the stone he had round his neck. It looked and felt the same

'I think I know what that is – it's coltan isnt it? You use it in mobile phones.'

'We call it Bellenwire, that's black beauty to you. I only know it goes to the factory, we just get it out of the ground and put it in milk tins. It goes up to Zambia on the train. The company man comes with a truck and collects it and pays us by the tin. We'll show you our workings by the river, in the morning. Just don't tell too many people.'

He looked ruefully at Maria and her cousins on the other side of the fire.

'But I don't think we'll be able to keep it quiet much longer. It's not called the bush telegraph for nothing. Her whole family and their families will be out here soon offering to work for less than we get paid. No union here! I think it's maybe nearly my time to get off this particular gravy train.'

'How did you get on it in the first place,' said Jemal.

'Heard about it in Vic Falls. I used to work in a hotel there but there's not much work or anything at home at the moment so I hitched a lift to the P&P road camp and then set off and found this place. I bumped into the company man and as I have good English and Ovambo he grabbed me with both hands and I found myself organising this operation. I've almost got enough money to get to the UK now.' He looked speculatively at Annie.

She, not wanting to get involved in one of those all too common 'Can you get me a visa' conversations, leant back in her plastic chair and letting the talk drift over her head, looked around her, watching the embers from the fire fly up into the African sky. It was dark and the stars had come out. They were still largely unfamiliar, but with some effort she found the southern cross and mentally greeted it as a friend. Tonight, she thought, I am going to sleep under these stars. It was, she felt a magical experience she didn't deserve. Her very practical self began to look round for a good place to hang her mosquito net, but again she was distracted, this time by the sight of all the people around her.

While James and Annie and Jo and Jemal had been having their English discussion on their side of the fire Maria and Jo's young men and some of the miners were having their own conversation in the bushman Tsan language. Jeff, the driver sat between, trying to listen to both groups at once. Yet, thought Annie tomorrow we'll all recombine and get together and work as hard as we did today, just to get a job done. Human beings are splendid.

Dozing in the warm, she was pulled back to reality by Jeff and James talking and bringing something to show her. Jeff was holding a rather odd mosquito net.

'They sleep under these here,' he said, 'and they don't have enough for us. He wants us to sleep in that.'

He pointed into the shadows where the container she had seen earlier stood.

'There is plenty of room in there really and it is clean. It's called the lab and the company use it to test our stuff before paying us. And there really is a nasty mosquito round here that can get through ordinary nets and gives a very bad fever,' added James.

Annie took the net in her hands and looked at it. It was knitted, like tights rather than like the ones they used which were more like net curtains. As a result the holes were much smaller and the whole fabric was denser.

'This is a Kala Azar net,' she said. 'But there is none of that round here. You know; against the little black flies. Where did you get these.'

'The company gives them out, and they do work. But it really is little mosquitoes, not those black sand flies we have round here.'

To Jeff's obvious relief Annie agreed that she would forgo her night under the African stars and the whole Becana team were shepherded to the container. With a positively Victorian adherence to propriety the men and women laid out their sleeping-bags at opposite ends of the giant tin box. The men took the end that was obviously used for assaying the products of mining. There were balances and shelves with glass bottles and plastic containers with red labels on them. The women's end had long high tables against the end wall on which there seemed to be a lot of glass tanks and a microscope and a centrifuge.

Jemal, who was still trying to avoid Annie, was creeping away but though exhaustion was imminent Annie refused to submit. She still had no idea what a young man she had last seen outside a frozen phone box in Devon in January was doing in South West Africa in June, and she wasn't going to rest easy until she had some answers.

'Don't you try and disappear Jemal. I want a conversation with you, now.'

'You've given me some of the answers,' was his reply.

'That's not good enough. Let's start at the beginning. What do you know about Sal being ill? You know something. Then what happened to Vix? And then - how did you get here and why?'

The two of them sat down at a table in the middle of the container while everyone else was busy laying out their bedding. As two English in conversation in their own language, they relaxed and consequently their word rate increased and all the others except Jo, looking up and hearing them could barely distinguish an intelligible phrase.

Annie started.

'Tell me about Sal - she had malaria didn't she? I've worked that out, having seen it here, but how, in January in England?'

Jemal looked into Annie's tired but ruthless face and perhaps recalled his own mother, he realised that there is no arguing with a determined midwife. They are programmed to know that there is a process and always an end to things and thus rarely allow themselves to be put off or side tracked. He made the sensible decision that a pooling of resources might produce some answers where this puzzle was concerned. He was still wondering however, whose side she was on.

'All right,' he said. 'Sal. We think she caught something on the raid. We were RAN.'

'Ran?'

'"Release Animals Now." We set caged animals free, especially laboratory animals. We did a raid on the new research place and it was all wrong, no animals, but cages of insects and two chimpanzees.'

'When was this?'

'A couple of weeks or so before Sal got ill. What's this about malaria?'

'That would fit, Malaria takes about ten days to incubate, but it doesn't explain what you are doing here.'

'Well, we smashed the place up but we took a laptop and it had stuff about insect breeding programmes on it. We thought maybe they were trying to spread plague or something and we found an address here where they were sending stuff for breeding insects. But malaria's not serious is it? You sleep under a net. You treat it and take the drugs. Sal only died because they didn't know she had it, didn't she?'

'Malaria not serious!!' Annie was momentarily diverted from her current investigation. 'Do you realise it kills many thousands of people every year and most are children under five. And pregnant women are especially vulnerable because it hides in their liver and then they get so anaemic they just die. Just recently… Oh never mind. It's serious alright. Very serious and something needs to be done about it. As soon as a new drug is found the little beasts get immune to it. And we can't vaccinate against malaria. Did Sal get bitten?'

'Yes. She thought the chimpanzees had fleas but it probably was when we smashed the glass insect tanks.'

'Go on. Why are you here?'

'Like I said. We found this laptop and address labels to someone in the P&P office at the Becana road camp. RAN isn't just hippie groups breaking things you know. People in London looked at it all and sent me here to find out what was going on.'

'And what is?'

'Well I don't know yet, but whatever it is P&P are involved in some way. I joined the NID team to get a better look around.'

'You too! Everyone has their own agenda. Jo thinks there's something going on with the animals. All I want is to do is to get all the children on my patch protected and I'm not sure I'm at all happy at this piggybacking on my show.'

She sat back and thought a minute

'Look tomorrow we are going to finish this job properly. We will find all the children there are to be found, get them protected and you will do your job or I'll want to know the reason why not. OK?'

'OK!' he responded.

'I still can't make head nor tail of most of this. Yes I'm sure Sal died of malaria, but if you break into a medical lab and smash the vivariums and get bitten by a mosquito what do you expect? If the place had been full of snakes would you have let them out? Where's the conspiracy?'

Jemal didn't respond. She'd told him something new. That was enough for now. And she clearly wasn't ready to listen to anything else.

Annie stared at him.

'Look, up down or sideways I am bushed. I'm going to go to sleep. Tomorrow we do this job. Anything else you have in mind must wait. OK?'

'Like I said OK. I promise to behave tomorrow. You get some sleep.'

That is exactly what Annie did. Her mind briefly tried to struggle with the new information, but her body had other ideas. Within seconds of getting her head down she was sound asleep. Had she stayed awake she would have seen Jemal seek out Jo and the two of them sit talking for a long time. None of the rest of the team were awake when later that night the two of them carefully explored their temporary habitation.

CHAPTER SIX
The Dawning

The following morning, those sleeping in the metal shipping container were woken by banging on the door of their tin hut. Annie who had gone to sleep first, was already up and opened the door to be greeted by the unbelievable smell of fried bacon and eggs. James was standing there.

'We have to give a good breakfast to our guests,' he said. 'Come on, it's all ready.'

She looked back and saw that the stream of sunlight let in by the open door had roused the others.

'Breakfast is waiting,' she called to them and followed James.

He led her to a table, on which within the limitations of a camp kitchen, breakfast was laid out as it might have been in a four star hotel. In the middle of the table was a proper pot of tea.

'I told you I used to work in Vic. Falls. I was a breakfast chef at the Luxor and it's so nice to do something sometimes that doesn't involve mud. The tea is "English Breakfast." Enjoy!'

That was exactly what Annie did, joined shortly by the rest of her companions.

James seemed to have appointed himself as their tour guide. When they had finished their breakfast he shepherded the complete immunisation team off 'to look at our workings.'

Annie had been conscious in the back of her mind, the night before of the sound of water. It had been a dull roaring and her first thought on drowsily becoming conscious of it, was that she didn't think the motorway was so near. A moment's sensible consideration brought her to the idea of water. After all, the river, the Zambezi couldn't be too far away.

They followed James down a track and into a clearing by the riverbank.

Annie had got used to broad, but unpredictable African rivers. She had paddled a dugout canoe at a local safari lodge and viewed the more hazardous inhabitants of the river from the safety of the hotel jetty. She had enjoyed watching the river used as larder, laundry and bath to many of those who lived on it's banks and worried with them, about crocodiles and hippos getting too close. The broad fast flowing water was integral to community life.

She had however, never before seen what they came upon, by the river's edge. It was a piece of land that to Annie looked the size of a couple of football pitches. It had been cleared of vegetation and consisted largely of mud. Small canals had been built into the shore to channel the water from the river, through little traps and sieves and then back into it again. The whole thing reminded Annie of the seascapes she and her sister had built on the beach at Weston-super-mare, except the scale was so much larger.

James watched their reactions. He was very proud of his organisation and engineering.

'Since I arrived we've managed to get a lot more out, mostly by building all these little canals. We collect the gritty stuff they want in these tins.' He gestured toward a pile of small tins.

On closed inspection, in a previous life they had used to contain baked beans or condensed milk.

'They pay us by the number of tins we fill. One of our problems was the hippos and the crocodiles but we managed to get hold of some blasting powder from P&P and that seems to have frightened off the last few. Hippo steak is rather good by the way!'

Annie couldn't actually hear Jo boiling over but could guess what was going on in her head. She turned around just in time to catch Jemal firmly shaking his head at her. To Annie's surprise she shut her opening mouth and tried to look attentive and interested.

James went on, 'It's not that easy though. The new malaria is bad here. You saw our special nets. The people who used to live here got sick and their babies died, so they decided it was a bad place to stay and have moved over the border. They didn't like us clearing the ground. They were actually quite difficult, used to come out at night and break all my workings. They said they'd always been here and we were killing the river. It's a good thing they've gone we can get on with our work. You can't stand in the way of progress.'

Jemal spoke.

'And this stuff goes to Zambia, on the train, from Vic falls I suppose?'

'Well I expect they try to avoid the Zim border posts. It'll go to Livingstone, but that's not my problem. When I give the stuff to the P and P man and get our money then my job is done.'

'The P&P man? They collect it?'

'Yes.'

'Dear me,' said Jo. 'I think that makes us all company men doesn't it? They pay my wages, and yours Annie, and Jemal you're on the payroll too.' Her tone of voice was acidic. There was both disillusion and anger in it.

Annie decided it was time to get a handle on things again and remind everyone that this was her show and that they had a purpose.

'Listen people. Today is Immunisation Day Two. We are going to do the job we are paid for - whoever pays us. OK?'

Jemal responded, 'Yes it's OK I agreed that yesterday.'

'Me too,' said Jo. 'But there are questions to be answered.'

Maria was standing listening to all this and spoke to Jo in Africaans. Jo turned to Annie.

'We aren't the only ones with questions. Maria has been talking to her cousins and she wants some answers as well.'

'Right,' said Annie, 'Tomorrow is Sunday. I invite you all, and you Jeff,' she included the silent but attentive driver, 'to Sunday Lunch. We'll have it in the clinic. There is room and it's private. Everyone can have their say. Now let's get this show on the road.'

James too had listened to this exchange, but said nothing. He waved his guests off as they left and wondered about the future of his enterprise.

*

It didn't take too long to get the cars rolling but the atmosphere didn't have the jolly expectancy of the previous day. Jemal followed Jo to her truck and Jo directed one of her young men to join the ambulance. It seemed to cause a little argument Annie raised her eyebrows at Jeff.

'Don't worry, they are her guards, but this one is also a cousin of Maria's and also related to Inika, so he's alright,' responded the driver.

The concept of 'guards' gave Annie pause for thought. She had always thought of Jo's young men as her employees. Considering them as guards somehow put the relationship in a different light. Were they containing her, or keeping her safe? The question created yet another cloud in Annie's clear blue African sky.

They had a rough and ready route planned for the day, taking in various remote settlements that were way off the road.

Maria and the young man who now had changed from 'guard' to 'cousin' were talking animatedly in the back in what Annie thought was Lozi. Annie looked at Jeff and raised her eyebrows.

'The next village is Mulanga. Maria has relatives there. We had a big funeral in Becana, for a baby from there, just before you came. We used the ambulance. Lisa, who was here before you, loaned it. She didn't like the babies dying. Those two are talking about the babies dying, and Mulanga was one of the worst places.'

This was only the second bit of information on Lisa, her predecessor Annie had been able to gather. All Inika would say was that, 'Lisa was really a child.' Somehow it felt like another piece of what was becoming clear to Annie was a very complicated jigsaw.

Mulanga turned out to be just like any African village looked in the picture-books of Annie's youth. There was a big tree in the middle and round houses with thick grass roofs and mud walls. The trouble was it seemed to be unoccupied. The cars drove in and stopped beside the tree. Jeff did what they always did when the ambulance car arrived in a village on outreach. He picked up the lump of metal lying on the ground and banged on the car wheel rim hanging from the tree branch.

These makeshift gongs had become their way of announcing the travelling clinic's arrival in each village. Usually after a short interval, mothers and children would come out to greet them. Having been on the receiving end of Annie's 'Wash Your Face' anti blindness campaign that she was planning to tell her sister about in her next letter, the children would often be a little damp when they appeared, having just had their faces doused as their mothers' heard the gong announcing the arrival of the ambulance.

Today however there was no response to the clanging. Nobody came. The sound echoed around them and the only response was from a flock of birds who rose into the air, swirled around and moved off. They at least had heard the call and responded.

Maria's cousin, the guard, who turned out to be called Patrick said something in Lozi and looked at Jeff.

'He says, I told you so,' translated Jeff.

'So where is everyone?' said Annie. 'Have they just moved on?'

The Bushman people were known to up sticks and move every now and again. It was another cause for disharmony between the various ethnicities. A stable population meant a place became

SOMEWHERE. As far as everyone else in Becana was concerned, this moving around whenever you felt like it was a sign of primitive nomadism and not what people did nowadays.

An indignant Maria responded to Jeff's translation of Annie's remark.

'No no, this is a new place. Everyone was starting again here and my family were going to stay. The President when he came said we were to take the land and make it work. Look, come and see the fields, and the new house.'

They followed her as she led them all down the village street.

'Look this is the new house.'

Annie looked. It seemed very odd to her. All she could see was the bottoms of beer bottles sticking out of mud walls. Jo came up and looked.

'Don't you see,' she said. 'This is a bottle house. This is meant to last. This was going to be permanent settlement. Those bottle houses are a brilliant idea. Good insulation and no more broken glass on the ground, even if it does give everyone a reason to spend their money on beer,' she added.

'So,' said Annie, looking at Patrick this time and raising her hands in the universal interrogative gesture. 'I say again, Where are the people?'

Annie seemed to have opened a flood gate of explanation. Patrick and Maria both began to talk at once. The other two young men from Jo's truck, her other 'guards' also started talking in Africaans to Jo. She listened to them and was interspersing questions. Jeff seemed to be trying to get a clear explanation from Maria who was now crying. The silent empty village reverberated with the sound of the raised human voice in a babel of tongues.

Annie looked at Jemal. They were the two people present who could understand barely a word of the animated conversations going on around them.

'I've learnt that here, if we watch and listen and wait when everyone has had their say we'll eventually find out what is what,' she said.

They sat down on the ground in the shade of the tree, and watched and waited and as Annie said some sort of consensus was reached. The need for shade for all was by then acute in a temperature of 30C so the others joined Annie and Jemal and took the bottles of cola she was handing out.

'So what do we know,' she said, 'except that there are no children here to vaccinate.'

Jo began.

'It seems the people left some time ago. You can see that from the gardens. There are graves too, and they look small, like children's graves. This is another village near the river. You can hear it if you listen, but Bushman people don't like to be too near water and most of the people here were partly from Bushman families.'

Jeff continued.

'But Maria says they didn't just leave because of the river. They say the river is killing the children. There is a bad fever here.'

'You mean malaria?' said Annie. 'But why didn't they use nets?'

Maria who understood that comment responded indignantly.

'Of course they used nets. Lots of people here knew Inika and were related to her. She'd be very angry if she found out any of her nephews and nieces or godchildren weren't sleeping under nets.' She turned to Jeff and went on in Lozi. 'The nets didn't work. They still got fever and died. We knew in Becana that something was wrong out here. That's why Inika was so keen to come. Ask Jo, she knows.'

Jeff translated and Annie looked at Jo.

'What I know is this,' she said. 'I got interested because the fish and the animals were having problems. Like the guy last night said "Hippo steaks." It's my job to stop that. Then Inika started worrying about her relatives out here. That was mostly why we did the map. To find out what people knew. Now he turns up with his story,' she looked at Jemal.

So did Annie.

'Your story?' she said.

'What I know is this,' he said unconsciously echoing Jo's words.

Annie interrupted.

'Jeff and Jo make sure everyone understands,' she said.

Jemal went on.

'What I know is this. It goes back to England in some way. A girl in England died and I think they killed her man as well. I was sent to find out. Annie looked after them in England, then she gets a job here.'

'You mean Sal and Vix,' said Annie. 'Are you trying to tell me all that is connected with here?'

'It's got to be hasn't it?' Annie caught a look that passed between Jo and Jemal and made her own connections. She was angry.

'You really think I know something about this? No, don't answer that.'

She stood up.

'What I know is this. We are sitting in the middle of the bush in the middle of nowhere and in the middle of a complicated puzzle we don't understand. This is what we are going to do. We are going to all the other villages on our map, like we intended to, but to find out what is going on as well as vaccinate.

Jemal, you are going to keep a clear written record of every place we go and everything we see. This is still vaccination day I am not going home until we have found every child still around on this bit of our patch. I don't know what is going on here, but my job today is to look after the children and that is what I'm going to do. Agreed?'

It seemed to be. A subdued group got back into the vehicles and set off, the ambulance following the truck.

Annie sat in front of the ambulance, her mind racing. For some reason Jo and Jemal didn't trust her. Jemal hadn't told all he knew. Jo too had seemed restrained in what she said.

Maria in her distress seemed the only absolutely frank and honest member of the party.

Annie's own main emotion was fury. No one had ever questioned her professional integrity before. They might have objected to its inconvenience, when she had stuck her neck out but no one had ever suggested she could be dissuaded from doing what she saw as right.

They seemed to have the idea she was bribed by being given this job not to investigate further in England. Apart from anything else they seemed to have greatly overestimated her power and influence in the UK. Sal and Vix, Sal and Vix. What had been going on there? What hadn't she understood?

Well it was going to be an interesting meal tomorrow at the clinic.

A few kilometres further on, they came to the next village on their map. It was the same story as Mulanga. Clanging on the wheel-rim still hanging from the central tree produced no human response. Gardens, with growing vegetables needed weeding and appeared abandoned. Maize stood in small fields around the houses with no one tending it. They drove on and the story was repeated again. The fourth and last settlement on the off road route they had planned was further inland, a little away from the river. The track they followed was its usually dusty self and, as with all the others they had followed that morning, not marked on any official map.

They drove into another village. They were all now tired and depressed and hungry. They repeated their efforts to call the inhabitants but, by now weren't really expecting a response. The overgrown gardens they passed on the way in had told what was now becoming a familiar story.

'We need lunch,' said Annie. 'Let's have it here, even if we haven't found any work to do.'

They sat under the usual big tree and spread out the food. Annie had had a quiet conversation with James before they left their overnight camp and he had provided her with bacon and egg sandwiches, so as she could again avoid the universal millimeal. Everyone else seemed happy with the maize porridge and the good meat stew Maria produced to go on top of it. They looked at her.

'I'm sorry,' she said. 'I have tried, but I just can't get on with it. I wasn't brought up to it and I'm too old to change.'

She sat back, leaning against the tree watching the others eating and talking. As she ate her own sandwiches, Annie became conscious of another noise, from behind her, coming from one of the houses. It was a baby crying.

She got up and went to the doorway and looked in. It was dark, but from the far side of the one room came the cry again. It was the little wail of a baby woken from sleep. It sounded hungry. Annie had listened to the cries of many babies over the years and could interpret them. This cry sounded defeated and hopeless. This little one wasn't expecting any help or food to arrive.

Her eyes adjusted to the dark and she could see someone lying on the ground. She could distinguish a woman's head, with elaborately braided hair. The woman was swathed right up to her neck in the usual multicoloured cotton wrap. Annie went over, knelt down and touched the woman. She was cold. Her flesh had that inert feeling that told her that the woman was dead, and had been dead for some time. She pulled back the cotton wrap and saw a tiny naked baby sucking at a mother's breast that had long ceased to be of use. As she leant over to pick up the baby the light from the doorway behind her was excluded. Jemal had followed her in.

'Go.' she said. 'Get Jeff. Now.'

She looked around and saw another clean folded wrap on the ground. She spread it out and picking up the baby, laid it on the cloth. She swaddled it and then, cuddling it to her, walked out into the sun.

The others had heard Jemal's call and were coming over. As soon as they were near enough to hear, Annie started issuing orders, like a commander on a battle field.

'Jeff, from the ambulance I need NOW bottled water, glucose powder, and a dressing pack. Maria come and help me. The rest of you, the mother is in there but long beyond our help I think.'

Jeff was back very quickly with what Annie needed. She sat Maria down and gave the little bundle to her.

'Hold it close and keep it warm while I get this ready.'

The dressing packs were supplied prepacked and sterile by Katilo Hospital and intended for dressing wounds when running field clinics. They contained a collection of useful sterile oddments that were frequently used for purposes other than dressing wounds. Annie opened the pack and spread out the blue thick paper on the sand and the contents of the pack onto the paper. Into a plastic bowl she poured some bottled water and into this she tipped a little glucose powder. She stirred it in with the dressing forceps. To Maria she said.

'Lets have the little one now.'

She took the baby and settling herself on the ground unwrapped the bundle until she could see the wizened little face with its big eyes looking up at her. She knew that look so well. It was a newborn's look seeking its mother, hoping to fix her face in its mind for ever and ever.

'It's not me you're looking for little one,' she said softly to the babe. 'But let's see if we can get some of this into you.'

Taking a little plastic cup from the array spread out on the paper sheet and dipping it into the glucose solution, she began to drip fluid into the baby's mouth. The little face wrinkled up, almost in distaste and a small tongue appeared, but then after a lick of its lips seemed to understand what was going on and began to cooperate. It took Annie ten minutes of total concentration to get about an ounce of fluid (30ml) into the baby. That was all at the moment she felt it was safe to give. The baby, Annie thought, looked a little contented, a little more relaxed and perhaps less despairing.

'But still,' she said to herself, 'I'll be surprised if it weighs 3lb, old money. Under 2 kilos I'm sure. Still got its cord attached, but the cord is dry, so maybe it is three days old. Looks like a tough cookie though. Maybe we'll make it.'

She looked up to see all the others sitting in a circle around her. They had been watching her efforts. She looked at them.

'What I want to know is how this happened. Why was that woman and that baby left alone to die? Where are her people? What is going on here?'

Rather surprisingly they didn't all speak at once. There was a slightly uncomfortable silence as if no one knew where to start. A conversation she had had on her arrival in the area came back to Annie.

She had got on pretty well with Sister Hildegard, the catholic nun and matron at Katilo hospital, who had been there thirty years and had many stories to tell and was delighted to have a new listener. She was a particular fan of the Bushman people and their way of life but she also told of traditions she found when she first arrived and how they had shocked her as a young nun and how hard she had found it to understand them..

'They were still nomadic then,' she had said, 'and nomads can't carry sick people so when some one was going to die they'd leave them provisions for a good meal and move on. The sick and old were left to die alone. It still seems extraordinarily cruel to us, but it was their tradition for millions of years and it worked. They are the oldest surviving people on the African continent. I found it all very very hard to understand, but one custom I did manage to stop. If a mother died in childbirth if there was no other woman in the group lactating who could take the baby it was buried, alive, with its mother. That I couldn't have, so I let it be known the mission would take in any babies who turned up on our doorstep, no questions asked. If they survived their families could reclaim them when they were ready to. We kept one set of twins until their father was ready to marry them off.'

Annie looked again at her audience, the little bundle, now wrapped up tight in the way only a midwife can wrap a baby, was held firmly in her arms to keep it warm.

'Sister Hildegard told me some stories...' she said tentatively. 'Maria?'

Maria replied, this time in Africaans to Jo who translated.

'Nobody does that anymore. This was Newtown. It was to be a new start, a town of all peoples, all together. They were going to set up a cuca shop for the new road and take tourists on tours. But my cousin tells me, things went wrong. The babies and the children kept dying of the fever. Then the men got it too. And the animals started going and the river lost the fish.'

Jo continued now speaking for herself. 'I know Sister Hildegard's stories and her anthropology leaves a lot to be desired, but she has saved a lot of babies over the years and I think you may have it. The people from here have been badly frightened. That is a Bushman baby. They couldn't bring themselves to bury it with the mother as in the old days, but they couldn't take them with them either. What are we going to do about it all?'

'I will tell you,' said a determined and outraged Annie. 'What I know is this. The first thing is that this baby is going to survive. I refuse to accept anything else. OK? The next thing is that what is going on here is important. The French have a word for what we have to do. "Temoinage." It means "bear witness" which in this case means we write down, now, all we all know. Jemal get out your clipboard again.'

While he went back to the car Annie turned to Maria.

'Maria you take this little one in your arms and you do not put her down at all, under any circumstances, until you give her to Inika in Becana. Your job is to keep her warm and give her a very small drink of this mixture every hour. I'll put it in a bottle for you. When we get back to Becana, Inika will know how to get her safely to the children's ward in Katilo and get a message to Sister Hildegard. Are you clear? What I say is what I mean. You do not let this baby out of your hands.' With that she placed the baby in Maria's arms.

However the look on Jo's face as she translated made Annie realise that she was sounding very authoritarian. She understood that she needed to win hearts and minds here if she wasn't to be brushed off as another bossy foreigner interfering where she wasn't wanted and poking her nose into things she didn't understand.

She looked at the group in front of her. Jo and Jemal understood her language, Jeff mostly did but Maria, her cousin and the other two 'guards' could only understand the tone of voice.

She took a deep breath and began again, this time speaking slowly and calmly.

'Jeff,' she said. 'Tell everyone exactly what I say word for word.'

She went on, 'This baby is a new citizen of your country and it is my job, I am paid by your government to look after all citizens in this area. I am going try and make sure this baby lives. One day this little one will want to know where it came from. We need to write all that down now and give this baby papers.'

One of the guards interrupted and Jo translated. 'But you are paid like us by the company. It is to them we must talk about this.'

'I'm sorry,' Annie answered, 'but I don't see it like that. My duty is to the people, at the moment to this baby, who needs a name and everything we know about it written down.' she paused. 'I suppose we'd better weigh it and find out if it's a boy or girl, I forgot to look.'

'I looked,' said Maria. 'She's a girl and her mother has put a red and green cotton plait around her body.'

Annie's complete neglect of what other people thought important about a new baby made everyone smile and some of the tension seeped out of the gathering.

'Jemal, write for us, her papers,' said Annie. She looked around. 'She needs a name. Can we call her Morning Newtown? It is the morning and this Newtown is her village. I would guess her date of birth as about three days ago. Does anyone know her poor mother's name or family?'

No one did, or was prepared to say so. It took a little time but with everyone contributing, eventually the following document was prepared to accompany the baby.

'And we'll need two copies Jemal. One for us and one to go with the baby.'

Jemal, who had hardly said a word, gave her a look, put a new piece of paper on his clip board and began a fair copy.

Morning Newtown Shadicongo
Female
date of birth approx:
place of birth: Newtown, Shadicongo, Becana province, Katilo district
Weight 2.1kg...............
Parents names unknown
Distinguishing marks: A red and green plaited cotton cord around her body.

Medical notes: date............. Time 10.00
Morning was found on............ at 11.30 lying in the arms of her dead mother in a house in Newtown, Shadicongo. There were no other people in this deserted village. She appeared dehydrated and hungry, under weight but otherwise healthy. Umbilical cord still attached. She was initially given 30ml water and glucose by cup and spoon. The intention is to repeat this treatment hourly until she can be transferred to Katilo Hospital.

Those listed below were witnesses to this event.
A list of the names of all present followed. Jo's young men at first refused to have their names added to the list, but Maria spoke sharply to them in Lozi and they gave in.

Annie looked at Jeff.
'What are we going to do about her mother? Do we bury her?'
Everyone was however quite clear about that. She was to be left where she was and they would inform the police in Becana that evening. That way there was a chance someone would come up with a family name or relatives and she could have a proper funeral.

'So if there's no more to be done here people, we need to move. We've work to do.'
Maria got up, still holding the newly named Morning and went back into the house.
'She has to say goodbye to her mother,' she said. A few seconds later she returned, still holding the baby. 'Scissors,' she said.
Annie understood. She had seen the baby's mother. Picking up the scissors from the blue paper of the dressing pack, still spread out on the sand she followed Maria back into the mud and straw roundhouse. It was suddenly cool and dark again. They knelt beside the dead woman and while Maria placed the baby on her mother for the last time Annie cut one of the long braids from the dead woman's head. She gave it to Maria who wrapped it in with the baby. The two womens' eyes met. Their ability to communicate in words might be limited, but what they were doing now was beyond words.

They were trying to give this tiny girl as much as they could, to help her hold her own in the world. Something from her mother was part of that. Annie knew that by the time the baby went to Katilo hospital she would have an amulet of her mother's hair firmly tied around her neck and no one would dream of trying to remove it. It seemed the right thing to do.

When the two women emerged into the sunshine again they found the others had finished clearing up and loading and were ready to depart.

There was a discussion. Surely they should head straight back to get help for the baby Morning. Annie however was adamant. A quick two hour dash would get them and her to Becana but how would everyone feel if in a few months there was a measles or polio outbreak in the villages that would miss out on their vaccinations if the team went on this mercy dash. This was the only day in the year that it was made possible to do mass immunisation and as far as Annie was concerned it was going to be done.

'We can't sacrifice all the other children on the road for her. We must do them as we planned. This little one is tough and Maria will look after her.'

It was her final word and it was accepted. The vehicles set off.

*

Morning's home settlement was less than a kilometre from the new hard road and so in no time they found themselves on tarmac again. There were two stops that afternoon in small roadside hamlets, both based around a new cuca shop and bar, recently built to service those driving along the equally recent new black road. A modest but satisfactory number of children were immunised and recorded by Jemal on his clipboard. By four o'clock, before twilight the two cars drove into Becana.

'Straight to the clinic please,' Annie said.

All the action and activity of the previous morning was gone. The clinic and its surroundings were quiet and deserted. Inika was sitting alone on the concrete step with a cup of tea in her hand.

Annie was extraordinarily glad to see her. This tall Ovambo woman had been her rock these last months as she found her way around in this, to her, so strange African world. This was Inika's place and she understood it.

Or at least Annie sincerely hoped she did, because she herself hadn't a clue what was going on. She was beginning to realise how difficult the last two days had been.

'Though,' she said to herself, 'I have piloted my fleet successfully through all its hazards and brought my crew back into harbour with an additional member to boot. She added a mental aside to her father, 'In my book two ships is a fleet, so there.' He having been in the Navy, for much of her childhood she had been and still was inclined to think in marine similes.

What among other things was bothering her was that she seemed to be a source of suspicion and mistrust to the others in her team. This was so unfair. And there were so many other questions needing answers. There really is something very wrong here, she thought.

These thoughts flashed through her mind in seconds as the weary group tumbled out of the cars in front of the clinic.

Inika had watched them drive up and immediately understood the bundle Maria was carrying. An abandoned or orphaned baby arriving at the clinic was less common than it used to be, unusual but not unknown and procedures existed to deal with such infants.

Inika looked at all of them. In a land where there isn't a universal common tongue the ability to read body language develops very quickly. Inika could see Maria with Patrick the cousin /guard standing beside her. She could see Jeff leaning against the ambulance, Jo, with Jemal and the other two guards standing close together a little away from the rest. Finally she looked at Annie. Annie looked back at her and found to her total embarrassment that tears were running down her cheeks and they wouldn't stop.

'Tea,' said Inika. Tea worked. A little while later they were all crowded into the clinic and Annie tried to tell Inika some of the story, but they both knew the priority was to get the baby to proper help before dark.

'You transfer her,' said Inika. 'You are tired. You need to see her settled.'

'But,' said Annie. 'Her mother is out there, and something terrible is going on. And they,' she looked at her companions from the last two days. 'They seem to think it's something to do with me.'

'That's stupid. You must take the baby to the hospital. The policeman will drive you. Jeff can't. He has to tell them about her mother.'

'But there's more, much more. Jemal has written it all down. The papers are with today's number sheets. Keep them. And I've said we'll have a Sunday Lunch at the clinic tomorrow for everyone to talk and find out.'

'It's you who says "Tomorrow is another day,"' said Inika. 'Let's get you and that baby away, I'll say Manyana.' Her voice was the firm voice of a nurse holding a patient together and preventing panic. Annie understood and took herself in hand.

Very shortly afterwards she found herself being helped into the back seat of the police car. Maria followed her to the car. She had obeyed instructions and had never put the baby down. She placed her in her Annie's arms and stepped back. She smiled.

'Strong one Sister,' she said. 'She'll be OK now.'

The police driver was young and spoke little. His silence was a relief to Annie. She turned her mind to the little bundle in her arms. Slowly unwrapping the tiny person she spoke to her.

'Well, little Morning, it's evening now and how are you?'

The little face responded to her voice and looked up at her. Maria was right thought Annie. This young lady knows things are getting better. She wrapped the baby up again but kept her face visible and began to sing to her.

In such circumstances her only song was, 'Green grows the rushes oh.' Her mother had sung it to her, and it goes on a long time and you can go round again. Over the years she had found it ideal for baby comforting. Singing also had the merit that it prevented her thinking about anything else, for now at any rate.

Katilo Hospital, not unused to orphan infants, took the baby from her and competently sorted her out. 'I think she just needs feeding up,' said Annie. 'And she had no immunisations. Here are her notes. That's all we know about her.'

Having left her little charge snuggled into an incubator, for the night anyway, her name, Morning Newtown written on a piece of card stuck to the front of it and the twist of hair visible on a thread round her neck, Annie found herself shepherded back to his car by the policeman.

She realised he wanted to be back in Becana because that was where he thought the action was and he was missing it. She sympathized, but wasn't at all sure she really wanted to be where any more action might be ever, anytime.

They were about to get into their police car parked outside the main entrance of the hospital when a young woman came rushing out.

'Sister, sister,' she said. 'This came for you. An email. It was on the other system. It's from your nephew and he says it's urgent. Inika is my cousin,' she added inconsequentially. 'I work in the office here.'

Annie was startled as the piece of paper was thrust into her hand but unsurprised by the facts that: 1. There was another system which no one had told her about and

2. No one considered email at all private. Unless stuck down and sealed messages were everyone's property. And,

3. That because she was now considered part of Inika's community she got special treatment.

The West hasn't a clue about networking, she thought. The piece of paper said

'Dear Auntie Annie, Mum is very worried. What's going on? No letters. Get in touch. It's urgent she's bugging me. Max.'

Oh dear, it was true, she hadn't written for a while. She couldn't write jolly stories anymore and she couldn't think what she really did want to say. Trust Julia not to hang about. She must have have bullied Max into finding this new email. Actually, she mused, I suppose my own networking isn't that bad.

In the car on the way back, there was no baby to sing to, so she had no excuse not to think.

Her mind was all questions. Was there something going on up near the border? Something engineered, which was frightening the people away, or was it just the usual effects of development?

James and his mining was obviously causing disruption but the upside was money and wages. Every town and city and mine through the ages was built on land which once had been farmed or lived on. People survived and moved on.

She understood Jo's point of view, wanting to set up a network of rangers and promote tourism and keep the land the same, but who for? She wasn't at all sure the indigenous inhabitants wouldn't prefer a mine with good wages. Jo's idyllic tourism park with ethnic villages had the faintest hint of separate development about it…

But those odd nets and the bad malaria and the dead babies. How could that hippie girl Sal be involved in this?

The man who had at least some of the answers was she was sure, Jemal. She had yet to have a serious conversation with him and he knew something. There had to be a reason for an apparently indigent traveller to appear half way across the world with a job in the same place as she was offered one. If nothing else, who had paid his fare? Yet he kept avoiding her and now they were all suspicious of her. And as the guards and Jo had said 'We are all company men.'

This was the question which refused to stop nagging at her.

Had she been bought, bribed, and shuffled out here to keep her quiet, even if she hadn't known about it? And more to the point, should she have known about it? Hadn't that job offer, her dream, been too good to be true? Should she have asked more questions back at home? But a gift horse was a gift horse wasn't it? Or was it a case of 'No such thing as a free lunch?'

'But you don't expect international conspiracies to raise their heads in rural Devon,' she replied to herself. 'You really don't.'

The phrase 'International Conspiracy' caused a gelling of thought. 'Well I may not have asked questions then,' she continued her internal conversation with herself, 'but I sure as hell am going to now. No one is going to make that sort of fool of me.'

That seemed enough thoughts for the time being. Annie leant back and looked out of the window at the road, at the dark. It was a pleasure not to be doing the driving and be able to watch the bright eyes of small animals reflected in the headlights and then get a look at them as they turned their heads away. She saw a civet cat and momentarily her tired mind wandering, she recognised it as a fox, the like of which she was used to seeing when out at night, on call, in Devon country lanes. 'No wrong continent,' she said to herself and finally re-rooted herself back in the here and now.

When they entered Becana it was very black. The generator had been turned off for the night. Annie could hear some noise of revelry from one of the bars on the far side of the camp but over this side all was quiet and no lights showed. Everyone seemed to be in bed.

The policeman dropped her at the end of the little alleyway leading to her house.

'I'll watch you in,' he said. It was obvious she wasn't to go anywhere else and she was now body achingly tired. Sleep, her own bed, 'and my own mosquito net,' she mentally added was what she knew she needed.

'Tomorrow is another day,' she thought and smiled to herself. 'If nothing else I'm spreading clichés and truisms all over rural Africa.'

CHAPTER SEVEN
Sunday Lunch

The sound of the single church bell woke Annie. The church and the bell belonged to the Catholics but its sound was used by all denominations in Becana to call to their members on a Sunday. It was a late awakening for Annie. She realised how tired she must have been. She also realised she had committed herself to providing Sunday Lunch for an indefinite number of people, most of whom preferred food she didn't like and it all had to be organised within three hours. 'Not a problem,' she told herself. 'Breakfast first, and anyway there is no one to talk to today till after religion has had its say.'

She took her coffee, her sliced up fresh mango and her chair out onto the porch. She sat admiring the bougainvillea that clambered all over her little wooden house. She had seen it at home in pots in Devon garden centres labelled 'delicate.' It wasn't a phrase that applied to it here. It rampaged all over everything, Like Russian vine at home, Annie thought, and it comes in so many colours. Sitting where she was she could see the usual purple leaf like flowers, but also brown and yellow and pink ones and, as far as she could tell, on the same plant. 'Enough of gardens,' she thought. 'It's time to consider the day to come.'

The problem wasn't going to be her feeding of the 5000 at the clinic, well more than 10 anyway, she corrected herself, but sorting out what they had found yesterday and putting together all the rest of the story.

What was really going on?

Was, whatever it was, something that needed to be stopped?

If so was it any of her business?

It wasn't her country, and though she had learnt to love the place and people, in the months she had been here she knew she had only a very superficial knowledge, of a small part of this growing complicated new country.

But surely there were absolute rights and wrongs?

Weren't there times when anyone from anywhere had a duty to intervene?

She could recall at least two favourite quotations repeated often by her father. One he said, was from Albert Einstein and went something like, 'All that is needed for evil to flourish is   for those who look on to do nothing.' And it's Sunday today she thought. What about that Samaritan 'passing by on the other side.'

Annie took herself in hand. 'That's enough religion and philosophy for now. It may be Sunday but my main job at the moment is to feed the people.'

As she had told her sister she had created something of a tradition of 'Sunday Lunch' at the clinic once a month, so hustle and bustle around the place was expected.

Social integration at mealtimes was a real problem in this new country. Leaving aside the nastiness from her point of view of millimeal porridge, there was the problem of how to integrate those used to sitting on the ground around a communal dish and who ate with their fingers with those used to sitting on a chair and using plates and cutlery. Annie found sitting on the ground plain uncomfortable after a lifetime of chairs and eating with one's fingers was a skill she had tried hard, but not too successfully to learn. She had felt it important to try partly because to do it wrong caused offence, but also because in doing it properly you didn't spread or collect gastroenteritis.

What you were supposed to do was bring all your fingers together and by kind of poking get a small lump of porridge from the dish. You then used this as a sort of wrapper for a bit of meat or sauce from the centre. You then popped this bite sized morsel into your mouth.

Unacceptable bad manners involved letting your fingers touch anything in the big dish which you didn't pick up or letting your fingers touch your mouth and then putting them back in the communal dish for your next mouthful. Several months of trying had caused Annie to come up with a personal solution. She, when invited to such a meal, would immediately say how bad she was at finger eating and would ask that they put hers on a separate little plate so in this way she didn't contaminate the communal dish and put them all off the good food. It usually worked and she would get lots of advice on how to manage once people were sure her fingers were nowhere near their supper.

Today, however was going to be more complicated. She had to integrate the two customs, and everyone had to feel comfortable or she wasn't going to get her answers to all the questions that needed asking. Inika she was sure would provide a big pan of millimeal and stew, but what could she do so she wouldn't look like the foreigner just ordering food up and then interrogating people.

She mentally reviewed her larder and the contents of the freezer compartment of the fridge the government provided for the nurse 'in a remote posting.' They also provided a food allowance which remained an embarrassment to Annie when so many of the children she saw in the villages didn't even have the basics.

Looking at her watch she discovered it was now past 9 o'clock. This meant the generator had been on for an hour so it would be safe to open the freezer without defrosting its contents and see what she had. And that's another skill I've learnt, she said to herself, managing fridges and freezers on only twelve hours electric every day in temperatures of 30C.

Coffee drunk and mango eaten she went back into her house to look at her stores. Inspection of fridge and vegetable rack produced only one conclusion and as she thought about it Annie was rather pleased with herself. She had enough of everything to make a giant Shepherds Pie and she'd get someone to let her put it in the old army oven to brown on top. Culturally speaking she could describe it as her home country's version of millimeal and stew, only using potatoes and upside down, with the meat on the bottom not the top. A very large part of her precious sack of potatoes would be used, but this was no time for meanness, she thought. And I'll do them a pudding using millimeal. After all it's only cornflour. We'll have a sort of orange and lemon meringue pudding without the pastry and I've still got some of last weeks biscuits and half a dozen eggs.

Decisions once made, their implementation didn't take long to the experienced housewife. By the time Inika called round to discuss things, all was humming nicely on Annie's stove.

Inika's first words puzzled Annie, 'You Ok? No problems?'
'No, it's all coming on nicely,' she said gesturing to the stove.
'No problems in the night?'
'What do you mean?'
'Frank slept in your hammock. It seemed a good idea.'
Annie paused and recalled. Frank, he was the policeman. Her hammock was at the end of her garden so she could lie in the shade in the afternoons. So she too had been guarded. Her mind was dragged back from the pleasures of the stove to the realities and purpose of the day.

'There really is something going on isn't there? We can't just ignore it can we? Go back to the way things were three days ago? I love this job. I don't want anything to change.'

'We did that, for too long I think. You've changed things.'

'But I haven't done anything except my job.'

'Lisa being sent away so quickly and then they sent you. That's stirred something up.'

'They, they. It's always they. Who really are they?'

'Talk at the clinic. It's private there,' said Inika looking over her shoulder.

Annie had known that that these little wooden houses weren't sound proof. She was always aware of all her neighbours' activities. Suddenly she realised that the reverse was also true. Every word she said could be heard by any one nearby.

The two women looked at each other and conversation reverted to food, its preparation and management and finally its transportation over to the clinic. They used a very old perambulator which once had been a Queen of its kind with big wheels and a sprung body. It hadn't carried a child for many years but the big wheels meant it was easily pushable on the sandy paths.

Eventually everything was assembled at the clinic to both hostesses satisfaction. The long table had both chairs and the clinic examination couches set around it. Participants could choose their seating, on a chair with their legs under the table or sitting on a couch cross legged at table level. Plates and spoons were there for those who wanted them and cola for all.

'No beer,' said Inika. 'It's Sunday.'

'No beer,' replied Annie. 'It's the clinic.'

The food itself looked good and welcoming. In such a climate there wasn't so much emphasis on it being hot to the table, but on its being freshly cooked, as with few fridges and hot temperatures it went off quickly.

By midday Jo had arrived at the clinic but she only had Patrick with her. Her other 'guards' were absent.

'The other two aren't around,' she said. 'They just weren't there this morning.'

Most of the others who were expected were already assembled inside. Maria, who had helped transport everything in the pram, wheeling the shepherds pie and pudding from Annie's wooden house on to Inika's rather larger bungalow to add the millimeal stew to her load was now tidying the pram away in the back room.

Jason the tiny bushman caretaker had been waiting at the clinic. He, by means of waving his broom and shouting at them had excluded the train of children following behind Maria, hoping for a titbit. He helped her lift the pram over the threshold. He had every intention of being in on anything that was going on. From his point of view, after all as a Bushman this was his land and as a Caretaker this was his clinic.

Jeff was also there. He had abandoned usual driving garb of official blue trousers and shirt with epaulettes in favour of his Sunday best, a brightly coloured traditional long robe. He had arrived straight from the Catholic Church. Frank the policeman, Annie's Guardian of the Night was also waiting.

What Annie didn't know was that prior to settling in her hammock the night before, he had been out to Newtown and supervised the burial of the unknown woman who was Morning's mother.

Annie looked around and counted heads. Five, seven including herself and Inika. Minus Jo's two men but even with the expected arrivals there would be plenty of food. But food, she thought, was only half the story. She knew who needed to arrive if they were going to get any answers. That was Jemal. She looked at Jo and realised she was thinking the same thing.

'He promised he'd come,' said Jo. 'He had some stuff to show us and went back to his place at P&P to get it.'

Inika looked up from the table where she was laying out the food to her satisfaction. Millimeal and stew was at one end and Shepherds pie at the other, but in a concession to everyone's sweet tooth the lemon and orange pudding was in the middle.

'I've got everything you wrote yesterday. I took it from Jemal. Safer here with the clinic numbers.'

'Safer, safer, safer from what? That is what I want to know. No one will say anything,' exclaimed an exasperated Annie.

She was interrupted by the sound of a truck, rather screeching to a halt, outside the clinic front door, followed rapidly by banging on that door. Annie was startled. Someone had locked the front door. It was never locked when anyone was inside. This was more conspiracy theory.

Inika however went over to the window and peered carefully out from the side of the ancient curtains. Rapidly she went over to the front door, unlocked it and flung it open.

A very bloody but still beturbaned Jemal was standing on the doorstep. Behind him was one of the white flatbed trucks sporting a P&P logo. It was parked practically on the clinic porch. They all crowded to the door and could see another very bloody body lying in the open back of the vehicle. Nobody needed to say anything.

Quickly both men were brought inside and Annie heard the key being turned again in the front door. As she looked at the man carried in from the truck she realised it was James, largely because she recognised his floridly vivid shirt from the day before. His face was so bloody and bruised it wasn't recognisable.

Having repossessed one of the couches from the feast table James was laid on it and Annie and Inika began to look him over. He had clearly been badly beaten up. One eye was closed, his nose was swollen and not the right shape and his lip was badly split. His clothing was caked with blood, though it wasn't clear where it had coming from. He didn't appear conscious.

Jemal, still standing but very unsteady, grasped at the wall and spoke.

'They were going to kill me. He just came by. He wanted to talk English again,' he said. 'He was on his way here and would give me a lift. They jumped us at my place. We, I, stole their truck. He saved me from a lot worse.'

Those were the first words spoken since the injured men had come through the door. Annie and Inika heard them as they took the scissors to James shirt and trousers. Jeff and Frank, the policeman also heard them and exchanged looks.

Frank took the truck keys from the swaying Jemal's hand. He and Jeff moved towards the main door. Jason, who had observed the silent communication followed them and locked the door again behind them. Jo and Maria, just in time, caught Jemal and set him gently down on the floor, his back against the wall.

'They'll move the truck,' said Jo to Jemal, 'so they can't find you.'

James's body when exposed was bruised and grazed but had only one bleeding wound about an inch long which oozed rather than poured blood. Inika looked at Jemal.

'Bottle or knife?' she said.

'Bottle,' he replied.

The difference was crucial. A bottle wound an inch long couldn't be that deep and if not pouring blood could be dealt with. A stab wound with a knife wasn't so easily sorted out. It could have gone deeply into an internal organ and might need immediate transfer.

When Annie had first come to Becana, the only injuries she had ever repaired were those caused by childbirth. Though she was known in England for the quality of her sewing in such private places she had never until her arrival here, embarked on stitching up any other part of the body. However having learnt how to deal with the aftermath of a Saturday night in a place with eight bars and little other entertainment and also with the usual repairs needed by men and women engaged in agricultural work, the phrase she used to herself with a smile was 'transferable skills.' Stitching was stitching whichever bit of the anatomy benefited from ones needlework.

She and Inika were very good at sorting out the bad from the worst. This in practice meant deciding which wounded had to be quickly transferred to Katilo hospital for x-rays and such and which with cleaning up and sewing up and anti tetanus and antibiotic injections could be shut up in the police station for the night until reviewed, when sober, in the morning. They had become rather proud of their skills and held follow-up clinics to see how well their stitching worked and how small the scars were, their work had left. Though unconscious at the moment James seemed to come into the repair and retain category so they got to work.

'He was talking earlier,' went on Jemal.

'You said that once before,' said Annie to him, suddenly recalling Sal and was shocked at the ferocity of her tone. 'What in God's name is going on?'

'Let's leave God out of it. There are too many versions of him loose around here. Anyway man is causing this,' said a pale and now shaking Jemal.

Annie and Inika continued to concentrate on James and by the time Jeff and Frank had returned from their mission to hide the truck they felt they had done the best they could, though their casualty still wasn't conscious. The policeman and the driver came back in and also sat down on the floor beside Jemal.

'Don't worry, it's on the far side now.'

Inika looked and said to Annie, 'Under the windows. Can't be seen.'

Very soon they were all sitting on the floor, James included, who had been lifted off the couch and laid beside them, still unconscious. There was a feeling among those assembled that the time had come to begin, though no one was sure what they were at the beginning of.

'Jemal, you start. What do you know? What are you doing in Africa?' said Annie.

'I was sent. We found this computer on the raid and no animals.'

'What raid? What animals?' said Inika and Annie almost simultaneously.

Jemal still pale, looked aghast at the cultural complications of explaining animal liberation and breaking and entering to present company.

'That's the point. There weren't any. Only two old chimps. You explain.' He said this to Jo.

'Well,' she said as she took up his tale, 'He told me all this the other night. You remember that tin hut, the container, where we slept at his camp.' She gestured at the still unresponsive James.

'In England there was another place like that and Jemal and his friends broke it up and smashed the glass tanks. A girl was bitten by one of the insects they let out and she died.'

'Sal,' said Annie, 'and was it malaria?'

'We think so. We think,' said Jo looking at Jemal, 'that it or rather they, the insects, have been deliberately bred to spread malaria. That's what they were doing in England and why babies are dying here.'

She looked around her and repeated what she'd said in Afrikaans.

Maria spoke.

'They are too small, the new mosquitoes. They aren't the same. Ask him. Ask Patrick . His baby died. They are too small.' She put her finger and thumb together and looking at Annie said again, gesturing and repeating, 'Too small, too small.'

'There is some thing else,' said Jo. 'Two years ago now, you remember don't you Inika? We had the "relationship project". We took DNA swabs from all the Bushmen - to construct family trees, to see who was related to who. It turned out that everyone is mixed up now. Almost everyone was someone's cousin, Bushman, Ovambo, Portugese, Thimbukusho were all mixed in. Even I turned out to have some Zulu ancestry. Annie, your predecessor Lisa, did most of it, took the swabs. I just saw the results and the report at HQ on Montgomery's computer...' her voice trailed away and she went quiet.

Something else clicked in Annie's mind. 'The P&P nets,' she said. 'They don't let these new mosquitoes in do they?' She looked at Inika. 'We found specially fine nets, the ones they use against Kala Azar flies, when we were vaccinating. They had been given to some of the girls who had P&P babies, by their men. They were the only ones near the river who still had live babies.'

The usually laconic Inika was roused to speech.

'You mean someone is making specially little mosquitoes to get through the nets to kill our babies? Why?'

She was looking at Jemal as she repeated 'Why?' This time there was a certain menace in her tone. Those who had fought and who had friends who had died for the independence of their country were well prepared to leap to the defence of the next generation if they felt called upon to do so.

'It's not me. Don't look at me like that,' said Jemal. 'I came to stop it. Well, to find out what it was anyway. Ask her. She's the one who got the new job.'

Annie found attention turning towards herself, but it was Inika answered for her.

'No it's not her. She works with us. For the people. You! You've just come.'

The threat in her voice was still there and Jemal continued to look scared, but Annie, though so deeply grateful for Inika's words felt she had a case to answer.

'It's true. I did get a new job. I did look after the girl in England who died, but we don't have malaria there so I didn't recognise it till I came here. And they did offer me this job just after she died. And it was too easy to come here. I really do think they wanted to get rid of me from England because of that girl who died. He says they killed her man.'

She looked at Jemal.

'They found him cut up in bits, in bags by the side of the road in England,' he responded. 'You were easier to buy.'

'But I didn't know I was being bought,' said a despairing Annie.

The rest of the audience had each gathered most of the discussion from one source or another. It was Frank the policeman who asked the proper police questions.

'Who?' he said, 'and why? And him,' he said looking at James. 'What's he done?'

They all looked at James and realised he had his eyes open and had been listening. He spoke.

'The Who who did us were your guys,' he said to Jo.

Jo replied, speaking to Annie rather than James.

'I didn't know, either, I was being bought, or I think I didn't. I saw that survey two years ago and made a remark about DNA profiling to Monty. Then this fabulous conservation job turns up here and we are doing good work. And my guys have worked hard.'

'And so have I, but we both have been conned, not bought. And I haven't beaten anyone up. They were your guards. Did you trust them?'

Jo looked at Patrick who was standing beside Maria looking increasingly uncomfortable.

'Mr Monty paid us well to look after you and help you. We want good jobs with the conservation when this is done. He,' he said looking at Jemal, 'is an enemy. He is a spy. We were told to stop him, but Maria is my cousin and Inika is my aunt and my baby died too and so..... I couldn't do it when Maria said no. But I couldn't stay with them either. Look what happens. He was supposed to be dead,' he said looking at Jemal. 'We were to pretend an elephant did it. He's a foreigner so he wouldn't know they were dangerous.'

'That would be plain murder,' said Jo, seriously shocked at what men she had regarded as her friends had been ordered and were apparently prepared to do.

'None of this makes any sense. DNA testing, malaria, dead babies, murder, animal conservation - which certainly isn't working, by the way. Think of the river and him,' said Annie looking at James.

Jo turned to the Sikh.

'What, who is behind it all? Do you know Jemal? And James. Did he just get in the way? Why?'

Jemal, who was looking if anything paler and less well than the now awake and alert James, began to speak.

'In London they told me to look where the money was. The only real money round here is at P&P. Everyone is dependant on them. They are building the road. Everyone thinks it will be wonderful and tourists will come and there will be jobs and money for everyone. It'll all be green and beautiful. Think about it though, the road will join everything up. What is over the border? And on this side too. Stuff they can dig up, that's valuable. Stuff that we've never heard of. What do they need to be able to dig it up? Empty land. Ask him.'

Jemal was looking at James.

James found it was his turn to speak. His very proper English accent still produced a smile in Annie.

'You know my country, Zimbabwe. Many of us have moved on. I found a place where I could earn money. People have always dug up the earth for stuff. Gold. Diamonds. It was much easier to dig up our stuff when the little people, the Bushmen went away. They always move on anyway. There is lots of bush out there.'

'But it was their bush.' It was Jo who spoke. 'And what about the animals. Hippo steaks!' She spoke with a vicious scorn. 'And the stuff you dig up, that's one of those new minerals, casserite or something isn't it. They use it for mobiles. And get children to mine it in the Congo.'

'But I didn't do that,' said James. 'We had wages, and I don't know what the stuff is anyway. I just dig it up and get paid.'

'But the Bushmen didn't get paid, they just got driven off. And if what we found out is right, they are being killed off as well, by malaria. They didn't get those special nets did they?' said Jo. 'Who gave you those nets?'

'The P&P man. And I did rescue him,' James went on, looking at Jemal.

Inika interrupted.

'You know that tin box you said you stayed in? There's one here, in Becana. Is it full of glass tanks and tiny mosquitoes too, like in England?'

Jason the caretaker spoke to Jeff and Jo translated into English.

'Yes and there is broken glass there sometimes, like scientists' stuff, left outside.'

Jason then said something else to Jeff, who looked at Inika. She heard and understood.

'He says you know,' she said to Jo. 'Your Montgomery goes in there.'

A silence followed this statement. Looking at him it was suddenly very easy for the others to imagine Jason wielding a poisoned bow and arrow against an enemy.

A babble of recriminations and counter accusations followed. Anger was in everyone's voice. No one was sure who was accused of what. Everyone seemed to think it was someone else's fault but no one knew exactly what the trouble was. Something was wrong.

Inika spoke, looking at Maria.

'Food,' she said.

Annie realised she was right. They all needed to eat and to share the meal. She got up off the floor and with Maria went into the other room. Still laid out there on the table, was their carefully considered meal which had been interrupted by the arrival of the bleeding James and the shaken Jemal. It looked abandoned and was cold, but it was food and it looked very good to Annie and Maria. Their eyes met and they both realised how hungry they were and therefore presumably everyone else was as well.

They carried the two dishes in, one of meat and millimeal and the other of potato and mince and set them on the floor in the middle of the circle. Annie put a few plates and spoons and forks down as well. Everyone dived in taking whichever food by whatever method they chose.

'I'll tell you one thing. You two aren't going to manage anything of that.' said Annie, looking at James and Jemal and the two dishes.

'Wait a minute.'

She went back into the other room and returned with the pudding. Having scooped out some of her lemon meringue pudding into two blue plastic bowls from a dressing pack she gave them to the two young men and watched as they spooned it with care past their bruises into their damaged mouths. She suddenly realised that in this land, strange to her, this particular food from her homeland was actually familiar to both the battered young men, though they had grown up on opposite sides of the world. She briefly mused on the ramifications of cultural imperialism.

As people ate, tension abated. A calmness developed as all those present realised that they were in the middle of a drama in which they all had a part.

'There is a saying where I come from,' said Annie.

' "All that is necessary for evil to flourish is for good people to do nothing." I think that is what has happened to some of us. Things were too good and we didn't ask the questions we should have done, soon enough. Now evil is out there and getting bigger and we are going to have to do something about it.'

'It's got to be done quickly too. Before anyone knows what we know and comes for us,' said Jeff, who with Inika had also fought for his country. They were perhaps the only two in the room who understood determined lethal violence.

'What do we know, if we put it all together?' said a pale and shivering but attentive Jemal.

Jo spoke, partly in English and Afrikaans, translating as she went.

'I think there is something I know that is so evil it's unbearable. I have to tell you about it. But it didn't work out. That "relationship project" was hoping that all the Bushman, the Khoisan would turn out to have the same genetics, the same ancestors. That would mean they could get the same diseases. It would mean you could give them an invented disease that other people wouldn't catch and they would all die or move. But it turned out that everyone is mixed up. There are no pure bloodlines any more. Everyone is everyone's cousin so it wouldn't work. I can remember the last line of the report which I read, which, by the way was sent to England.' she said looking at Annie. 'It said something like "The proposed approach isn't feasible we therefore suggest adopting an alternative strategy with an entomological base." I didn't understand at the time but I think that means the mosquitoes.'

'But they can bite us all and we get better, if we get the drugs,' said Inika, using her childhood Afrikaans in a shocked understanding of aim of the project.

'But only if you can get to the clinic,' replied Maria. 'If the things are so little and can get through the nets, then everyone is ill and then people die because it's too far, especially for women and babies, like in Newtown yesterday. And when we are pregnant we lose the babies and both die.'

'So what they wanted to do,' said an appalled Annie, 'was to selectively kill off or drive off the Khoisan and leave the land empty for mining.'

'And they were giving us the old nets with big holes to give to people. And they knew they wouldn't work,' said Inika.

'And paying us to treat the sick while actually making the people sick themselves,' said Annie.

The two women looked at each other and understood their mutual affront and fury.

Apart from being a murderous plan, this was an attack on them as professionals, on their identity as carers of the sick and vulnerable. They had both been trained and had both spent their lives and energies implementing that training. It was what they both stood for. Being a Nurse and a Midwife was what they both were. Neither was prepared to have their identity so mocked.

'Nobody does that to me or my people,' said Annie.

'They're my people,' said Inika.

'They're mine too if I'm responsible for them. Someone out there is getting at them, and that I will not have. And making fools out of you and I.'

'We aren't fools,' said Inika. 'We'll get them.' She, ever practical considered the immediate problem, and continued. 'We need to break that other tin hut that's here in Becana.'

Jason spoke in Afrikaans looking at Inika and Jeff, 'And the other one, where you slept. Where he worked,' he said looking at James. 'That's for my people to fix.'

Jemal spoke. 'In England it was cold. When the glass was broken the insects all died in the air. It won't be the same here. If they get out they will just fly off and bite people and give them the new malaria.'

Inika listened and had an answer. 'We can spray them here like we used to do the houses. The old DDT stuff is still around, in the tin shed with the tanks the men used to wear on their backs, but they stopped us using it.'

Jason spoke, repeating himself, 'And the other one, where you slept. Where he worked. That's ours. We, us, out there. We can burn it.'

It had become clear that a pragmatic conversation was developing between Inika, Jason, Jeff and Maria as to how to deal with the immediate threat to their kith and kin and homeland.

The room now seemed to have divided into two camps, those whose life and heritage was here and those who came from somewhere else, the foreigners. Somewhere in the middle was Jo and she was crying.

Jo had been silent throughout this last practical conversation. To no one in particular she said, 'But I love Montgomery. We are going to be married.'

Annie heard her and responded with perhaps a little too much vitriol.

'You silly, silly girl, you are a scientist. You've got an education. Can you really do that? Think. Someone has made a fool of you too.'

'But I love him.'

'What on earth do you mean? "luv him" How can you? I thought love was about trust. Is it love if he tricks you into acting against what you believe in?'

'You don't know that.'

'They say he was seen going into the container here. He had the report. He gave you the job.'

Jo sought some tool to fight back with and replied.

'This was all organised in England. Your country not mine. You took the job too.'

'Yes I know. I think they were afraid I would say something back home about the girl who died. So they gave me the job here. Well they seriously over estimated my influence in the UK. Nobody ever took any notice of whatever I said back there.'

She was now talking to herself as much as anyone else, but realising Jo's distress responded to her.

'Look we've all been tricked and bamboozled. Who knows what your Monty thought he was doing. That's a discussion for another day. But today please, please, please, don't be a wimpy girl in love. Be a woman, an intelligent professional one at that. What matters now is what we know and what we do about it. We have to make a stand.'

They had been talking fast and furiously in English and had been ignored by the others. James and Jemal too had been talking to each other in English, but quietly about mining and mobiles and right and wrong.

They all looked up as they heard the clinic door being opened. Frank was letting Jason and Jeff out and locking the door behind them. The two Bushmen, one so tall and one so small were on their way to deal with what they regarded as their part of the problem. Inika was standing up looking at them all still sat on the floor.

'You talk too much,' she said, 'while we fix things. There is going to be trouble. It's time for foreigners to go. And you girl,' she said looking at Jo, 'must decide who you are loyal to, your country or your man. Are you one of them or one of us?'

This was the first time since she'd arrived in Becana Annie had even implicitly heard the colour question referred to. Rather surprisingly, given her own ethnicity, it had never been, even a baby elephant in the room. It did however seem to be time to talk about it now. There came a moment when even the most sensitive spot had to be probed, for the better healing of the whole.

'Inika that's not fair,' said Annie. Her family have been here for four generations.'

'Yes but she didn't grow up like we did, did she? We used to be her lot's servants.'

'And she has lost the power that you have gained. You are equal now. Nobody can help what they were born. It's what they do later that counts.'

Annie looked around the room and listed in her mind the people present.

Frank, the six foot tall Thimbukushu policeman.

Inika, a traditionally built very black Ovambo African woman.

Maria, a thin pale African woman with elaborately plaited hair.

James the Zimbabwean, also an African but with a completely different face and build.

Jo, the only white face present

and finally

Jemal, the Sikh who was born in London.

She thought of Jason, the tiny pale brown skinned bushman who had just left with Jeff the driver and a very tall bushman who was said to have a Portuguese uncle.

She took a deep breath and launched, voicing both the thoughts of a lifetime but also those that had crystallized during the last few months.

'Jo, and Frank, please translate for me,' she said. Then she went on.

'Listen. Everyone is a citizen of somewhere. Look at me. I'm black, my parents were white. They adopted me as a baby, so I think white. I have a white sister in Australia. My grandparents lost their families in the concentration camps in the war, just because they were Jews. They made sure their children believed that all people were just that. People, equal citizens of the world. Look at Jo. She is white, but an African born and bred to the fourth generation. She thinks more black than I do. And my white parents' English ancestors put her white Boer ancestors in other concentration camps, here in Africa and ever so many women and children died. We are all people of the earth. We mayn't speak the same language. We may not be the same colour but we were born under the same sun. And we must respect each other if we are to survive.'

Annie was mentally smiling to herself as she spoke. She had on several occasions said something like this before, but saying it in the UK she had always remained slightly equivocal on the subject of the sun, usually substituting the word sky for sun. She particularly recalled the last time she had been called upon to make this point.

It was at a weekend doing emergency obstetric training in February in very wet west Wales. Local reaction to the Eastern Europeans newly arriving in Wales provoked the speech.

Here, it was really true, they were all born or at least living under the sun. She wanted to go on and make the point about sitting on the London Tube and trying to guess the language being spoken by the person next to you, but the challenge of conveying the concept of an underground railway and the diversity of London to this audience, in the centre of rural Africa was too daunting. She was saved from the attempt by Jo, pausing every now and again to change languages and be sure everyone understood.

'It's alright. I can speak for myself. Yes I am an African and a trained professional and a scientist. All these make me one person. But I'm female and I do love Monty and we are engaged and I want a family. That's another person. Some of us,' she said, looking at the single childless Annie, 'may have made other choices. I don't know what Monty is doing in this mess, but that is for another day. And incidentally some of us also believe the animals have a right to this planet as well. That's for another day too. But I am with you. This is my land and it has to be safe for its citizens.'

She repeated her last sentence once more in Afrikaans and Lozi looking at Maria and Frank who it seems had already got the gist of what had been said.

Inika looked at Jo.

'Alright girl,' she said.

Annie's review of the personnel present had caused her to look more closely at Jemal. He wasn't well. She gestured to Inika and they both went over to him. He was hot, pale and sweating. It was clear he was ill.

Annie spoke to him. 'Have you been taking your anti-malarials?'

'I didn't think I needed to. I'm not white I won't get it.'

Annie paused, took a breath and then spoke.

'You, you… young idiot. You're English remember, a foreigner remember. It takes people who live here years to be immune and they still get it in the rains. You're going to need hospital and a drip.'

Inika intervened.

'Like I said it's time for the foreigners to go. And as for you,' Inika went on looking at Jemal still with some animosity. 'Well lets hope it was a big one bit you.'

There was a thundering on the front door of the clinic. Voices could be heard shouting .

'It's beginning,' said Inika to Annie. 'You are going to have to take the ambulance and them,' she said looking at James and Jemal, 'to Katilo. Out the back with you.'

CHAPTER EIGHT

What happened next.

Out the back they went. The two wounded and damaged men were walked to the ambulance and helped into it. Annie got into the driving seat. Frank the tall policeman got into the front passenger seat.

'He'll see you to the road,' said Inika.

'I'll not be coming back, will I?' said Annie looking at Jo.

'I think maybe you won't,' she replied. 'Maria and I will keep your things safe till we can send them. Listen out there, you can't stay.'

It was true. The sounds of an incipient riot were to be heard. The usual Saturday night noises of alcoholic over-indulgence were supplemented by angry voices and revving engines.

'Go while we've still got the electric,' said Inika.

Annie stood there, for a moment indecisive. How had they got here? Wasn't this her fight too? It was her clinic after all. Here she was running away and they still didn't really know what was going on. And she had loved this job. She had loved being welcomed, being useful. Now they were telling her she had to go and no one was going to give her time to say her goodbyes.

There were tears in her eyes as she looked at Inika.

Inika saw them. The two women regarded each other. There seemed to Annie so much to say. They were in some ways so alike but their experience was so different. No one successfully told either of them professionally or personally what to do. Neither took Authority too seriously. Yet Annie realised whereas she had rarely in her lifetime, heard a voice raised in anger, though she might over the years have diffused the odd potentially violent situation she had never, ever, either faced, instigated or participated in serious planned violence as Inika, when a freedom fighter had done.

In the end it all came down to a few words.

'I have learnt things from you sister. But them,' said Inika, jerking her head towards the ambulance, 'They must go, they won't be safe and they need the hospital. You know they do.'

She paused. 'We wish you well.' and smiling added, 'Manyana maybe.'

Frank the policeman did as Inika said, but as soon as the ambulance was clear of Becana, he asked her to stop and he got out. Before he did so he turned and shook her hand.

'We thank you for helping the people,' he said and disappeared back into the dark.

As she drove along the new tarmac road she watched Becana receding in her wing mirror. First she saw the lights go out, and then a few minutes later a flickering appeared in the dark sky behind her. Finally there was an explosion which was loud enough to be audible within the cab of the ambulance. She understood. They had burnt the container. She only hoped they knew what they were doing and had burnt the container, not the clinic or anything useful or any people.

It took her forty minutes to drive the dark road to Katilo hospital. The glow in the sky behind her remained, but the drive itself was uneventful. She watched the bright eyes of the small animals at the roadside looking towards her as they were lit up by the headlights, but to her relief she encountered nothing larger than a civet cat. In its own way this dark night drive was her adventure. 'I'm not running away,' she thought. 'I do have two patients in the back who genuinely need hospital care and if I'm honest I don't want to be part of what's going on back there. I don't like breaking things. There has to be another way. That's not my way.'

As she turned off the grey tarmac onto the dusty brown earth road that led to the hospital she was concerned that, at this hour the problem was going to be to get the night watchman to rouse enough people to help her.

She couldn't have been more wrong. As she drew the ambulance to a halt outside the hospital front door it opened and half a dozen people came hurrying out. The Dutch couple, the nurses who usually had a bath and towels waiting for her were among them, as was the guard and the nun midwife who she knew from her antenatal meetings. She also saw another ambulance car waiting on the drive.

She gave a very rapid report on her two patients and found them whisked away from her care to the treatment room. She herself was ushered across to the convent side of the compound.

She had only been there once before when she'd met Sister Hildegard, what now seemed many, many months ago. It was Sister Hildegard she found herself facing now.

'Thank goodness you are safe, my dear. We were just about to send a car for you, but it was difficult to get anyone to drive out there. What is happening? We can see the fire in the sky.'

Now Annie had liked Sister Hildegard. But she also knew from Sister Anastasia the nun midwife, that Sister Hildegard had happily run an apartheid style convent for many years with both black and white nuns, right up until independence and that the change that independence had brought had not been easy for anyone.

In addition P&P had just paid for and built a new ward at the hospital. In the light of the conspiracy theories of the last two days Annie decided that caution was required and decided to keep her comments to a minimum and say as little as possible. She confined herself to the basics. This woman might be running an African hospital but she was still her line manager after all and therefore, by definition, not to be trusted.

'Well it's Saturday night and things got a bit noisy there. I brought two transfers in. One injured and one foreigner who hasn't taken his anti-malarials. He helped on vaccination day and I think he got bitten.'

'And that baby, two days ago. Is something going on out there? Whatever my dear, you are not going back. We will give you a room here and you can work on the wards till the end of your contract. It's too much the wild frontier out there at Becana. I'm not risking a foreign volunteer. It would be too sad and difficult if anything happened to you. And you could be so useful here. Sister Anastasia never gets a night off. Now off to bed with you. I've put you on a late shift tomorrow so you can have a lie in.'

More than a little startled at the arbitrary change in her job description from Community Sister-in-charge to on-call hospital midwife, Annie found herself shepherded out across the compound and back towards the hospital. She was shown to a small brick built room very near the hospital main door. It was very reminiscent of the pictures she had seen of monk's cells in medieval monasteries back in Europe.

Annie looked around her.

'If she thinks I'm one of her novices and part of her convent empire, she's got another think coming. My contract isn't with her,' she said aloud. 'But it's getting very complicated and I'm exhausted,' she thought to herself as she sat on her bed. 'I know I can't go back to

Becana, but that's my decision. I don't want to work on the wards, here or anywhere. It's not my style.'

She considered the interview with Sister Hildgard and continued with her thoughts. 'She thinks she's God. Well I suppose she does think she's his deputy here. And somehow I don't trust her motives. Can one accuse her of being a "Vicar of Bray?" To have survived here at all, at the convent she must have learnt, at least to bend with the wind.'

Having started on this proverbial mode of thought she found herself unable to stop. 'There is an African saying about that, but I can't remember it at the moment. I suppose we are somewhere between, "Don't look a gift-horse in the mouth" and "Keep your friends close but your enemies closer."

The next morning she awoke, as usual restored by sleep, to find her emergency bag that she had kept in the ambulance car at the bottom of her bed. She was a little puzzled, as it was always supposed to stay in the ambulance. She presumed it had been brought over as it had her name on a large label tied to the handle. She opened it. All was as it should be, but the side pocket where she kept the inevitable paperwork bulged rather. Unzipping it, the first thing she found was a bundle of all the forms from the vaccination days together with the diary kept by Jemal of their findings. Someone, Inika probably had put them in there before she left. Her mind turned from the trivia of her new employment regime, to her real concerns.

Were they any wiser at all about what was going on? Was everyone alright back at Becana? They were her team, her people. How had Jason and Jeff got on at the camp by the river with the second container? Where did the buck stop? Was it about mines and mobiles? How far did the biological warfare go? She remembered the talk of DNA and the chimpanzees in England. Were they seeing a sort of genocide here? Above all, who was responsible?

She rephrased that to herself.

'Who is the enemy?'

Looking down she saw the second thing in the side pocket of her bag was the email from her sister Julia that had been thrust into her hand, the last time she had been in Katilo, when they had brought in their little survivor, the baby called Morning.

That was two, no three days ago. 'Oh hell,' she thought, 'this email needs sorting before that sister of mine calls out the guard or phones the Embassy or something.' She paused in her thoughts. 'Max.

That's who I need. He'll find me some answers, but first I need breakfast. I'm starving. Then I have to see how James and Jemal have survived the night.'

She was about to set out on a search when there was a knock on her door and breakfast arrived in the hands of one of the Dutch nurses. It was wonderfully Dutch, with orange juice, cheese and ham and fresh white bread and coffee with milk.

'You gave us a busy night,' she said.

'How are they?' Annie asked.

'Well we had to transfer the Indian guy with the turban. He needed blood and more meds than we had. Anyway it's safer to transfer foreigners. We don't want them being ill and complicated here and the other one, the Zimbabwean went with him, as his friend. Your baby went too. Apparently the social workers in Bundu want her where they can see her. They don't want anymore of Sister Hildegard's unofficial arrangements. Eat your breakfast and come over to my place.' She smiled. 'Towels are out, water is hot and that woman isn't getting your nose to the grindstone just yet. I've found a hospital uniform that I think will fit.'

'Thankyou and again thankyou,' said Annie and meant it. 'Any news from Becana?'

'No more visitors in the night, but the rumour is that the constabulary from Bundu are on the way out there in force. We, here, are all pretending we know nothing about it all and not mentioning you.'

Annie looked puzzled.

'Well I think Sister H. feels you shouldn't have been there in the first place and doesn't want to be blamed. She only let you go out there to oblige P&P. Now she is covering her tracks. She does rather think that the heathens at the end of the line should be left to their own devices. I'll see you in a bit. OK.'

'So,' thought Annie as she ate her breakfast, 'I'm alone and unaccounted for am I? And I've got the evidence. I'm not sure I like that. On the other hand it may be better to be invisible for a while.' She looked again at Max's email. 'Well somehow I must make sure someone knows where I am.'

She finished her breakfast and headed over for her bath at the Dutch nurse's house. She emerged clean dry and uniformed as a hospital nurse. Caps were still in vogue in this part of Africa and not having worn one for more years than she cared to count Annie found securing it a challenge. 'But at least,' she thought, 'no strangers will notice me here, dressed like this.'

She was conscious of the stares of the other residents as she passed by. This was a small isolated hospital community and the arrival and then departure of ambulances in the night let alone the admission and rapid departure of battered foreign patients was definitely the topic of the day. Annie could be a source of information but not too many of those who lived in the hospital compound could speak English so they regarded her with frustration as much as curiosity.

Sister Hildegard had said 'a late shift tomorrow' and so before Annie knew what was happening she was taking report on the maternity ward and found herself the sole qualified midwife in the hospital.

Try as she did to remain aloof, it was only moments before Annie found herself involved with affection and concentration in the work of ensuring that the women and babies in her care in the ward got the best she could arrange for them.

Later that evening as Annie was delivering the baby of a very young girl Sister Hildegard put her head around the door of the labour room.

What she actually said was, 'What's she doing in here?' as she looked at the mother of the young woman, whom Annie had invited in to be with her daughter as she gave birth.

'Well I don't speak her language,' said Annie, 'and she needs her mother.'

Their eyes met and a brief unspoken conversation took place. Annie would work to her fullest capacity in this new role, but in her own way and by her own rules. Sister Hildegard would respect her autonomy and let her do the job as she saw fit. An understanding was achieved.

It has to be said that Sister Hildegard had spent many years as head of her establishment and knew a vocation in action, religious or otherwise, when she saw it. She was wise enough to step back and let things happen.

Sister Anastasia, the midwife nun also knew a good thing when she saw one and on Annie's arrival had immediately put in for and achieved acceptance on an emergency obstetric training course in the capital.

As she said to Annie, 'You won't be here for long and it'll be me again when you go. It would be good to know the new ideas and maybe I can get Her to agree to some new equipment.'

The old midwife's attitude to her superior wasn't overflowing with respect and Christian charity, but Annie who had heard stories of how, in the pre-independence days the black nuns had been expected to act as servants to the white ones and weren't often allowed into the white nun's living quarters, understood her attitude.

This did however mean that Annie found herself entirely in charge of the midwifery in this small corner of a tiny African country. The task was absorbing and all consuming. Becana and its problems retreated to the back of her mind.

'Well it's not as if I can do anything about it anyway,' she thought to herself, 'and it is really their business not mine.'

The work of a midwife in a rural African hospital was rather different from that which she had been doing out at Becana. As a result Annie constantly found herself reconstructing her knowledge to fit the new circumstances.

"Steep learning curve" and "back to basics" are my clichés of the week she thought to herself as she trudged down to the end of the hospital compound. Beyond the bursting and blooming vegetable garden was the Maternity Waiting home. One of her new duties was to do a daily antenatal check on the residents.

It was usually evening by the time she got there. After doing her checks and seeing who new had arrived that day, she had come to love sitting in the sunshine at the end of the vegetable garden , under a banana tree, surrounded by carrots and peppers and papayas and tomatoes that grew so fast she wondered if she could see them getting bigger as she watched.

This wasn't quite as idyllic as it sounds because in order to do this she had to take extensive anti mosquito precautions, covering her exposed hands and feet with insect repellent.

This smell combined with the cooking smells and unintelligible but usually jolly noises of conversation from the women in the Waiting Home made for an hour of gentle slightly smoky contemplation amidst the verdant greenery at the end of a working day. In years to come, she recalled the time with great affection and in these current days she found it very precious.

Maternity Waiting Homes were a new concept for her. In England she had spent a great deal of time at antenatal classes telling young women not to turn up to hospital too soon in early labour as, " if they weren't in established labour" as the phrase went, they would be sent home, again, in the jargon of the service "to await events."

This is a fine idea when most people have cars, an efficient and free ambulance service exists, and is supported by a sound telephone system and a good road network.

Things were a little different in Katilo District. There might now be one nearly complete tarmac road, but most settlements were well away from it. Few cars existed and there was no subsidiary transport such as donkeys or horses. When Annie had asked about this, she was told that any horses and oxen, who used to pull carts died from Rindepest and so there was no point in getting anymore. As she had found out at Becana the telephone line was spontaneous rather than reliable and a mobile network was still a dream.

This situation created real problems for women in the last month of their pregnancy. Most were well aware that it was wiser to deliver their babies under skilled supervision, but the challenge of achieving this was considerable. One, not entirely ideal solution was the Maternity Waiting Home.

Annie had heard stories of Maternity Waiting Homes being set up by International Charities at considerable expense in other countries which had remained deserted and unused with much disgruntlement and recrimination all round.

It may be very laudable to try and prevent mothers dying in childbirth, but to try and do it by corralling all pregnant women, or even those considered at high risk of difficulties, to live in or near the hospital until nature takes its course, is unlikely to succeed. As it is a social intervention rather than a medical one, such establishments have to consider the society in which they intend to function.

In rural Africa, for example, the woman is the head and heart of her household and if she isn't there, her absence is felt by all. It is a very mature and skilled woman who can arrange for her absence to be covered for perhaps several weeks without her family, her household and perhaps her business suffering. Children have to be fed, washing done, food gardens attended to and husbands kept happy and the money has to be kept coming in.

Annie knew all this and was delighted to discover that at Katilo, the concept seemed to work. She had no idea what proportion of the pregnant women of the area made it to the Waiting Home but she enjoyed the time each evening she spent there, checking the women and offering advice.

Most of those who were there, it seemed to her, had made a wise decision to take up residence. She had recently found a set of twins sensibly awaiting their time, within their mother's womb and thus, "Fingers crossed" thought Annie, avoiding the perils of prematurity. Their actual delivery she was aware was going to raise other issues about transfer to the District Hospital at Bundu. 'But that's not today's problem,' she said to herself.

There were also several very young mothers-to-be who found themselves mothered in their turn by a couple of much older women expecting respectively their ninth and tenth child. Both these groups of pregnant women were considered by all the medical and obstetric authorities in the world to be at high risk of life threatening problems at when they gave birth.

Living arrangements in the Waiting Home were very primitive. The women had a floor space for a sleeping mat and little else, but the building in which they slept was brick built. It was the old disused black nun's dormitory from apartheid days. It was mosquito proof and, being within the hospital and convent compound, safe from unwelcome visitors.

It was also right next to the vegetable garden and the mothers-to-be both cultivated for the hospital and harvested for themselves from the garden. They cooked their meals in the open air outside the building on little wood fires using the garden vegetables supplemented by occasional meat provided by the hospital kitchen. This service was also, crucially, provided free.

As everyone knew, the last person a mother will spend money on is herself. In her eyes there is always a worthier cause, be it school fees, a husband's needs or new clothes for someone else. As everyone else also knew, this is a very short-sighted belief as a family in Africa without its mother is lost. It is condemned to poverty and frequently disintegration. If a mother dies in childbirth, usually her baby does too and other young siblings may well follow them to the grave with none to exercise that indefinable something, a mother's care.

As Annie visited daily she could see most of the women benefitting from the rest from their usually enormous workload, but this in turn produced its own problems. Once rested, such women will not sit idly, watching the world go by. The hospital compound contained a substantial population to whom one could sell things. Individual skills would be utilized. Small cake cooking enterprises would grow up and flourish briefly until the cook had her baby and returned home.

The hospital authorities usually ignored or welcomed such enterprise. However there was one such project that produced fury in Sister Hildegard and from time to time chaos within the hospital.

At regular intervals a new inhabitant of the Waiting Home would start brewing the local maize beer which was then sold to the hospital staff and conveyed by them outside the compound to anyone else who would buy.

Sister Hildegard had had the bible text, "The devil will find work for idle hands." painted on the wall of the yard where patients waited. It was the brewers she was aiming her fire at. She had, Annie thought, a very good point.

The beer was potent and unpredictable in its effects. Even in Becana, where due to the wealth of the navvies working the road, most alcohol was of the branded type and arrived in bottles and cans, it caused enough problems. When overindulgence was due to local home brew, the problems were the most intractable.

It was becoming a pleasure to live in an atmosphere free from the effects of alcoholic over indulgence. It did mean she had no qualms, when doing her antenatal checks in keeping a sharp eye open for anything resembling a plastic dustbin or any large container which might contain a potential brew. If her suspicions were roused she would then mentioning it tactfully to the night porter who would in his turn would wander around the more remote corners of the compound looking for such a container and then maybe it would in the course of the night have an accident and cease to hold liquid.

Microbreweries apart, Annie was convinced that here at least, in Katilo, the Maternity Waiting Home was doing what it was supposed to, which was to prevent the deaths of some mothers and babies. It was however very difficult to demonstrate this statistically to the authorities who funded it.

Sister Hildegard and Annie had had a conversation about that, which Annie continued to mull over. It began when Sister H had tried to enrol Annie in her job of completing the annual statistics for the local authority. They were both convinced the Waiting Home had a value but as Sister H said, 'It's a case of proving a negative and how do I do that?'

Annie vaguely recalling a lecture she'd had the previous year in Devon about evaluation techniques, replied, 'We need some clever help. Someone who can work out ways to measure difficult things.'

'What about your young friend, Jo Schmidt. If she can do all that work on animal populations she ought to be able to devise a way to measure what the waiting home is doing and prove it's doing its job.'

Annie had been amused by and was a little suspicious of Sister Hildegard's attempts to get Jo within her orbit, but in this instance she had a point.

It also has to be said that when you live in a remote area with limited resources you use what is available. Sister Hildegard was an expert at using what she found and saw Jo as a new tool she could use. 'Not I hope,' thought Annie considering her recent adventures in the bush, 'a new mineral she can mine.'

However without getting involved with statistics and science, it also remained difficult to convince a good few of the residents themselves that they had benefitted from the Waiting Home. When safely recovered from the birth, they would say to Sister Anastasia, 'You see. I didn't need you. I'd have been fine at home.'

Sister Anastasia found she could do little more than give an exasperated sigh.

And thought Annie, they were partly right. You couldn't know. She herself found it hard to believe that three weeks of rest and good food didn't improve a woman's chances of having an easy birth and a healthy baby. She was also sure that being under the hospital roof prevented some of the stranger rituals of village birth and ensured a clean delivery, and so prevented often fatal infections to mother and baby.

However a woman might well be glad to be still alive but she might also question how useful was this was if, when she went home she discovered her other children sick, her husband involved with another woman and her garden, on which her family depended for food, neglected.

The fact remained that in this part of the world, a hospital delivery, or even skilled care at the birth for all, was still a dream. For many women the earth floor of their hut was where their birth would take place.

The local health workers had a list of conditions which put pregnant women at risk of a problem and for which they were supposed to send these patients up to the next level of medical care, but this involved them being able to spot the problem in the first place, which wasn't easy for the incompletely trained, often male worker. Having found a problem the worker then had to persuade the woman to go to the next level clinic.

Having worked at Becana. "in the bush" as far as everyone in Katilo Hospital was concerned, Annie strongly sympathized with the local workers in the villages, so far from support and backup.

The concept of risk wasn't easy to explain. If they over predicted the risk, to cover their own backs, then they were haunted by the cry, 'You see I was fine.'

More importantly, many of the risks of childbirth aren't predictable and never will be forseeable by anyone. The mantra she used when teaching in the UK came to mind. It was applied to the acute life threatening complication of a baby with stuck shoulders.

"50% of events are unpredicted and unpredictable."

What it meant, in practice was that no amount of risk assessment, or good antenatal care and selection of women at risk was a substitute for emergency care immediately available when disaster struck. In a rural area, this meant access to an ambulance to transfer women, to blood transfusion services and a surgeon and an operating theatre.

The months of experience had given a reality to Annie's reading about what the statisticians called Maternal Mortality. It had been some time since she had first talked about it in a letter to Julia. Since then the raw reality had become evident to her.

Her current problem was these unborn twins she had just discovered. The official plan for their delivery was that the woman, Mrs Abdela would live in the waiting home until labour started and then be transferred by ambulance to Bundu district hospital where facilities for the twins existed.

This plan had been hard fought for by Annie but she had severe doubts as to its feasibility. The mother-to-be had only agreed to come into the waiting home, when it became obvious to herself she was unwell and only then, because she lived not too far from the hospital and could keep some sort of long range control of her affairs.

Her consent to transfer in labour had been given to Annie in such a way that Annie had her doubts she would be told when labour had started. In addition these twins would be a third and fourth baby and so the labour was very likely to be rapid.

This meant when the mother finally admitted labour had started, a moment came when a judgment had to be made by whoever was in charge. Would it be was safer for the mother to stay put and the babies be born in a medical facility, albeit inappropriately equipped, or risk a roadside delivery with no facilities at all, on the way to the 'big' hospital where there were incubators and doctors?

Given her knowledge of Mrs. Abdela's attitude Annie had read her textbook and done as much planning as she could. She had witnessed a good many sets of twins delivered and delivered one set herself, but in a UK consultant unit with two senior midwives behind her doing the "Lefthand down a bit" support and a paediatrician standing by for the babies. That had gone well. They hadn't even needed the paed., she thought and remembered with much affection, Charlotte and Emily each weighing 5lb 8oz. or 2.5kg and therefore not even technically underweight.

'But, she added to herself, I have no intention of repeating the experience here unless absolutely forced to do so.'

She was very clear what, here, at Katilo Rural hospital they could do, or more importantly, in maternity terms, couldn't do. They couldn't do a caesarean section to save either mother or baby's life and they couldn't give a blood transfusion. There was an occasional hospital doctor but he wasn't a surgeon and didn't operate. Katilo shared him with another rural hospital an hour's drive away, where he actually lived, so if he wasn't on the premises when a crisis occurred it was quicker to transfer the drama immediately to Bundu than wait for him to arrive. They did at least now have good, well serviced ambulances for such transfers.

P&P had seen to that when they first started the road construction and their workers began to have accidents.

Sister Anastasia having run the maternity ward at Katilo for years was clear about its qualities and deficiencies, but unsure how to remedy the latter. Before she had gone off on her course to the capital she and Annie had sat down with the WHO guidelines to try and work out where Katilo fitted in. The guidelines hadn't helped much. The best they could come up with was a request for portable oxygen to be available in the ambulances for when mothers were transferred.

The teaching in all the books was clear. Skilled support at delivery was essential, to prevent and recognize problems, but what actually saved a mother's lives was a surgeon and an operating theatre and a means of reaching them.

They came to the conclusion that so long as they had a good ambulance and the new road that was all they could hope for.

The devastating consequence of choices which had to be made in such circumstances was shortly demonstrated very graphically to Annie.

Late one afternoon Jo's familiar green and yellow wild life truck drew up outside the front door of the hospital. Annie had seen it come in and gone out to meet it wondering if Jo would be aboard. She was, but also was the palest skinned Koisan lady Annie had ever seen. She was obviously very pregnant.

'She's one for your Waiting Home I think. She says she's due soon,' said Jo. 'She lives miles off the road. We met her doing a survey near the river.' Jo's heavy emphasis on the last three words conveyed to Annie that this young woman came from the area of their adventures on vaccination days. 'And,' added Jo eyeing Annie's uniform, 'What are you doing dressed like that?'

'It's Sister H's idea,' said Annie. 'She is determined I should clearly belong to her and so be invisible. It seems I am a temporary lay novice! Anyway let's have a look at your passenger.'

The tiny thin girl was no more than five foot high. Her pregnant tummy looked stuck on with glue like some detachable appendage. The alarm bells started ringing in Annie's head. She had never ever before seen a woman with such a pale, translucent skin. It was almost as if one could see through her.

She held out her hand and smiled, 'Come,' she said. It seemed to work. The woman took her hand and allowed herself to be led into the clinic and sat down. Jo followed.

'Can you translate?' said Annie.

'Only sort of,' said Jo.

'Well we need someone here who can do it properly.'

Annie stuck her head out of the clinic door and called the porter.

'Jo, tell him who or what language we need to talk to her properly. I think it's going to be important.'

While waiting for the translator to arrive Annie did her usual antenatal check and tried to find out the girl's name. When asked, the girl gave her the answer in the clicks of her native language and the best attempt Annie could make at it came out something like 'Kala.' The girl smiled and accepted the midwife's attempts with good will.

Unusually, when starting her check, Annie's first concern was not the baby's wellbeing but the mother's. Looking at the girl she suspected severe anaemia. She knew that she was lucky in that she had a clever tool that she hadn't had access to in the UK. This would give a reasonable instant estimate of iron level from one tiny pinprick of blood.

'Jo, hold out your hand, you are going to get your iron level done, OK?'

'Er, Ok,' said Jo well used by now to Annie's somewhat dictatorial ways.

With the aid of a little pantomime acting Annie explained to Kala what she was going to do to Jo and that then she was going to do it to her. The girl smiled and understood that she was being reassured, so the finger pricks were carried out. A small spot of blood was put on a glass microscope slide and spread out. The slide was then put in a hand held tool a little like half a pair of binoculars. There was a gauge on the side and Annie slid the newly taken sample up the coloured gauge until she got a match. She showed Jo and Kala Jo's result.

'See that's good. She is more than eleven and it looks nice and red. Now you Kala.'

The sampling was repeated. Annie looking at the result she knew she hadn't been mistaken. The sample didn't match. It was paler than the palest colour on the gauge. The lowest measurement read " under 4gm/dl."

In the UK, 10.5 g/dl was considered the magic number above which it was safe to go into labour. Even in these days of HIV with a level under 7gm/dl you got a blood transfusion. 'And we don't do transfusions here. We have no blood,' Annie said to herself.

Firmly fixing the reassuring smile to her face she showed Kala her result.

'Yours is a little thin,' she said, 'a bit pale,' and to Jo. 'Please go and hurry the translator up.'

It was a few minutes before Jo re-entered the room, this time with a woman Annie recognised as the school teacher whose baby she had delivered in the clinic yard at Becana. As she had told her sister Julia in a letter she was unusual in that she was both Koisan and a qualified teacher.

'We're lucky,' said Jo. 'She was visiting a friend on the wards.'

'And how are the children and Dawn,' asked Annie smiling. The usual obligatory few minutes of family enquiries were engaged in and then Annie spoke to the school teacher whose easy name was Miriam, trying to sound reassuring but nevertheless also trying to convey what she felt was the urgency of the situation.

'Could you tell her that we have tested her blood and it is very thin. She needs to go to Bundu where they will make it thicker. It is very important she goes before the baby comes so we don't have much time.'

The secure happy look disappeared from Kala's face as Miriam spoke to her.

'She wants to stay here and have the baby here.'

'I'm sorry she simply can't. Listen it is important we don't say anything to frighten her, because she mustn't go into labour till she is somewhere where they have blood available. We simply don't here. Say something to cheer her up.'

There was some very fast discussion in clicks. Jo watched and Annie looked at her.

'You getting this ?' she asked.

'No,' replied Jo. 'About one word in four. But she is worried about money I think.'

Annie spoke directly to Kala, looking at her. 'It's Ok. I'll send you in the ambulance and P&P will pay for everything. I have money from them for special cases.'

She gestured to Miriam who translated. There was more discussion and finally Miriam turned to Annie and said, 'She says she will go if you'll come too.' She added, 'she is very anaemic isn't she.'

'Absolutely Yes,' said Annie. 'Life-threateningly so, but I say again, don't alarm her.'

'And the baby?'

'I expect it's alright, but I don't intend to find out. The mother is our concern. If she doesn't get blood neither of them will make it. She has to go, now, tonight and I can't go with her. Unlike the Starship Enterprise the whole command crew cannot leave the ship every time there is a crisis and today I'm the only qualified one here.' Realising she was being incomprehensible Annie went on, 'Sorry it's an old TV series at home.'

Miriam laughed, 'We not that much of a backwoods,' she said and turned to Kala and spoke.

Amidst the clicks Jo and Annie heard the words "Captain Kirk and Dr McCoy."

When Miriam turned back to them she was smiling. 'She understands. We have Star trek on video at the school. She will go. Can it be tomorrow and we will get her family here.'

'No it can't. It has to be now. I'm trying to be tactful but what I am saying is if she goes into labour there isn't enough red blood in her to carry the oxygen around her body and she will simply die of heart failure. She could easily start in the night, look at her Miriam. She's very near her time.' Miriam looked and understood.

'Shouldn't you put a drip up or something before she goes?' asked Jo.

Annie again spoke, trying to sound quiet and unfrightening, so as not to alarm Kala.

'That is the very last thing I should do. A drip, if it isn't blood will simply dilute what little red blood she has and mean even less oxygen gets to her heart and to the baby. Goodness knows how she is managing to sit up and talk now with a haemoglobin that low. All I can do is give her a big dose of iron pills and vitamins and send her in the ambulance with what oxygen we've got.'

There was silence in the room but Jo and Miriam looked at each other and were convinced.

'Look,' said Annie, 'she's agreed. You two stay with her. I'm going to organize the ambulance. I will be back very soon.'

Nevertheless it was half an hour before Annie returned. She had written a referral letter, raided the petty cash for enough currency to satisfy Bundu hospital admission office and got the night porter to put Katilo Hospital's second to last cylinder of oxygen in the ambulance.

Finally she had tried to ring Bundu Hospital to warn them of the transfer. She had been unable to get through. The line was obviously down again. This wasn't unusual. 'A tree or an elephant, I suppose,' thought Annie. Bundu was used to receiving casualties so she wasn't over-concerned. She re-entered the room pushing a wheelchair with pills and water in her hand.

Jo said, 'Miriam's going to go with her.'

Annie sighed with relief and gave her instructions and the letter and the money to Miriam. Kala took the pills and swallowed them without a fuss. She looked extraordinarily dainty and pretty with the blue beads that were plaited into her hair hanging around her pale face. She was very reluctantly sitting in the wheelchair as she was pushed to the ambulance.

'She says she can walk ,' said Miriam.

'Not on my watch she doesn't, with a haemoglobin of about two and 38 weeks pregnant,' said Annie. Her parting advice to Miriam sitting in the back with Kala was, 'Keep her sitting up. She simply mustn't lie down.'

Kala and Miriam's exit in the ambulance was watched by a fair number of the hospital community. Jo and Annie were both rather smug and pleased that here visibly demonstrated was the fact that the ambulance could be used for all citizens including the Koisan peoples, who some still considered not quite as human as everyone else.

It was with a sense of a job properly done that Annie sighed again with relief as she watched the ambulance drive out of the compound. She turned to Jo.

'Let's go to my room. I think the phrase is, "a lot of catching up to do!" What on earth's been going on since I left Becana?'

But Jo was still concerned about the Kala's transfer and continued to pick over the bones of the decisions just made as if she were a cat worrying a dead bird.

'Are you sure she couldn't have stayed? What would Sister Anastasia or Sister H done? Surely she was better nearer home and her own people?'

Annie was a little annoyed.

'Listen girl. This is Auntie Annie's potted guide to maternal care in a developing country.

In the UK, in a biggish city of perhaps a quarter of a million people, where I used to work we had about 8,000 babies born in a year. According to the statistics we should have lost one mother every 2 years. When it happened, and I saw it once, it was a major thing and it was carefully investigated.

That statistically was a Maternity Mortality rate of 10 deaths per 100,000 births.

Here we have a population of perhaps 20,000 and 600 births a year. You and I ourselves know of two mothers who have died in the last two years and I'm sure they aren't the only ones. You know it's not sensible to do the stats on such little numbers but anyone can see there is a big difference between two deaths in 600 births and two in 100,000 births.

'Surely that's just the way it is. Different climates, diseases and things.'

Annie sighed and rather crossly went on.

'No. It is not like that. The thing is all the books and now all the work I've done tells me that these deaths are easily preventable. There is a nasty little pie chart that all midwives working in foreign countries know.

It says that women die of bleeding, birth problems and infection in that order. All those are fixable. Blood transfusion, surgery and antibiotics, deal with them. It's called Emergency Obstetric Care and that's what Bundu does. It's the best idea anyone has come up with yet.

'Can't we do that here?'

'I knew you were going to say that. Think about it. The only thing that saves a mother's life when a baby is stuck or she is bleeding to death is a surgeon. But a surgeon standing in a rural village field all alone is no good. They come with baggage. They need a theatre, anaesthetists, nurses, beds - a proper hospital. We aren't that.

Even if we had all that, there wouldn't be enough work out here to keep a surgeon busy. Like any skill if you don't use it you lose it.

Even out here, in the Bush, the death of a mother is a rare event even if it's not as rare as it should be. When it happens when a mother dies is everyone thinks, "Oh dear. What a tragedy," and moves on.

What do you want your surgeons to do the rest of the time. You can't just put them in the deep freeze and get them out when needed.'

'Can't we do anything here?'

'Well Sister Anastasia and I did talk about about blood transfusions before she went on her course. You know we do give very small amounts of blood to children in the ward who usually have had malaria and are anaemic, but that is planned, by appointment and the doctor comes to do it and brings the blood with him.

The point about maternity is that happenings are nearly always an unpredicted emergency so the doctor wouldn't be here. And we'd have to keep the blood here and safe and useable and that means a blood bank and that's too complicated for us. In the end she said we should count our blessings and make do.

'And her so called blessings?'

'They are real. Much more than most rural hospitals. We've got a tarmac road all the way to the surgeon and thanks to P&P, good ambulances.'

'And if they go?'

'They can't take the road away. Anyway that's tomorrow's problem and not mine. Listen. I once read an article that said that the number of mothers dying in childbirth each year is the same as a jumbo jet falling out of the sky every day, killing 1500 mothers. I thought that made the point rather well, that it's only when you add them all together you see the problem. They go on about finding a cure for cancer, but the point about mothers dying is that we know most of the answers. It's not science that's needed, it's organization. It's very difficult to get people to see that.'

She paused.

'Can I get off my soapbox now? Oh and by the way, we have just been talking about the mothers here. If we sort them out then maybe we might start work on preventing their newborns from dying.'

Jo was contrite.

'I'm sorry, but I had to understand. I do now. She had to go. But do you think it was anything to do with the mining and the little mosquitoes that she got so anaemic? Or did she just not eat right?'

'Now you want a lesson in malaria in pregnancy too.? That is too clever for me. But I think Kala may well have had malaria that didn't show up on tests. You must know more about that than I do with all your animal stuff. You know that picture in a circle of the lifecycle of a mosquito?'

'Yeah?'

'Well at one stage the little things go into the liver and hide and do loads of damage to the red cells without pregnant women testing positive for malaria - always supposing they get anywhere to be tested anyway. Then they get suddenly, hugely anaemic. It happens because women are immunosupressed in pregnancy. They have to be, to let a baby, an alien, grow inside them.'

'Ah what you mean is hepatic schizonony'

'OK show off. You're the one with the university education!'

'Anyway because of that, what you said, the new idea is we treat all women three times in pregnancy for malaria regardless of whether they think they've got it or not. It's called IPT (intermittent presumptive treatment) but we haven't got it going here yet.'

'I suppose it doesn't matter whether they were the big or the little mosquitoes that bit her. Malaria is malaria.'

'What matters to me,' said Annie, 'is that if they are doing what we think they are, they are trying to make fools of us by ruining the nets programme. They want to make sure some people get malaria. The nets are crucial. If people stop believing they work, the children won't be made to sleep under them and will start dying again from ordinary malaria.

We were beginning to make headway. All of us were trying hard.'

Annie saw the smile on Jo's face.

'Alright, I am trying hard to do medicine here and they are just taking the Michael. Just to clear the land and to make money. I'll not have it. They will not make fools of us.' she paused. 'Did you find out any more?'

'We were right about the container. It was full of insects in vivariums. It made the most wonderful explosion, just after you left.'

'I heard it and saw the sky. It looked like something out of Rebecca - Mandalay burning.'

'You would be appalled at the amount of broken glass in the sand out there. Inika had all the men out with rakes trying to clear it to stop the children cutting their feet.'

With very little imagination Annie could see her former colleague marshalling her forces.

'That woman should have been a general.' she said. 'And the other one, the container by the river?'

'Just the same. It's been dealt with too.'

'What did the police from Bundu say? They told me here, half the force had gone out to Becana.'

'Frank's no fool. He stood outside the police station under his blue lamp, looked them in the eye and swore it was the Angolan bandits coming over the border. Everyone backed him up.'

Annie looked again at Jo who had become such a friend and thinking about their last conversation, wondered if she dare say anything. Tact and discretion never having been part of her makeup she plunged in.

'And you and Monty?'

Jo was abrupt in her reply.

'We had a conversation. He's been offered a good job by P&P in Thailand. He's going. I'm not.'

Not content to leave it alone Annie pressed further,
'Did he know?'

'Yes he knew, and yes I was a fool. He just thought they were expendable in the greater interest. They were only Koisan, he said, not real people.' Jo looked at Annie. 'How does one get it so wrong? I could never spend my life with someone who thought like that.'

'What do I know?' said Annie. 'I've never found a permanent man, but you mustn't be so hard on yourself. He was charming and good looking and there aren't many men around for you to choose from and he got you your dream job. And at your age sex is very good. You just never gave yourself time to get to know him properly did you? It was all too quick.'

'You are right about that. We met one night and by the next morning it all seemed settled. There were bits that were magic and I hate being just me, alone again. Being two even if he wasn't here all the time made us something.'

Annie was about to go on when there was a knock on the door. She went over and opened it. The night porter was standing there. She looked at him. Something about his face told her what he was going to say.

'Oh no,' she said, 'Mrs Abela,'

'Yes Sister. Anabel said to fetch you. She's in the labour room with her.'

'Jo you'd better come too,' said Annie. 'You can translate. You are about to see what shouldn't happen. When the planning doesn't work.'

It wasn't far across the sandy compound to the labour room.

Though basic, to anyone who had worked in NHS hospitals in the 1950s the labour room looked familiar. The glass fronted cupboards, the fittings had a Made in Britain look about them, There was no formica in sight, but a lot of good stainless steel.

They went in. The heavily pregnant woman was pacing up and down the far wall. She paused as they entered and looking at them and steadied herself and began to breathe in and out deeply.

Annie turned to Anabel, the novice nun who was also a student nurse and who was in charge of the ward for the night.

'Why didn't she tell us? She could have gone in the ambulance. These twins could have had proper care.'

'She says that girl was sick and she didn't want to catch anything and anyway she was Bushman and she wasn't going to ride with her.'

'Well, "Que sera, sera,"' said Annie. The glance of experience told her that it was now far too late for a transfer to Bundu anyway. She would have to see if all her contingency planning worked. Putting her hand in her pocket, she took out her keys and held them out.

'Anabel, take these and go to the cold room. In the small frig there is a little red box. Take it out and put it in one of the two cribs you will also see in there. Bring both the cribs, just as they are back here, All we need is in them. And ask Jackson to come here.'

But Jackson the night porter, an old hand at such emergencies, was already hovering.

Annie spoke to him.

'Can you go and wake up Rudy and Erica and get them here. We need all hands on deck. You'll have to take someone to stay in their house and babysit their little boy.'

'Aye aye Sister. All in hand.' He grinned at her. 'Good to have you aboard.'

And she remembered, he was an old navy man.

The room emptied except for Jo and Mrs Abela who was now between contractions and leaning against the wall.

Annie walked over to her and stood in front of her. She held out both hands and took the woman's in hers. She spoke in English.

'Mother, we are just going to have to do it ourselves. What is really important is you listen to me and do what I say.'

Jo who understood her role was standing behind Annie and repeated what she'd said first in Africaans and as that didn't produce a response, then in Ovambo. Mrs Abela smiled back and spoke. Jo translated but looked a little puzzled.

'It'll be fine, Sister. I will do just what you say. God will look after us. And the one with the feet first, he is fine. He is my nephew.'

Annie replied to Jo.

'She's the aunt of my breech baby, the one I delivered when I'd only been here two days. Well at least she believes in me. I wish I had her confidence and I hope her friend upstairs is paying attention.'

To Mrs Abela she said, 'Now mother, you don't think it's going to be long do you? You are doing fine. When the waters go, though, I want you on the bed. OK?'

'Yes Sister. It's fine. Don't worry.'

The response made Annie realise she wasn't appearing as calm as she should. She stopped, took a deep breathe and spoke again.

'There will soon be people in here to help us and look after the babies. Don't take any notice of them. Just keep your eyes on me and listen to me. OK?'

'That's better sister,' said the mother-to-be. 'We'll be fine.'

The room began to fill up. Anabel returned with the prepared cribs. The two Dutch nurses arrived, relaxed and well used to being roused from sleep.

'Hey this is your show you know,' said Erica to Annie. 'I'm no midwife.'

'I'll need you to take the babies from me and sort them out,' said Annie. 'Rudy, could you get the synto drip ready in case we need it for the second twin. All the stuff is in the crib.'

Very quickly the room began to look like it should when awaiting the arrival of two probably small babies. Hot water bottles arrived, and clean towels were wrapped round them, for even though the temperature outside was 25C it was still a lot cooler than the 37C of the babies' current residence.

Such oxygen as was available was fetched as was the suction equipment which was a rather efficient foot operated model recently donated by UNICEF. The drip was set up by Rudy, just in case and put to one side. Annie's carefully prepared sterile instrument packs were opened and made ready. Two little metal cradles stood clean and made up, awaiting their residents.

'One last thing,' said Annie to Mrs Abela. 'It would be nice to get a needle into your arm, just in case we need it later. OK?'

Within ten minutes all was in place and the bustle stopped. All was quiet and eyes turned to the mother-to-be.

Annie smiled at her,

'We're ready now. In your own time.'

Jo translated and then said to the assembled company, 'It's like we've laid out a birthday party.'

'It IS a birthday party you amateur, in fact two,' said Erica, the Dutch nurse looking up, from minding her warming cots and clean baby wrappers.

Annie heard the change in the note of Mrs Abela's breathing. A sort of grunting note emerged from the woman's mouth. The two women exchanged looks. Mrs Abela nodded.

'It's time to get on the bed I think, don't you?' said Annie.
She turned to Anabel and called her over.
'It's your time to learn. Come, help, beside me, here.'
Together they helped the mother-to-be onto the single hospital bed, which they had turned parallel to the wall so as to make a broad delivery couch. With the support of pillows Mrs Abela could sit up, leaning against the wall but both Annie and Anabel could reach out to where they needed to.

Mere seconds after they had made her comfortable there was a quiet pop and everything got very wet. Mrs. Abela's face crinkled up and the noise familiar to all midwives was heard, that of a mother about to deliver a baby. Annie turned to Anabel.

'Watch,' she said. 'I'm going to talk through what I do. One day you'll find yourself where I am now and this may be the only time you've seen it happen. OK?'

Anabel nodded.

'First, we know nothing about how these twins are lying, which way up they. Yesterday, when I checked, the first twin was head down. Let's hope it's the same today.'

She went on.

'The idea is that the first twin is an ordinary delivery, so you just let it happen. Don't let the mother try to push. Just let it happen. Now you hold the towel and as soon as I've cut the cord you take the baby over to Erica and come straight back to me. Ok?'

As she spoke there was a bulging visible and shortly afterwards some dark curly hair was seen.

'Thank goodness. Head first,' said Annie and to Mrs Abela, 'Steady now. Don't push on any account. Just let it happen. Jo tell her. This is very important, for the second baby.'

With the next contraction a small person slithered out into Annie's hands. She put the baby down on the bed and taking the clothes peg like clamp and scissors from Anabel, she clamped and cut the cord, making sure she kept a clamp on both sides of the cut. As the scissors went through the twisted white spiral the baby let out a cry. Annie picked it up out of the puddle it was born into and put it onto the dry towel Anabel held out.

'Over there now,' she said. She turned to the newly delivered mother. 'Well that one sounds fine,' she said.

Mrs Abela said something and Jo translated.

'Boy or girl?' she said.

'Oh dear, I forgot to look,' said Annie. 'Erica?'

'He is a he, beautiful and all of 2.5kg I would think and listen to him,' said Erica from her station by the cot. All present could hear this new African protesting loudly at having his warm and comfortable existence disrupted by the "blooming buzzing confusion of birth."

'Anabel, back here, now,' said Annie. 'This is the tricky bit.'

Ananbel having seen many births was unfazed by the beauty of a newborn and was actually already back at Annie's side. She was an avid pupil.

'Our next job is to try and find out which way the second twin is lying. Watch. I palpate like this, very, very, gently,' she said demonstrating. 'What we don't want to do is upset anything good and natural that is happening. See,' she said cupping her hands, 'Here is the head. Number Two is sensible and coming head first. Now we wait.'

Rudy was hovering in the background holding his drip stand.

'No,' said Annie. 'We wait. Let her body reorganize itself. We wait, a little while anyway, to see if contractions start again.'

The room was quiet. Mrs Abela said something to Jo who opened her mouth to translate.

Annie understood and interrupted.

'NO don't try to push. Wait. Wait till it happens.'

To Anabel she said, 'Always avoid doing an internal now unless you really need to know something. If you accidentally break the second bag of waters, if there is one, before the contractions start again, then baby can come any old way, arm first or something, then you're in trouble. And today it's just us, there is no help to call, so we leave well alone. OK?'

'But the other baby,' said Anabel. 'Shouldn't it get out as soon as possible?'

'Yes it should. Its oxygen supply is now compromised, but we can cause more problems by interfering. Let's just hope it's a sensible child. There is one thing we can do though.'

She turned her head and called out.

'Erica can you bring Number One Son over and give him to his mother please.'

Erica brought the dried and swaddled infant over and put him in his mother's arms. She pulled the towel back from his face and the new mother looked at her new son.

The whole room witnessed the magical moment when mother and baby first look into each other's eyes and the bond is made. As mother looked at baby, so nature reasserted itself and the contractions began again. Erica lifted the baby from his mother's arms as she concentrated on producing its sibling. The second baby appeared in exactly the same way as the first.

'Another he,' thought Annie checking this time. This one didn't cry out though when she cut the cord. Ananbel took him quickly to Erica.

'Don't worry,' said Annie. 'He looks fine, he was kicking. He just needs a little longer to find his lungs.' Seconds after she spoke a cry was heard and everyone in the room except Annie and Rudy relaxed.

'Anabel, back here. We still haven't finished the job you know,' said Annie. 'For twin ladies this is the most dangerous time. If her overstretched womb relaxes she can bleed to death in seconds. I've given the syntometrine to contract the womb, now we wait again. Watch those two cords.'

As she spoke both Annie and Ananbel saw the clamps on the end of the cord slide a few inches down the bed followed by a small trickle of blood.

'We're in business,' said Annie. 'See. Cord lengthens and there's a separation bleed. The afterbirth is ready to come.' She put her left hand gently but firmly on Mrs Abela's abdomen and held the cords in her right. She pulled very gently and with a gurgle something that looked like a large red dinner plate slithered onto the bed.

'See,' she said again, 'Both cords embedded. I think we've got it all. Now let's put the drip up.'

Rudy stepped in and did his bit, connecting the IV bag and tubing to the needle already in Mrs Abela's hand while Annie and Anabel did their tidying up which involved a gentle inspection, a quick wash and a clean sheet for the new mother to sit on.

'You see. No damage down there. The babies were smaller than her last one so she got away with it, and next to no blood loss either, perhaps 200ml.' She looked at the new mother and finally risked a smile.

'Mrs Abela you were brilliant, marvellous, splendid. You did it just right. I think all will be well now. Anabel will give you a wash and help you feed those babies while I go and write all this down.'

Jo, who had been hovering, translated and then said, 'Can I stay?'

'I'm sure you can, but ask the Mother,' said Annie, musing to herself that the cuddling of new babies was a very good treatment for a broken heart.

Anabel, now on familiar ground, was taking over. Both she and the mother of the twins were glowing with pride. Annie watched for a minute or two and convinced all would be well retreated.

The astonishing thing was that when she sat down at the desk in the next room with the hospital's birth register in front of her, she looked at her watch and realised the whole drama had only take an hour and a half from start to finish. It wasn't yet midnight.

Filling in the register was immensely satisfying. It was another old leather bound book, continued from before independence, like the one at Becana. She filled it in and signed the entry, but she left a space below her name for Anabel's signature as second midwife.

'She'll be the one to look at this in years to come,' she thought, 'not me. She should have her history.'

She continued her musings and then smiled as she remembered her last twin delivery. This is what they call reflective practice these days I suppose, but that little episode would have given Krista and Lizzie at home complete apoplexy. I didn't check on the babies' heartbeats once. But there was no point. Our priority was the mother. The babies just had to look after themselves and I'm glad to say they did. I will say that for African babies they do know which side their bread is buttered and do try not to make trouble!

It was sometime later Jo came in bearing a cup of steaming tea.

'I put sugar in it,' she said. 'That was amazing. Rudy and Erica sent this. They said goodnight and have gone back to bed.'

She handed over the steaming cup and a small glass.

'Ah,' said Annie. 'Rudy's no 1 Schnapps. I am honoured.' She picked up the glass and tipped it into the tea and took a sip. 'That hits all the spots,' she said.

She looked at Jo.

'Now do you see why the one in charge can't leave the bridge! If I'd gone with Kala, there would have been no one here with the experience to deliver those twins?'

'Have you done them often?'

'An honest answer is, never unsupervised. That's why I had Ananbel there. I was just repeating word for word what my seniors said to me the only time I've done them before. I just needed to say it all out loud, to get it right and she did need to see. It's the only way you learn in this game.'

'Why did it go so well do you think?'

'Well we've had her here for three weeks and we'd been feeding her good red meat and iron pills and vitamins every day so at least she had reasonable blood levels, not like Kala. And she believed in me and I believed in her and I'd done my homework and I suppose in the last resort someone up there was keeping an eye on us. But will I be glad tomorrow when Sister Anastasia and Sister Hildegard are back!'

She went on.

'You remember what we were saying earlier? You see the problem. That mother'll never believe in an emergency now. And that could have gone so wrong. The babies could have been breech, they could have got stuck and she could have bled and died. We were very very lucky.'

There was a sparkle in Jo's eye, familiar to anyone used to emergency work. She was on an adrenaline high.

'Do you think it's all over now and we can go to bed ?' she said, but Annie could see she was a long way from sleep.

'I do sincerely hope that is it for the night. What we've seen today is the rule in midwifery. It's either feast of famine. It's never calm and regular throughput. Come on, I've finished here. Let's look in on them.'

And so they did and there they were, the two new citizens fed and asleep. Their healthy and now also almost asleep mother was still smiling from ear to ear being watched over by Anabel. The young nun had brought in a comfy chair and was obviously intending to bed down for the night next to her charges.

'Call me if there is any problem ,'said Annie. 'You're right to stay with her. Sleep well.'

The two who felt they didn't belong in this circle of cosy warmth crept out.

Back in her room Annie tried to pick up the conversation from where they were when they'd been interrupted but somehow things seemed to have moved on.

Jo looked at her friend and mentor, a new calmness in her face.

'Look,' she said. 'I know, I was a bit broken. I seem to be fixed now. I am going to chalk it up to experience and move on. I don't know what watching those babies arrive did to me, but it did do something. I really am OK.'

She went on.

'What we really need to do is talk about the mining and the mosquitoes and P&P and James and Jemal. Our bush telegraph out at Becana said they'd gone to Bundu with the Newtown baby. Do we know any more about them?'

'I don't,' said Annie. 'They whisked them away while I was asleep, that first night here and since then, my nose has been kept almost unremittingly to the grindstone. Sister H seems to be a great believer in "The devil finds work for idle hands." She doesn't know and doesn't want to know what's been going on, but she sure isn't going to give me any time to do anything except work. Both she and Sister Anastasia are off on jollies in the capital and I'm left holding the baby. Sorry bad pun. Babies. You saw tonight what it's like. Also according to Erica she hasn't told anyone I'm here.'

'Ah I know about that,' said Jo. 'Frank let it be known you'd gone on holiday to Vic. Falls and weren't expected back for another week still. I thought that was a brainwave. Stopped everyone looking for you.'

She eyed Annie.

'Don't kid me though, you are enjoying the work. I can see it in your eyes and I watched you tonight.'

'You're right, I know. And it stopped me thinking about the bigger problems, which I suppose now we've got to.'

They sat there in silence for a few moments, then both started speaking simultaneously.

'OK you first,' said Jo.

'Well,' said Annie, 'It seems to me though we don't really know everything, you lot seem to have put a stop to things out there for the moment anyway. Direct action has its uses.'

'Yea but it's not that easy. My guys who beat up James and Jemal are still out there, and still being paid wages by P&P. They haven't dared come back to see me though. And there is P&P. We just don't know how far they'll go. They are a big, huge international company. What we also don't know is whether this is a maverick individual up to something, or does it go all the way to the top?' continued Jo.

'We know more than that,' said Annie. 'Think. They must have a whole establishment in the UK for Sal, the mum who died of malaria, to catch it in the first place. And someone was worried enough to sent Jemal out here to find out what is going on. And if what he said is true, a murder was done. What has your Monty said?'

'I thought we established that,' said Jo a bit firmly. 'He's not my Monty any more.'

'Don't be so touchy. Your ex- Monty then. Keep to the point.'

Jo smiled wryly.

'You're a harsh woman when in pursuit of the truth Sister Larriot.'

'Oh for goodness sake what else is there?'

'Kindness, softness, maybe love and don't you start quoting Keats at me. I did O level too.'

'Never went a lot on him anyway. Silly boy, died young. As we were saying...'

'Alright - Monty, when I finally cornered him I made him tell me. He said his job was, was coordination. The labs in the containers were set up before he arrived out here. The work is very low level. There are no scientists or anything. The stuff arrives from the capital by post and is put into the tanks. In about 10 days there are little mosquitoes ready to go. His job was to release them in the right places and make sure the right people had the protective nets. As I said, he seemed to think it was a good use of resources.'

'And he's going you say? Just as well. What would Inika do to him?'

'I see your point,' said Jo. 'Yes. This job in Thailand. After he reported on the destruction he got his marching orders. It's officially a transfer. The paperwork and job offer came from HQ in the UK. It's more money too.'

'You see what I mean,' said Annie. 'It's not run from here. It's got to be bigger than just this little bit of Africa.'

'So what's our Plan of Action?'

'There's two things, the mining and the little mosquitoes. We may have got the latter sorted, here anyway, for the moment, but we need to go and see the nurse guy at P&P. I know him. I talk to him about the paternity of Becana babies from time to time. He needs to know about the need for the nets with tiny holes for a while. The mining I'm not sure about. What do you think?'

'I think we don't know enough. I think any mine has got to be community owned and managed. I think the people have to choose between the animals and the mining or find a way they can coexist. We need to know more, and mostly what Jemal knows.'

'I think you mean a trip to Bundu? And meanwhile I think I know someone who can do some research for us. He's clever at things like that. My nephew Max is in my house at home and he managed to get this to me.'

She showed Jo the email thrust into her hand the day she'd brought the baby Morning in. Jo read the message, "Dear Auntie Annie, Mum is very worried. What's going on? No letters. Get in touch. It's urgent she's bugging me. Max."

'You don't give them much do you? They are your family.'

'Well it's hard to explain. I've never been away before and it's not as if I'd forgotten about home. It's just reality is here. This is the now. But it seems they remember me and are getting a bit annoyed. I will have to email him in the morning and I'll ask him some complicated questions about mining and mobile phones and then maybe we can organise a trip to town. Bosses are back tomorrow. I'll have some time. OK?'

'That is the beginning of a plan,' said Jo.

'Now do you think can we go to sleep?' said Annie. 'Have you come down from Cloud Nine a bit? It is late and some of us have to be up with the lark or whatever they have here.'

They settled and slept.

It was late the following morning Annie finally found time and made her way to the hospital office. She sought out the young woman who had defined herself as Inika's cousin, when she had thrust that last email into her hand.

Slightly horrified at her neglect of her roots Annie realised that that was a while since the email had arrived.

She found the young woman she was looking for and holding out the email spoke.

'I must reply. They will worry.'

The young woman looked back at her, looked around her and seeing that no one else was in sight said, 'This way sister.'

Annie slightly bemused at her conspiratorial attitude followed. At the end of a corridor they entered what looked like a broom cupboard. Following the young woman past the pails and brushes and behind a colourful cotton curtain, she found herself in a very small space with a table and a computer.

'This is ours,' she said. 'The staff's. The Convent lot think we are simple and they won't give us time on the hospital system. They don't want us using it too much. With this, ours, we can do shopping and email and internet and things. This is wireless and we have a modem. They are too stupid to work it out. We just use the hospital connection and electricity. Inika's uncle In Bundu found this computer and got it out to us. My nephew set it up. We call it Kat's (for Katilo you see) Internet Cafe - only there is no cafe.'

Annie listened with amusement to this recital. There was nothing like being on the inside. And being given the OK by lnika obviously got you in. She recalled one of Max's comments along the lines that though knowledge is power these days, access to that knowledge is the real power. She remembered his final words.

'People will always find a way Aunty.'

He was definitely right, as was clearly being demonstrated in front of her.

The young woman logged on and got her to the email screen.

'That's all very well,' thought Annie. 'But where do I start.'

'Oh look,' said the Inika's cousin. 'There is another one for you.'

CHAPTER NINE
Communications

email: Max McClaren to his Aunt, Annie Larriot

Dear Aunty
We have had rumours here that you are missing. Mum's had a phone call. One of your friends came to see me. She works in Admin. at your hospital here. They had a fax from P&P asking for further details of your next of kin. As that's Mum, I thought I'd better get in first. I actually don't believe you are that easy to rub out. Mum says they were calling it 'loss of contact'
But to save me from Mum, reply if you can. Attached is her email.
Max

email: Julia McClaren to Max, her son

I knew I was right to be worried. I've had a weird phone call asking if I've heard from Annie. The implication was that she was missing, but they called it loss of contact. What's going on. You find out. Has she been kidnapped or something? I was never keen on that job.
Mum

email: Annie Larriot to Max, her nephew

Dear Max
It was clever of you to find this email, which I now have access to. Please tell your mother I am well. No I'm not that easy to rub out and (what a chance to say this) reports of my demise (or kidnap) are premature. There are complications here though, which it is important you keep to yourself. I need you to do some research. Just reassure your mother and tell her to keep schtum about me. Forward this to her if you want. It is important you don't say you've been in touch with me or where I am, which given the email I expect you can guess. Let them wonder.

Then find out as much about the minerals they use in mobile phones as you can. Where are they mined, cost etc. Anything about the guy from P&P would help too. His details etc are on my contract in the desk in my bedroom at the house. TACTFULLY get in touch with Rosina. Her sister in Aus knows your mother. She is a mine of information. Ask her about a traveller boy called Vix. I don't want to say more yet till we know this email works long-term.

Annie

email: Max McClaren to Annie Larriot
Aunty

I won't forward Mum's reply! Some of it is unrepeatable. Basically she says she's glad you are ok, and who do you think you are, a John le Carre character and will you please get out of there and come straight to Oz. She was going to give you a round the world ticket for your birthday anyway. And you are half way there already. She has a point.

I hope you are alright, really. And Mum is just OTT.
Max

Report of Police Constable Francois Ruhumba to his HQ in Bundu for week 27 20..

Four incidents to be reported.

1. Attended the village of Newtown at the request of the NID team responsible for that area. They reported a deceased woman alone in a hut with a live female baby. The NID team had already arranged for the admission of the baby to Katilo Rural Hospital, from where she was subsequently transferred to Bundu District Hospital. On reaching the settlement the police team found it to be deserted. It was impossible to discover the woman's identity. The NID team had provided the information that death appeared natural, probably in childbirth or from malaria. The woman was therefore buried in the deserted village graveyard by my team. Some personal effects from

her house are held at Becana Police Station, should any relatives come forward.

    2.Incursion of Bandits into Becana Camp
    Disturbance on Sat …
    Saturday night at 22.00 I was made aware of an unusual level of disturbance on the periphery of Becana Camp. Myself and a group of other concerned citizens attended. We found strangers breaking into a facility which is owned by P&P. As we arrived there was a large explosion. It seems that an attempt to blow the doors off the metal container in order to access the contents, had gone wrong. The explosion completely destroyed the container and damaged its contents beyond repair.

    The force of the explosion frightened the thieves. They then fled into the bush. We were unable to detain any persons. None were recognised by myself or my team. Because of this we believe they were from over the international border, intent on robbing a secure P&P store known to hold valuable equipment.

    There were no fatalities or major injuries in Becana camp as a result of this incident.

    3. Two foreigners were transferred by ambulance to Katilo the same evening with suspected Malaria. They both assisted on NID day.

    The other foreigner resident in Becana is the nurse midwife Sister Larriot. She is currently away, believed on holiday at Victoria Falls.

    4. Several hours later, in the early hours of Sunday a loud explosion was heard in the North, some miles away, near the border. Fire was visible in the sky. There are no known villages in the area. I and some citizens from Becana attended the scene at first light. A second P&P container was found in a similar condition to the first. It was destroyed. There were no people present, but it appeared there had been some sort of settlement there, near the river. There was evidence of excavations having been carried out. It is presumed the thieves continued to this store when chased away from Becana. They however repeated their mistake and again destroyed the store rather than just blowing the doors off and looting it.

5. Reports on the follow up to incidents 2 and 4 are known to you, having been attended by the Police Team from Bundu and reported on by Sergeant M....

Email: Karl Burgdorf, Head of ops., P&P Becana district to Charles Coniston-Brown Research Officer P&P UK

Jim

I have to report the devastation of the research project in Becana district. Both laboratories have been broken into and gutted. The police state that there were bandit incursions from over the border. Our own intelligence tells us otherwise. Some, no doubt, distorted reports of the purpose of the research are said to have reached local inhabitants who have taken direct action.

I strongly recommend that Dr Montgomery is transferred to another field of operations immediately, as he is apparently associated in the local mind with the laboratories and therefore must be considered at risk. Should any harm befall him, a white scientist working in the bush, police investigations would inevitably have to be extensive and might well involve a detailed examination of P&P ops here.

Extraction activities have currently ceased. All local casual workers have dispersed. Most were from over the border and of dubious residential status so we anticipate no comeback from that direction. I understand there is soon to be a meeting with tribal elders to discuss how they wish to use the area of land adjacent to the river. I have been informed by London that they wish us to attend and monitor the outcome. Covertly or otherwise is yet unclear.

We, here, are unsure how rumours about the purpose of the research spread but checking our records, several new employees have arrived from the UK recently, one of whom has a home address in Devon, England. He acted as a volunteer on the recent local recent vaccination days (a community effort supported by all local civil employees). He will therefore have had contact with the Nurse, Sister Larriot, sponsored by yourselves. She is presently unavailable, said to be on holiday in Victoria Falls. It seems extremely likely that any intelligence leak originated in the UK and not locally. I suggest you investigate.

Karl

email: Charles Coniston-Brown Senior Research Officer P&P UK to Karl Burgdorf, Head of ops P&P Becana district

Karl
All points well taken.
Attached is paperwork for a transfer for Dr M. to Thailand with immediate effect, to supervise the research project there. It is noted that this is a promotion in the light of his sterling work in the bush in Becana under such difficult circumstances. Please convey the Company's gratitude to him when you inform him of his imminent move. A substantial relocation allowance will, of course be payable as he is required so rapidly in Thailand.

Please ensure a suitable fully accredited representative from P&P attends the elders meeting. P&P's objective should be, under all circumstances to prevent the meeting opting solely for a wildlife sanctuary and banning mining activities. Given the intelligence leaks, damage limitation, from P&P's viewpoint, involving an exemplar community mining project with wildlife protection is an idea. It would make for good global publicity.

Intelligence leaks have been traced to the theft of a computer from the research lab in Devon UK. Shortly after this theft a Mr J Singh applied to P&P with an unverifiable CV and what have proved to be false references. He was given a job in Becana because he said he had relatives locally. Please terminate his employment.

Sister Larriot is only supported by P&P, not employed by us. However, she is employed by the convent medical service at Katilo Hospital. Some discussion with our mutual friend Sister Hildegard may be indicated.

Can you see any further details that need tidying up?

Jim.

email: Max McClaren to Annie Larriot

The other stuff as promised. Yes there are several minerals they use in mobiles and they are mined in your neck of the woods. World prices rise and fall but the cheaper you can dig it up the more money you make. There is a whole debate about ethical mining and I have to say us Aussies do the right thing.

There is also other stuff they dig up that's very trendy. They are called rare earth elements and they are needed for the magnets for windmills and all sorts. They all come from China so everyone is madly looking for another source.

As your access to the net is probably limited I haven't attached lots of stuff but here is a rundown of what I've found. I hope this is what you need:

I have a date with Rosina next week, for a meal. Apparently she knows her way around a stove.

Max's guide to what can be dug up and what people do to get it:

1. Mobile phones (and lots of electronic stuff) contain minerals called tantalite and columbite, hence the coltan you asked about.

2. 50% of the stuff comes from Oz and is responsibly mined over in Western Australia. I told you we were the good guys. It's also mined in Canada and Brazil, but the only places it is processed into the tantalum metal they use is the US, Germany and China.

3. As we all wanted mobile phones the demand rose and the price went up. 'Worth its weight in gold' is a quote used and they mean it literally.

4. It can be dug up in lots of other places, notably the Congo. It is also very easy to get out of the ground, just like panning for gold as they did in the gold rush in the 1860s in Oz. It's called artisanal mining. As a result lots of people started digging it up and recently the price has fallen. The Aussies have even mothballed one of their mines

5. This low level mining is what concerns people. It's very basic capitalism. The stuff is moved along the line, everyone taking a markup and no-one controlling anything. When it finally reaches some very responsible mobile phone maker, even if they do care, they can't tell where it came from, like you can with diamonds, or what people have done to get it. It is now possible to 'fingerprint' the coltan to see where it comes from, like the diamonds, but it's a very expensive process and nobody wants to have to do it.

5 There is lots of stuff about coltan v. gorillas (ie destroying wildlife habitat) and child miners in the Congo and coltan funding armies in Central Africa and displacing people to get at land. That's why mining it in Oz is better, we're organised and respectable.

6. Attempts are being made to regulate all this. The Americans have a bill pending and some official body is trying to make governments accountable for their licences (ie not take bribes) but nothing really is happening 'on the ground,' like where you are. If you are a respectable company, you don't want to be associated with child miners or war, so the principle of regulation seems to be that if they destroy the market for the non respectable stuff then only big respectable companies will mine it.

7. This is only one thing they dig up. It's the currently fashionable one, like blood diamonds were a few years ago. The next thing is going to be stuff called rare earth elements. The west are desperate for these as most are at the moment found in China. Nobody is sure where else they can be found, or what they can be extracted from. Science hasn't caught up with mining yet so everyone is hanging on to any mining concessions they've got hoping (figuratively speaking) they are sitting on a gold mine.

That do you?
Max

email: Annie Larriot to Max McClaren
Max

Thanks for all that. Some of it I knew or guessed. Here, I've seen the panning by the river, and they are killing the animals to feed the miners, but more importantly they were trying to move people off their land. I won't go into that now, but it seems to have been sorted out locally.

As to respectable mining in Oz. Don't be smug. I've lived longer than you. Do the words uranium and Aboriginals mean anything to you? I have to say that to me it looks a little like the big fish eating the little fish to stop the little fish undercutting them and pinching their profits. Capitalism red in tooth and claw?

Annie

email
Max McClaren to Annie Larriot

Aunty

Pots and Kettles!! I did history at school and I am born Aussie. As they say 'We grew here, you flew here.' (I know you haven't yet but don't forget, Mum does want you to.) What about Marilinga and Woomera then. That was in your time, 1950s. Land round there will be uninhabitable for 1/4 million years because of those Pommie H bomb tests.

I've been to see Rosina and had a lovely dinner. I have no idea what you two have in common though. She was onto your mission. She actually said 'And what does Annie want to know now?' This is what I found out.

The man who gave you your contract whose initials come out as JCB is currently Head of research at the new facility and linked in with the hospital as you know. Melanie says he has fingers in many pies. She met him again recently at a dinner and they were talking about travellers. He is very against them and was offering further support to her monitoring group. She tactfully declined. Apparently earlier this year he lent some men as muscle to move some stones to block gates and prevent the caravans getting onto her local common. These guys rather alarmed Melanie and her lot. They were hinting that for a consideration they could arrange 'things.' The implication being that gratuitous violence was their everyday stock in trade. Nice phrase that, never used it before, says just what I want it to!

I have to say I was amused by all the above. It's so frightfully English. You will all ruthlessly man the barricades to prevent incursions onto your tiny tiny little bits of green land but you will do nothing to damage the invader or put him out of business on a permanent basis. You just want him to go away. 'Live and let live, but do it somewhere else.' While you are trying to repel boarders you will probably arrange clean water and welfare benefits for the besiegers and their dogs. Us ex-colonials have seen and felt that benign yoke.

Re the traveller called Vix. He was in the news here a couple of months ago. He was found in bits in a bin bag by the road. It was labelled 'bikie business' and no-one has been arrested. There was a big hippy funeral and lots of the vans were impounded and then released again. When I asked Rosina about him she gave me a funny look and started talking about the head of her group, some Brigadier or other. It was then I got the negative vibes about JCB. The brigadier guy had made enquiries among his old contacts and to quote Rosina he said Mr JCB 'was not the right sort to mix with,' and not to let the group become involved with him.

Not sure what that means BUT really listen. I really do think you should be very careful. This stuff is real. These big companies won't stand for being thwarted. They'll eat you up too. It's not all hippie peace and love you know.

Max

**email
Annie Larriot to Max McClaren**

Dear Max

OK. I'm sorry. Pax re uranium and the H bomb tests and colonialism. I would remind you, however, I'm not that old and never was personally responsible for transportation. We all have things to answer for. Mind you, you never felt any 'benign yoke' either. As you say independent Aussie born.

Anyway, it's the here and now I have to deal with. You are right, I will take things seriously. I think people have been murdered in the UK because of all this. I got given this job to get me out of the way.

I understand the info from Rosina but don't you mock her lot. Many of them, if not veterans of Greenham Common at least supplied the Greenham women with food, baths and old carpets to keep the mud at bay. It's not PEOPLE they are against, but what some people decide to do. Nuclear missiles or travellers in their backyard are equally unacceptable. They do so many quietly useful things in the community and their organisation is superb. If they are wary of JCB then he and his are something to be wary of.

No-one has ever given benefit payments to the dogs. That is a persistent urban (or do I mean rural) myth. And there is nothing wrong with a sense of fair play and a dislike of violence

And I would say if it hadn't been for us hippies you wouldn't have the greens and what rules we have got.

As to action on the ground. We have a visitor from home who knows a lot. But not enough, he's in hospital with malaria at the moment. I'm trying to work out a way of visiting him.

Tell your mother. Not sure what. But reassure her. My adventure. Have to do it my way. Never been free before. Don't annoy her.

Annie.

email: Karl Burgdorf, Head of ops., P&P Becana district to Sister Hildegard , Mother Superior, Katilo Convent and Medical Supervisor Katilo Rural Hospital.

Dear H

We have recently had a request from a sister company of ours asking us to look for a rural African hospital in which they can trial their new oxygen concentrator system. The objective of the system is to free up small hospitals from dependence on the delivery of oxygen cylinders. The very simple machine concentrates the O2 in the air and gives an acceptable % for most low level therapeutic use. We wondered if Katilo would be interested in being the guinea pig?

We have a small local difficulty. I don't think UK got it right when they sent us that new nurse. She has been active among the bushman, and though I have no evidence I feel she may have had some input into the recent disturbances. She isn't one of us and is unused to our ways. Should you feel able, the firm would appreciate her relocation.

best wishes
K

email: From Karl Burgdorf, Head of ops., P&P, Becana district to Charles Coniston-Brown, Senior Research Officer, P&P UK.

Jim:
A few things still.

Jemal Singh, currently in hospital in Bundu will have his employment status terminated. He will then have no visa and will have to return to the UK.

Sister Larriot, similarly will also find her contract foreshortened. Both should arrive in the UK within the next month.

The Elders Tribal meeting will be attended by P&P in an official capacity. We will instruct Jo Schmidt, who works for a local conservation charity which we support, to draw up a plan allowing tourism, wild life conservation and at present anyway, an artisanal mining programme. It is considered that once a mining concession is officially established, then should expansion in the future be deemed appropriate, this process would have been facilitated. Karl

email: Charles Coniston-Brown, Senior Research Officer, P&P UK to Karl Burgdorf, Head of ops., P&P Becana district

Karl
Planning sounds fine. We will tidy up this end.
Jim

email: Sister Hildegard , Mother Superior, Katilo Convent and Medical Supervisor Katilo Rural Hospital to Mrs Susan Dopke, Personnel Officer for Nursing, Bundu District HR Department.

Dear Mrs Dopke
    I have recently heard from Mr Burgdorf from P&P. He is looking for a hospital to trial some new equipment. I attach a computer link for you to view the scheme they suggest. I shall of course be contacting the medical director to discuss the details.
    I would appreciate your advice on another matter. We have a midwife working for us on a volunteer contract named Sister Anne Larriot. She is enthusiastic and extremely capable. Her work out in the bush at Becana was dedicated and she has very efficiently taken charge of the maternity unit here, in my absence. I have great respect for her work and if asked would give her an outstanding professional reference. But, in the local context, and it is a big but, she seems to have got herself involved in politics.
    It has been suggested to me, with no evidence, I may say, that she may have had an input into the recent local disturbances in the bush. I had understood that the police considered these were incursions from over the border by bandits.
    I am also concerned about her health. Her over-involvement in local issues is putting her at serious risk of professional burnout. Your suggestions would be helpful.

Hildegard, Medical Supervisor Katilo Rural Hospital.

Letter, by Hand
Jo Schmidt to Annie Larriot

Dear Annie

This will reach you via the beer delivery man who is an old Africaaner and some sort of cousin of my father. He does his own thing and owes allegiance to no one but Midas and Family!

I can't write too much as he is already revving his truck engine, but he called by specially on his way back from the border to see how I was. He says he will stop at Katilo and give this to you. Being a loyal member of the Kerke he will get satisfaction out of annoying Sister H by stirring up the dust with his truck in her so Catholic compound.

Something weird has happened. I have had a formal letter offered me a further contract to plan a joint programme involving mining, wildlife and tourism. It is a dream job and might be the answer to us here. Somehow they don't seem to realise what I've been involved in. Monty obviously kept very quiet about me. I suppose it was in his interests to do so. P&P must be paying, though the letter is from the wildlife trust. My instincts are to accept. I need to talk to you though. What more do you know?

Bush telegraph tells me 1. The twins are very well.
2. Jemal has been officially sacked and will have to leave the country as soon as he is fit to leave hospital. James is still visiting him in the hospital in Bundu.

Inika sends her love and says give her greetings to her cousin who does the computer. I think that's Inika-speak for 'She'd better look after you or else.'

You were right. I am my own person and I am learning to be alone. I shall try to take things slowly next time, but it's so easy to get sucked in.
love
Jo

Routine monthly communications envelope from Bundu Hospital Admin Dept to
Sister Hildegard , Mother Superior, Katilo Convent and Medical Supervisor Katilo Rural Hospital.

Dear Sister
Please find enclosed this month's doctors' rotas, new pharmacy order forms, and the latest memoranda from HQ.

Enclosed also are the following:

1. Termination papers for Sister Anne Larriot. I gather from Mrs Dopke it is her time to move on. She has one month's paid holiday due to her and it has always been customary for VSO volunteers, who we've had in the past, to spend their last holiday time in our country travelling and seeing something of the area. To facilitate this I have arranged a room in the nurses' home in Bundu be made available to her for that month.
.2. Information letter and medical reports on the Koisan lady known as Lala Kai.
I believe Dr Hasan, the duty doctor that night is contacting you direct.

signed
Helvi Mawano, (Mrs) Administration Officer.

Emergency Department, Bundu Hospital.

Report on admission and treatment
Patient 3672 known as Lala Kai.

This lady of Koisan ethnicity was admitted by ambulance from your facility on ... at 22.00
Diagnosis: Prima gravida, probably at term. ? in early labour.
Subsidiary findings :Anaemia.
Observations on admission: T36.4 P120 R26 BP 120/90, Fetal heart not heard.
Investigations: Routine antenatal bloods taken. Haemoglobin 2.8gm/dl.

Treatment: Blood transfusion ordered: IV infusion of normal saline set up while awaiting arrival of crossmatched blood and transfer of patient to maternity ward.

Outcome

While awaiting the arrival of the prescribed blood this lady showed signs of congestive cardiac failure. She collapsed, became unconscious and in spite of determined efforts by the casualty staff she died approximately 30 minutes after admission. In view of the absence of an audible fetal heart no heroic measures were taken to deliver the baby.

Mortuary card
Patient: Lala Kai hosp no. 3672

The mortal remains of this patient will be released on presentation of this card.
In the event of non collection, the remains will be retained in the facility.

CHAPTER TEN
Each to their own.

It was some days after her own and Sister Anastasia's return to Katilo that Sister Hildegard sent for Annie. The arrival of the monthly envelope from Bundu had crystallized the need for her to act. In front of her lay Annie's termination of contract document and the medical reports on Lala Kai. She wasn't looking forward to the task she had set herself.

Annie entered the room, still wearing her semi-novice-nun nursing uniform. Things had been quiet since the return of the bosses she thought, and that had been nice. Handing back her responsibilities to Sister Anastasia, she had given her a detailed and exhaustive account of the twin delivery and received suitable praise. She had also described her action on the transfer of the little Koisan girl with blue beads in her hair, as she continued to think of Lala. She had been slightly surprised at the noncommittal response she had received. On thinking about it, she'd not heard from Miriam either.

Since the letter from Jo had arrived she'd had no news from anyone. The deliver of said letter had caused the drama Jo predicted.

Annie was wondering if this summons to see Sister Hildegard was in some way connected with that incident.

The arrival of an alcohol bearing truck into the heart of the hospital courtyard had been bad enough but when it had been augmented by theological discussion with the truck driver who mentioned the 'Anti-Christ in Rome,' "unamused" had understated Sister Hildegard's reaction.

While Annie sat herself down on the hard, high backed wooden chair reserved for visitors, Sister Hildegard had been rearranging papers on her desk. She handed to Annie the black edged mortuary card that had come from Bundu.

'I thought you ought to see this,' she said.

'Oh dear,' said Annie, reading it and looking up. 'What happened? We transferred as quickly as we possibly could. I borrowed from the petty cash to make sure there would be no financial fuss when she got to Bundu.'

Sister Hildegard handed over the medical report. Annie read and reread it and then read it a third time and then lost her temper.

'For goodness sake. They are supposed to be the experts. They practically murdered her. Bundu is supposed to be where we send them. That's what emergency obstetric care is about.'

'I also had a phone call,' said Sister Hildegard. 'He said, please would we not send any more moribund patients. He asked why we didn't put up an IV before she left here and what sort of antenatal care were we doing out here?'

'I hope you told whoever rang that they were incompetent killers and you were going to report them to the Ministry and demand a Maternal Mortality Meeting,' responded a furious Annie.

'I'm afraid in my position I do have to be a little tactful. What's your considered professional view on this.'

Only a very slightly chastened Annie replied stiffly, 'My report and rationale are in the transfer book. And I stand by them, recorded contemporaneously I may add, as we're supposed to do. I'd just got it written before the twins kicked off.'

'I know but you need to lay it out for me, in detail. We need to officially record our position here at Katilo, if we are going to make any sort of comment.'

'Well,' said Annie, somewhat calmer externally, but inside still boiling. 'It's fairly simple. She was brought in by Jo, in the late afternoon. Her team had found her in a village way down by the river and the girl's mother asked them to bring her in. The mother said she was "too white." The girl herself had never seen a nurse or a hospital before. She was very young, maybe 16, a primigravida, very obviously near term and really extremely pale. On our little Hb 'scope' she came out at 'below 4gm/dl.' Though she was cheerful and 'well' I considered her a candidate for immediate transfer. We were very lucky in that Miriam, the school teacher from Becana was in the hospital visiting a patient and came to translate. Inika and I had delivered Miriam's last baby, so she was happy to help,' Annie added.

'Anyway we got the girl's consent and understanding and wrote her name down as Lala Kai which sounds a bit like how you say it. Miriam agreed to go with her. Everyone here was brilliant. They had the ambulance ready in no time, with oxygen. I wrote a transfer note, gave Miriam money to get her admitted and sent her on her way. I did try to phone and warn them, but as usual in the evening, there was no line.'

'Bundu specifically complained that that no IV was put up and no fetal heart recorded.'

'Both those were clear treatment decisions by me, and I stand by them. The mother, not the baby was the priority. Looking at her it was clear to me that if she went into labour she would die. You could practically see through her she was so pale. I wasn't going to alarm her by finding out whether or not her baby was alive. She said she could feel it moving. As to the IVI. Her circulation was holding its own, just, on an Hb of under 4. If I'd put a drip up of anything except whole blood I would have diluted her blood still further, without any adding red cells. Her heart would have got even less red blood and therefore oxygen and wouldn't have coped. It didn't did it? How could they have been so stupid in Bundu?'

She looked at the medical report and answered her own question. 'They ordered the blood, didn't they, but the nurse just did her routine job on admission, didn't she. No-one said not to put anything up except blood so she put up a drip and ran a bag through as one normally would. And sent the girl into heart failure. Do we know if the doctor saw her before the drip was put up?'

'The report doesn't say. Maybe he didn't. And they will try and cover their backs.'

Annie searched through her memories of her reading.

'Do you know the *Three delays framework* they use with maternal mortality stuff?' She didn't wait for an answer and went on.

'It goes Delay 1: The decision to seek care. Delay 2: The reaching of care. and finally Delay 3: The receiving of appropriate care.

Our poor little lamb ended up the victim of the first and the third. We, here, avoided delay two. We got her to care as fast as was possible. We, here, did the right thing and some half asleep nurse in casualty in Bundu just did a routine job without stopping to think.'

Annie looked down again at the report and went on,

'If you can't depend on colleagues, it's all nonsense. If I'd gone with her then it might have been ok. Or if she had died it wouldn't have been by mistake.'

Sister Hildegard listened to Annie's raging and then spoke.

'Now listen to me, you know very well about maternal mortality. It's your subject. What you seem to have forgotten is that every single mother's death is a tragedy for someone. There are children, a husband, parents. This particular mother has got to you personally. You are too angry to be professional. You do know though what has to be done. That's to have an enquiry and learn from the mistakes made. If everyone starts throwing accusations about everyone else will cover their backs and nobody will learn anything. I will make sure a proper maternal mortality meeting is held.'

But Annie wasn't listening.

'If only I'd gone with her... She was so young. But I was in charge here so I couldn't. That was the right decision too. Otherwise no one would have been here for the twins.'

'Who are doing very well and their mother,' said Sister Hildegard.

'That's not the point.'

'Perhaps my dear you are being over ambitious. Try and hear what I'm saying. This is sub-saharan Africa. You know the numbers. A mother here is so many more times more likely to die in childbirth than in the West.'

Annie sighed and tried to see Lala Kai as a statistic and failed.

'No you don't quite understand. She did creep into my heart, that young girl, but what has made me so angry is the mistake that killed her. She might well have died anyway, but the point is that incompetence actually killed her.'

'I repeat,' said Sister Hildegard. 'We can guess what happened. You and I both know it was late at night. There will have been no doctor actually in casualty when she arrived. They would have had to call him. She will have been seen by a nurse first who will have done the observations. Do you want to punish some poor night nurse in casualty? That's not the way and you know it.'

'But she was going to be a mother and she is totally and unnecessarily dead. And she was so young and beautiful and hopeful and she trusted us. And we sent her to a strange town and a strange place and she died there. She's alone there now, without family or anything.'

Annie had a sudden flashback to the other dead mother she'd seen recently, Morning's mother. She at least was buried in her own ground on her own land. She spoke again, still furiously impassioned.

'I'll tell you one thing. She's not staying in that morgue because no one can afford to collect her. Bodies are there for years sometimes. She's one of ours and we'll have her back and we'll bury her in her own village, where she belongs. Please can we fetch her and take her home?'

Sister Hildegard looked at Annie and decided that sometimes concession was wise.

'I was thinking it is time the spare ambulance was serviced. It needs to go to Bundu. And you are due a little time off after your hard work here. I'll give you a letter and you take the mortuary card, then you can bring her back, when you bring the ambulance back. You will stop here and we will take her into the chapel and bless her and then you will take her to her village for a funeral.'

Annie looked straight at her boss, a little startled at gaining such easy compliance. Sister Hildegard went on.

'But there is a condition. You have to promise me that if I let you go to Bundu to collect her you will not start throwing accusations around. There will be an enquiry, but it will be a proper, no blame, maternal mortality meeting and you are not to prejudice it in advance and upset everybody. Do you understand?'

Annie did, and something went click in her head. Professionalism reasserted itself.

'I do know you are right, really, but that little one, she got to me and this is the second dead mother in a month. I think I've had enough.'

'I have been concerned about you,' interposed Sister Hildegard.

Annie, as she usually did, just charged on.

'I'll tell you something. I just can't do this anymore. I can't do my bit right and have other people do their bit wrong. I need to be proud of my profession. They should have got it right in Bundu. She might not have made it, but they should not have done the completely wrong thing. They screwed up.'

'There is a word for where you are,' said Sister Hildegard. 'It's called burnout. If you're going to work here you have to learn where we are at and work to move on from there.'

'The trouble is,' said Annie, 'I know what should happen and I can't live with it not happening any more. The botching is too much.'

'Sister Larriot, Annie,' said Sister Hildegard with a firm kindness, 'you have done a great deal for us here. You have re-inspired the community out at Becana and you have enabled them to get their ambulance back. In the hospital here you are much liked and respected. But you have to accept that some people are just innovators, blow-ins I think is the current term. They make their mark and move on. Other people carry on their work and ideas, day to day. Maybe you are a blow-in. Maybe you have given all you've got to give at the moment.'

Annie looked at her.

'I can't do it any more,' she said. 'I'm sorry. That little lass with the blue beads in her hair is the last straw.'

'Look,' said Sister Hildegard. 'Don't be so absolute. But if you feel you must go, then you must. I don't see why we should call it a resignation though. You are entitled to holiday and I think you need some sick leave to recover. I'm also told that it is normal for volunteers to have a month free in country at the end of their contract to look around and travel. If we add all that up that brings us more or less to the end of your contract. I shall of course give you an excellent reference, not as I understand it, you need it, as you are going back to your old job aren't you?'

Annie felt a sudden flush of relief flood through her body, but she couldn't bring herself to say anything.'

Sister Hildegard had recognised the body language.

'I think,' she said, 'you should do as we've agreed. You should take the ambulance to Bundu and do what needs to be done. When you've seen the funeral through, come back here to us and I will have done all the paperwork necessary to send you on your way. It will also give everyone here a chance to say their goodbyes to you.'

Both Annie and Sister Hildegard felt a little surprised at the outcome of their encounter. Both had, metaphorically at least, girded their loins for a unpleasant task.

Annie was good at her job and to dismiss her, however kindly and with however good a reference, was still a dismissal and going to hurt and was fundamentally against Sister Hildegard's principles.

Collateral damage was not something she normally considered acceptable.

However, P&P were bigger than Annie, who after all was very short term and peripheral in her input. P&P were for the moment essential to the welfare of the hospital and therefore the people. Also she and Karl at P&P, had both been born in this country had gone to school together. They had been friends for over 40 years now, from long, long before independence, and they knew what was best for their country.

Annie was a foreigner, and it had to be said, not being white, didn't really understand the politics. It was better she went and it had been a delightful relief to Sister Hildegard that all found she had to do was accept Annie's decision to leave. She had been spared handing over the hemlock cup or delivering the stab in the back.

Annie too was rather surprised she had apparently got carte blanche to take an ambulance, go to Bundu and fetch Lala Kai's body and take it out to the village for burial, especially as she had just effectively resigned early from her contract.

Almost by accident she had achieved of two of her objectives. She could now visit the hospital in Bundu and talk to James and Jemal.

She had also got a chance to go back to Becana.

She was annoyed with herself with resigning, but deep down she knew her time here, in this country was over. She also had a feeling there was tidying up to be done back at home and this was one of the reasons she needed urgently to talk to Jemal.

She would have been surprised if she had read the paperwork that had been sitting in front of Sister Hildegard while they spoke. She was to remain ever innocent of the fact that she had been about to be dismissed anyway and also of the fact that her skin colour had been a factor in the event.

'Not being one of us' had always been part of her life and she had learned to celebrate it. Being adopted in itself had made her different. The fact that she had been, as a child, the only black face in her Devon village had been secondary. An outsider, she had found, saw more of the game. As many such outsiders, she was unconscious of the carapace she had developed for her own defence.

Having been given an official 'OK,' preparations for the trip to Bundu were quickly made. Annie tried to make her own private preparations and went again to see her young computer friend.

She asked if a message could be got to Inika to tell Jo that Annie would be in Bundu shortly. Assurances were given that all efforts would be made.

The following day, Annie in uniform, and Jackson, the ex-navy night porter who had been present on the night of the twins birth, set off together for the District Hospital at Bundu.

In the ambulance, Jackson had put a stretcher, a very proper shroud and a spare sheet and blanket taken from Katilo's store room. 'To wrap the body in,' he said. 'They'll not give you a dead rat in that place.'

Annie carried the papers and the mortuary card tucked into her bag and, lent by the Dutch nurses, a small suitcase with her 'mufti' and overnight things.

The first stop was the garage where they left the ambulance.

Jackson then escorted Annie to the hospital. It felt familiar to her. The clerks behind the desk were still in the 'walled in mode' rather than the 'welcome' mode now more common in England. They had a good barrier of glass and wood between themselves and the people they were paid to serve.

'Well we do that bit better at home, these days,' thought Annie as she watched Jackson speak to the reluctantly attentive clerks. Suddenly she found she had a room with a key which was hers.

'See you tomorrow Sister,' he said. 'At the mortuary by 8.00 Ok? Before the day gets hot.' With that he disappeared.

This African nurses' home didn't seem so different from its UK version except in its dilapidation quotient. Though, thought Annie I seem to recall one, on a course in London, was pretty terrible. It had cockroaches. At least here I have sunshine. And it's one up from where I've just been in Katilo. There's a wood floor here, not earth and I've got a balcony.' The balcony in question was a communal one and ran the length of the floor. On opening her door on to it, Annie found the space outside the adjoining rooms, and in fact all the way along the floor, garlanded with everyone's washing, drying in the afore mentioned sun. The colours in the display were less brilliant than that she'd see on the rows of market stalls, as African cottons however bright they are to start with, fade quickly. Nevertheless the muted display gave Annie great pleasure.

'Anyone with taste prefers washed denim anyway,' was her passing thought. 'I am going to take so many pieces of that stuff home with me. There are just so many patterns.'

She changed out of her pseudo religious uniform and emerged from the room a normal looking human being. She set off in search of the men's medical ward where Jemal should be.

She found him. Enquiring for the foreigner with the turban made the task easy. Sitting beside him in a far corner of Men's Medical was James. Jemal raised an eyebrow on seeing her.

'Dr Livingstone I presume,' he said.

'That's my line I think,' said Annie.

'Actually if it's anybody's it's mine,' said James smiling in welcome. 'My country, my continent, but who is quibbling. "What news from the Rialto?"' He spoke to Annie.

Jemal in his turn, looked puzzled, but Annie smiled, ' "There are more things in heaven and earth Horatio...."wrong play, but same author I believe.' She looked at Jemal, 'I can see you have to live in

Africa to get a decent English education these days. Anyway how are you?'

'Very well now, but trying to look ill so they can't deport me. I've been sacked.'

'We're both a bit stuck,' said James. 'Don't know what to do or where we're at in this game. I'm in a church hostel.'

'The police come and see me every couple of days. So far the docs have said I need to stay here, but not for much longer I think,' said Jemal.

'Well, I've not been sacked, or I don't think I have.' Annie paused for a moment and briefly recalled her recent interview. 'But I'm going home too.'

'What happens next?' said James.

'We need to compare notes. Have you found out any more?'

'He's got some info,' said James who in spite of Jemal's scowls, had decided Annie was family. She had become, in some way, his honorary aunt. 'He got me on the email to UK.'

They were so engrossed in their conversation that they didn't notice a fourth person approaching the bed.

'Well you three are causing a little sensation in this place aren't you?'

They looked up and found Jo standing at the end of the bed.

'You look as if you are plotting world revolution.' She turned to Annie. 'Your message got to me so I've come.'

Annie looked around her and realised, that indeed they were the centre of attention and that this was no place for private conversation. She raised an interrogative eyebrow at Jo who replied.

'Inika's not the only one with contacts. I've a cousin in this town and we can borrow his house. Will they let you out?'

'I think so,' replied Jemal. 'If I can give them an address. The nurses 'll be glad not to have policemen wandering round their ward and trying to chat them up and get free medicines out of them.'

'You'll need to get them to give you anti-malarials or we'll be back here again in five minutes, well ten days.' said Annie.

*

It all seemed to work. The nurses were indeed delighted to see Jemal go and so be able to exclude their other unwelcome visitors. They did the necessary communicating and form filling and even provided a weeks worth of pills for their patient. The address Jo gave for Jemal caused the ward sister to look twice at her.

'Our foreigner is going to a good home then, with other foreigners,' she said.

Jo was annoyed and showed it.

'I'm no foreigner,' she said. 'This is my country too. And these are visitors who have been doing our country a service.'

Her sharpness produced unconvinced grunt in reply. However the woman gave Jemal his pills and his papers and they left the ward, very conscious of the stares of its remaining inhabitants.

'What was all that about?' said Annie.

'Well my cousin lives in a rather good bit of town. It used to be a no go area for non- whites. The address put her back up.'

'Rather good bit of town' understated it as far as Annie was concerned. They had piled into Jo's truck with Annie and Jemal in the front and James in the back.

They drove down the main street, with its accumulated rubbish and noise. They went past shops with windows full of goods and no customers, then past the bank and then past the market, packed with stalls selling what people actually needed. Finally they passed the makeshift, lean to huts by the roadside on the edge of town.

Jo then turned off down a broad clean tarmac avenue and, as she stopped outside a walled garden pressed the remote control in her hand. The gate opened. They drove in and it closed behind them.

To Annie it seemed like the smartest of English Country House Hotels, the kind she'd only seen on television, except that there were Jacarandas and Bourganvillias in the gardens instead of Hollyhocks and Delphiniums. Roses were apparently common to both she noted. The lawns seemed to be manicured rather than just mowed.

Jo led them indoors through the house and onto a veranda. They realized they were looking out across the wide, wide river.

'And who lives here,' said Annie in a tone that expressed the views of all three visitors.

'As I said, a cousin, works for the UN and is away. There is no one here but us.'

'Someone keeps all this going,' said James.

'I know but they are all away this week, except the man who waters the garden. I don't do servants,' said a slightly aggressive Jo. 'Can I get you all something to drink?'

The luxury was intimidating and rather dampened conversation while the visitors looked around them. Jemal seemed to feel the least out of place.

'I went to India once, to see some uncles. It's a bit like that there: the contrasts,' he said.

'Some have better bits of God's garden than others,' was James comment and then, realising the possibilities he turned to Jo. 'What's your kitchen like. I've been scrounging, practically begging and all he's had is millimeal porridge since we left Becana. We are both starving.'

'All yours, master-chef,' said Jo grinning and glad of the break in tension. 'It's all yours. Do your worst.'

'Listen,' said Annie. 'Please can we get down to business? There is so much to say. Your stomachs can wait. I've, maybe we've all, got a funeral to go to tomorrow.'

'OK. Two minutes,' said James. He reappeared almost within the stated time with a tray, glasses, a jug with water, ice and sliced lemon in it and also fruit, bread and cheese. 'We can't think empty,' he said. 'And anyway, sorry, but I couldn't resist a real kitchen.'

Even Annie realized they needed food. They ate. News was exchanged.

'And did you hear what has happened out at Becana?'

'I went to see our baby we found,' said James. 'They say she's doing well.'

'There is more stuff about P&P from the UK,' said Jemal.

And finally

'A funeral. Whose?' They all looked at Annie. She told her end of the tale of the death of Lala Kai.

'And we really thought we'd won that night,' said Jo.

'I know,' said Annie. 'But we didn't necessarily have to lose like we did. I'm still angry, but I have promised not to make a fuss in return for being able to take the lass to her home village to be buried.'

'The Tribal Council meeting is there tomorrow too,' said Jo. 'I have to talk about my scheme.'

'Hmm,' said Annie. 'He who sups with the devil should use a long spoon.'

'That's why I need to talk to everyone.'

'I know my job in this team has largely been to make lists,' said Jemal, now well fed and smiling. 'So let's get it all written down, what exactly we know. Then it'll be clear what to do next.'

The piece of paper they constructed was always thought of in Annie's mind ever after as 'Plan Mosquito.'

Jemal, recorded the input from each one of them as they said it. It was true once it was all written down, the bigger picture became clear to all of them.

Plan Mosquito

1. From Jemal:

The Group who sent me here, have set themselves up to keep a watch on the environment and try to keep a check on what is happening on this planet. P&P who are a construction and mining conglomerate suddenly started employing entomologists and fitting out biology labs. A stolen laptop told my bosses a lot. I was sent here to check it out on the ground. We know what we found. An attempt to clear the land of people in order to dig it up unhindered. We're not sure why P&P suddenly took to genocide. It's not like them, they are a respectable multinational. Their research though, is all being done in Devon in the UK, but parcels of insects have been sent to other places, like Thailand for example.

2. From Annie

Coltan, the stuff James was digging up is used in mobiles as we know, but Max, my nephew says there is lots more stuff they are looking for and hoping to find. At the moment it's called "rare earth elements." He suggests the valuable thing to P&P is not so much what they are finding or looking for now, but hanging onto the right to look for stuff in the future as even they don't know what might be useful one day. It depends on what is invented.

He also says, from another contact of mine, that the man running things in the UK, the one who gave me my job, isn't to be trusted. He doesn't mind working outside the law.

3. From Jo

I've been offered this chance by P&P to construct an ecotourism scheme involving wildlife and the way of life of local people. There's a sentence in the proposal about developing the area to its full potential and for the benefit of the inhabitants. That lets the mining in.

4. From James

You mustn't be against progress. I was digging the stuff up and making a good living. There was the beginning of a new way of life there. We were getting organized. Without mines we wouldn't have coal and gold and silver. That means money and trade and electricity and cities. Village life is hard. This way of life stuff is just a method of keeping the people under. The old regime, down the road, made a speciality of it. Progress is good.

The resulting piece of paper clarified everyone's minds. For the first time the scope of the conspiracy was clear, but it didn't make finding answers any clearer.

Jemal's contribution from his London employers showed how global some of the arrangements were and also gave some clue to the fact that somehow the UK end of things had got out of control.

'We, here, are just one cog in their wheel. They are worldwide. Look how quickly they could move Monty. In just a few days he was gone. We can't do anything,' said Jo.

'Yes but remember the words of my generation. 'Small is beautiful and the Personal is Political,'' replied Annie

'I never did understand what that last one meant,' said Jo. 'My mother used to quote it.'

'Brief digression for education everyone,' said Annie. 'What your mother meant by it, is that every little aspect of your life is influenced by the system you live under. If you don't like your life, then it is the system you have to change. That's the way your life will improve. Feminists invented it. They wanted to say it wasn't just "natural" for women to stay at home, be domestic slaves and have no power.'

Jo suddenly noticed the mutinous expressions on James and Jemal's faces.

She laughed.

'Don't go there,' she said. 'You still have much to learn about the other half of the human race. Substitute the word "blacks" for "women" and you'll see what she means.'

Annie ignoring this exchange, went on.

'It works here too. Think about it. Breaking up the mossie labs in those lorry container places dealt with the immediate problem, but real baddies can soon think of something else. How much better if, at this Tribal Council do, control of what happens is seen to stay with that Council.'

'But P&P can just buy people. It's what they're planning to do with me, again,' said Jo.

'She's right,' said James. 'They can, but it's much less easy to do if everyone realises they have a say and can argue. In my country, over the border, we used to decide local things at Council. It doesn't work any more because people are being beaten or bought. But it did work, for a long time.'

'Trendy word is "transparency" I believe,' said Jemal. 'P&P are a respectable company. They don't want to be associated with breeding lethal mosquitoes or killing rare wild life.'

They looked around at each other. A consensus seemed to have been reached. James voiced it.

'So we are all going to turn up tomorrow, in the village, for Lala Kai's funeral and the Tribal Council. We will be seen to be there and we will stand up and speak. I think Jemal and I will be safe, this time, because we will stay in the open, in public. We won't be caught unawares. If we travel with Jo's truck, everyone can see we are sort of official.'

'I will come with the ambulance and Jackson. We'll bring the body, young Kala, our Koisan lass to be buried and meet you at the Tribal Council. It'll all be at Becana won't it?'

'No,' said Jo. 'It won't. Too much authority there. Becana is old army settlement from before independence and it's got a jail. Too much history. It'll be at Shadicongo. You remember, the second stop on NID day. They feel in control of their lives a bit more out there and it's also where the girl's aunt runs a Cuca shop.'

'I have to stop first at Katilo,' said Annie. 'The nuns say she has to be blessed. But we ought to be out to you by late morning, especially if I say her family are waiting.'

'And,' she added, 'I have to be back at the hospital here in Bundu tonight. I have been given a room there. I meet with Jackson to get the body released at 8 o'clock tomorrow morning. If we are into conspiracy, I think I should stay there, where I'm supposed to be, though,' she said, looking round the luxurious room and over the veranda at the view of the river, 'I think I'll be missing out.'

'The rest of us will all stay here,' said Jo.

'With a bath and hot water and towels?' said Jemal.

'And the kitchen,' said James. 'It'll be "A night to remember," you'll see.'

'I seem to remember, that was the name of the first film about sinking the Titanic,' said Annie.

'Sorry,' said Jo. 'But I think you are right. You do have to go back into town. I'll take you. What's it like, the nurses home?'

'Not like this,' replied Annie, 'But I've stayed in worse.'

'Sister, I promise,' said James, 'to bring you the best picnic you've ever had, tomorrow, to make up for the meal you are going to miss tonight.'

The four, were a disparate bunch, but they had developed the camaraderie of musketeers that comes with a common cause.

Nevertheless, thought Annie, each of us has their own agenda.

James and Jemal, the young men were simply looking forward to the adventure. For both of them it was a foreign land where they were doing their own thing. They may have had an ideological base for their actions, but it was adventure they were chasing.

For Jo it was more complicated. This was her country, her home and she had made her decision to commit to the place. History meant the future was going to be "interesting" as the Chinese might say, but it was her history too and she was going to be part of it.

And me? This isn't my place, but it has been good to me. Now I'm leaving it, but for what? I had respect here. I decide to do things and they get done. My world is bigger now. Am I ever going to be able to settle back home in England?

It was also clear to her that there was stuff to be sorted out back home. The end of the story was back there. Once that was dealt with, she wasn't sure she wanted to go back to being what she had been. The role of the piece of grit in the smooth functioning wheel of her Local Health Trust was an exhausting one

'Ah well,' she thought and smiling recalled Inika's catch phrase. 'Manyana is the answer I suppose. Or "Sufficient unto the day is the evil thereof" will also do nicely.'

They said their goodnights and Jo loaded Annie into her truck. 'I'll have supper waiting for you Jo, when you get back,' was James's final remark.

The two women were silent in the truck. Finally Jo turned to Annie.

'Why did you never get married?' she said.

'And where in the depths of your subconscious did that come from?' said Annie.

'I just wondered.'

'The answer's not that easy either. Why do you really want to know?'

'You know why. What am I doing wrong? Deep down all I want is a house and a man and babies. Why did you avoid going down that road?'

'Well I looked after my father for a long time after my mother went. That meant I learnt about looking after men, always putting their welfare first and so on and I didn't really like doing it, even though he was my father and I suppose loved him and of course they had taken me and my sister in as a babies.'

'But children, and sex.'

'There was enough of the latter and you must remember on the child front, that there is a sensuality in holding and feeding babies and I do it every day. I sometimes think that the daily contact meant the need for my own didn't become acute enough to make me do anything about it. And they are a terrible responsibility I'm not sure I want. Does that help?'

'I'm not sure. I need to think.'

'I can quote you plenty of sayings to make you wary of taking the plunge.'

'Go on then,' said Jo.

'How about, "It starts when you sink into his arms and it ends with your arms in his sink." I can go on and on. I was a different sort of Sister, back then, still am really.'

'But surely,' replied Jo, 'there is some man, out there, who'll share, who believes in equality, who'll want what I want?'

'I honestly don't know, but I do think it's obvious that you need to wait till you really know someone and can trust them. Men are just human beings, good, bad, selfish, cheerful sad. If you don't wait, a couple of years down the line it's all heartache. On the subject of equality I've another quote for you.'

'Go on then.'

'Just remember Ginger Rogers did everything Fred Astaire did, backwards and in high heels,' said Annie.

It had the effect Annie hoped. Jo relaxed and giggled and then roared with laughter.

'Who said that?'

'It came from some American cartoon. It used to be quoted a lot. Not one your mother told you then?'

'No but if she'd known it she would have done.'

'Look all I can say is this. Where "lurv" is concerned don't disengage your brain before pressing the start button,' said Annie. 'And can I add that your absent love life isn't our most acute concern at the moment. I'm not being mean, but tomorrow we have big events to deal with.'

Jo looked at her.

'Don't be so grumpy. You have helped and you know you have,' she said.

By this time they had reached the main road outside the hospital and Jo parked her truck.

'Do you want me to come in with you?'

'Frankly my dear you show up too much. You've no camouflage. For once in my life I am the anonymous one.'

'OK,' said Jo. 'Pax. No mutual insults guaranteed. We'll see you tomorrow. And.. er.. thanks.'

Annie took her bag and walked in through the main hospital gate. She found her way to the Nurses Home. She hadn't meant to be so sharp with Jo, but no one, she reflected, seemed to realise how stretched she herself was. There wasn't a great deal of her left emotionally to act as agony aunt to anyone. She was tired, probably hungry and definitely alone and a long way from the familiarity of home. At this moment the woman who never found it too hot in Africa, would have greeted a thick white clammy damp mist rolling off Dartmoor with tears of joy.

The night was uneventful and brought sleep. The morning was a new day and Annie woke full of her accustomed bounce. A quick look into the communal shower room made her realize she could wait to wash. The canteen however produced good strong tea with sugar and also bread and fruit. At seven forty-five am she was in her Katilo uniform, outside the Nurses' Home waiting for Jackson.

CHAPTER ELEVEN
Confrontations

Somehow she had thought reclaiming a body would be difficult but it was easy. They walked up to the counter in the mortuary foyer. She produced the paper work and a tall man in an apron took it and disappeared through a door. Shortly afterwards a trolley was pushed back through the door. On it was a body roughly wrapped in a white sheet.

Annie had been able to get a glimpse through the door as it opened and had seen wooden racks, like bunk beds, but in fours. There were bodies stacked on them, definitely unwrapped.

She looked at Jackson who was holding the stretcher from the ambulance.

'You must check it's her Sister, whatever the labels say. They do make mistakes here,' he said looking fiercely at the trolley pusher who was not the man who had disappeared with the paperwork but a boy, Annie guessed, of about 14. 'He and his grandfather run this place. His father died in the war and they got this job afterwards.'

A second trolley was produced. The Katilo stretcher was placed on it and Jackson laid out the red blanket they had brought with them. Annie unwrapped a little of the head of the body in front of her. She could see dark plaited hair and blue glass beads. She didn't need to look any further.

'It's her,' she said.

Together Jackson and the young boy lifted the very small corpse onto the red blanket and stood back. Annie realized it was her duty to finish the job, so she laid the shroud they had brought with them over the sheeted body and folded the red blanket as tightly as she could around the girl.

'You'll need this,' said Jackson, holding out a piece of what in her other life Annie would have called "farmers twine." 'We need to tie it round the feet and neck. Even with the new road it's still a bit of a bumpy ride and we don't want her unwrapping herself.'

A little startled Annie did as she was bid and the trolley was wheeled out to the waiting ambulance. The stretcher was lifted off the trolley and into the vehicle where it was laid on the floor. Jackson then tied it to the supports inside the ambulance.

They were ready to depart.

The journey took about an hour along the very empty new road. It was so early in the morning that the elephants had yet to move away into the bush. She counted perhaps forty of them of all sizes standing under the few trees she could see, a very little distance, barely a netball court away, from the edge of the broad new road. The very big ones were flapping their huge ears to create a breeze. In the distance behind the elephants she could see antelope of some sort. She still wasn't sure of what kind. A question to Jackson produced a wildlife lecture that lasted them until they turned into the Katilo Hospital compound and spared both driver and passenger from more complicated conversation.

As they drew up outside the main door Sister Anastasia came out. Annie got down to greet her.

The nun said, 'She is for us now. You go, get breakfast. Come back in an hour and a half and she'll be ready for you.'

She'd no sooner reached her room than there was a knock on the door. Opening it she found someone she didn't know bearing a breakfast tray. The stranger informed her that Anya, the Dutch nurse, had sent a message saying she had left the towels out for her and then left.

It was therefore a clean and well fed Annie who reappeared by the ambulance exactly an hour and a half later. She found a transformation. There was no coffin, but the inefficiently wrapped body was now dressed in its shroud and a settled within a nest of blanket in a long canvas hold-all with handles at the side. Kala's face was visible, her hair neat and the blue beads shone in the sunshine. Her hands were crossed over her chest and the arrangement of the shroud and draperies intentionally concealed her advanced state of pregnancy.

Annie's astonishment showed on her face.

'She was never baptized,' said Sister Anastasia. 'But she was one of God's children. She just hadn't yet had the chance to find him. She is entitled to our love.'

The theology was lost on Annie but the sentiment she understood. A very young woman who had been going to be a mother had died. There had to be respect shown to her on her journey out of this world.

Sister Anastasia smiling at Annie as she climbed into the cab of the ambulance said, 'Be careful out there,' and inconsequentially added. 'We saw the TV in the evenings on my course.'

They were half a mile down the road before Annie picked up the reference and then continued to wonder for some further distance what Sister Anastasia, a nun who as far as Annie knew had never been further than Bundu had made of the local TV diet of violent American cop shows. One at least had clearly got through to her.

'What do you mean, it's wasn't that bad out there last time I was here,' said Annie in response to a mumbled remark from Jackson..

'It is wild out there,' said Jackson with emphasis.

'What do you mean?' said Annie. 'Lions and things?'

'No,' he replied. 'The people, they are wild. We are going beyond Becana. They do their own thing out there.'

They continued in silence while Annie considered this statement and looked out of the window at the flat, now familiar landscape.

There was an added poignancy to the journey for her. She knew that this was probably her last trip into the bush. This journey mirrored the one on that vaccination day to Tundi and the second village, Shadicongo, where the people had been cross because the Becana team had arrived late.

This village was apparently their destination today. As far as Jackson was concerned it was beyond the end of the universe. Yet the romantic words, 'in the bush' had in the last months fulfilled all her expectations, even though these had been largely derived from old 1950s movies seen on afternoon television in England.

In truth the sights, the big sky, the elephants, the noises, the drumming, the singing, the villages with their round houses and the children rushing to greet any vehicle that came by, had been all she had wished for. These scenes were her great adventure. Regardless of what the day was to bring, Annie intended to take it all in and lock it in her brain, her memory and her heart. This, her big adventure she felt was drawing to a close and it seemed unlikely to her she'd ever have another.

She pulled her thoughts back.

'A touch too early maybe even metaphorically, to pack my bags. We've not sorted this yet. There is still more to come and more to do. And we have a funeral to attend,' she said to herself.

They had begun to notice people standing by the road side watching for them. The watchers didn't wave but raised their hands in a solemn sort of greeting.

'Ah we're expected,' said Jackson. 'Your friend has got the news out then.'

Annie was startled. She had been at pains to keep all talk of her hospital visiting activities in Bundu to herself.

Jackson just smiled back.

'It's not called bush telegraph for nothing Sister,' he said, as he swung the vehicle off the tarmac onto a track of sand and grass which threaded between trees. The trees weren't big, but they closed off the sky and they were suddenly in shade. The vehicle had to slow to a crawl, not only because of the terrain but also because of the number of people on the track walking ahead of them, who, as they approached, had to retreat into the trees to let them by. The people then reemerged from the track side undergrowth and continued their journey, but with a greater urgency now as they followed the ambulance.

'Nobody wants to miss anything,' said Jackson.

The vehicle suddenly emerged from its shadowy tunnel into a broad circular clearing. In the middle was a very, very large baobab tree. Beyond the tree Annie could see two vehicles parked. One was Jo's green and yellow truck. The other was a shiny white Toyota Landcruiser with the P&P logo on the side.

As their car approached the tree several older people stood waiting to greet them. There was a tall man, about forty, obviously in charge, several very old men and two middle aged women, one very small and one very tall, both in full ceremonial dress with headdresses well arranged.

Annie looked at Jackson questioningly.

'That man's the local chief, just come back from college in Jo'burg, with a fancy education, they say. The old men are the local elders and the women must be our girl's relations,' he responded.

They stopped the car and Annie got out and walked towards the group. She spoke directly in English to the women, holding out her hand as a greeting, hoping someone would intervene and translate.

The man Jackson had called the chief intervened.

'They don't understand you know. We don't all speak the Imperialist's language.'

Annie realized that they were going to dislike each other rather thoroughly. Not a good start she thought. She introduced herself to him and turned back to the women.

'They don't understand you know,' he repeated with his very Oxford accent.

Annie looked at the two women again and then smiled.

'But she does,' she said.

Standing silently behind the two women was Miriam. Annie spoke again and Miriam translated as she had done at the hospital.

Once communications were established the funeral arrangements took on a life of their own. Everyone seemed to know what to do. Annie found herself following the chief and being led along by the two women, with Miriam beside her. In front of them all, were the men carrying the body on the stretcher from the ambulance.

'He talks a lot,' said Miriam looking at the not very ritually clothed chief, in his dark business suit, but in deference to tradition holding a long hunting spear. 'But he's only just come back from abroad. He is the chief though. What he says goes. He will be good for us as a people, so long as we watch him. We need more people like him with education.'

What Annie didn't know was that this was, in many ways a repeat performance for all concerned except herself. At that funeral her predecessor Lisa had been the nurse present. The difference today was that this funeral was on Khoisan territory and carried out by Khoe rules. There was no choir and no Christianity. A grave had been dug a fair way outside the settlement. It pointed west. Those accompanying the body stood, with the sun behind them as the young woman's body was lowered.

The grave was filled in by the men with their spades. More men then came up with large containers of water and poured them onto the grave mound, and then, again, a high fence of thorn bushes was built around the site.

As they walked back towards the village settlement and the shade of the big baobab tree the chief took on the role of educating Annie and walked beside her lecturing her on local custom.

'We do thank you for bringing her home, you know. Did you understand how important it was she should come back?'

'I didn't,' said Annie, 'but this is her home and so it was where I felt she should be. That hospital mortuary is a terrible place.'

'Well our reasoning is that if the dead aren't comfortable they will return to bother the living. Especially in this case the unborn boy will come back to trouble us. We pour water so that the burial should be "cool." In the two years I spent at Cambridge I watched the English and their burial customs. Now you have watched us.

There are very few places where the people are free and follow their old ways. Very few know the old ways now. Sometimes we must make them up to suit our circumstances. Even here, in this part of Africa, we too, are now all mixed up, but as you have done so well in the UK, we also have to blend into a whole but somehow maintain our individual traditions. There are the equivalent of Scots and Welsh and Yorkshire men here. We retain our consciousness of origin in spite of the 'Unity in Diversity' our leaders in the South talk about. I wondered, by the way, about you, looking at you,' he said. 'Where do you fit in?'

The suddenness of the confrontation shocked Annie.

'Nobody has been so rude as to say anything like that since I arrived in this country,' she said. 'I was brought up to believe that making personal remarks is rude.'

'You misunderstand my dear. They may not have spoken, but they wondered. I too have problems with who I am. I, as they say, "have seen Paree," but here I am, back on the farm. Maybe we are both misfits. I really don't mean to be rude but I want you understand that nothing is really true. We interpret reality to suit our own truths.

An extremely annoyed Annie responded as best she could, with the feeling she hadn't a clue what he was talking about.

'If you must know, not that it is any of your business; I suppose I would say I am what some people call a coconut. They mean it as abuse in England, but I am proud of what I am. I am black on the outside but I was brought up white, so I think white. It means I can see and understand so much more than most people. And anyway - what about you, standing there in your ridiculous suit, speaking English with your so proper accent. Who do you think you are?'

'As I said maybe we are both misfits. I am not actually interested in your personal adjustment to the world. What I am saying is we remake reality all the time. What we are about to do in this meeting is going to be that.'

'I am not a misfit, I am me.'

'I'm not talking about you, but about my people here and reality and the future. What I need you to remember is that all truth is relative and we are going to reconstruct reality in a minute.'

Something clicked in Annie's head.

'Do you know what has been going on?' she said.

'As I said. What is going on? What is reality?'

Annie's feeling was that reality was a pompous idiot and she was looking at it. She looked at him again and saw an amused smile on his face. She rephrased her thought to pompous patronizing idiot.

He continued.

'Let's get this show on the road.'

Annie dropped back in the procession to walk with Miriam and the other women.

'I told you he was clever,' said Miriam. 'We need him.'

Everyone it was clear was expecting alcoholic beverages. The thought of being alone out here, in the bush, with a drunken mob rather obviously alarmed Jackson who was waiting by the ambulance, keys in his hand.

It didn't work out like that though. As they all processed back to the Baobab tree Annie's conversationalist, the Chief took centre stage. He stood under the tree and as everyone gathered around him, began to speak.

'We have buried our sister. Now we must talk of the future, then we will eat and drink. Let us get ready.'

A slightly rebellious crowd, both male and female, settled themselves on the ground, in the shadow of the tree and waited. Miriam and the relatives of the dead girl went into one of the houses. Tradition said they had to sit inside the dead girl's home and receive visitors.

Annie rejoined Jackson and looked around, trying very hard to record the scene in her mind. She had some feeling that what was going to happen should be remembered as history.

She could see the baobab with all the people sitting to one side of it. The shape of the crowd was clearly delineated by the shadow of the tree. She had grown used, over the months, to watching crowds shuffle around the central tree as the sun and therefore the shadow moved. Some village meetings were very long and to keep in the shade was a priority for audiences in temperatures of over 30C. Under the tree were several benches obviously ready for occupation by important people.

On the other side of the clearing, Annie could see people were erecting straw fences and roofs around the trucks in an attempt to keep them in the shade.

'Why don't they park them on the track where we came in, under the trees,' said Annie. 'It's cooler there.'

'They have to be seen,' said Jackson. 'They're afraid of having them stolen.'

'And who by exactly?' said Annie, reviewing the size of the crowd. 'It looks as if the whole population is here.'

'They, the trucks, have to be seen too. It shows what you can command, if you can drive up. And everyone knows that actually P&P have paid for all three of these cars. And anyway there are the bandits from over the border you know.'

'I didn't think they were real,' said Annie. 'I thought we just invented them when convenient.'

'No they did exist. They may come back one day, who knows?'

Annie turned again to look at the scene in front of her. She had the feeling it was a stage set and that the chief, at least, understood the principles of direction.

As if on cue, from out of one of the traditional round houses filed, in a line, two more men in suits, one of whom looked Chinese. Behind were Jo, Jemal and James and to Annie's astonishment Jason the tiny porter from Becana clinic, dressed in some sort of ceremonial cloak.

They were escorted to the benches and sat down.

'What's he doing there?' asked Annie, speaking to Jackson, who was sitting beside her in the shadow of the ambulance.

'Didn't you know? He is a senior elder among these people.'

This news put a slightly different complexion on things for Annie. If Jason was as Jackson said, a power in this land then the Chief probably did know what had been going on and probably knew about the malaria and the mosquitoes. Jason had after all been instrumental in destroying the container laboratory out here by the border. She became surer and surer there were layers of complexity here that she was missing. She needed to concentrate. She brought her mind back to current proceedings.

The Chief had stood up and was speaking in English. He was making the introductions.

'Mr Burgdorf you all know, he has grown up with us and now works for P&P. He has brought Mr Wang, from P&P head office to talk to us about their future plans.

Jo Schmidt is also known to us and has been working surveying and counting the animals in the bush. Mr James has been working by the river and I understand that Mr Jemal has been working with Jo Schmidt and knows something of what has been happening here. He will keep a record of what is said and decided.

Finally I call on Jafeta, our elder to talk to you.

Annie had always regarded Jason, as she knew him, as the least satisfactory member of the Becana team. He was idle and elusive and never spoke English, though he clearly understood it. Watching him now, was a revelation. He stood and spoke with authority in the click language of his people. Annie had no idea what he was saying but he was listened to. She understood his last remark from its intonation. She would have translated it as 'Any Questions?' and there were some.

Various members of the audience spoke, some in Africaans some in Khoe clicks. Jafeta responded carefully to them all. His audience seemed satisfied.

The chief then stood.

'Mr Wang would now like to talk to you. He comes from Hong Kong in China and works for P&P. He will talk in English and I will translate into Khoe.'

Mr Wang then stood. He too wore a business suit and tie that wouldn't have been out of place in any city office. His physiognomy may have been Chinese, but his English had the clear twang of the BBC world service.

'I am honoured to talk to this council today. I thank you all for coming to listen to me. What I wish to talk about is what P&P can do for this area in the future. As you know we have been here building the new tarmac road.'

Some of the crowd clapped this remark and it became clear to Annie that many people understood what was being said, even when only English was spoken.

'And we support your clinic and Miss Smith's project here.' He nodded to Jo.

'It has been a happy partnership I think. We would now like to move on and build on these foundations. In the future we would like to bring more money to the area and so enable your leaders to build new facilities for you, like schools for the children.

We understand however that your people have perhaps the oldest way of life on the planet and P&P has no desire to disturb your ancient traditions or practices.

Your way of life is precious. It is the way you people have lived for many centuries. The desire not to change this has been part of our plan. The world does change though. It has been discovered that you also have some very valuable minerals on your land. It isn't gold or diamonds, like they have further south, but something in the mud of the river that the world pays well for, at the moment.

What P&P would like to do is pay your people to allow us to dig up this mud. We would bring in our own people in to do the work and they would live at the P&P road camp and wouldn't disturb your way of life out here. The money we would pay would build new schools and clinics, pay teachers and nurses and your way of life would not be disturbed.'

The chief then stood and spoke in Khoe.

'Well that's more or less what he said,' said a voice and Annie looking behind her realised Miriam had appeared on her other side. 'I had to hear what was going on,' she said.

As the chief finished James stood up, without waiting for an introduction.

'Some of you know me, he said in English, my name is James and I am a foreigner from Zimbabwe so Good morning.' He repeated himself in another language Annie didn't recognise.

'I can do Bantu and Xhosa as well if you like, but I'm not good on Khoe or Africaans, so if everyone is happy, I will talk in the official language of both our countries English.'

There was a murmur of assent from the crowd.

'Some of you here, were with me when we worked the river. We made money didn't we? We had it to spare for clothes, for things.' He looked at the crowd. 'You, Jobe, he said pointing at a man, 'You bought your wife a sewing machine, didn't you?'

'Oh yes,' was the response, 'and now she wants money for another for her sister. They are making stuff for everyone.'

'That's what I mean. It gave us money to do things with. If you agree to what Mr Wang says there will be no money for you. It will all go to the top and you will get what they choose to give you. A school and a teacher will do for your children, but what about you? I have seen it in my country. The Chinese come in, build a factory, run it, live beside it, bring in their own food and don't even talk to us. The foreigners in my country even have land there, but they stay away from us, the people. They stay separate. We get nothing, no jobs, nothing.

It will be the same here unless you make something different happen. Make them give you jobs and teach you how to do them. Don't let them bring a village of foreigners in and hide them away in secret camps. Get the work yourselves and get paid for the work yourselves.'

There was a murmur of agreement from the crowd, who seemed to understand most of what was said. One or two people asked questions of Jafeta.

The Chief then stood and spoke in Khoe. Amidst it all Annie only recognised the word 'apartheid'. She looked questioningly at Miriam.

'He is clever,' she said. 'I did say. He has translated what James said, but he also said to remember that another word for separate is apartheid.'

The Chief then turned to Karl.

'Perhaps you could tell us a little more about the scheme you plan with Miss Schmidt.'

Karl, experienced at meetings, seeing the way the wind was blowing, determined not to be outfoxed said,' I think Miss Smith should present the plan herself.' and gestured to Jo to stand and speak.

Jo rather suddenly found herself centre stage.

'What language would you like?' She said. 'I can't do Khoe very well.'

'Your mother tongue will be fine my dear. Africaans is well known to us all,' said the chief.

Jo blushed and Annie found herself muttering 'Bastard' under her breath.

Jo however was not to be put out of countenance that easily. She launched out in both English and Africaans as Annie had seen her do many times. It was clear, very quickly that she was a favourite of the crowd.

'You know me too. Some of you think I prefer the elephants to people.'

It was obviously a familiar joke and raised a laugh.

'You know too, that I believe that your way of life is special. The Bushman way of life is the way people lived when the world began. We need to keep it safe, but I understand what James was saying. Money in the hand buys things. I can think of one way to do both. That is to get visitors to come here and see this place. The rest of the peoples of the world know they have lost something, with the coming of the cities. Tourists will come here and pay to stay in guest houses in villages and pay to be taken out to see the animals. This is a plan that works in other places.

But this new mud means new things. I've an idea about that too. Sister Larriot, over there,'

Jo pointed and Annie watched the heads turn in her direction.

'Has a sister in Australia and she told me what happens there, with the gold and the tourists. They have big industrial mines there now, for the gold, like in the South, here, but in the beginning they got it out of the river just like you do the new mud. They dug the gravel from the river, panning it and swirling it in the water and collecting it in tins. But now thousands of people every year go to the places where it all began in Australia and pay real money to do it themselves in the river. We could make that part of our program here.

Nobody has said today what this mud is used for. I'll tell you. They use it in mobile phones, which as we know, don't work out here yet. Everybody in the world will soon have one.

We could also ask,' she went on, looking straight at Karl, ' that as well as a school, P&P get them to give us a mobile phone mast. P&P are a big company and Telecom would listen to them.'

The Chief seemed to feel she'd said enough and stood up to intervene. He turned to Karl and Mr Wang.

'May I summarize the feeling of the meeting,' he said speaking in English. 'As you know, in these times, the National Government is unlikely to go against the feeling of an assembled Tribal Council of Elders, especially when the proceeding are reported on the net and available from the International Council of Indigenous Peoples website and other such organisations as our careful recorder,' he nodded at Jemal, 'will make sure they are.'

A look of understanding appeared on both Mr Wang and Karl's face. Both had been unclear as to what a turbaned Sikh was doing in the middle of this assembly. They now realized that though silent, he was in fact their nemesis.

The Chief continued.

'We are most grateful to P&P for telling us of the new opportunities this mineral from the river brings to us. We see this as a local opportunity for development. We are grateful for the suggestion that our way of life can be left undisturbed while mining takes place. We have however learnt that that time cannot stand still. In the last two years we have watched the road creep through our bush. Very few were paid to help build it but now we all use it. It has changed the way things happen. We would like the plan for mining to be different.'

He nodded to Japheta and the old man began to translate into Kxoe as he spoke.

'We have a list of things we ask in return for giving P&P the right to dig the new mud from our land. We accept their kind offer to support a tourism and eco-project locally but also, if industrial type mines are built, we want an assurance that all miners will be local people. To begin with foreigners may come in, but to teach local people what to do. Wages will be paid to the people themselves, who do the work.

Secondly we would like a new school and teacher, out here in the bush.

Thirdly', he looked at Jo and nodded, 'we ask for a commitment to extend the mobile phone network through here, right up to the border.'

Annie recognised her moment and raised her hand. To Miriam she said.

'Come along, we're on stage I think.'

She stood up.

'Can I say something please. Miriam will do the Khoe for me,' she said looking rather firmly at the Chief.

Slightly startled he said, 'The chair recognises Sister Larriot.'

Annie, a little amused in her turn that his surprise had caused him to revert to a more formal meeting procedure, walked over to stand under the tree and face her audience.

She began.

'As well as everything else asked for today I would ask for one more thing. I came here today to bring a young woman and her unborn baby home to be buried. I have seen another dead mother very recently and her baby is still in Bundu hospital. These mothers died of malaria because there is a new mosquito out here, that can get through the nets we have and bite us. I ask that P&P promise now, to give everyone the new nets with tiny holes.'

She paused for Miriam's translation to catch up.

'Some of you will have seen them. I also ask that for one year they spray the houses and the clinic and the school to get rid of these new tiny mosquitoes.'

As Miriam continued her translation Annie turned to Karl and the Chief. Behind her a rumble of agreement was heard.

'I think that makes a fourth request' said the chief. 'Would you care to respond on behalf of P&P.'

Mr Wang gave a brief nod to Karl who stood up in his turn.

'I think we can manage that,' he said.

'Is that a clear promise of committed funding?' said Annie.

He looked at her exasperatedly.

'I did just say so.'

'So, for what I asked, P&P will buy and supply enough nets for everyone, all families. They will be delivered to the clinics,' she persisted.

'Yes, yes.' Karl was now annoyed. The day had not gone according to plan and now he was being bugged by an irritating middle aged nurse. He was very hot and his face was very red.

The Chief intervened.

'Thank you for those assurances,' he said with a bow and then turned to Annie. 'And thank you Sister Larriot for your contribution. We are most grateful.'

He signalled to her to return to her place by the ambulance. As she and Miriam passed him he bent his head and whispered in her ear.

'Geese and golden eggs. Gently, gently, my dear.'

Annie did understand but still was deeply furious. Did he have to be so patronising?

The Chief turned to the scribe.

'Mr Jemal you have written a record of all that was agreed today? Do you need any subsidiary information? You will let all interested parties have a copy of your record?'

Jemal, still silent, nodded.

The Chief turned again to the men from P&P, who looked, if possible, even hotter in their business suits, for as the crowd had moved around the tree to stay in shadow, somehow the benches for the visitors had stayed put and they were now in full sun.

'We must thank our generous supporters and friends from P&P and look forward to a fruitful partnership.'

With a gleam in his eye the Chief added, 'We would invite them to stay and spend some time with us. It is perhaps now time to relax.'

Karl's look of alarm was real.

'We thank you for your kind invitation,' he said. 'But Mr Wang has a flight tonight to Hong Kong, so we must move on.'

Japheta then processed forward and spoke in Kxoe to Karl, holding and shaking his ceremonial spear. Karl obviously understood and whispered to Mr Wang. Both men bent their heads in acknowledgement and followed Japheta as he led them to their cars, followed by other equally traditionally dressed Kxoe hunters.

'I think Jafeta enjoyed that,' said Miriam to Annie, who raised her eyebrows in an unspoken question.

'He was giving him a sort of Bushman bon voyage. But years ago, when Jafeta was in the Bushman Brigades, Karl was his officer. He used to have to salute him and incidentally clean his boots every day'.

'Ah,' said Annie. 'To quote another prophet of the age "The times they are a changing."' She looked at the departing suits. 'I think those two will be glad of the air conditioning in that Toyota.'

Meanwhile the Chief was addressing the crowd and the crowd was making preparations for what it saw as its delayed wake. Annie had another quick mental picture, somehow tangled in her mind with her nephew. He didn't actually say "Let the wild rumpus begin" but that was definitely the thought behind his statement.

The crowd also saw it in that light.

'Well what now?' said Annie.

'Back to Katilo,' said an obviously nervous Jackson, 'before they get too happy out here.'

'No,' said Jo, 'Back to Becana first. We have to tell Inika and Frank. They didn't come today as this isn't their place or their Council but they need to know what went on. Then to Katilo to drop you off and on to Bundu so Jemal can type his stuff up and email it and get it out there as soon as possible.'

'No,' said the Chief, who had joined them. 'First you all come with me. We need a little refreshment and a little debrief. I think.'

He led inside a nearby round house. The moment they entered they felt coolness created by the thick insulation of the straw roof. On a formica topped table, in a bucket of water, waiting, was a bottle of whisky, which Annie recognized as a single malt and in an adjacent bucket several bottles of cola. As he removed his jacket and tie he said, 'No ice for you I'm afraid. I'm sorry but we had to turn off the generator. We didn't want to look too sophisticated to our visitors, did we?'

As they all sat down and took a coolish bottle of drink, Annie looked around her and finally expressed her thoughts.

'That was all fake wasn't it? You all, except me, knew exactly how it was going to go, didn't you? It was all an act, a pantomime.'

The Chief responded.

'It was neither charade nor a pantomime, my dear, it was a performance. And I hope it achieved all our objectives.'

'But…' She wasn't sure what her ' buts' were, but was equally sure that some sort of remonstrance was required. 'Weren't you just using the people as cannon fodder? To rubberstamp what you wanted. Aren't you, we, just another elite, know all, self-selected group, making what we think are the best decisions, maybe for them, maybe for ourselves.'

'Don't underestimate "the people" my dear, I don't. Everyone in that audience understood the issues in terms of their own lives.'

'That was, if I may so sir, a beautifully managed meeting.' It was Jemal who interrupted Annie.

'You may indeed, all plaudits accepted. Did we forget anything?'

'I can't think of anything. They know we know about the labs and the mosquitoes,' replied Jemal. 'They know Jo knows about the abortive DNA plan and they also know you here, won't say anything if they keep their side of the bargain. We just have to make sure their promises and the minutes of this meeting are out there in the ether as quickly as possible.'

'So nobody is going to be held to account for all that wickedness?' said Annie.

'It's not appropriate, not helpful. The problem has been dealt with. Now we move on. We will keep watch though, monitor them,' said Jemal.

'Listen young lady,' said the Chief looking at Annie, 'I am older than you.'

'Not by much,' she thought, but remained silent.

'Can I quote to you someone whose name I can't at this minute remember. He said "The only thing worse than being exploited by a multinational is not being exploited by one."'

'He's right,' said Jo. 'We need them.'

'The phrase is "Added Value," my dear. They have to be prevented from just galloping in here and taking what they want and then leaving. Also, incidentally, prevented from murdering us, but development cannot be stopped. When they leave, we want to be doing it for ourselves, and to be doing more of it here, so as more of the money stays here. Today, we all cooperated and, I think, cooked their goose nicely.'

Annie slightly exasperated still, turned to the two members of the group who had yet to speak. 'James?'

'I'm with him. You can't stop it, you have to manage it.'

'And you Miriam?'

'You know what I think,' she said, not a little embarrassed by having all eyes focused on her.

The Chief leaned back, holding his whiskey glass. He was now in expansive mode.

'As I said, at Cambridge they lectured us on indigenous peoples and for the best part of a century or so anthropologists have been eulogizing about the indigenous bushman and his way of life. Suddenly indigenous doesn't mean what it used to, not that I thought it really ever did, but it was and still is, a useful stick for beating authority about the head with.

Most of those 19C anthropologists had never been here and were using their perceptions of this culture to reinterpret their own. My favorite of these non visitors was a man called Kropotkin. He used stories of this way of life to create his dreams for communist Russia that never worked out. He wrote something called *Mutual Aid* and would have been proud of our activities today. Look around you.' He smiled at Annie, 'If we include your Australian sister, we have had all five of the world continents represented here today doing the arranging of the affairs of this small part of the world.' He winked at her, 'Haven't we done well.'

'He's still a patronizing bastard', thought Annie. 'But he's a just and honest patronizing bastard.' What she said was.

'Well, I don't know. All I can say is the Women's Institute in Devon couldn't have done a better job of getting done what they wanted done.'

'I regard that as a serious compliment my dear,' he replied.

'But, whatever anyone says,' she went on, 'when I get home I am going to make someone accountable, somehow for what was done here. It was mostly done to mothers and babies,' she said as if that settled the matter. 'They are the ones who die of malaria.'

Proceedings were brought to a halt by Jackson, who had remained beside his charge, the ambulance. He stuck his head through the door.

'Sister, we have to get back. They are getting very happy out here and it's getting late.'

'He is right,' said the chief. 'But, I think a few elementary precautions are required. Our friends shouldn't have had time to arrange anything, but we will see you safely on your way. We will make sure you have good company to Becana and then the constabulary can take over.'

Thus it was that the Watcher who had indeed been contacted by Karl, reported back that instead of two lone vehicles setting off in separate directions he saw a convoy leave the settlement.

It consisted of, in front and behind an open flat bed truck, each with perhaps twenty very happy singing men and a drummer aboard. Sandwiched between the two were Jo's green and yellow Land rover and the Katilo ambulance. As the four vehicles drove along the track the two trucks sung and chanted by turn, each answering the other as the drummers competed in rhythm and word.

'What are they saying?' Annie asked Jackson.

'You don't want to know,' he replied. 'They are wedding songs.'

Understanding, Annie just sat back and with the windows of the ambulance open, absorbing and enjoying the sound of the song and the response as it passed over her head between the two trucks.

Any ideas the Watcher may have had about arranged traffic accidents, elephant collisions and bandit attacks were perforce abandoned in view of this vociferous escort. The four vehicles were allowed to drive unhindered up to the square between the police station and the clinic in the centre of Becana.

Annie got out of the ambulance and walked up the steps to the familiar clinic front door. Inika was waiting and as Annie held out her hands to her she heard a noise from behind. She turned and looked and saw all the men were standing up on the two open trucks. Inika put her hands on Annie's shoulders and turned her round to face the men.

Miriam appeared beside her.

'They want to say good bye,' she said.

The men sung and drummed and sung. Miriam laughed,

'They are singing about the little woman who is so fierce but brought their sister home and looks after their women and children as if they were her own.'

'What more could I ask for,' thought Annie and she would not have been human if the tears hadn't begun to run down her cheeks.

As she stood there, the scene before her became permanently etched onto her brain. Thereafter she could always hear and see the men standing on the flatbed trucks. She could feel the muted strength of the late afternoon sun on her skin. She could see the African sky. It was fixed for ever in her memory.

When, in the future, from time to time, she did recall it, the moment returned complete with the responses of all her five senses.

The men finished singing. Goodbye was said to Miriam as she climbed into the cab of the leading truck. It was the first of the goodbyes which were to wrench at Annie's heart over the next few days.

Both she and Miriam realized they were unlikely ever to meet again and yet Annie had been her midwife, had brought her baby into the world. That baby's delivery Annie knew would never just become amalgamated with all the others in her memory as deliveries, with the years, were inclined to do.

As she stood and waved farewell to the trucks, to Miriam and to the singers, Annie looked across the square and saw the blue light above the police station porch. She regarded it with the affection of familiarity. To her it said something unequivocal and uncompromising about right being right and wrong being wrong. Those fundamentals of life seem to have got very complicated lately.

CHAPTER TWELVE
An Ending

'So things went well then, out there in the bush?' said Inika. She kept her arm around Annie's shoulders and the two of them went into the clinic together.

'There is so much to say, and I'm supposed to be back in Katilo with the ambulance tonight,' said Annie

'That I can sort,' said Inika. She went out to talk to Jackson. When she returned she said, 'Done. He'll explain to Sister Hildegard that you are staying one night with us to say goodbye and that Jeff will bring you in, in the morning. Jackson has gone now.'

By this time Jo, Jemal and James had also got down from the other truck. Annie saw Frank the policeman appear from nowhere and speak quietly to Jo. She got back into her truck and drove it under the police station arch into the yard behind and then into the garage.

'Don't worry, said Inika.' We just don't want nosey eyes to know who is where, do we? Now, we have food. Come in, all of you. I see,' she said looking at James and Jemal, with a slight sharpness in her voice, 'our foreigners have recovered since we last saw them.'

It felt ages, Annie realized since she'd been here. This was the place where she'd spent those magic months, dealing, each day, with what came in the door. It was where she'd learnt all her new skills. She was just very grateful to have one more chance to see the place.

Maria appeared carrying what looked like supper. She started spreading it out, as they had done before, on the floor of the big room.

'And we have potatoes for you sister' she said 'and a cake for pudding.'

Annie looked around. The only participant in recent adventures not present was Jason, the porter, the man she now knew as Japheta the senior elder.

'Jason?' she said to Inika.

'He'll be back tomorrow, in time to sweep the porch and maybe do some work.'

'I suppose you knew he was who he was?'

'That's why he has the job.' Inika replied.

'Of course,' thought Annie, 'an official paid job, one of the few, so it's not menial employment, it's an honour. Just like the grandfather in the mortuary in Bundu.'

It was an evening of exchanges. News went both ways. It wasn't exactly a victory celebration, more about comrades in arms exchanging battle stories. Other people came in to join them. Their faces were only faintly familiar to Annie, but all seemed to know something of what was going on. By the end of the meal everyone present knew everyone else's story. The picture was clear. Mutual self satisfaction prevailed. A vote on Becana's Best results in order, would have produced the following list:

'You mean they've promised us a mast so we can have mobiles?'

' Everyone is going to get new nets.'

'There are going to be proper jobs.

The promise of a new school in the bush wasn't very relevant to anyone present and the creation of the eco-tourist scheme, only to Jo.

It wasn't unlike the Community Midwives Meeting back home, thought Annie. Once a month, there, everyone exchanged news. Everyone had their tales to tell about their most odd encounters, the latest most inaccessible home delivery and the location of a new cafe on the patch. It used to be called gossip and discouraged, now it is called 'sharing' or 'reflective practice' or some such jargon phrase and considered an essential part of professional life.

She looked around her for a few moments and considered.

'There is no substitute for people talking to each other, especially when sharing food,' she said to Jo, who like her was now sitting back and watching the proceedings.

'It's all going to work out here, you know,' said Jo. 'Like you say everyone has to talk to everyone else, then it'll be fine.'

'And you, will you work out here? Will you be fine?' Annie looked closely at the young woman, who had been her friend but also her mentor.

'Yes, you know, I think I will. I've got a place here. I'm going to be a useful bridge between the groups. And this eco-tourism thing is really important. It could be a template for lots of other schemes.' She smiled at Annie, 'I've learnt from you – throw yourself into things, work hard and don't look round.'

'Am I really like that?' asked Annie. 'I was going to say how much you've taught me. I'll never accept "no" or "can't be done" as answers ever again. I'll never forget the day we filled in the swimming pools. Somehow at home, I couldn't imagine making things happen in the same way. But I'll give it a try now.'

Inika had been watching them from across the room

'Don't worry,' she said to Annie. 'She's a good girl and this is her place. I'll look after her and one day we'll even find her a husband and invite you to the wedding.'

'I think,' said Jo, 'with me under Inika's wing, you needn't worry about me. I might have to though. It'll be like having an Aunt with a hundred eyes. She knows everyone.'

Annie also got some other answers she was seeking. She had been waiting to question one individual in particular since the vaccination days but every time she was just getting round to cornering him events would intervene. This evening she finally got her chance. He was sitting down so Annie went over to him and stood in front of him. This meant that for once she was looking him in the eye, instead of being towered over by a 6'2" beanpole made even taller by his turban.

'Exactly who and what are you,' she said to Jemal. 'I first meet you. It's the middle of the night and you are a traveller, living in a van in a country lane. Then you appear here in the middle of Africa as a clerical helper apparently employed by the enemy. Today at the meeting you seem to be some sort of international guru. Well?'

'I could say the same to you, you know.' The voice had all the resonances of home. Her original analysis held good. "Tottenham with a touch of Trowbridge" caught it exactly.

He went on, 'I meet you in a country lane and the next day Sal dies. Then here you are, paid by "the enemy" looking after the people who are dying of this new malaria and giving out ineffective nets. Even today, again, it wasn't entirely clear where you stood.'

Annie was astounded.

'Do you mean to say you doubt my, my honesty, my integrity? How dare you. Nobody has ever questioned my ethics before. My actions maybe,' she said recalling her various run-ins with Authority, 'but my motives never.'

'Actually, No I don't really,' he said, 'but I'm trying to show you how careful we have to be. I got beaten up you know, and got malaria.'

'The latter was your own fault. You should have taken your pills,' she responded, 'and anyway, who is we?'

'There's no easy answer to that either,' he said.

'You'd better think of one,' she said crossly. 'You can't just go round impugning someone's integrity like that and then go wishy-washy and nebulous on me.'

He smiled. 'The Bushmen got it right,' he said, looking up at her from his seat on the floor, 'You are fierce. Peace. OK. All I'm trying to say is that it doesn't do to splash information around until you know who is who.'

Annie was not to be diverted. 'Then who are you?'

'OK, ok, I'm a sort of researcher for an organization that keeps an eye on things.' He replied.

'And that tells me exactly what?' she said.

He sighed.

'Right. Let's try again. There are a lot of big corporations as well as governments out there. The market value of, say Apple or Microsoft is about the same size as the economy of Portugal. These companies are so big that half the time they don't know what they are doing. Or more likely what individuals are doing in their name.'

'So what, the NHS budget is bigger than that of many small countries. We all know that, but it doesn't have a cadre of spies to keep an eye on it.'

'Perhaps it should, but that's another story. Listen. There are organizations and individuals, some green, some humanitarian, some maybe from the corporations themselves who want to know what is going on. They support my lot. Our work is to get everything out there. We don't conclude or judge, we publish. Nothing we do is kept private; it all goes on the net. Good solid data, no opinions. It's there then for the people to see.'

'The people. The people. That's so easy to say. Who do you say they are then?'

'You know that. I've watched you work. You believe in everyone, every single person, however big, however small, whoever they are. The people are us, all of us. The whistle blowers who send my lot info are people. For every obscure document we publish, there is a person out there who sent it to us and another one who understands what it is about. That's two people. When the evidence is published then more people can read and understand and that changes the public debate and maybe events. ' Jemal paused. He had run out of steam. He looked up at her and said, 'And you could sit down you know. I'm getting a crick in my neck talking to you.'

'Now you know how it feels to be a small person,' said Annie, 'This is my way of making a small person bigger. But you're right.' She sat down beside him. 'You know who you remind me of? A TV hero of my youth; Wolfie Smith.'

He laughed. 'I do know. The Tooting Popular Front. My Dad loved it too. I hope I'm a bit more competent. 'Power to the people' is what we are about though.'

Trust was suddenly there. Each briefly, mentally stood back and looked at the other and each was amused by what they saw.'

'We'll be discussing cricket scores next,' said Annie'

Jemal looked puzzled.

'It's the cliché, she said. 'The Indian and the African in a foreign bar. We are so English and so not. This is definitely a foreign land even if there is no alcohol.'

'Londoners United?' he said.

'Well maybe,' she said. 'I was born there too. But don't distract me. I'm trying to understand. What we were arranging today was about here, very local. What you're talking about, well, that's all a bit big isn't it? That's sort of global.'

'Everything is global now,' he replied. 'And about control. Knowledge may well be power, but the opposite is also true. Ignorance is being controlled and being helpless.'

What about today! What's everyone most happy about? The chance to get mobiles out here in the bush. With the info and knowledge people here could have put a case to Telecom and got a mast ages ago. It's suited P&P or maybe the government not to let it happen. Stopping people talking, communicating. It keeps them down, powerless and ignorant. But in the long run people won't stand for it.'

'Like Kat's café,' said Annie.

Jemal looked puzzled.

'At the hospital at Katilo,' said Annie, 'It's a secret internet café for the staff. They've got wifi, in a broom cupboard. I email my nephew from there.'

'Do you mean to tell me that just down the road there is a connection which we can get at? I can get my stuff off? Why on earth didn't some one tell me.' His exasperation was very evident and gave Annie pause for thought.

She looked at him.

'I'm not sure I got how important computers are to all this.'

'The net is everything,' he said. 'It's the absolute new freedom, provided everyone has it. It's our job to make sure they do. Now this place 'Kat's.' Can we use it?'

'I don't see why not. They let me in there.'

'You see there is something else you need to know. Whistle blowers aren't popular. By definition, being a little person with a story to tell, means you are vulnerable. It also means Power thinks you are easy to silence. Lots happened today at that meeting. Those minutes have to get onto the Indigenous Peoples website. That's important and P&P know that will happen. But a lot wasn't said was it?'

'About the mosquitos and labs and such,' said Annie.

'And Jo and Inika and the Chief and everyone here don't really want P&P upset do they? They want the deal.'

'Yes.'

'But what was done has to get out. For goodness sake they were trying to go for genocide.'

'You don't have to convince me. When I get home I'm going to shake a few trees. The French have a word for it "Temoinage."' said Annie.

He looked at her.

'You do need to be a bit careful,' he said. 'These people don't muck about. Bearing witness is all very well, but one doesn't want to do it posthumously.'

'You exaggerate.'

All he said was, 'Vix and Sal and there have been others.'

Annie was a little taken aback.

'Anyway,' said Jemal, 'can you use a memory stick?'

'I don't think so.'

'Well you will be able to, by the morning. I'll teach you. Then I'll copy the stuff. You can send it from Katilo to your nephew. I'll encrypt it. It'll be safe.'

'Whoa, whoa. Explain.'

'Look, when James and I emerge in Bundu I'm sure I'll be arrested and deported. I have no visa now. I'll be searched and anything I've got on me confiscated. We need another route out for the stuff. I think that's you. Encryption means the stuff is unreadable without the key, so nobody can blame you. If asked you can just say you were doing a friend a favour and didn't see anything wrong.'

'And in the UK?'

'Once you're home, you'll be contacted. Then you can send it on.'

'You've got it all worked out, haven't you.'

'I hadn't until you told me about this Kat's place.'

'How do I know all this is ok? You might be getting me into God knows what. Trying to start World War Three or something.'

'You know, we both know, it's about trust. You looked at me and I at you. We both know the other is OK.'

'Yes, I suppose, but perhaps I think it shouldn't be like that. We should both be more careful.'

'Look when there's time I'll give you my talk on person to person communication, but not now,' he said and looking up. 'I think we've had all the time we are going to get.'

Annie looked up too and could see the others had been watching them both talking.

'We are both Londoners born,' she said to those watching. 'We come from the same place.'

'You talk so fast, no one else can understand,' said Inika.

Jemal stood up. 'I have to get all today's stuff written up,' he said. 'If it's ok I'll go over there in the corner and get it done.'

The rest of the gathering watched the tall lanky man as he took himself to the far corner of the room. He settled down on the floor and got a small notebook computer from inside his jacket and then from another pocket he produced the more conventional notebook he had used earlier in the day, at the meeting. As he settled down to his task of transcribing his words from the older to the newer type of record, everyone else turned away, and continued their conversations

'What happens next?' said Annie. 'What about you James?'

'Don't worry about him,' said Jemal looking up briefly from his computer screen. 'His grandmother had the intelligence to be born in Hackney. In London,' he added looking round at the other mystified faces. 'I talked to my lot when I was in that hospital. They say they can get him into England and give him a job.'

James, Annie thought, had been looking immensely pleased with himself all day. Now she understood why. He, at least, had got his heart's desire from this adventure.

Jo too seemed happy. She'd said so earlier. She had a plan for her future. Annie turned to Inika.

'Are you OK with how it's all gone? Do you think it's all sorted?' she said.

'We are going to be fine here now,' said Inika. 'The phones, the nets, jobs and wages. With the new road, things will grow. Becana will get bigger. Maybe they'll make us an A grade clinic and I'll get A grade wages.'

Annie surveyed the rest of the people present. There was Maria who had been with them when they found the baby 'Morning', Frank the policeman, Jeff, the clinic ambulance driver whose job she had fixed and who'd seen her through far more sticky situations than she'd ever told her sister about.

There were other people here too. If she looked hard at them she could recall when she'd known them. She could recognize the mothers of at least two malaria babies she'd treated, and the two very small children who she'd injected every day for ages because they'd been licked by a rabid dog. They miraculously seemed to bear her no ill will for the pain she'd inflicted on them. There were men present too. She could see the huge guy on whose chest she had developed her suturing skills after he had been in a bar fight. There also was the old man who fell in the fire, remarkably sober for him. Most satisfyingly from a professional point of view, was the presence of the young man she had transferred to Katilo, when unconscious, sitting beside him on the back of an open flatbed truck . She had never spoken to him, but had got him to a safe place and he had recovered. As she'd told her sister, it was largely because of him, Becana got its ambulance back.

The sense of mutual self satisfaction was still in the air when the clinic door opened and the senior school children came in with the usual tall African drum.

'We can't let those Bushmen be the only ones,' said Inika and the teenagers began drumming and singing. It was one of those songs with verses and a response. Annie couldn't really follow the words but both the rhythm and intention were clear. The audience added a line or so from time to time and the drummer, a lad who looked about sixteen seemed inexhaustible.

What amazed Annie was that somehow everyone here seemed to think she had caused all these good things to happen. She turned to Inika.

'It wasn't anything I did. Everyone else did things.'

Inika gruff and brief as usual replied, 'Maybe. But something was you. If you hadn't come, it wouldn't all have happened.'

Well I don't mind being a catalyst, thought Annie. She suddenly realized she was bone tired. The ever watchful Inika had noticed.

'Stand up and say something,' she said, 'then you can go and sleep. We'll put you in the other room. You'll be safe in the clinic. This party will go on for hours yet.'

So Annie did. Then she settled herself on the examination couch in the delivery room and fell fast asleep to the sound of the drumming and singing in the next room.

She was woken as it was beginning to get light by James bearing a cup of tea, followed by Jemal carrying his computer.

'We thought we'd better wake you kindly,' said James, 'before your IT lesson.'

Annie sat up and watched as Jemal showed her how he loaded files onto a memory stick and then showed her how to download them again.

'I can do attachments once I've got it on the computer, but I can't believe this thing is so tiny.' She said looking at the memory stick.

'That's its merit,' said Jemal. 'This is what we do.' He threaded the tiny plastic cylinder onto a leather thong and handed it to her. 'It's a necklace now, put it on. No one will see it.'

Annie put it over her head and tucked it under her somewhat crumpled, slept in, uniform. It really didn't show.

'Do what I've showed you and email it as an attachment to your nephew. Tell him to save it as it's data for someone's PhD. He'll understand that. Then you keep the stick safe and someone will be in touch. That is belt and braces I think,' he finished.

Her next visitor was Inika. 'They'll want you back early today,' she said, 'but we've some things for you to take. Come with me.'

Annie followed Inika over the sandy main street of Becana to the police station opposite. Frank, the policeman was waiting there in his so English, so familiar police station. Yet another colonial DIY kit thought Annie as she looked affectionately at the building with its blue light over the door, knowing it was for the last time.

Frank was standing behind the wooden counter. He had a bag in front of him. It was the size of a shopping bag and sewn from the usual bright patterned fabric.

'It's for you,' he said. 'We thought you should take it to Children's Services. It's the few things from Newtown, from where we found the baby.'

Annie opened the bag and looked inside. She found a hand mirror, two necklaces, a half carved marula nut and a small beaded purse with papers inside it.

'We found her papers in the end, they're there.' he said. 'It seems she used to make a living by doing these.' He picked up the round hard nut and showed it to Annie. She had seen the finished article in the tourist shops. The carved nut was eventually hung on a leather thong and sold as a necklace. They were carved with a traditional pattern of deer chasing each around in a circle. On this particular nut the deer never completed the circle. The carving was never finished. All three people present looked at it each recalling the empty abandoned village and the dead mother with the living child.

'Her daughter will want this one day,' said the policeman.

'Remember,' said Inika to Annie, 'this little citizen in particular wouldn't be here at all if it wasn't for you.'

They replaced the things in the bag and Annie carried it back to the clinic and packed it in her holdall.

By this time too, Jo was up and about, talking to James and Jemal. She came over to Annie.

'I shall have to take them straight to Bundu, she said, 'I'll see them both onto a plane. Jemal is hoping if he is deported they'll pay his fare. I ask you.'

'Knowing him, they probably will,' said Annie.

'But it means Goodbye here,' said Jo. 'I won't be able to stop at Katilo on the way.'

After Jo came Inika and then Frank and Jeff and then other faces she had been less close to, but who had been part of her time spent in this life, in this place.

Annie recalled the pain of these moments of goodbye years and years later. It was in another country and another time and she was talking to someone who'd worked in emergency aid for a many years. The woman had then inexplicably to Annie, given it all up to take an office job.

'I couldn't do it any longer' she'd said to Annie that day. 'I just couldn't bear to say goodbye one more time.' Annie had understood exactly what she meant. There did seem something wrong with a world that let one put such hard work into relationships, make such intense friendships and then cause them to be so abruptly terminated.

It was so early that the rest of Becana was quiet. It was barely light. There was no usual morning bustle and only the occasional finger of smoke arising from the odd, isolated breakfast cooking fire.

'After last night, no one will be up for hours,' said Inika, 'so we'll get you off safely.'

This concern for 'safety' seemed a little unnecessary to Annie but she found herself rapidly hustled into the ambulance and, with Jeff and Jo driving, the two vehicles set off.

She knew now that this really, really was her last time along the road. She thought back and remembered it when she first arrived. This stretch had still been an unmade road then, with no tarmac. She could recall the haze in the sky as you drove and saw the sun through the yellow film of dust that your vehicle had stirred up. Yet now the road stretched in front of them, black and smooth. Still, on either side the bush remained. She noted the familiar landmarks in her mind as they passed them. There was the place where the beer lorry had been stuck for three days. This was the bit where the elephant crossing the road had scared her so badly that night. That track, over there, went to a clearing with a few round huts built on the sand, but where she'd found a young woman working away on an old treadle Singer sewing machine. She'd had no electricity or water but an incredibly well organised household with a marvellous vegetable garden and children whom she marched to the road each day to get a lift to school in their home made uniforms. Her ambition had been to make enough money to get a solar panel and a cooker. Annie had bought some hand sewn straw panels from her, for her own garden in Becana and learnt from her how to make her own Papaya tree grow.

On the other side, she saw the track, where one night, having been roused by urgent banging on her house door, she and Inika had to persuade the policeman to drive his car out in the dark. To their amazement they had found, up a track, an abandoned VW camper van and an unconscious man whom they had transported first to the clinic and then on, to Katilo. It had turned out he was a Zambian nurse hoping to work there, but he'd not taken his anti malarials and having had his spleen removed after a motorbike accident had caught bad malaria. He, she remembered, had never recovered, but Sister Hildegard had arranged for his mother to come from Zambia and take him home.

All those lives she'd briefly touched. People living in ways she'd never have been able to imagine had she not left England and seen for herself. Whatever anyone's motivation for sending her here, she thought, it had been an amazing privilege and she would be eternally grateful for having had the experience.

An hour later, having waved goodbye to Jo's green and yellow truck on its way to Bundu, the ambulance turned off the road to the Katilo compound. It stopped outside the familiar main hospital door and parked behind another ambulance which Annie recognised, by its dusty condition as her transport of the day before. As she walked through the front door, carrying her bag, she looked back. In the windscreen of yesterday's ambulance, on the passenger side, about half way down was a small round hole, which anyone who had ever watched a TV cop show would know was a bullet hole. Jeff looked at it too.

'I told you I'd keep you safe,' he said. 'That Jackson doesn't understand the bush.'

Internecine rivalry between drivers wasn't Annie's concern. Jackson's wellbeing was. As she opened her mouth to protest the man himself emerged from the front door and took her bag from her. He saw her face,

'Let's call it bandits,' he said. 'Sister Hildegard wants to see you straight away.'

She looked back at Jeff. He raised his hand in a wave, got into his vehicle and drove off. She watched for a moment as her last link with Becana and the bush life disappeared.

'She is waiting,' said Jackson.

Annie felt she was, having slept in her clothes, a little crumpled for an interview with her boss. Jackson however would brook no delay.

'Now, she wants to see you now,' he repeated.

Sister Hildegard was waiting in her office and greeted Annie with a tense smile. She looked her up and down and said, 'Well we can give you a clean uniform anyway, but there isn't much time. We've booked you on a flight to Jo'burg tonight.'

'I thought I had a room in Bundu for a month,' said Annie.

'You are welcome to spend a month at the order's guest house in Jo'burg, but it has been decided you should leave the country tonight.'

'Not by me it hasn't,' said Annie, who momentarily forgot her manners as she sensed Authority wielding a heavy hand.

Steel was audible in Sister Hildegard's reply.

'No maybe not, but it has been decided at a level, way above both our heads, so we will comply.'

Annie knew an immovable object when she saw one. She was also a little shaken by the bullet hole in the ambulance windscreen. Had she travelled with Jackson the day before she would have been directly in its line of fire. 'Exit strategy' was the phrase that came to mind.

Everyone was concerned for her safety, perhaps they had a reason. Maybe strategic retreat was required. Anyway, if she couldn't stay here, she wanted to go home, proper home. She had no energy left for a new strange place. She looked equally firmly back at Sister Hildegard.

'Maybe it's for the best,' she said. 'But, in that case, I want to go back to the UK as soon as possible.'

'Not a problem,' was the reply. 'An international flight goes the following day. One night in the guesthouse in Jo'burg and you'll be on your way. I must say, I think you've made the right decision.'

They were conversing using the code of civilized social intercourse which never really says what it means or feels, but their own meanings were clear to them both. This understanding, in its way led to a less confrontational, more cooperative turn to the conversation.

'There is a little paper work to sort out, and I imagine you'd like a bath and change of uniform. We will lend you one for the journey as you'll need one to stay in our house in Jo'burg.'

'And my packing? 'said Annie.

'Oh, that's been done. We have your things here in the convent'

She rang the little brass bell on her desk and a lay sister unknown to Annie came in.

'Could you take Sister Larriot to my bathroom, sister, and show her where we've put out spare clothes for her?'

Annie was astonished. She had never ever before, in her time at Katilo been allowed, let alone invited, into the convent section of the hospital compound, where the nuns lived.

She followed behind her guide and found herself led through a door into a big bedroom with one high window. It looked just like a nun's cell from a movie, except bigger. Another door led off it into what she found to be a surprisingly lovely bathroom. It too, was big, with a bath and a chest on which a set of clothes was laid out. There was a window here as well, with a gauze curtain in front of it hanging right down to the floor. Annie looked around her again and noted with amusement the fact that the bathroom door had a key in it. So a Mother Superior was allowed privacy, if no one else was.

The sister who had accompanied her gestured at the towels and uniform and then backed away. 'I will return in a while to fetch you,' she said.

As she closed the main bedroom door behind her Annie heard the key turn in the lock. She understood. She was a prisoner until it was time to leave.

This was not good. She had a job to do. She looked around. Further observation of the room had her lifting up the gauze curtain. Behind it, she found, not a window but a half glass door. Of course, she thought, someone had to be able to get in to clean without going through the convent rooms. The Mighty always have an Achilles heel if they stop cleaning up after themselves. She tried the handle and it wouldn't open. It was locked. Un-phased she went to the bathroom door and removed the key she seen in its lock. She looked at it. MH25 was engraved on it. It was the commonest of the lock and key numbers at Becana clinic. At least half the rooms could be opened with key MH25. 'I'll bet...,' she thought, and tried it in the glass door. It turned.

She took the key back to the bathroom door, locked it, removed said key and put it in her pocket. She then put the plug in the bath and turned the taps on. While waiting for the bath to fill sufficiently for verisimilitude she planned her route to the Office and Kat's café.

The bathroom door led, she could see, to a path through the back of the garden to the wall and then into the hospital compound. She had from time to time noticed the gate and wondered where it went. She had, not ever, envisaged being on the other side of it.

Once the bath was full enough she turned the taps off and let herself out into the garden, locking the door behind her.

As swiftly as she could, without appearing to hurry she reached the Office, and to her relief her friend, the young woman, Inika's cousin was behind the counter.

'They are sending me to Jo'burg tonight,' she said. 'I just need to tell them at home.'

Her voice obviously conveyed a greater intensity than her words. She was quickly ushered behind the counter and into the broom cupboard. She was soon in front of the computer, looking at the email page.

'I have to go back to the desk,' said the girl. 'Call me when you've done.'

Annie found she had been well taught. Having unlooped the memory stick from round her neck, it took only moments to load and attach the contents. Her message to Max was brief.

'I'll be in the UK very shortly. Keep attachment safe. It's the data for a friend's thesis. I mean safe. Annie'

It took seconds more to press the send button and then close the program. In another four minutes she was back in the bathroom with the garden door relocked behind her.

The bath now looked really welcoming. The clean clothes laid out were however puzzling. It seemed, more or less a full novice nun kit. As she examined them, Annie mused. She says I need it to stay at the house in Jo'burg. Then enlightenment came. She's getting me out in disguise, she thought. Few know I'm here and few will know I've gone. Well it has its advantages I suppose. What's one uniform more or less?

She undressed and, removing the memory stick, hid it in her shoe. She was clear in her mind, in spite of emails, this little gadget needed to get back to the UK safely and intact.

Immersion was wonderful, after two days and a night in the same clothes. There were no fancy bubbles in this spartan bathroom but the soap and flannel and hot water were more than adequate.

Clean and dry she dressed in her new clothes. She held the memory stick in her hand and wondered where to hide it. She looked over at the chest where the clean clothes had been laid out for her. There was a last bit of that kit she had yet to put on. It was a cheap white metal crucifix about four inches long which was hung on a strip of black leather. They were worn by all the non nursing nuns. The nursing ones refused to wear them as they saw them as a yet another bit of weight to carry around all day and a genuine hazard in terms of cross infection. She remembered being shown one and being asked by Sister Anastasia to support the request for an alternative. As a result the nursing nuns had been given small crosses to wear under their uniforms. As she held the big cross in her hands Annie realised it was intended as part of the disguise and concealed the fact she was who she was, a nurse.

Well two can play at that game, she thought. She turned it over. It was, as she remembered, a hollow mould, to keep it lighter, but backed with fabric so as not to mark the uniform. She peeled back the top edge of the fabric and found that Jemal's memory stick slid very neatly into that hollow.

It was a slightly self conscious, fully clad 'Annie, the nun' who pulled the plug out of the bath, cleaned it and then unlocked the door from the bathroom to the bedroom. She looked at the key and on impulse put it in her pocket instead of back in the lock. It seemed a perfect memento of a place and time where locks and keys had been so much part of her life. MH25 was after all, the number of the original pharmacy lock at Becana which, quietly, late one night, she had swapped with another. One that she hoped was maybe unique and certainly was less common. After all, she thought, dressed like this, I have to be a little bit wicked, just for my own self respect.

It was clear that Sister Hildegard's intention was to get Annie out of Katilo as soon as possible, with as little evidence as possible that she had ever been there. Almost as soon as Annie was out of the bath, food appeared, laid out on a little table in the bedroom. When Annie had eaten it, the lay sister reappeared and shepherded her back to see Sister Hildegard.

'Ah better now I see,' she said. 'I did want to say goodbye and give you my blessing. We really have been most grateful for all your useful help here.' Unknowingly she echoed Inika's words as she said, 'Without you some of the changes of the last few months wouldn't have happened.' She surveyed Annie's outfit. 'You look very well dressed like that. Should you ever care to make it permanent we'd be delighted to hear from you.'

A startled Annie smiled.

'I'd never be able to obey enough orders,' she said. 'But thank you for the compliment.' She looked hard at Sister Hildegard. 'You are worried for my safety aren't you? That is what these clothes are all about isn't it?'

'To stay in the convent in Jo'burg you do have to be in uniform, as I said. But..'

'But?' Said Annie raising her eyebrows.

'But, that was a bullet hole in the windscreen. It may have been a random bandit attack but. again, I prefer not to put temptation in people's way and I think you may be a temptation to someone. As you are going it is better to go as quickly as possible. The car is waiting.'

Annie did understand. She too had been shaken by the sight of that hole in the glass windscreen. It didn't take much imagination to see that the bullet would have gone straight through her had she been in her usual seat and was at this moment presumably still embedded in the upholstery.

'The car' Sister Hildegard referred to wasn't Annie's usual transport, one of the ambulances, but the official sister's car with darkened windows. She found herself settled in the back with her somewhat meagre luggage beside her. As she saw it, she had one more task to complete before she left the country. She leant over to the driver. 'The hospital at Bundu, please' she said, 'just quickly before we go to the airport.'

The driver, a man unknown to Annie, looked dubious. It hadn't been his original instructions, but Annie had used a tone of voice that brooked no argument. It was the tone that had persuaded many a reluctant baby into the world and saved many a mother from the surgeon's knife. She used it now and forty minutes later the car drew up outside the hospital.

They remembered her on the baby ward, even in her new outfit, and took her over to a crib.

'No incubator now you see. She is coming along fine' said the ward nurse.

'What will happen to her? said Annie, 'I've got some things from her mother for her. They found them out at the village.'

'Children's Services will find her relatives in the end. They nearly always do. I'm afraid the things you've brought will need to be officially accepted by the social worker. Look. Why don't you give this little one her next feed while we fetch someone official to take the things from you.'

Thus Annie found herself with the baby in her arms, feeding her formula from a bottle. This was a task she frequently did at home, but oddly enough, she realised, she had never done in Africa. Where almost all babies were breastfed, the opportunity rarely arose.

The tiny brown face looked up at her seeking something she recognised, something she couldn't find.

'Sorry, little one,' said Annie, 'I know. I'm not her either. But you are doing well you know.'

The baby reacted to the voice and relaxed a little in Annie's arms, sucking greedily on the teat.

'Gently does it. Little Morning. I do wonder what will become of you.' Annie went on chatting quietly to the baby as she fed her, winded her and then continued the feed. She looked up and saw an older woman in the doorway, watching her.

'I'm from Children's Services,' she said. 'They say you need to see me.'

'I have to leave for home, England, tonight,' she said to the woman. 'I wanted to say goodbye to this little person, but mostly to give someone these things. When they searched her mother's place they found them and they need to be kept for her. It's that there,' said Annie gesturing at the coloured bag at her feet, as her hands were still busy with the baby.

The woman picked it up and looked, experiencing the same emotions as the others had done the previous day, at the few things in the bag.

She looked at Annie.

'You could be her Godmother, her sponsor, you know. You did find her. We could put you in the file officially. She's going to need all the help she can get. A foreigner to pay her school fees when she gets that far, might be very useful.'

This seemed absolutely right to Annie. Her name and address were officially recorded in the file of Morning Newton as an interested party and Godparent. The paperwork took a little time so Annie finished the feed, changed her charge and wrapped her tightly before putting her back in her crib. Morning, with a full stomach looked once at Annie from big brown eyes, then closed them and fell asleep.

'She's going to make it you know,' said the nurse as she watched Annie sign the forms in the file, 'and she'll be glad of you one day.'

Annie's driver from Katilo suddenly appeared in the entrance of the ward, looking anxious and impatient and rather large.

'I've got to go,' she said. 'There is a plane.'

She followed the man to the car and sat on the back seat with a head so full of thoughts that the next time she became aware of her surroundings was as they turned into the airport.

Bundu did have an airport. It was a little airport, though technically it was an international one as flights went to several African countries. It also had a terminal building, but it wasn't an airport like Heathrow. There was only ever one plane arriving or departing at any one time and everyone there seemed to know everyone else. The Katilo car was greeted with respect and Annie found herself waved through all formalities and driven straight to, what looked to her inexperienced eye, a rather small plane.

She was escorted to her seat and brought a glass of orange juice by the stewardess.

'We'll be a little while yet, sister', she said. 'The other passengers still have to go through customs before they can board. Just call me if you want anything.'

Annie looked around her. It was definitely a small plane. The jumbo jet she arrived on held 500 people this one held less than fifty. As she watched the other passengers began to walk past her down the aisle to their seats. She was startled to see a familiar turban coming towards her. Behind Jemal walked a man who was clearly a policeman. She looked up at Jemal as he passed, but he gave a quick shake of his head, so she did as she felt she'd been bidden and didn't greet him. She presumed he had achieved his ambition and was being deported at government expense. I do hope James is OK was her first thought. Then she smiled at herself. She had begun to regard those two unlikely companions as an inseparable pair and her friends.

The flight was very short, barely an hour. Annie found herself treated as a VIP and ushered off first, down the aeroplane steps into a buggy. This drove her directly to the exit gate where two sisters, clad as she was, were waiting for her. They all smiled at each other but it rapidly became clear that the three of them had no language in common. The sisters spoke to her in Ovambo and then tried German and then Afrikaans. All Annie could do was reply in English. She felt very foolish. Nevertheless the three women managed to exchange some sort of civilized greeting before relapsing into silence.

It also became clear to Annie that though her hostesses had a great curiosity about their visitor, they had been instructed to leave her alone. Her food was served to her in her room and though a sister came to fetch her for evening prayers and sat beside her in the nun's chapel little attempt was made to question her. The language barrier completed her isolation.

Sitting in the chapel, listening to the nun's evening prayers turned out to be an unexpected pleasure. They sang, as the school children at Katilo did, unaccompanied except for a drum.

On returning to her room from the chapel, as she got ready for bed Annie realised someone had unpacked for her and laid her night things out. A touch of cynicism returned after the comfortable warmth induced by the singing.

Did they kindly unpack my things for me, she thought, or search them? She put her hand on the crucifix around her neck, with its hidden electronic gizmo. 'Well I suppose it is called a cell,' she said aloud to herself and undressed and got into the bed. She did however sleep with her hand on the bulky cross still hung around her neck.

The day started extraordinarily early for Annie. It wasn't yet light when her breakfast appeared and before she knew it she was back at another airport again. This time it was the familiar experience of a large international terminal, with departure desks and airline symbols and noise and announcements and something she hadn't seen for a while, shops selling shiny new things.

Her escort of two nuns and the driver took her over to the check in desk and handed over her ticket and her meagre luggage. Annie produced her passport and in no time she had her boarding pass.

'Do feel free, sister, to use the first class lounge, while you are waiting. We like to take care of our special travellers,' said the female check in clerk. Annie did realise that the offer was made to her borrowed nun's habit rather than her person but still smiled and thanked the woman.

Her three escorts gently hustled her towards the departure gates, the traveller's point of no return. Annie well understood that they were anxious to get rid of her and that once she was through security and in the departure lounge then she was no longer their responsibility.

Unpoliced freedom appealed to Annie too. What's more on the other side of the security arches and scanners she could see a fully organised lounge of shops anxious to part travellers from any remaining currency they may have.

Mutually meaningless farewells were said and Annie, putting her purse and her passport and the cross in the little tray proffered to her. She walked through the scanner arch and promptly set off the alarm. She was startled as were her escorts, who having withdrawn as she went to the arch and scanner, now returned, crowding towards her and watching.

The searcher looked at her, and she looked back a little confused. A cotton summer nun's uniform didn't leave much room for contraband. Then she put her hand in the pocket and felt the key MH25, the key to Sister Hildegard's bathroom back in Katilo. She took it out and held it up. The searcher smiled and nodded, but a voice from behind her called out. She turned and saw the older of the two escorting sisters holding out her hand. There was a look of both relief and anxiety on her face.

I knew they'd been looking for something, thought Annie, but I can't believe it's this key. They must have been told to make sure I don't take anything compromising with me.

She walked back to the nun and handed her the key.

'So sorry,' she said. 'My mistake.'

The walk back through the security arch was silent. Once through Annie picked up her things from the tray and turned to wave goodbye. The three were watching her and as she waved, they too raised their hands and turned and walked away. Annie stood looking at the receding backs until they were out of sight round a corner.

She sighed a relieved sigh and then headed for the shops.

From various outlets with familiar names, she purchased a complete set of clothes, including underwear. She paid for them all on her credit card which hadn't seen the light of day since her arrival in Africa.

Next stop was the 'ladies'. Carrying her newly acquired carrier bags she retreated to the largest of the cubicles and locked the door. In a moment she'd stripped off and begun to dress in the new finery. It all felt very good. She looked at her discarded bra and knickers with some affection. They had stood by her, but they were sad garments now. Cold water, rough soap washing and sunshine drying had done their work. They were only fit for the bin, which was where Annie put them. Disposal of the nun's uniform was more complicated. After some thought she folded it all up and put it in the biggest of the carrier bags. Sitting on the lid of the toilet, she carefully peeled back the fabric on the reverse of the crucifix and retrieved the memory stick. She then resealed the space and added the cross to the bag with her previous outfit in it.

Ten minutes later the novice nun had vanished and a small black woman appeared, clad in khaki coloured trousers and a flamboyant gold and red long-sleeved silky satin shirt. This was Annie's version of the standard travelling gear for the middle-aged female traveller. Around her neck, under the shirt, on a newly bought rainbow shoelace hung the memory stick.

Thank God for plastic, thought the newly liberated Annie. I'm human again.

CHAPTER THIRTEEN
Home Sweet Home.

She felt a great deal more secure on a big plane with, to her mind, the proper number of seats. She looked around and couldn't see Jemal, so she presumed they'd send him on another airline and dismissed him from her mind. A sense of security made her both tired and hungry, and so she slept for most of the flight waking up each time they brought her food, eating it with relish and then going back to sleep again.

With the dawn of the new day came the old life. She looked out of the window as the plane descended towards Heathrow. England and London appeared as they always did when returning from somewhere where the sun shone. They looked miserable. The sky was grey. She wasn't sure if it was raining, but looked as if it might be.

I do understand why there was a British Empire, thought Annie. Who'd want to stay in this when you can have 30C and giraffes and bananas on trees? Such thoughts put her in a somewhat truculent mood. After she'd collected her suitcase, she walked through the double doors and viewed the waiting crowds lining the barriers.

Waiting for their loved ones, she thought. I'm a bit lacking in that department. I wonder what's here for me.

The first thing she did see were two very visible nuns in a familiar, if somewhat warmer looking version of the get up she'd been wearing the previous day. They were watching the travellers, obviously searching for someone. To quote the old song, thought Annie, 'It ain't me babe you're looking for.' She put her head down and walked steadily past them. In her new clothes she was invisible.

As she reached the end of the concourse she became aware of a persistent voice.

'Aunty Annie, Will you slow down. I'm trying to meet you.'
She turned and saw Max.
'How on earth?' she said.
'Got your email, worked it out. Drove your car up and here I am.'
She looked at him.'
'And I am so very, very glad to see you. Thank you.' She looked back for a moment. 'There is something you can do for me though, immediately,' she said. 'You see those two nuns. Can you take

this bag to them and hand it over. Just say someone, you don't know who, asked you to give it to them.'

'More conspiracy is it?' he said. 'Then you'd better wait around that corner hadn't you? Or they'll see you.'

He did as she asked and was quickly back. Picking up her case he continued, 'Let's get out of here and home.'

He had with great thought provided a warm fleece for her to wear and settled her in the back seat of her own car.

'It's still the crack of dawn,' he said. 'You go back to sleep till we reach home.'

She realised he didn't want her breathing down his neck as he drove her precious car. She understood. She'd felt the same when driving her father's car. Rather surprisingly, warm in the back seat, she did sleep again and next became aware of her surroundings as the car drew to a halt and she saw her own front gate.

As she got out Max was already unlocking the red front door. Annie sensed home. She both saw and smelt her old house and her old life. She walked past her nephew into the sitting room and sat down. As he followed and looked at her he saw tears begin to stream down her face.

'Tea,' she said. 'I need a tea from a proper teapot. Go, there's a good boy.'

Max returned minutes later bearing a tray with teapot, milk and mugs.

Annie looked up at him, 'I feel like Mole,' she said.

He looked puzzled.

'Don't be silly,' she said. 'Your grandfather read it to your mother and I all the time, when we were children.'

'Ah yes,' he said, light dawning, 'she read it to us as well, but it doesn't work the same in Oz. But you're right, she cries too, at the bit where they find the baby otter and the god Pan is there.'

Annie sat back in her chair and drank her tea while Max fussed around and lit the fire,

'Listen' she said, 'Sit down. Now I'm to tell you a story.' And she did. She related the whole conspiracy as she knew it, from Sal's death to the bullet hole in the ambulance windscreen.

'Well Mum was right about one thing' said Max. 'You need to get away. I think that holiday in Oz. just got closer.'

'No. Don't you understand? Somehow we have to sort out the last bit, the bit that's happening here. It was here it was all plotted.

That girl Sal died because they were breeding dangerous insects in a lab here, in England, not in some foreign land. And that poor boy Vix who everyone says is dead. We've got to do something. That man who gave me a job is part of it. And he made a fool of me too. I'll not forgive that.'

'We?' said Max. 'I'm volunteered am I?'

'Yes you are. You know you are.'

'Alright, but I just wanted to say, firstly; nobody asked me, and secondly, you, me and whose army are going to do all this?'

'We need a plan,' said Annie.

'I'll tell you one thing,' said Max. 'Your friend Jemal said "belt and braces," about that memory stick. I think we should improve on that. We need more copies in safe places. I'll put the stuff on several discs and we'll post them, to Oz for a start, to my college address and anyone else you can think of who will keep it for us.'

'Why do you think that's so important?'

'Well. Let's not behave like a bad movie and have everyone chasing one copy of the magic formula. Think. If, as he said they would, they got his copy off him do you realise the only other copies are here, one in my email from you and one around your neck. That's not clever. If they, whoever they are, work it out that could make us a target. I'm going to do those copies now, while you think about what else needs to be done.'

Annie handed him the little electronic amulet still on its rainbow shoelace. He sat down at her computer on the other side of the room. In less half an hour he stood up and stretched. He held out five discs to show her.

'What shall I call them. I need to write on them, 'he said. 'We do need to be able to recognise them again.'

She'd had time to think while he'd been working.

'"A snake in the grass,' she said. 'Write that on them. It sounds like a movie title but I know what it means.'

He looked at her.

'That bastard who gave me the job. He's the snake. Let's just get them addressed and in the post. Five copies. Well that's one to my godfather, Henry West, you remember him, you spent ages talking to him at my leaving party. He used to be my bank manager. He'll keep it safe for us.'

Max went on, 'Two to addresses in Oz. Well out of harm's way. One to my college address and the fifth?'

'Lets keep that hidden here as a backup, till Jemal's lot get in touch. Put it in a CD case on the shelf with the other CDs,' said Annie.'

'Which one, remember you have to find it again.'

She thought for a moment and then smiled, 'Put it in with Mick,' she said. 'He won't mind and I'll remember.' Max looked puzzled and Annie got out of her chair and went over to the shelf. She reached for 'The Stones greatest Hits'. 'It'll fit in there,' she said.

Max raised his eyebrows at her.

'Well, 'she said defensively, 'Those songs, played very loud, with all the windows open are a great help in troubled times.'

'I'll take your word for it,' he said and put the disc in the case and back on the shelf. 'Now what else is in the great plan?'

'It's not easy is it? The obvious thing is the police – but we've nothing to tell them. All we have about Vix is hearsay and Sal was doing a break-in when she got infected. And they'd probably got all the right permissions in that lab. Somehow the rule of law doesn't seem to have anything to offer.'

'What do we want to achieve?'

'I want that bastard who gave me the job and sent the insects to Africa. I want him well and truly screwed,' said an impassioned Annie. 'Don't you look at me like that. You could say this is both personal and professional. He made a fool of me and he was killing my patients.'

'And,' said Max, 'We need to get the data you brought back, out there in the public domain. For the future, that's everyone's best answer.'

'That bit's not up to us,' responded Annie. 'We just have to wait. I know they'll get in touch. That Jemal is a serious individual. That bit needs to be done right or it won't be effective.'

'Be honest,' said Max. 'What you want is revenge in your little world here in Devon. The bigger picture doesn't interest you.'

'Not fair. Retribution, maybe. Just deserts perhaps. Anyway I don't really understand the global stuff.'

'That's not true either,' said Max. 'But never mind. What are we going to do about the here and now?'

'Well, we both know who knows everything around here, don't we. I think it's time to go and tell Rosina I'm back, via the post office.'

'Don't you want to sleep?' said Max. 'You've just come half way across the world?

'I was asleep all night on the plane,' said Annie. 'And this thing has to be sorted somehow before I can really be back, in this life again. It's not real here yet.'

On the way to Rosina's, having completed their transactions at the post office and despatched the discs to their varied destinations, they discussed actually what to tell her and how to approach her.

'As I told you in the email,' said Max, 'her lot have some concerns about Our Friend anyway. He has some very rough acquaintances.'

They found Rosina in her garden weeding her vegetable beds, with earphones in her ears. They had had to come round the back of the house to find her, and then attract her attention. When she saw them, she was both startled and wary.

She made all the right welcoming noises, but Annie could read the reservation in her eyes. Annie and Max however had made their plan and refused to be put off by her lack of enthusiasm for their presence.

They launched into the local story, about Sal and Vix and the lab. They were rather more vague about Africa. She immediately picked up on the story of the break in at the lab.

'I know something about that,' she said. I'm a 'Friend of Taunton Zoo' and last year we got given two new, actually very old, chimpanzees. It was kept quiet where they came from, because the police didn't want the animal rights lot rioting. But they did come from Coniston-Brown's research place. After all the pictures in the local paper he decided they had to be moved. The Zoo got them free, with a financial donation, provided their origin was kept secret. I've been to see them. Apparently, once upon a time they were in a circus. It's so obvious that they so they love the Zoo with all the crowds to perform to. It's a good arrangement, a nice old age for them and a bonus for the Zoo. They are bringing in the crowds.'

'So he's wriggled out of any consequences of that then,' said Annie. 'But what went on there wasn't right.'

'Those vandals did break in you know. If your girl hadn't done that she wouldn't have been bitten and died,' said Rosina.

'We knew you'd say that,' responded Annie, 'But what was going on there was so wicked.'

'So you say but it was all to do with 'a quarrel in a far away country among people of whom we know nothing', to quote my latest

OU text, she said, gesturing towards her headphones. 'I'm doing a degree you know. But I repeat it all has nothing to do with us here.'

'Don't you believe us?' asked Max.

'Yes of course, but I don't see what I can do or what you two want of me. That quote was from Neville Chamberlain. He couldn't do anything either.'

'I'll tell you what we want,' said Annie. 'You know everyone. We need to know who to talk to. People need to know what went on in that place. They need to know about that Coniston- Brown and anyone else involved. He's got his finger in too many pies. Look how easily he got the hospital to agree to let me go off. What else could he get up to? He can't be a good man.'

Rosina thought about it. She would concede they had a small point.

'Look. I've got one idea. I think you need to talk to the Brigadier. He knows of you by the way. I've mentioned you to him before. He says you delivered his somewhat wayward granddaughter. Jessica Elston out at Wenlock?'

'His granddaughter was she? I remember her. That was the homebirth with the hypnotapes and a Staffordshire Bull Terrier in attendance. A long night.'

'Well, you're in his good books. She praised you to the skies.'

'I got stick for that one too,' said Annie, 'They said I should have brought her in, but she did OK in the end. Anyway, you think he'll listen and understand?'

'Yes I do. He really does know everyone and certainly used to be a power in the land. I'm going to ring him now. He only lives over the other side of the common,' she paused. 'It might be nice if you come, one day, just to see me, not simply to mine me for info, and contacts,' said Rosina.

Annie had the grace to look shame faced and Rosina noticed.

'Oh never mind,' she said. 'I'll make that call.'

Their next encounter was with the Brigadier, who on Rosina's insistence invited them straight over.

He lived in a house that took Annie's breath away as she looked at it. It was a crenulated 18C villa with bow windows, covered in wisteria, perfect in every detail. They drove round the sweep of the curved drive and parked outside the front door. As she was admiring the immaculate garden, the door opened and a very tall thin man invited them in. They followed him into a big drawing room whose disorderliness was at odds with the neatness and care lavished on the outside of the house.

He greeted them with that old fashioned courtesy which seeks to establish common ground with a visitor. He shook hands with them both and then spoke to each in turn.

'Miss Larriot. I believe you know my grand-daughter and great grandson?'

'Yes indeed,' said Annie. 'How old is the baby now?'

'Nearly two and walking. His mother still talks about you and the night he was born.'

'Jessica. Yes, she knew exactly what she wanted. She was a young woman of character and courage, that's why she achieved it.'

'I think, maybe you helped?' he said.

'Yes, but that was all. Helped maybe. It was her achievement, you know.'

Having checked out Annie he turned his attention to Max.

'Australian, I understand?'

'Yes sir, I'm here to do my masters. Computers.'

'I worked in Australia once, in what your generation calls their 'gap year'. My father sent me to work as a jackeroo on a sheep station near Mudgee. I gather the sheep have gone and it's all vineyards now.'

'Indeed. Some of our best reds comes from there. My father works on the export side.'

'Yes. We all drink Australian wine now. Good stuff.'

The conversations seemed to have established their credentials and they were invited to sit down and offered a sherry. The Brigadier noticed Annie looking around the room.

'Can't get worked up about the inside you know, now I'm on my own,' he said. 'Outside's different. House keeper comes tomorrow she'll put it all this back, ship shape.'

Annie, however, wasn't assessing the Brigadier's housekeeping standards, she was looking at the spear mounted over the fireplace.

'I think I've seen something like that before,' she said.

'Ah, that's from the Kalahari. Ceremonial spear. Spent time there too. They gave it to me when I left. Splendid little people. Knew every inch of their own ground. Amazing field craft, the men and the women come to that.'

'Well,' said Annie, 'you may not believe it, but it's about them, among other things we wanted to talk to you.'

They told the story again and this time left nothing out.

The Brigadier may have been reduced, by retirement to running a local residents association and organising siege defences against the summer invasion of new age travellers but in his heyday as a young colonel he had marched at the head of his troops, through alien cities with his regimental band playing their bagpipes. At the time he had the respect of his peers.

When such people get older they discover that those they trained are now at the top of the tree. As a result they also find that the powers in the land have a tendency to call them 'sir' and listen carefully when asked for favours or information.

'Hmm. I can see your problem. Do you have a strategy?'

'My problem,' said Annie, 'is that man Coniston-Brown. The African end is sorted out, I think. They, there, will deal with that. We, here, have got the data safe, for collection.'

'Sensible that,' interrupted the Brigadier. 'Stupid just to keep the one copy.'

'But that man, Coniston-Brown,' went on Annie. 'It all started here in Devon, at his place. There must be a way of making him accountable.'

'I have heard something of him. He has friends who are not quite right. The Association ..' he said, but the perceptive listener could hear the word 'regiment.' ' The Association,' he went on, 'no longer has dealings with him or his contacts. Leave it with me. I will call some people. I have heard that he has been seen in McMarne's.'

'McMarne's?' Annie looked puzzled.

'It's a very expensive exclusive gambling club in London where the rich go to lose money and find excitement. You have to have an extremely large surplus income or be very clever to be seen there often.'

'You think he may be in over his head financially? That's what all this is about?' said Annie.

'Maybe,' said the Brigadier. 'You must trust me. I will get back to you.'

Annie was in bulldog mode and not inclined to be fobbed off so easily, but as she opened her mouth, the Brigadier, a man also not inclined to be pushed further than he was prepared to go, turned to Max.

'And you, young man. What is your role in all this?'

'Communications, sir,' said Max, 'and guard duty. After all this, I have to get my aunt to my mother in Sydney in one piece or I'll answer for it.'

'Splendid. Every leader needs a good Adjutant. Now I must see you on your way. ' He looked again at Annie. 'I will get back to you,' he said.

They got into Annie's car and drove away. Annie had a feeling she had been patronised.

'And you didn't have to call him 'sir,' she said to Max.

'Don't be so prickly Aunty. They expect it, old men like that. And anyway, I liked him. I thought you'd met your match there, by the way.'

Annie remained inarticulately silent but definitely annoyed.

'Can I add,' said Max, 'this Aussie, I thinks things are getting more Olde Worlde and Agatha Christie every day.'

'Don't be ridiculous,' said Annie. 'And don't you dare cast me as Miss Marple. I'm not that old and anyway… You need a whole lecture on female opportunity you do. Listen, while you drive.'

From Jane Austen onwards middle class women have found them selves chained down. Their sons and grandsons had adventures and founded empires. Those poor women just had to sit at home in a drawing room and await news. It must have been a terrible life. A few escaped, but if they went abroad as wives, they were inclined to die in childbirth. There were some wonderful eccentric Victorian women travellers. But that is what they were, travellers, not working, not doing a job. It took Florence and Nursing before respectable middle class women could find escape and adventure and a decent job of work. Think of your great-grandmother. She festered away in that vicarage until your great grandfather was called up and then she found herself running the parish and an orphanage the government dumped nearby and she still found time to start a mother and baby home. They gave her an OBE remember. But circumstances gave her the opportunity. My generation are very lucky. We can get a training, get away and do something useful, even if in my case it took some time. As for Miss Marple,' went on Annie who was sensitive to this particular jibe, 'she barely made it out of St Mary Mead, not to Africa and back and anyway, can I remind you, she is fiction, this is reality.'

The speech bridged the time gap until they drew up at Annie's front door. Her diatribe had put her back in a good temper.

'Sorry,' she said to Max as he locked the car and followed her in. 'But you know me. I don't like being talked down to.'

'Yes, Aunty' said Max, 'and by the way I've always felt you had a raw deal staying here to look after Grandpa.'

'Ah well,' said Annie. 'I did owe them you know. Who knows where we'd be if they hadn't adopted your mother and I.' She paused, 'Anyway now I will go to bed.' 'We've done all that we possibly can do, until someone gets in touch with us. Now I can sleep.'

The following morning brought a highly coloured envelope through the letter box and onto the mat. Max picked it up.

'It's for you Aunty. Someone knows you're back.'

Annie opened the letter and looked bemused.

'What do you make of this?' she said.

Max took the envelope held out to him. It contained three sheets of paper, two plastic bracelets and two cardboard tickets.

'Wow,' he said. 'It's tickets and staff passes for Splendival. They cost a fortune these days. It's this weekend too. Who do you know?'

'There's this as well ,' said Annie. 'I think it's from Jemal and what on earth is "Fairy Tale Splendival"?' she said looking at the heading on the piece of paper.'

'Posh, sanitized festival camping for the largely affluent middle classes and their small children. It's so they can pretend it's a real festival and they're not getting old.' He paused, 'No maybe that's a bit unfair. They want their children to hear the music they heard when they were young.'

'Like Glastonbury? Your grandparents took us when we were tiny.'

'Well, sort of, but without the edge. It's not dangerous and it is commercial. Not in aid of Amnesty International or anything. It wants to make a profit. It has a Pimms tent and up market shopping. It's very safe. Hey! Lets have a look at that.'

She held out the other piece of paper which seemed to be a flyer for a cafe.

It said ' Kasbar café. Leave your children and come and have dinner with us.'

'What with those bracelets and this, I think we might be going as staff,' he said. He showed her the illustration. There was a man in sultan type costume at the door of a draped tent and other vaguely draped figures attending diners who were sitting at low tables.

'There's another thing,' said Annie, 'If they are all English middle class affluent and such, won't Jemal and I rather show up?' She looked down at her brown arm. That's hardly a secret rendezvous. We are trying to be discreet.'

'No,' replied Max, 'I think that's the point. Look they, whoever they are, have thought of that. We're part of the staff of this café. He showed her the flyer. You see we'll be in costume, dressed up like everyone else.'

'Dressed up, like everyone else?'

Annie spoke with mounting horror. To those who wear uniform as their official daily wear, the word 'costume,' bodes ill. They particularly loathe appearing as anything other than completely anonymous on their days off.

'Don't worry. Everyone there does it all the time. It's part of the game. They even have a theme each year. Look at this,' he said looking at the flyer, 'this year it's fairytales. You'll see they'll all be wearing wings and things. It's a way for the well behaved office going types, accountants and bankers and such to let their hair down without any real risk. And for their children to spend time getting excited and making costumes at home with the aupair. Then they take them to Splendival and let them go feral because they don't have all their childcare on tap and have never learnt how to manage their children themselves.'

'That seems a little harsh. How do you know all this?'

'My course. The married ones and the lecturers have been talking about it for weeks. The honest ones are gritting their teeth.'

'Do we have to sleep in tents too?' said a dubious Annie. 'I've only spent one night back in my lovely own bed.'

'Well even camping isn't what it used to be what with popup tents and air mattresses you can inflate from your car engine, but by the looks of this we are ok. It says here 'caravan allotted.''

'We?' said Annie.

'Most definitely yes, we,' said Max. 'Tickets cost a fortune. A poor student like me couldn't afford to go.'

'So all that sarky criticism of those who do go, was a touch of the green-eyed dragon?'

'All I've said is true,' he said. 'Doesn't mean it couldn't be fun. Got any sleeping bags in that attic of yours?'

*

Thirty-six hours later saw the car loaded, entirely inadequately to Annie's mind, with what Max said they needed for a weekend at Splendival. Their supplies included at Max's insistence a fair part of the content of her sewing bag and several rolls of tape and some safety pins.

'Don't we need to take food?' said Annie.

'Don't worry we're staff. We'll get vouchers for free and anyway we're working in a restaurant. We are only going for three days. The less we take the less we lose.'

'You have a point,' said Annie, who was still smarting at the thought of the possessions of hers she had never managed to recover from Becana. None were important, but they were hers. And they were lost.

The car journey got extremely boring as they realised everyone was going the same way and that the last five miles were along a narrow lane down which no one was going to drive at more than four miles an hour. An acerbic comment from Max about 4x4's seeing more of the countryside than they'd seen all year, was ignored by Annie, who had never got beyond regarding a car as a coloured tin can with four wheels that got you from place to place.

When they finally reached the gate, they simply showed their passes and bracelets and were told to park their vehicle in the car park and given a map. Max consulted it.

'Look our base is by that helter skelter. I'm going to unload our stuff here and then go and park. You wait here with it and I'll be back in a few minutes.'

Annie found herself abandoned, surrounded by sleeping bags and rucksacks. She looked around her. She was standing on a bit of raised ground, on the sloping side of a hill which descended down to the valley below. All around her were hills. She knew from the map that just over those hills was the sea, but you wouldn't know it. This valley was secret, hidden.

She turned and looked behind her and saw for the first time the castle in whose grounds the event was being held. It too looked as if it had escaped from some medieval picture book, and of course that same picture book might have been the inspiration for those who built it. This castle, in its own time was built as a fantasy of what the architect thought a medieval castle should look like.

Turning her back on the castle and looking at the fields below, her next impression was of rows of flags on tall flagpoles, hovering above all the activity taking place below them.

They weren't national or recognisable flags but lovely coloured silky ones, blowing in the wind. Annie could see several rows, each consisting of perhaps ten tall poles. Every row stood in a different field and had a different theme colour, but the individual flags themselves also varied in shade and tone and pattern.

Orientation markers, she supposed to help people find their way around amidst the confusingness of the green open fields. As she watched, the flags were caught by the breeze and became fully extended. The impression was extraordinarily lovely. The whole scene reminded her of the background she'd seen in pictures in a medieval book of hours. She was sure whoever had designed this had the same sort of pictures in his or her head and had tried to recreate their own version of it. To her mind they had succeeded.

Max came up behind her.

'Amazing, isn't it,' he said. 'Us Aussies aren't used to real live castles. That's not cardboard or Disney, or been unloaded from the back of a truck and bolted together.'

'No,' said Annie. 'That's the real thing. Well sort of. According to the book I read in the car it was built as a sort of fantasy too. It's been standing there for more than 300 years though. It must have seen so many comings and goings. I wonder what it makes of all this. I don't feel it would disapprove.'

'Less whimsy Aunty. Let's move. It's over there we have to be. By the helter-skelter. That, at least, is 21st Century and did come off a truck and I hope was properly bolted together, seeing as we are sleeping next to it.'

They picked up their bags and headed out across the open grassy ground to a sort of island in the middle consisting of a helter-skelter and beside it a festooned yurt type tent and almost obscured behind it two small caravans.

Annie was unrolling her sleeping bag in one of the caravans when there was a knock on the door. She opened it to see a tall man wearing a very much more elaborate turban than she was used to seeing him in and some sort of Aladdin/sheik costume. From this party getup however there stared out the familiar face of Jemal.

Annie threw her arms around him and hugged him. It was something she had never done in Africa. He too was grinning all over his face. They didn't quite know what to say to each other. There was so much ground to cover and yet there seemed no way to start. In the end Annie opted for the conventional.

'Max can I introduce Jemal. Jemal this is Max, my nephew.'

'Ah,' said Jemal. 'The other end of the email. How do you do.' He held out his hand.

'Hi,' said Max, taking it, 'It's good to meet you. As they say, I've heard a lot about you.'

'Well how did you get out? Did they pay your fare? Where's James? Why are you dressed like that? Why are we here?'

The ice broken and contact re-established, Annie discovered she had a long string of questions.

Jemal began to answer.

'Yes, they did pay my fare as I was officially deported as no longer having a job or a visa. That was very satisifying. James is here too. He's holding the fort at the café.' He briefly smiled to himself. 'I'm dressed like this, because that's how you are going to be dressed shortly. We are staff here and it's part of the ambiance that we dress up. We are here because my bosses thought the debriefing and handing over of data had better be done as quickly as possible, for your safety. Once it's out there, there is no point in making you a target.'

'Target?' said Annie.

'I can't believe it's a real problem or you'd be anybody's target,' said Jemal. 'But the boss is insistent and remember that ambulance windscreen. Jo told me about that.'

'Yes, but that was Africa.'

'Remember Vix. He was here.'

'Yes but he was a traveller. He knew those sort of people.'

'Not really. He was butchered and the only motive anyone can think of was because of what he knew. So we are being careful.'

'OK, but why here, I mean, at this weird festival.'

'Well my bosses were coming. They all have families too and were booked in to this thing. It seemed a good anonymous place to meet. Sorry you've got to work part of this weekend, but we have put you on the cash desk. The only way we could get tickets for you at this late stage was as staff. By the way, I've brought your costumes over.'

Max was already exploring the armful of costumes Jemal had dumped on the bed.

'If you think I'm going round looking as I've escaped from Sydney gay pride week you've got another think coming,' he said.

'Don't be so uptight,' said Annie who, also was turning over the pile of bright and shiny fabrics Jemal had brought, had suddenly acquired the holiday spirit. 'I'm sure we'll find something to suit you.'

'Look,' said Jemal. 'Plan is this. Café opens at eight. My lot will be here at seven and we can all sit and talk. Why don't you just go out and look around. Maybe Max will see an image that appeals to him. You should see James! You will later.'

Annie had very vague residual memories of the Glastonbury |Festival when she was a child. A lot of what she remembered had involved being frightened and lost, so she looked around with interest.

'If we walk up to the top,' said Max, 'we ought to be able to see the sea.'

They set off across the wide open field, aiming at the other side of the valley, but progress was slow because there were so many distractions. Everything around them was so watchable. There were adults variously attired, usually accompanied by several rather small children. Both adults and children were engaged in finding activities to occupy the small people.

There were plenty on offer. There was, of course the helter skelter which had a permanent queue snaking out from its base, but she could see no other fairground rides. What there were however, were many, many stands and tents just doing things with and for children.

'Well it is a Children's Festival I suppose,' thought Annie. From where she stood she could see kite making, and face painting and storytelling. There was a bubble man handing out small pots of bubbles and blowing big ones himself.

One of the more entertaining, ongoing activities was the construction of a cardboard castle from any old discarded boxes. It got bigger as she watched.

Dispersed around the field, were iron bedsteads, the like of which Annie was sure she'd last seen in IKEA. Here they had been provided with cushions and mattresses and draped with curtains and bunting and looked reminiscent of illustrations out of Alice in Wonderland.

The idea apparently was that any passer by could lounge on them and listen to the music while watching the world go by. Each was a different colour and they enchanted Annie. She picked on one with red and gold cushions and settled herself. It was near a small bandstand on which someone she vaguely recognised as a character from a children's television show was performing to an audience of loud and enthusiastic children largely under the age of five.

'Look, you wander for a bit. I just want to sit and watch, if you don't mind.'

'Tell you what I'll get us a drink and see what's on the main stage,' said Max and departed leaving Annie on her red and gold sofa.

She looked around. It was impossible not to make comparisons between parental behaviour here and in the country of her most recent residence.

Carrying children in an African village where no roads, let alone prams or pushchairs existed, was an art form in itself. Annie had watched women carrying their children on their backs in various types of child sling. They successfully supported an infant of up to two or more years old entirely by tying a length of fabric with particular knots. They were so safe that the child would be secure while the mother walked miles. It was a serious skill. Annie, when she was in Becana, had fun trying to learn to tie slings and carry children herself. On the whole, she was only successful with infants. Any child that could crawl or walk felt more secure doing so.

Admittedly, in rural Africa, this skill was almost exclusively practised by the mother, whereas in front of her she could see many fathers carrying children. There was a new phenomenon in evidence, too. One that Annie had never seen before.

A good many men and women come to that, she thought, as she looked around, seemed to be pulling small carts. They were of the type used in city parks by the gardeners and more often, pulled along behind mowing machines. They were four wheeled trailers with proper inflatable tyres. Many were decorated with ribbons and tinsel and upholstery and all contained cushions, blankets and often more than one child, either awake or asleep. They looked expensive, but Annie could see the point. The ground was too rough for pushchairs, which anyway always tipped over and never held enough of the required equipment to run an outing for several children. The carts reminded her a little of the old, huge, sprung prams which would easily hold three children, but for which there was no room at all in a modern house. She remembered the last time she'd seen such a pram. It had been in Becana, to carry food to the clinic for that final Sunday Lunch.

As she watched the always moving, busy, noisy crowd, most of which was under four foot high Annie noticed one small girl standing alone. The child had also been watching Annie. She finally came over.

'I can't find my Daddy. Have you seen him? He was here and now he's gone. He's got his wings. I wanted to watch Igglepiggle.'

To Annie she didn't seem upset, just a little confused.

'Well why don't you sit here, with me and we can watch for your Daddy together. You'll see better by staying still and I expect he'll be looking for you. What does he look like?'

'He's orange,' she said, 'and he's got a golden head and a dragon and he's got his wings now.'

The description wasn't reassuring, but the child was very self possessed and calm, so Annie made room for her and the two of them sat watching the people passing by. The child obviously knew who she was looking for, but Annie felt, the description she had given didn't assist a total stranger trying to identify her relative. On the other hand as she watched the adults in the crowd she could see wolves and woodchoppers and knights and playing cards and quite a lot of pirates. Minutes later she realised she should have had more faith in the literalness of a child's description.

'Ah Daisy, there you are,' said a very tall man clad in Guantanamo type orange overalls with a USAF logo on them. He was also wearing a golden helmet and brown fairy wings and had a dragon on his shoulder. He was exactly as his daughter had described him. He was also pulling one of the carts Annie had noted earlier.

'Daddy,' said the child and flung herself at him. He picked her up and sat her in the cart, then spoke to Annie.

'Good this year isn't it.'

'I've never been before. It's all new to me.'

'Much better this year. Many more things for the children. They've got it right I think.'

'Would you mind if I asked you something?' Annie paused briefly, but went on. 'These carts. Are they a new idea? They're just garden trailers from the garden centre aren't they?'

'Yes, they may look like that to you, but to us parents they are a mobile canteen, changing table, baby sitter and bedroom.'

'But you have to pull them around. They look heavy.'

'Not so heavy as a child on your shoulders – and anyway you can only carry one child at once. I've got three and these places are big. They do get tired.'

'And in the evening you can take them to the stage to hear the music?'

'Yes but not only that, you see, this one is particularly good. When it hasn't got sleeping children in it, the side comes down and it turns into a sofa. You can sit down comfortably and chat where ever you are,' he said.

Suiting his action to the words, he stood the small girl up and said, 'Daisy, look there's Bob the Builder. You go and watch. I'll stay put. I can see you and your brothers too from here.'

The child now entirely secure set off to go the few yards to join a crowd of similar children sitting and watching a full sized man dressed in the costume of a tractor.

The man turned to Annie.

'I'm on child-watch this afternoon. My wife is having a sleep. And you?'

'Oh I'm working here, in the Kasbah Cafe.' said Annie. 'My nephew brought me down.'

The man made himself comfortable on his portable sofa and leaning into one of the various bags aboard produced a beer for himself. 'You?' he said.

'Thanks but someone's bringing me one. But tell me more. Your costume for example?'

'You want my cover story? Right! Well, with all the cuts the US Air Force can't afford planes any more and has started training dragons for secret missions. One of my boys has come as a dragon. See – I'm the dragon trainer.'

Annie did see and hoped there were many more Dads out there like this one in front of her.

When Max returned bearing a Pimms and a lager he found Annie and the orange clad stranger deep in conversation. The topic appeared to him to be distinctly medical and unsavoury and to involve babies. He held out the pint glass of Pimms laden with strawberry and cucumber and mint.

'That sort you out?' he said, 'Would you believe it. A Pimms tent at a Festival. "Times they are achanging."'

The orange man stood up and took his leave.

'Nice to meet you,' he said. 'Must go and round up my lot. See you around,' and looking at Max and Annies's tshirts and jeans added, 'There are some good stalls you know, where you can hire a costume.'

'Well, that's us told,' said Annie. 'I think he feels we are letting the side down, but he's a lovely man.'

They drank and watched in a companionable silence.

A little later Annie turned to Max.

'It's so gentle and safe here,' she said. 'Africa is full of happy children too, but it seemed as if I spent most of my time there trying to keep them out of danger. Here, it's safe.'

'I think that's drink and sunshine talking,' said Max, 'not reality. Come on it's time we got some food and you had a walk around.

They continued their aimless wandering and were mellowed by their afternoon of people watching. They sustained themselves, in Annie's case, after the Pimms, by a really good veggy-burger with more relishes than she thought possible followed by a creamy strawberry ice, and in Max's case by a large glass of a very cold and obscure german lager and a steak pie. Fed and comfortable they meandered back towards the helter skelter and their caravan, in time to change for seven o'clock.

On the bed lay the pile of clothes Jemal had left. Max looked at her and them.

'I give in,' he said. 'I'm happy to be a nice discreet, run of the mill pirate. No parrot, no cutlass, both legs and no hook. OK? What about you?

Annie was turning over the pile of female clothes. She had observed that ladies of a certain age at this gathering seemed to have rather limited options.

There was a standard fairy costume, white gauze and silver glitter in front of her. She also rejected a dress with a large gathered skirt and tight bodice. It was reminiscent of the costumes worn by the Herero women in southern Africa on celebration days. It had always bothered her that these were copied from their Dutch mistresses and were fundamentally servants' clothes. Finally at the bottom of the pile she found something else. The dress was made of cotton but covered in tiny patterns in bright colours and fitted rather than loose. There was a headdress to go with it. Inhibitions overcome, they both dressed up and began to enjoy the sensation of pretending to be someone else.

As they approached their destination, the 'Kasbah Kafé' in their new get ups they had their first chance to take proper look at the establishment in which they were to work. Annie couldn't help but laugh.

'What's so funny?' said Max, still slightly sensitive in his new persona as a pirate.

'Very mixed parentage that place,' she said. 'Look , it's got a little turban thing on top like out of Ali Baba and a streamer flag and lots of draperies but really, it's a Mongolian yurt. It's built of woven wool and wooden poles, and then, see, outside it it's got a very English row of little round clipped bay trees and laurel bushes in pots. A thoroughly modern mongrel. I do like it.'

They entered the tent and looked around. There were two men sitting on cushions at a low table at the back who stood up as they entered but their attempted greeting was interrupted by a sudden fanfare. Jemal in his Grand Vizier costume, was banging a wooden spoon on a baking tray. They all stopped, a little startled. When he was sure he had everyone's attention, he whipped back a curtain and James walked through. He was carrying a cake with a sparkler candle in the middle. It glittered and hissed as it did its thing and James placed it on one of the low tables.

'For you Sister, my sister' he said. 'Welcome home.'

To Annie's great embarrassment there was a little gentle clapping.

To distract attention from herself, she looked at James and laughed outright. He, too was in costume and was clearly doing a Johnnie Depp/pirates of the Caribbean imitation.

'I'd forgotten,' she said, 'you are a chef. And now I suppose you are captain of your own ship?'

'Definitely so,' he said. He looked her up and down, 'And you seem to have become a grand Ghanaian lady.'

James was a big man and he picked her up and hugged her.

'It's Splendival to see you again,' he said. He put a slightly ruffled Annie back on her feet and said 'Come and meet the bosses. We've told them all about you.'

Annie suddenly remembered Max. She turned around and caught the grin on his face.

'James. Can I introduce you to another pirate, my nephew Max. I think we are both on your staff for the weekend. If it is me he is laughing at, you can work him extra hard.'

In a minute or two all participants were properly introduced and sitting around one of the low tables with tea and slices of the cake, which, once the firework had been removed and it had been cut, turned out to be an extremely tasty lemon drizzle.

Annie, meanwhile, was watching 'The bosses' so called by James and Jemal. They were two white men, in their late thirties or early forties and they weren't in costume.

'We were told off earlier, for not dressing up,' she said.

'Ah, but we're Dads here,' said the older of the two men, 'We don't have to do the costume routine.'

'I saw a good many well camouflaged dads earlier,' she said. 'I think you are perhaps a little chicken?'

'It's possible,' he said with a smile. 'Maybe a little, but, you see, as soon as we've done our talking we'll take your stuff away and get it out there.'

'We might be arrested on the motorway, don't you think, if we're driving along dressed as pirates or cops or robbers,' said the second man who had a ginger beard. 'By the way, you look great in that outfit. It's one of my wife's. She's Ghanaian. Jemal gave us an idea of your size and she sent that down with the other costumes. She said you didn't sound like the Mother Goose, Fairy Godmother type, so she sent you her Kente dress.'

That analysis at least was correct, thought Annie, but it did make her wonder what had been said about her. She was also wondering about these men and their credentials. She voiced her concerns.

'Look, we've come, partly because we didn't know what else to do and I know something has to be done. How can you help? Jemal said you publish things? How is that going to work? Who are you really?'

Ginger beard started his answer with her last question.

'Both of us in our other life are university teachers in computers. That's what we get paid for. Because of our job we understand the power of information. It's a cliché to say the internet has changed the world, but it has. We try to do our bit to see that the change is for the general good.'

'The general good? Who decides that? Some educated or rich middle class male elite as usual?'

'Aunty!' said Max, slightly shocked, 'Don't you remember, "Knowledge is power." '

'Of course I do and I remember what you said too, access to and control of that knowledge is the new power, or something like that,' replied Annie. 'And don't patronise me please.'

'Control, being bosses. No, that is not what we're into,' said Gingerbeard. 'We are trying to open things up, get things, information, ideas down to grass roots.'

The older man spoke.

'It's about the people. Democracy. Our organisation publishes all secret documents it is sent, in such a way technically, on the internet, that no one country or company can suppress them.

The information is there, then, for any interested person to find. One of the problems is that these days, life and the world are so complicated, that it takes another expert in the same field to look at something and work out what's wrong with it. In our university world that's called 'peer review'. What we want is a sort of world wide peer review. Everyone to have an informed opinion on everything, or if not that, at least everyone who can, to have an opinion on what they understand, and then inform the rest of us. They can only do that if they have the data, the facts, uncorrupted by interpretation by interested parties. If we manage that we can make use of everyone's skills for the betterment of all of us. Sort of pool our knowledge.'

Annie looked at him. This at least did make a sort of sense.

'Examples,' she said.

It was Gingerbeard who replied.

'Look, in the UK for example, all that basic data that came out about the railways being badly maintained under privatisation. We published stuff, maintenance schedules and such like, that were sent to us by men who worked on the railways and were scared for the safety of the public. That basic data allowed journalists, who knew that field to write articles and tell us what was going on.'

'That hasn't changed anything,' said Annie. We still have loads of companies who just work on the principle of confusion to sell us tickets.'

'It's not our job to change things, just to get the info out there and get people talking.'

'The word is transparency,' said the older man. 'We think that only with true transparency can the people decide what they want.'

'Are you telling me all this stuff is sent anonymously?'

'Well, mostly. It has to be.'

'Anonymously? Shouldn't those who tell you be accountable for the information they give, be prepared to sign their name at the bottom of the page? I'm accountable for all my practice, as I know to my cost, regularly, when I get hauled over the coals,' said Annie.

'Being a whistleblower can be dangerous you know,' responded the older man. 'In some places, people don't just get hauled over the coals. People have died for what they know. Our job is to help those who want to whistleblow and keep them safe by keeping the source anonymous.'

'But still someone has to be the boss. A manager has to make judgments about what to publish and what to hide, surely?' said a not entirely convinced Annie.

'We try very hard not to make judgments, but if some country or organization is trying not to publish, something our lot think that's a reason for putting it out there, for those people who understand it, to comment on it.'

'Aunty, calm down, these really are the good guys,' said Max

'How do you know?' replied his still suspicious aunt.

'I know enough to know some of the other things they've published. I've heard of them from college. Sometimes it's big things, like the number of civilian casualties in Iraq, or that stuff about Global warming emails, but sometimes it's little things, like pointing out that it is your Royal Mail in this country that was trying to stop us looking up our postcodes for free. Or in Oz, pointing out that what was a bill to stop people looking at child pornography on the net, can be used by a government to threaten access to all sorts of other sites too.

'And they want the stuff we have from Africa?' said Annie looking at Max, but it wasn't he who replied.

'Yes,' said Gingerbeard, 'and we'd like you to tell us all you can about what you think was going on there. We had some ideas from the animal rights people, but no real facts. That was why Jemal went out. Your data and your testimony could be very important.'

'Temoinage,' said Annie with a smile. 'I was trying to explain the "bearing witness" idea to someone not so long ago. I was saying then – it's the old   quote –"All that is needed for evil to flourish is for the good man to do nothing." '

'The good person surely,' said the older man smiling. 'But we try vey hard to protect the witnesses. No individual in this age can stand up against a big company or a government.'

Jemal spoke,

'I put stuff on that memory stick you wouldn't believe. Apart from all her animal census data, Jo managed to get emails from UK to her boyfriend and a copy of that report about the DNA. There was entomological stuff about the mosquitoes from the broken labs too and all your vaccination day data about coverage. Stuff from James about how they got the mined stuff over the border and when I was at P&P I too found some emails and some accounts which seemed to have little to do with road construction.

They knew I had something and I was searched so that not one piece of paper or disc was left in my stuff. They even took my rucksack to pieces and gave me a new one. What they got may make them feel safe.'

'And they searched me too,' said the hitherto silent James.

'They – again?' said Annie.

'Well. This time it was the customs men in Bundu, but I don't know on whose instructions, do I?' said Jemal.

'All right, I'm convinced,' said Annie to the two men. 'I can see that you'd had better have it. 'She unlooped the rainbow shoelace from around her neck and handed to Jemal who examined it and smiled.

'Max,' she said.

He produced his disc from inside his pirate ensemble and gave it to Gingerbeard. 'We made other copies,' he said, 'and posted them to various places yesterday morning. Just as well. Before we left I checked my email. It's been hacked and corrupted, so they got the first copy.'

'Sensible,' said Jemal. 'But, Annie how did you get yours out? Didn't they search you too?'

'Yes but they gave me new clothes in the convent. Sister Hildegard. dressed me as a novice nun. She wanted me out of the country and I think now, looking back, she was scared for me. Anyway novice nuns wear big cheap hollow tin crucifixes. I just peeled off the green baize on the back and slipped the stick thing in. Nobody touches a nun's cross.'

There was laughter from the men listening to her.

'You are a natural born spy,' said the older man. 'We should find you a job.'

'No thank you,' said Annie. 'All I want is my old job back and everything normal again.'

Even as she said it she wasn't sure she really meant it. There had been drama, excitement lots of things happening these last months. She went on. 'But it's here I'm concerned about. This is where the wickedness began. And that man who gave me the job. He has to answer somehow. What are we going to do about that?'

'Look, tell us the whole story and we'll try and have some ideas.'

'I suppose it started, the first night Jemal and I met at the traveller camp, but you know about that. That girl died and suddenly I was offered a dream chance to work abroad for a year. It was such a wonderful, once in a lifetime thing, I didn't look too hard and grabbed it with both hands. I realise now it was to get me away because of anything I knew about Sal.

That in itself was a mistake. They, whoever they are, always overestimated my knowledge and influence. I knew nothing and never really have known what is going on.'

'No,' said Jemal. 'I think they always intended to silence Vix and when he was found, cut up in those bin bags you might have asked some questions?'

'I don't suppose so,' said Annie. 'Mostly people like me just get on with the bit of life they understand.'

Her story moved to Africa. Annie continued her tale. James and Jemal butted in with their bits of the story. There was a mutual recall and reliving of events which resulted in the contact between the three of them becoming welded into a friendship that was to last many years.

'It's only when something is so absolutely wicked and wrong and insulting to one's professionalism that finally you are pushed to stand up,' said Annie as she concluded the tale.

'It was the nets that got to Inika and me. We worked so hard to get every child sleeping under a net and it turned out our work was largely wasted. They knew the nets we were supplying for the river villages wouldn't work. Then if you stand back a little further and think, the real wickedness dawns on you. They were killing, mostly children to make their parents move on, just to clear the land, to dig it up, for money.'

'Perhaps you could call it 'International Capitalism,' said the older man.

'I call it wicked greediness,' said Annie.

The two men to whom they were telling of their adventures listened and made various notes.

'And he was definitely Chinese?' They asked about Mr Wang, from the meeting in the bush.

' Oh yes,'said Jemal. 'Though his English was very good. He was flying back to Hong kong the next day, we were told.'

The storytelling moved on to their return, to copying the data and the hacking of Max's email and finally the visits to Rosina and the Brigadier.

' " McMarne's," you say was the name of the club where Coniston-Brown was seen?'

'Yes, said Max, 'The Brig says you have to be rich or clever to go there.'

'Indeed. It is also owned by a very well to do Chinese businessman. I think we are beginning to sort this story out,' said Gingerbeard.

'Yes,' said the older man. 'I was always concerned that P&P, who on the whole, are a responsible lot should get involved in this sort of thing. But, if we've got sub contractors and Chinese money and Chinese connections in the UK. Add the chance for a local to make a quick buck on coltan, and a vulnerable scientist with gambling debts and there you are. Bioengineered mosquitoes and a genocidal plot to murder indigenous children.'

'Do you mean to tell me all this really has been about debts? Money. How ridiculous. If you haven't got it you don't spend it. If you really need it something will turn up. It's only a tool. I've never understood greediness for money so long as you have enough for today, what can you do with the rest – just buy Thneeds.'

'Thneeds?' asked Max.

'It's a children's book. Dr Seuss. Things you don't need. Should be compulsory reading for all children over five once a week,' said Annie.

'Well that's a quick destruction of the capitalist way of life,' said Gingerbeard.

'Never mind about that,' said Annie. 'What am I going to do about Coniston-Brown?'

'Do you have to do anything? It sounds to me as if your Brig will cook his goose,' replied Gingerbeard.

'Not enough,' said Annie. 'It's personal. Someone has to tell him in words of one syllable what he actually did. He didn't just persuade people to move on. He killed mothers and their newborns. I saw some of them. They didn't need to die. In the last resort we are humans. All the edifice of everything is just made up of humans doing their thing. That means every human is equally valuable, whether born in a bush village or a palace. I'm a midwife. That's what it's about for me.'

This speech produced a silence but Annie was on a roll and not to be stopped. 'You see, I know you're going to duck the issue aren't you.' She continued, 'This little story about a tiny corner of a small country has got bigger and bigger. Somebody once told me that St Theresa was a saint of little goodnesses. Well here it's little badnesses. Each tiny one allowed someone else do something worse. That man has to be told what his little badnesses led to.'

It was Max who spoke. Everyone else, slightly embarrassed, felt it was only for family to intervene in this diatribe.

'Aunty, that's a lot of philosophy for one night.'

'Well, I'm sorry. All those months and no native English speakers and having to sit still for so long on the plane. I've had plenty of time to think about 'the world, the universe and everything' and nobody to spout off too. You haven't answered my question' she said looking at both Gingerbeard and the older man.'

'I'm sorry,' said the older man. 'We did say all we did was put the info out there. Give us time to think. We will get back to you I promise.'

James, who had for the last few minutes been wandering around the tent adjusting this and that and generally fidgeting spoke.

'Everyone, we have to open. Listen there's hungry people out there.'

It was true. The chattering of a queue was audible at the curtained doorway. The two middle aged white men stood up. Gingerbeard spoke.

'We'll go now. We're going to take this stuff this evening to London and sort it and put it all out there. We'll be back late, but anyway I will see you tomorrow. If you can put up with the family I'll buy you all lunch tomorrow, when we're back. We can continue to reconstruct the universe. OK?'

Goodbyes were said, the men left. The curtain doors were opened. Customers flooded in. Annie had a pleasant evening, sitting at the cash desk taking the money and watching people eating and mostly enjoying themselves.

When the last guest finally left James, Max and Jemal sat down at one of the tables with the two girls who had appeared and waitressed all evening. Annie looked at the five of them and felt too old. They were settling down to one of those intense conversations that the unattached young have. It was part exploration, part discovery with loads of sexual sparking.

They don't need me here, she thought. She spoke aloud.

'Will you finish cashing up for me. I've about had it, but I'd love to have a walk around. Look at it all in the dark, before bed. It really is a little like fairyland. 'No,' she said as Max began to stand up, 'I really prefer to do it by myself. I'll see more of what I want that way.'

Her tasks delegated, Annie walked alone through the draped entrance into the open field. It was transformed. The helter-skelter still glowed bright with its multicoloured lights, but now it presided over a quiet empty field. There wasn't a child in sight. The teeming hordes had gone. All the tents around the edge, that earlier had been overflowing with constructive activity were zipped tight shut. This field, even including their café had gone to bed. It was the grown ups time now, thought Annie. So let's go and see what they are up to.

She walked towards the castle and the sounds coming from the main stage. As she got nearer the noise swelled and the crowds reappeared. The smell of barbequed meat was in the air. There was a Ferris wheel with its own Hurdy Gurdy and its own very long queue of preadolescent youth awaiting their thrill. Children weren't absent, but the tinies were asleep in the carts pulled by their parents or older children. They really were asleep too, she noted, and oblivious to the screams of the teens on the Ferris wheel and the general cacophony of overexcited pleasure.

As she continued to wander on towards the main stage the background noise declined and the offering of the band became more dominant. She stood on the steps of the castle and looked down towards the stage and at the fields full of people below her. It was dark and late but everyone seemed set to party for many hours yet. The performers on the stage, so tiny and far away, were singing to their audience who were singing back and waving their arms in unison. Everyone seemed to know the words. There was a mass hysteria of participation, with everyone in the crowd trying to belong and be absorbed into some nebulous undefined whole. The songs were vaguely familiar to her, from her youth but music had never pulled at her heart strings as it seemed to for most of her contemporaries. If there was such a thing as a musical gene she was sure she didn't have it.

As she watched from her vantage point she could see subsidiary entertainments going on There were fire eaters and jugglers and dancing and apparently St George and a dragon.

That's more in my line she thought and set off down the side of the main crowd.

Her first discovery was a tent where ballroom dancing was going on. There was an old fashioned jolliness in the air. She bought herself a drink and sat down to watch. It seemed to be an establishment intent on teaching everyone to variously waltz, foxtrot and quickstep. Music was provided by a man with an accordion. The instructors who didn't have partners were soliciting members of the audience. The teachers were young and clothed very properly as for a tea dance in a provincial town hall. A man approached Annie and before she could protest, whisked her off her feet. She could ballroom dance. Her father had taught her and her sister so she relaxed into is arms and followed his lead.

'Who on earth are you?' she asked, as they spun around the makeshift ballroom.

'We're students, from the teacher training college. We thought it would be fun to remind people how it's done. '

'I think it's marvellous,' said Annie. 'I'd forgotten how to dance like this.'

'You haven't forgotten,' he said. 'Concentrate. Let's show them how it's done.'

Annie did concentrate as she had been told to and found the freedom exhilarating. Her body rapidly recalled what to do, so she surrendered to the moment. For once, no thinking, no brainwork was involved, just simple physical coordination. For the next few minutes they whirled and turned and promenaded. The accordion player watched them and adjusted his music to their exhibition display. Shortly they were the only couple on the floor. When eventually the music stopped and as she and her partner clapped each other Annie realised the tent audience were also clapping the pair of them and that they had given a more or less solo performance. She was too embarrassed at being the centre of attention to take the floor again.

'But I did enjoy it. I really did. Thank you,' she said.

Still laughing she moved on down an avenue of stalls all open and alive, all trying to sell their wares to the late night revellers. Everything on display seemed to tinkle or glitter or glow in the dark of the night. There were earrings and water toys and fancy cakes and mobiles made from flattened knives and forks and a stall selling ukuleles and panpipes.

At the end of the line of stalls there was an area of open ground where various theatrical acts were doing their own thing and largely ignoring each other. Field theatre, rather than street theatre, thought Annie to herself as she watched.

Each act captured a group of supporters around it who, when the performance ceased, moved on and reformed around another attraction. She watched a Punch and Judy show acted by adults, without their box-stage. Surprisingly, the dog dragging his sausages ran off to considerable applause. The universal story worked without the puppets.

There was also a juggler with fire sticks who successfully, if terrifyingly threw his tools high into the air and caught them. Brief 'Health and Safety' thoughts passed through her mind and she smiled. It was nice to know that even back home in safe quiet England there were still small corners, where risk escaped assessment.

She turned around and found herself facing St George and a Dragon and a Jester with bladder and on a stick. The Jester shook his bells in her face and then hit her on the head with the bladder. It was heavier than she expected and she was momentarily dazed.

'A maiden, a maiden,' he shouted and pulled her into the action.

'A dragon, a dragon', called St George and waved his sword at the crowd and the large man clad in green scales.

'Fe fi fo fum I smell the blood of someone, not an Englishman', called the Dragon and pressing a plate on his chest produced a very African sound of a lion roaring. The small crowd of onlookers clapped.

The mummers surrounded Annie and she found herself centre stage. The green dragon was behind her. He put his arms around her and held her rather tightly. She wriggled but the grip held firm. St George was facing her and she suddenly recalled the actual words the Dragon had just spoken and remembered that other set of Englishmen who used the red cross on a white background as their emblem. She struggled further, again to no avail. Suddenly alarmed, she called out.

'Stop! Let me go. I don't want this.'

'Ah ha she speaks, the infidel maiden speaks,' cried the Jester and Annie felt her wrist twisted behind her back.

'Quiet or I'll break this arm,' said a quiet very undragonlike voice in her ear. 'We've been hunting for you.'

'Help' she called to the audience and felt a pain in her arm that brought tears to her eyes. They clapped her authenticity.

'St George to the rescue,' said the man himself and lunged towards the Dragon, who retreated in front of him. He continued to advance as the Dragon retreated and Annie realised they were leaving the arena and going into the darkness under the trees.

She could hear the Jester addressing the audience in their wake.

'And tonight people maybe the dragon gets the girl. Who would you rather have ladies, the man or the animal?'

With a final shake of his bells, he bowed.

'Goodnight all. Sleep, or whatever, soundly,' he said and made his exit, retreating towards the darkness where his fellow troopers had gone before him.

Annie could hear the applause from the audience he left behind him and summoning up all her strength let out the loudest, most anguished cry for help she had ever produced in her whole life. She heard a final burst of clapping.

'See Paki bitch, they think it's the act.' The Dragon spoke as he twisted her arm further. 'Shut it.'

He pushed her in front of him deeper into the darkness. She could hear St George and the Jester following.

'Keep going,' called the Jester from the rear. He had a high squeaky voice. They pressed on and Annie heard the sounds of the field behind her fade. 'Too quiet here, keep going' went on the voice.

The epithet more than anything else had shocked Annie's mind back sharply to her predicament. Her sense of soft warm communal pleasure was banished by the two short words.

'These are not nice people,' she found herself thinking.

Her arm hurt a great deal and as he pushed her forward the Dragon twisted it again and she involuntarily cried out.

'I said shut it,' was the response and she tried hard to bite her lip to avoid provoking him again.

As they went further into the trees, new music became audible and then increased in volume. To her surprise, still dazed from the bang on her head from what had definitely not been an air filled bladder Annie recognised the words being sung ever more loudly.

'I've got twenty acres and you've got forty three.'

The Wurzels! The realisation that the musical accompaniment to her predicament was played by a group who, some would say, were to Devon, her current home, what the Beatles were to Liverpool, did not contribute to her sense of reality.

She had heard them often as a child and never liked them. There was a rustic lack of inhibition in their performances that had frightened her then. It didn't reassure her now. Their sound did however allow her to work out that they must be somewhere behind the folk music stage and therefore not too distant from the Kasbah Café.

'This is far enough. Let's have a look at her,' said the squeaky voice again. The Dragon pulled at the Ghanaian headdress. It came away in his hand. He threw it aside. Annoyed he buried his hand in her hair and pulled Annie's head back.

'She's no spring chicken,' said the Jester

'Nice bit of dark meat though,' said St George. 'We'll have her. All of us. Do her good. Darkie slut.'

There was a brief pause as the other two men understood the opportunity in front of them. St George put out his hand and grabbed the neckline of the borrowed dress and pulled. It ripped straight down the front.

'And the rest,' he said, his voice gruff with arousal. He grabbed again at the remaining sheds of fabric hanging on around her waist and threw them aside.

'That's better,' he said. 'Spread her against the tree.'

There were no objections. His companions obeyed. They too were caught up in the lust of the moment. Something very nasty was in the air. She was their prey. They had hunted her and they'd have her. A pack must conform to it's rituals of power.

St George pulled off his tabard and unzipped his leather trousers. His penis emerged and he moved towards the exposed Annie, held conveniently available for him. The other two men had her arms and legs. She had very little defence but as he got close, the flabby white skin of his chest pressed into her face. As his hands fumbled below, she opened her mouth and taking a good solid lump of flesh between her teeth she bit as hard as she could and hung on as long as she could.

'I've got a brand new combine harvester and I'll give you the key.'

He hit her head and she let go. He jumped back and taking up the only other weapon immediately available, the wooden sword of St George. He swung it and hit Annie, hard. She felt her arm break as he made contact and she screamed. The Dragon, who had been holding the arm up, let it go and it swung useless at her side. The extreme pain in her scream somehow dissipated the sexual tension. The penis was no longer erect.

The Jester, who up to now had supported St George in this carnal search for gratification intervened.

'You've got something a friend of our wants. Hand it over,' he said, 'or we'll start again.'

Through her pain it dawned on Annie that this wasn't just a random attack on her because of who she was, but was part of the whole Becana business.

Somehow that improved things and she collected her wits. A little late perhaps, the fight or flight reflex had kicked in. Her perceptions were sharpened by adrenaline. She became aware of a rustling above her head in the branches of the tree. For this reason she wasn't quite as surprised as her enemies were, when there was a sudden explosion of activity from above and St George lay flat on his back apparently unconscious. Standing, largely on top of the inert wannabe rapist was a man in orange overalls. He picked up the discarded wooden sword and swung it at the Dragon. It made contact. The creature let go of Annie.

'Run,' said the orange man. 'Run.'

Holding her broken arm against her chest she tried. Behind her she heard the sword make contact once again and heard the pained squeal of the Jester's voice.

'That's all of 'em,' said the voice behind her, 'lets go.'

She felt an arm around her. As Annie had worked out earlier, it wasn't very far to where the helter skelter and the café stood. Less than a minute later the pair of fugitives emerged from the trees into the familiar open field.

'I don't think they'll follow us,' said her rescuer and acquaintance of earlier that afternoon. 'It seems as if a man can't even have a quiet smoke in a tree these days,' He looked at the nearly naked Annie who had blood trickling down her face from where she had been hit and who was using her good arm to hold the broken one against her chest.

'Hang on,' he said.

They were near one of the curtained and cushioned sofas they had sat on together that morning. He went over and taking one of the curtains in both hands pulled. It came away. He took it back to Annie and wrapped it round her.

The adrenaline of escape was still in her veins.

'The café,' she said. 'My friends will still be there.'

He looked at her, still standing, now no longer naked but almost more bizarrely swathed in a large satin curtain, embroidered with characters from Alice in Wonderland. He simply picked her up and ran across the field. Some commotion must have been audible to those inside the empty tented café for as the orange man with his bundle approached, the curtain doors were pulled back and Max and Jemal emerged.

They didn't understand, at first what they were seeing but the orange man pushed past them straight into the café.

'She was attacked. She said to come here.'

Looking round he laid her down on one of the low cushion sofas that had earlier been the diner's seats.

Annie, for whom the jiggling run across the field had caused acute pain was unable to speak and had tears running down her face. She just lay where she was put. The two young women she had watched being such competent waitresses earlier were still there, and she discovered still competent.

They looked at her, gently unwrapping the curtain. They understood the implications of her torn clothing and could clearly see her damaged arm. They covered her up again and stood protectively close to her.

'She needs an ambulance. Now,' said the first girl.

'That's a broken arm, at least,' said the other.

James appeared carrying a glass.

'Here's some brandy,' he said, 'buck her up.'

'NO,' both girls spoke loudly and in unison. Then more gently one said, 'That's wrong, you mustn't. She might need an anaesthetic,'

'To set the arm,' said the other. 'It's an ambulance she needs.'

Max had heard her the first time and was already on his mobile making the appropriate call.

James looked so stricken that the second girl said to him, 'Let's just have some warm water and wash her face'

He retreated behind the counter into the kitchen feeling very incapable, but returned shortly after with the requested bowl and cloth.

Annie had heard all the conversation but seeing as everyone was doing what she thought they should be doing, she didn't waste her limited energy trying to speak. She just watched them all fussing around her and relaxed into the safety of it.

The orange man approached.

'You're OK.' Then, looking at the battered woman in front of him, and realising what he'd said, rephrased his words. 'What I mean is they didn't manage it. We got away.'

Annie smiled at him and nodded.

Max had finished his call.

'They say they'll only be a few minutes. They had an ambulance on standby for the Festival.'

He turned to Annie's rescuer.

'What happened,' he said.

'I was just sitting up in a tree having a quiet smoke and listening to the music when these guys appeared dragging her, underneath the tree. They were really going for her, but she bit one of them and then he broke her arm. That's when I managed to jump in and we ran.

Then I realised we knew each other, from this morning, when she was kind to my little lost Daisy.'

He went on to tell Max everything he saw. Moments later they all heard the sound of a motor engine, grinding rather, as it made its way across the field. The orange man raised his head and listened.

'I've got to go,' he said.

Max looked at him puzzled.

'It's my night off. Wife is with the kids. I've been smoking see and I'm a teacher. Must go. I did get there in time, really I did. Goodnight.'

As the ambulance, signalled to by Jemal with a torch, drew up outside the tent, the unknown orange stranger disappeared into the darkness towards the distant music. He was replaced by two florescent clad paramedics, one male and one female. The male made a gentle inspection and seeing the distorted shape of her arm said, 'We'll get you something for the pain.'

His colleague brought over a long blue and yellow bag and extracted a mask from it. Annie, still with tears running down her face, began to giggle.

'They don't usually laugh until we've given them some,' said the female paramedic to her patient.

Annie responded with a further feeble giggle.

'I'm not in labour,' she said.

'She's a midwife,' said Max, who ad been hovering attentively. The female paramedic understood and grinned at her.

'Never mind, me love,' she said. 'We won't hold it against you. Now breathe in and enjoy.'

When, years later Annie would relate the story of the attack on her by the medieval mummers who were trounced by a trainer of dragons for US Air Force. She always added the detail that, as she was driven away in the ambulance, still wrapped in a satin curtain covered in embroidered playing cards, the last bit of music she heard as they left the festival site was one other song she recognised.

'I'm the urban spaceman baby, I'm making out, I'm all about.'

'It seemed,' she would say, 'the final surreal touch to the whole adventure.'

*

Your nephew tells me,' said the policeman standing beside the hospital trolley on which she lay, 'that you say you were attacked by St George, a Dragon and a Jester. They broke your arm and threatened you with rape and that you were then rescued by a large man in an orange jump suit wearing a golden helmet and brown fairy wings'

'Yes,' said Annie.

'And that's all you know about your attackers and your rescuer?'

'Yes. They took me by surprise. I wasn't expecting it. I was just having a nice time. It was so quick.'

. 'Perhaps we should be testing you for hallucinogens?' he said.

Annie was still in pain and now annoyed as well.

'Let me tell you I have never in my life taken any illegal substance. I am a   midwife and I don't do that sort of thing. If all you can do is insult the victim then for goodness sake go away.'

Even though she was lying on a narrow hospital trolley, she tried very hard to turn her back on him. The nurse looking after her intervened.

'You'd better leave it until she is out of surgery,' she said. 'She really is still in a lot of pain.'

CHAPTER FOURTEEN
Another Ending

The next person Annie remembered seeing was Max. He was anxious.

'Mum is going to kill me you know. She's sent tickets and you are to be on the plane as soon as possible.'

Annie smiled. She could imagine her sister's furious comments. If Julia had something to say she said it and it was wise on the part of anyone she saw as a target to duck her missiles. She wasn't a diplomatic citizen.

'Anyway I can get out of here now they've fixed and plastered my arm,' she said. 'Where did you spend the night?'

'Back at Splendival. If you remember they wouldn't let me in the ambulance so I followed in your car. When they'd put you to bed I went back to tell the others how you were.

There was a lot of carryon back there, about the attack. Security guards everywhere, but of course they found nothing and nobody. All those guys had to do was take their costumes off and fade into the crowd.' He paused, 'James and Jemal send their regards. Jemal made sure his bosses knew what happened. They had no trouble. Spent their night in London. All our info is safe and where it should be. Attacking you was a waste of time.'

'It hurt too' said Annie waving her Plaster of Paris arm at him, 'and goodness knows when I'll be able to go back to work.'

'You are not going back to work you are going to Oz. OK,' said Max.

'Maybe, when this is really done' said Annie. 'I don't run away, ever.'

'What about a strategic retreat?'

'Again. Maybe. I just have a sort of feeling this isn't over yet.'

'What do you mean?'

'I'm not sure. I think it's a case of " It's not what you know, but who you know" and, she said, cradling her newly plastered arm, 'And I suppose, in this case, who knows you and who they know.'

Max looked confused.

'I don't know what you are talking about. But after last night, you might at least have the decency to be scared.'

'Well I know what I mean,' she said. 'And anyway I got away. Right won through.'

'Bullshit. That was just luck,' he said. 'He's vanished too, by the way. The orange man.'

'Well he would wouldn't he? He was a teacher. Didn't need any questions, did he? Let's get out of here. They've given me an Out Patient appointment back at home in Devon. It's in two days, just to check the plaster. That's going to be embarrassing. Explaining this in my own hospital to people I know, especially when I'm still supposed to be in Africa.'

Max was fidgeting and Annie looked at him sharply.

'You've got something else to say, haven't you?'

'I rang Rosina. And, well, she went over to your house the day we left for the festival. Just after we'd gone. Someone had got in and there's a mess. Rosina got the police and such but we were lucky not to be there.'

'Nonsense,' said Annie. They obviously waited until we'd gone and then went to look. It was only after that they came after us at the Festival. They are intelligent you know. They're not looking for trouble.'

'Are you sure? Look what happened to you?'

'Oh that was just time and place and opportunity. The ambiance – mood music and the dark.'

'For goodness sake Aunty. They've been in your house. You, hell, we, must be careful.'

She could see he was scared but she somehow wasn't.

'It's all over now anyway. We know that. There is nothing to be gained by going for us and this is England you know, not some remote bush village.'

He simply stared back and the phrase 'mutinous silence' made sense to her.

It was a quiet journey back to Devon. Annie slept most of the way having been well sedated by the ward staff.

'Let's hope he's a smooth driver.' They had said to her as they gave her the tablets, still doubtful about such an early discharge. 'Your appointment at your local hospital fracture clinic is in two days. They'll check the alignment then.'

She awoke as they drew up outside her own front door and Max hooted the horn. Rosina came down the path to greet them. Annie was a little disconcerted. She thought she was going home to her own fortress and was not expecting to find it occupied by others. Getting out of the car and walking up the path she looked at her little house.

It had clearly been in the wars as had she. The boarded up side window made it look a bit as if it was winking at her. She smiled back. It had obviously had an interesting weekend as well.

Rosina was looking very concerned.

'They haven't done too much damage,' she said. 'They seem to have been after technical stuff. You'll need a new computer.'

There was a howl from behind Annie and Max could be heard quietly swearing as he locked the car. Rosina hovered round Annie. She sat her on the sofa and retired to the kitchen to make the obligatory cup of tea.

Max, meanwhile came through the front door precipitantly, dropped the bags he was carrying in the hall and disappeared upstairs.

Annie looked around her. She could see there had been serious attempts at cleaning and tidying. A lot of things weren't quite where she left them only two days ago, but all things considered her little hobbit hole had survived the impact more or less intact.

Rosina returned with mugs of tea and the inevitable plate of homemade cake.

'I called Cathy. You know, I met her at your leaving party,' she said. 'She came over with another friend and they cleared things up a bit. The main damage seems to be the computer, but you'll get a new one on the insurance.'

As if on cue, Max came downstairs holding his laptop with both arms close to his chest.

'They didn't get this,' he said. 'I hid it in your airing cupboard in the middle of the clean sheets, Aunty. At least my dissertation is still in existence.'

'I've been talking to Julia,' went on Rosina. 'I don't think we have actually spoken for years, not much since she left for Australia. It's all been letters and emails.

You are definitely sisters. She won't take no for an answer either. Adopted the pair of you may be, but I remember your father being much the same, when we were all young together, riding our bikes across Dartmoor. In fact I remember being very jealous of all the adventures he would arrange for you two.'

'Who do you think taught us to be like this? It's nurture not nature that counts,' said Annie laughing. 'Anyway what did Julia say?'

'She said to tell you that your ticket is at the airport waiting to be picked up and it is booked and unchangeable so if you aren't on the plane she'll lose 1500$. Max has the dates.'

'I think I give in and comply,' said Annie. 'Everyone needs to cool down. Like you said Max, a strategic retreat is indicated, especially after this.'

She glanced around again at her slightly battered sitting room but her eyes rested for longer on the VDU that had once been part of her desktop computer. It wasn't just broken, as if dropped while being stolen, it was smashed, well and truly, with vicious intention. Rosina saw her looking at it.

'I wanted to throw it out,' she said. 'But the insurance say they have to see it and then police want it too. I think everyone will be happier knowing you are a few thousand miles away in the sun.'

'Definitely,' said Max.

'Alright, alright,' said Annie, 'No need to go on. I've said I'll go. OK.'

The body is a very efficient machine if the brain responds to its demands. Annie well understood hers. It told her to go to bed and sleep. This she did, while other people around her busied themselves with what they saw as urgent business. Police and insurance men were dealt with and forms were filled in. Max contacted James and Jemal and arranged for them to come and stay in Annie's house once the Festival was over. The Brigadier, kept informed by Rosina, made some phone calls of his own.

Sleep did it's work and consequentially when Annie woke early, after two days in bed and twelve hours solid sleep, arm in plaster or no, she had already laid breakfast and was eating it when Max appeared.

'I smelt the coffee,' he said. 'I didn't expect you to be awake yet.'

'I'm fine now and it's my appointment at the hospital, for my arm today isn't it?' she replied.

'Welcome back,' he said with a smile.' I was a bit worried. All you've done is sleep for nearly two whole days.'

'That's all it needed. I'm fine. Now about today...'

They planned the logistics of the next twelve hours.

'If you drop me off for my appointment, then you can go and fetch James and Jemal. You're right, it would be good if they stay here while I'm in Australia.'

'Do you want to be picked up?' he asked.

'No,' she said. 'Rosina said to phone her and she'll pick me up. You'll still be on the road I expect. Anyway, after the clinic I've got to go to personnel and arrange my sick leave. All their stuff takes hours. You'd be hanging about for ages. It's a lovely day. I'm missing the African sun already. I just want to sit out in what we've got.'

As Max drove her up to the main door of the hospital Annie had mixed feelings. She'd been away for what seemed to her, eons of time, but the place looked the same. Now, also, she was coming back as a patient, which rather lowered her status, in her own eyes at least.

Old habits quickly reasserted themselves however.

As Max parked the car to let her out, she looked around and registering the increased number and type of uniforms visible. Her subconscious noted 'Flap on. Marines in charge.' An understanding of military procedures and ethos was part of working in this town she reflected.

The town loved the military, not least because many of them had served their time in either the Navy or the Marines and somehow never moved away. The hospital patients loved them because military female nurses still wore the uniform their civilian sisters had abandoned in the 1980s. This involved white caps and cuffs, lace edging, and black stockings, thus to patients the Naval Nurses were 'Proper Nurses'. The comments of Annie's military colleagues on the subject of their hospital uniforms were unrepeatable.

She said goodbye to Max and, dodging an exiting wheelchair, went up to the desk and handed her appointment card to the receptionist. He took it and examined it.

'Fracture clinic miss. You'll need an Xray first then,' he said.

He was a man she'd known for nearly twenty years. It took him a second or so to recognise her. Instead of her usual blue Sister's uniform, in an attempt to convince herself it was still summer she was wearing a golden yellow, short sleeved, long skirted, cotton dress. She wasn't going to give up on the sunshine till forced too.

'Ah, Sister Larriot, nice to see you back,' he said. 'Been in the wars though I see. Better warn you,' he went on as her entered her arrival on his computer screen, 'we're rebuilding again. New research block. So you can't get through the usual way but it's easy. Just down there, through those double door, turn left. Then go over the car park and through the orange door. It's on the second floor. It's simple, you'll see it. There's a lift. Be careful though, they've put in a new set of lifts. If you take the wrong one you'll end up at the top of the new tower.'

She reclaimed her appointment card and set off.

Reorganisation exercises were regularly engaged in by all British NHS hospitals. Their objective is only clear to senior management.

Annie had long suspected it was a ploy to keep all patients dependant, submissive and confused. Geographical insecurity creates anxiety. The obligation is on the patient to be in the right place at the right time. If you end up in the wrong place then you've failed. The fault is then clearly yours and not that of the system. You have demonstrated that you are incompetent and stupid and therefore feel suitably cowed.

In order to run a successful hospital, patients must be controlled, in case they should develop independence, raise their voices in protest and shout at the megadinosaur that enters lives when illness became part of daily existence.

'Disempowerment makes for compliance,' thought Annie, quoting to herself the sociology lecturer of the year before. 'But I'm Staff and I'm supposed to know where I'm going. I refuse to get lost.'

She did of course get lost. She made it through the orange door as her instructions had said. Then something went wrong and she found herself on a corridor with no sign posts or notices or directions. This wasn't unusual. It was another feature of being involved with the military. Where ever possible signposting was kept to a minimum. In these circumstances the only solution was to ask the way.

Annie knocked on and then opened a nearby door.

'Excuse me,' said the now very lost Annie, 'could you tell me where XRay East is?'

There was only one man in the room. In front of him, on the desk, he had a half empty bottle of whisky and a partly full glass. He seemed to be removing files from a cabinet and putting them into the boxes in front of him. He looked up at her.

It took a moment, but then Annie recognised him. That thick head of floppy fair hair which had caused a such a flutter in Rosina's chest was unmistakable. She realised she hadn't seen him since the leaving party when he had offered her what she had thought was her dream job.

She was shocked and tried to force herself to step back outside the room and close the door. She found she couldn't. She had, in her mind, been planning a showdown with this man whom she had demonised over the last few months. She had, however, envisaged the meeting happening on her own ground and conducted by her own rules.

An unexpected encounter in a seemingly empty wing of the hospital with the man who had recruited her to Becana wasn't her plan. Yet, try as she might, she couldn't do the sensible thing and walk away. Anger welled up in her as she looked at him.

'Mr Coniston-Brown,' she said.

He too recognised her. After all, he had been forced to retrieve her file from his desk drawer more than once in the last months. He had looked at the little passport photograph clipped to the top corner of the CV and had wondered why on earth this irritating little woman couldn't just do the sensible thing, get bitten, get malaria, die and stop stirring up trouble.

Neither of them could relinquish the contact made, yet both knew it would be wiser to do so.

'Do you know what you've done?' said Annie.

'I could say exactly the same thing to you madam,' he replied. He reached for his glass and took another gulp. He neither invited her in nor offered her a seat. She couldn't help what she did next. The compulsion was irresistible. She pushed the door fully open, went on into the room and shut it behind her. She stood there, back against the closed door with folded arms.

'Well I'm going to start,' she said. 'I'm going to have my say. Firstly, I know you recruited me to get rid of me because of the traveller girl. You wanted to keep me quiet.'

'Possibly,' he said guardedly. He was aware that to have this conversation was a mistake, but in the last forty-eight hours the edifice of his life had collapsed around him and the desire to lash out at someone was getting stronger by the minute.

The strength of this compulsion correlated negatively with the amount of whisky in the bottle on the table. He poured himself another measure.

'Well that was a mistake, for a start,' replied Annie. 'I didn't know anything then. But I want to know now.'

'You are just a nosy middle aged nurse. How could you cause such chaos?' he said wonderingly.

'I'm not "just a nurse." I'm a midwife and more importantly a professional. Your mistake was making a mockery of what I do for a living.'

'You are a ridiculous little person. And you've ruined my life.'

'Oh really. How could I possibly do that?'

Her exasperated tone finally tipped him over. He too was going to have his say.

'If you really want to know, I'll tell you. The hospital has rescinded its support for the research institute. They say 'in view of current reorganisation' there will be no place for the research institute in their plans, They say as a result of that, would I arrange to vacate my office here as it will be need to be reallocated. In addition they have withdrawn my hospital and university privileges. How could someone like you manage that?'

'It wasn't me. I don't have that sort of pull. It was you. It was what you were doing.'

'It's who you've spoken to. I seem to be on some sort of blacklist. I get no more official invitations. No one returns my calls. And that's not all I've had a letter from the charity board of the hospital requesting my resignation, "as they are reconfiguring the structure of the committee." I'm not accused of anything. There's no charge I can answer, but no one will be seen to associate with me. Nothing goes forward. I'm being obliterated, here in Devon.'

'Like I said,' responded Annie. 'They know. It's what you were doing. That was wicked.'

'Nonsense, complete nonsense,' he was almost shouting at her now. 'I was only helping out a friend, with a bit of lab work on the side and the money was useful.'

'But you know don't you, what you did? How did you get into it?'

He looked at her with a mixture of rage and alcohol induced self pity. The urge to justify himself was too strong to resist. He went on.

'It was just a pub conversation with a mining friend. We were at school together and we keep in touch. One does need to know what one's contemporaries are doing. You never know when you may need them. He told me about mining the coltan and how he needed to move those people on. They're nomads anyway. Tight little ethnic group. That's when the DNA idea came up.'

He took another drink and seemed to be settling into confessional mode.

'But then, after all that effort collecting blood samples, it turns out that wouldn't work because they aren't an exclusive group as everyone thought. All that separate development, tribal stuff the Boers put out is rubbish. There's been ethnic mixing for generations there. Everyone has been having it off with everyone else for centuries so there is no target DNA.

P & P put me on the payroll and that's when the malaria idea came up. They weren't difficult to breed, the little bugs. Limited release of tiny mosquitoes in that area. When their children kept dying then the nomads would pack up and move. That was the idea.'

Annie couldn't believe that another human being could really plan such things and then discuss them so casually.

'Can you hear yourself? You are talking about killing babies.'

He seemed unconcerned.

'Well they have too many anyway. Monty said they were, developmentally, barely part of the human race. We were reducing the world population. You can't talk. The company was paying you out there to teach them birth control wasn't it? What's the difference?'

Annie opened her mouth to reply, wondering where to start her lecture on the subject of half a century of women's reproductive rights and maternal mortality. She looked at him and realised he was incapable of hearing her, so she just said.

'Contraception isn't murder, you know. That is a rubbish justification for killing mother and babies.'

'I was reared an old fashioned Catholic.' he said with a grin.

'Don't be ridiculous. That's just...' Annie was left speechless at his arrogance.

'Oh for goodness sake, what's a few less natives when measured against progress,' he continued. 'That ore was needed. Anyway all that's over now. I'm finished here. I'll have to move it all somewhere else. This place was a bit provincial anyway. I need to be nearer, Oxford or London, more in the swing of things.'

'That's not going to be so easy either, you very stupid man,' said a now extremely angry Annie.

He looked at her, the drink was now clearly making its presence felt in his responses.

'What do you mean?'

'It's all out on the internet. All the data from the labs. The deaths, emails . Meetings with indigenous elders. Lists of who is on charity committees. Staff of P&P. It's all there for anyone to read and anyone in the know can work it all out. It's not just rural Devon that won't touch you with a barge pole. No respectable institution is going to risk their reputation by associating with you.'

'But we put a stop to that. Your house, and the Festival…..'

'I don't know who your "we" is, but us, my lot, we got the stuff safe out there in spite of those goons.'

He fell silent and sat and thought for a minute or two. A little local setback had suddenly become something far bigger. He didn't like the implications at all.

Annie couldn't resist twisting the knife in the wound.

'You're such a fool. Don't you realise that you were deliberately targeted. They, whoever they are, needed a tame scientist. You were blackmailed. Your school-friend Monty, he works for P&P doesn't he?'

He looked at her. She seemed intent on dismantling the few remaining the struts and props in his life

'What do you mean?' he said.

'Someone told me you'd been going to McMarnes and you owe a lot of money. McMarnes is owned by a Chinese business man. P&P have now secured huge Chinese investment for mining exploration. You were set up.'

He heard her this time and turning around, looked out of the window at the courtyard below. He spoke almost to himself.

'How could you, someone like you, know all that?'

He turned back. A viciousness had entered his voice.

'I should have just trodden on you like that criminal gypsy scum, when I had a chance,' he said.

The question he had so quietly asked himself wasn't expecting an answer but it got one

'I'll tell you how I know. It's not what, but who you know,' said a still incandescent Annie. 'Surely the old school tie mentality understands that. I have good friends too.'

The interchange had degenerated into a straightforward row. Both were angry and out of control.

'You are a nasty self righteous little bitch. I've had enough of you.'

'And you are a drunken fool.'

'Somehow you've screwed all my contacts. A man is his reputation. You've ruined mine, not just here, but everywhere – that's slander, I could sue you.'

'Not if it's true,' she responded and added rather childishly, 'And I hope you weren't thinking of driving home after all that whisky.'

There was a pause, while the opponents eyed each other. The man seemed to come to some sort of conclusion.

'You're a fool too,' he said. 'What makes you think I'm going home? If all you say is true, I've nothing to lose. I'm finished. This conversation stops now.'

He stood up and moved around the desk. He went to look out of the other window in the room. He was fiddling with the catch and eventually managed to throw it open wide.

'See,' he said, 'important staff are given keys to open their windows properly. Health and Safety can be defeated if you try.'

Something clicked in Annie's mind.

She knew she had gone too far.

She realised the danger.

This man was descending into despair. He was cornered.

She knew that sort of monomania which says 'if I can't have what I want then no one else can either.' She'd seen it once before.

Oh God, she thought, he's not going to do a Mickey Rooney on me if I can help it. I shouldn't have pushed him.

She remembered her mother saying 'You'll be sorry when I've gone.' They weren't, but they did all feel very guilty because they hadn't stopped her destroying herself. Here, playing out in front of her, she recognised the same pattern. And she was making it worse, provoking this response in him. Somehow she had to slow things down, get him back from the brink of whatever he was contemplating.

This man felt he was at the end of the line. This chance meeting with her had crystallised things for him. She had cruelly made him face truths that it would have been better not to have examined at this moment.

She continued to watch him as he sat back down at the desk and rummaged in its drawers. It's time I got out of here, she thought. It was as if he'd read her mind.

'Don't even think about it,' he said.

She heard behind her, the safety lock go clunk into place as he pressed the emergency button on the desk.

'We do this my way,' he said.

She could read his face and see his brain planning an exit. She didn't like what she saw.

A little late in the day, she started trying to reduce the temperature of their encounter.

'Perhaps things aren't really that bad,' she said. It sounded a pathetic response, even to her ears.

He looked at her and understood that she had seen into his mind and had some idea of his intentions. He also understood that she was scared.

'They are for you,' he said. 'And I repeat, this conversation stops now.' He couldn't resist continuing though. 'I am a scientist. That was a really clever solution to the problem. Good science. It took a real eye for detail to breed those bugs. It's just the liberal lefty moral lobby that won't wear it.'

'That's what matters. You are a scientist,' said Annie's voice. As her gut was saying 'You are a maniac who planned genocide,' the statement lacked conviction.

'That's the point. I'm not anymore am I,' he replied. 'You've lost me my reputation, my credibility. That's all a scientist has.'

Annie opened her mouth to respond.

'And anyway shut up. Shut up and I mean it.'

She realised all she could do was listen and hope he talked himself back to reality.

'I'm nobody now. It's all gone. Don't kid yourself that gets you off the hook,' he said. 'I'm ruined but I'm not going down in history as the crooked patsy of a Chinese syndicate.'

'Don't you see, you were tricked,' said Annie. 'You weren't to blame.'

'You don't believe that and neither do I,' he said. 'Looked out of the window lately? Notice anything as you came in today?'

Relieved that communications had been resumed Annie spoke in placatory tone.

'Well it looked as if there was a usual flap on. Marines in charge, I think.'

'Well madam, Things have changed while you've been away. We have terrorist protocols now, especially when one of the nuclear subs is in the dockyard. One dialled code on this phone from the right person and the whole shebang is let loose. Armed marines, naval police, dogs, the lot. They can shoot to kill these days if they feel a suicide bomber is loose.

This is nasty, thought Annie.

'I think you've just become my bomb,' he said.

'Listen,' said Annie. 'You mustn't…It's never that bad.'

He stood up. He had something in his hands.

'I said shut up,' he said. 'No one gave you permission to start jabbering on again.'

He came over to her. Before she realised what he was doing he had covered her mouth with a strip of duct tape. She reached up with her good hand to remove it.

'And while we are about it,' he went on and twisted that good arm behind her. Very rapidly he immobilized her with more tape. He ignored her plastered arm as he pulled the tape tight. She felt the plaster crack and pain shoot all up her body to her brain, bringing tears to her eyes.

'And another one for luck,' he said with a smile, adding a second strip to her mouth. 'That'll sort you out, you mouthy madam.'

Annie didn't quite yet understand the depths of her predicament. Had she been physically able to she would have smiled. Now I know what a 'captive audience' is, she thought.' Really this is taking the concept of shutting women up too far.'

Moments later all frivolity drained from her as she began to fully comprehend his intentions. He, having silenced her had acquired what he wanted, someone forced to hear him out, but unable to answer back.

'Now a bomb I think.'

He looked around him and saw a backpack and a denim jacket hanging and on that still fairly prevalent piece of government issue office equipment, the very solid circular wooden coat stand. He lifted them down and examined them.

'Ah yes. That looks authentic. Just like those the 7/7 guys had. We've all seen the pictures in the papers. Now,' he said looking at Annie, 'we need a few wires and a lot of tape to make it look good. And some sort of switch.'

Annie, who still had the use of her legs, tried to move. Though he was looking down at his handiwork, he heard her.

'Don't be foolish,' he said. 'There's a lot more tape. If that's how you feel.' He walked over and grabbing her by the front of her dress with one hand he moved her a few feet and pushed her up against the curly wooden coat-stand. He rapidly taped, round her waist and around the central upright. She was both uncomfortable and immobilized.

'That'll do,' he said, standing back and looking. 'Now, she's a witch at the stake. Most suitable. But I'll need her to walk later though,' he went on, speaking to himself rather than his now terrified audience of one.

He returned to his handicraft activity. In the drawer he'd discovered a pen torch. He found more wires by ripping them off the desk lamp. There was a clock on the wall behind the desk facing her, so Annie knew he spent a full five minutes in silence, cutting and sticking and fixing, before he spoke again.

'Did you ever make a 'Tracy Island ?' he said. 'I did, but no one ever gave me Thunderbird Three to land there. That looks fairly convincing I think?'

He held the holdall up for Annie to see. It did, terrifyingly so. 'Just like on TV' was the phrase that came to her mind. It didn't reassure.

'Pity I can't say 'and here's one I've prepared earlier.' I've always wanted to do that. But I really hadn't envisaged this outcome, you know. I wasn't prepared. Only way though. Can't go back.'

Her head was full of answers. She was sure, if she could talk to him, she could bring him down. She recognised this state of mind. Here was someone who had made a plan. He'd done his research, knew his stuff and therefore confidently expected the world to comply with the outcome he expected. If it didn't, then his only response was temper. The frustrated toddler who hits out and is then terrified by the damage he has caused was an analogy that came to her mind.

The trouble was, it was easy to pick up the angry toddler and hug him and cuddle him and convince him that he was still loved even if he had thrown the TV remote across the room and broken the window...

One couldn't do the same with a 6'2" male, particularly when you were immobilized and silenced. If only she could speak. But he'd made sure she couldn't.

Something must have shown in her eyes as he responded.

'No sloppy chit chat. Madam. I've made my decision. Leave me be. Taking you with me is the best I can do to get my own back. We're going out with a bang. Yes I know there's no explosive. But those marines out there with their nice shiny SA 80s, they don't know do they?

They'll just see you and me and the switch. They'll have no option but to shoot. Then it's curtains, all over, for both of us. Then they'll see what a perfectly ordinary guy was driven to by interfering do-gooders who haven't a clue about the real world.'

Surely in this day and age, thought Annie, shame and loss of face, they really weren't good reasons to kill yourself were they? Let alone someone else as well.

His look of thwarted intention reminded her of some of the women she'd seen through their first birth. They obsessively over planned. If they were school teachers, as they often were, they would have made a detailed birth plan and were very angry with everyone, God, providence, the midwife and themselves when labour didn't go according to that plan.

Annie had made a speciality over the years of talking these obsessive over-planners back down from their peak of anger and getting them to accept reality. Her aim had always been to make them feel good about themselves and thus get them to welcome their baby.

Her concluding remarks were usually along the lines, " birth is only one day in yours and this child's long life. There's years and years of days to come. Don't get so worked up about this one."

It frequently worked and a calmer look would appear on the woman's face. There was a comparison here, she was sure, if a somewhat tenuous one. The trouble was death really was only one day. You couldn't improve on it. It was a bit final. If only she could talk to him, she was sure she could get him to see things differently.

She had a feeling that he also knew that, and that was why he'd taped her mouth. He simply didn't want to give anyone the chance to talk him down from the rooftop. He had made up his mind.

She did realise that her own self-righteous anger had been what had pushed him over the edge and into making that decision. She had brought this situation on herself and at this minute she couldn't see any way of getting out of it.

It seemed a pathetic way to die. To be shot in error because some soldier thinks you are about to attempt to blow up something or other. What, she wondered could they possibly have here that would make security so strong. He seemed to read her thoughts.

'They've got a couple of 'terrorist' prisoners patients in. Being treated for something complicated. They are expected to be grateful and cooperative. There are also expected to be attempts by their comrades to silence them,' he said. 'So we are all at Level Three Risk.'

He put his completed pseudo backpack bomb on the desk. Beside it he placed a sleeveless waistcoat made from the denim jacket.

It bulged lumpily and had wires showing, connecting one pocket to another. Both looked alarmingly realistic to Annie.

'Right. Time to go, I think,' he said.' This is what we are going to do. I feel you should know the plan. When   we're ready I'm going to use my password to alert security, both on the phone and by email.

When I can see from this window that all force is assembled, we are going to walk out of here. All they out there will see, on all their clever monitors, will be two hooded suicide bombers with explosives and wires attached to them. I will be holding up the switch. We will walk down the corridor towards the isolation unit where they've got these guys. We won't be very clever. Any sniper with minimal skill will be able to pick us off through the windows.'

His reasoning was sound. She remembered the phrase from American police dramas. "Suicide by cop."

Had she had the use of her voice she would have pointed out the obvious fact that "Murder by cop" was very unfair on both parties.

'Right, we have to look the part now. Think of it as a fancy dress parade.'

He had been rooting around in a cupboard.

'Nowadays they pay us all to cycle to work so there's enough stuff to clothe a regiment in every office cupboard. This'll do I think. '

He pulled on a woolly hat over his very fair floppy hair until it was hidden and the edge of the cap reached almost to his eyebrows. He took off his standard, scientist at work, white coat and put on the denim waistcoat and then over it, a dark green fleecy jacket.

'Now for you,' he said. 'See what I've found. A headscarf, that'll convince them.' He produced a long dark red pashmina type wrap and waved it at her.

She couldn't fight back as he came and put the scarf around her head. He then pulled it under her chin, looped it round her neck, and then brought the long end back around her face leaving only her eyes visible. There was enough scarf left to secure it behind her head with the ubiquitous tape. He stood back and looked at her.

'Nice little terrorist extremist we've got there I think. In my white coat you'll do. Time to get this show on the road.'

He sat down at the big desktop computer and started typing. Annie watched. She could see the screen from where she was, but was too far away to read the words. He seemed to be sending an email. He pressed the send button and as soon as the 'sent' screen appeared he pulled out the power cable of the computer and picked up the monitor. He went over to the open window, and threw it out. It fell the four floors to the courtyard and shattered loudly on the paving below.

'That should attract their attention, now they've got the message,' he said.

He then went back to the desk and picked up the telephone. He dialled a set of six digits, paused and held out the phone to Annie. She could hear the familiar voice of the switchboard operator saying 'emergency protocol extension 5716. Will you confirm emergency protocol.'

He pressed one more button and then ripped the phone and wires out of its socket and threw them out of the window after the computer.

'Now we wait and watch,' he said. 'Let's see whether those drills we've all been forced to do while you were away have paid off. Officially they have ten minutes to deploy.'

It was extraordinary. He stood there at the window, watch in hand. It was as if he were the official instructor on an examination day. As he watched, he gave Annie a running commentary.

She didn't listen. As he had started talking she gave up on all thoughts of reaching into his psyche and turning him around.

It was time to concentrate on her own plight. She was damned if she was going to end like this.

Decision making in crises. Choices, even where life and death are concerned are not unfamiliar to any community midwife. It usually came down to when and if to call the ambulance. The trouble was here today there didn't seem to be any choices. And she was sure the ambulance was already outside awaiting the outcome of events.

She looked around her. The adrenaline rush of danger had sharpened her perceptions. Her brain raced.

Everything in the room and about him, her would-be executioner, appeared sharper and brighter. She understood what he intended to do now.

They were supposed to walk down that corridor looking like suicide bombers and get shot dead. He was going to wear that denim waistcoat with the very obvious wires and she was kitted out in this ridiculous headscarf which hid the fact her mouth was taped up. He was going to put his white coat on her and the rucksack on her back. Well at least there was a tiny flaw in his plan. His white coat was far too big. It would trail along the floor on her. That wasn't going to work.

When he had to undo the tape tying her to this umbrella stand, that was going to be her chance to run and she must take it. She needed to look as unlike a suicide bomber as possible to avoid getting shot. She was not going to put that white coat on.

'Right everything in place now. I can see snipers on the roof opposite and I think in that building over there. Your turn to get dressed for the party now, I think, madam.'

In front of her stood this very tall man with the woollen cap on his head pulled right down over his ears. The denim waistcoat bristled with wires, very visible to any watcher with a pair of binoculars.

He stood there, holding the backpack, non-bomb and his roll of tape. Carefully he put the home made switch into a pocket and began to undo the tape around Annie's arms. He released her good arm first and holding her wrist threaded her arm through a strap of the backpack. and then taped the arm back again across the front of the rucksack straps. He then turned his attention to her plastered arm. He removed the tape holding it and pushed it through the other strap. She retched with pain as he moved it and cried out, but her cry was inaudible. He taped this arm over the other, so it looked as if she was holding the bag close to her chest. As he did so, he looked at her face and sensed the silent cry.

'Ah ha, some pain at least I can inflict on you for now. That is pleasing,' he said. 'Sadly I think death will be instantaneous and you won't suffer anywhere near enough for what you have done.'

He stood back and admired his handiwork.

'Attention to detail, solid research. That's my reputation, was my reputation, before you came along. Ah yes one more thing. You are going to walk quietly beside me and not run.'

Annie's eyes gave him his answer.

'I'll show you why,' he went on.'

He went to the desk and came back with the nylon cord from hem of the green fleece he was wearing. He held it in two hands like a garrotte and stretched it out. 'Strong stuff,' he said. 'Unbreakable, see?'

He threaded it around her neck.

'Under the scarf. Invisible there,' he said. 'And now a nice slipknot I think.'

She felt him pull it tight around her throat.

'Understand ?' he said.

She did. He had her on a choke lead, like an unruly dog.

'Well?'

She nodded, tears from the pain in her arm still running down her face. Escape seemed impossible.

'Now the rest of that tape. Sticky stuff isn't?' he said conversationally, 'I am never without it though. Holds the world together.'

Pain or no pain, in some bizarre way Annie found herself agreeing with him. She too, had held large parts of her little house in Becana together with duct tape. She realised the danger.

Concentrate, she said to herself. You are a prisoner. Don't sympathize with him. He's a bastard. Don't collude, No Stockholm Syndrome for you. Keep focussed. Watch. There may still be a moment.

As he ripped off the tape holding her to the hat-stand he smiled and gave her injured arm a gratuitous little tweak. The pain ran right up into her brain and nullified any empathetic thought she might have been developing for her persecutor.

He held her, standing up straight and unattached to the coat stand and reached for something behind him.

'Now the white coat, I think. Then our dedicated little female terrorist will be ready to go,' he said.

As he draped the coat over her shoulders he realised his error. A great length of it simply trailed on the ground. A coat meant for a 6'2" man cannot be adapted, without at least a pair of scissors, to fit a 4'11" female. He frowned and looked about him, but, as he realised, Annie's legs were now free.

He saw his problem.

If he let go of the noose around her neck she wouldn't be captive and could try to run. This meant he didn't dare let go of the cord around her neck so he couldn't look for another solution or another white coat. He paused and looked at her.

'We'll manage,' he said. 'That headscarf is very convincing.' He threw the white coat aside and reaching over, pulled the surplus length of headscarf round to her front to try and hide the fact that her hands were taped to, rather than clutching the 'bomb'.

Annie though shaking with pain and anger felt a momentary frisson of triumph. A tiny victory and she wasn't sure how it would help, but a victory nevertheless.

'We are worth a Blue Peter Badge or a prize at fancy dress ball don't you think?'

Annie's own thoughts were of Red Riding Hood and the wolf.

'And at least she got away,' she added to herself.

He marched the two of them over to the mirror on the back of the office door. She looked at the reflection.

They were terrifyingly convincing. He was tall and not a trace of fair hair showed. The denim waistcoat looked like all those she'd ever seen on the TV news. She barely reached to his shoulder, but there she was, head suitably covered and apparently voluntarily clutching the obviously wired backpack to her chest.

'Now en avant. Let's go.'

He twisted the cord once more round his hand and Annie felt it tighten round her throat. He opened the door and propelling her in front him, they started walking. At first Annie tried to pull ahead but felt the noose tighten to the extent that she almost couldn't breathe.

'I told you,' he said.

She ceased pulling and dropped back to walk beside him. He put his hand, holding the noose cord firmly on her shoulder. The switch, now in his other hand was held aloft so any watcher couldn't possibly miss seeing it.

The corridor they were walking down was flooded with bright sunshine. It had windows all along one side, making the two of them the perfect target he had planned.

At the end was a double set of swing doors. Through the windows in the doors she sensed some movement. Her thoughts were racing. Every sense was working overtime. It wasn't the end. It just wasn't going to be. She refused to believe it. Life did not end like this. She strained every faculty. She saw every detail about her. Distant noises were audible, men's voices. She heard the sound of an ambulance siren abruptly curtailed.

'Be prepared, be prepared,' she said to herself and as an old Girl Guide had time enough to be amused.

As they continued their walk, side by side down the corridor, the image of Red Riding Hood and the wolf flitted once more through her mind. Again he seemed to read her thoughts. He looked at her and raised his eyebrows.

'All the better to see you with,' he said and they were his last words. As he spoke them, Annie heard the crack of breaking glass and immediately let her knees relax. She dropped to the floor.

Simultaneously she felt the power go out of her captor as he collapsed on top of her.

She had over the years watched a lot of police dramas. It seemed to her that at this moment her only choice was to lie absolutely still.

Play possum then nobody will shoot you to tidy up, she thought.

The trouble was, that as her captor was shot, his grasp on the noose had tightened and as he fell on top of her, the distance between her neck and his hand lengthened.

Neither hand nor neck could move, thus Annie found herself loosing consciousness as she was slowly strangled.

She felt the cord biting into the flesh of her neck and she could smell the firework smell of cordite. Her ears picked up peremptory commands and the sound of the swing of the double doors opening.

There was the unmistakable noise of military boots on the corridor floor as they approached. Try as she might to draw breath she was finding it increasingly difficult. Reality was beginning to go woolly and dark round the edges.

She fixed her mind on staying absolutely still.

'Play possum, play possum,' she repeated to herself and as alertness faded, her last thought was, 'Though it seems unlikely I'll ever get to see one, for real, now.'

She opened her eyes to find herself in the open air covered in a red blanket with an oxygen mask on her face and various people crowding around her.

She put her good hand up to her neck which was painfully sore. Her fingers could feel the line where the cord had bitten so tightly into her skin. Pulling off the mask she tried out her voice. It was scratchy and hoarse.

'How come I didn't get shot? That's what he wanted to happen,' she said.

Of the people crowding around her several had an answer.

The paramedic spoke.

'Don't worry about that now. Just concentrate on breathing. Good deep breaths.'

She did comply with that instruction and could feel the air going deep into her body. It tasted very, very good. 'Mostly of sea salt, still with a flavour of summer,' she thought inconsequentially.

A soldier, she recognised as a marine, huge in his body armour and still carrying his weapon stood in the background and watched her.

Meanwhile closer to her she could hear another voice. Her eyes found the speaker.

'Had we been called earlier,' said a senior looking and apparently annoyed uniformed policeman, 'we might have worked it out, realised it was all a fake. We have experience in these things, but troops I'm afraid. They don't assess. See a bomb, kill the bomber.'

He had been talking to someone behind him but then realised Annie was awake and listening turned to her

'It was obvious you were a captive not a participant. People from the hospital identified you on the monitors. No one believed the scarf, especially with your bare arms. The porter remembered that yellow dress because he was used to seeing you in uniform. But the military didn't know the explosive was fantasy. I still think you were very lucky they missed you,' he said. 'Collateral damage would have been an acceptable answer at the inquest. Not,' he added pausing and pondering, 'that I think there'll ever be one. It'll be 'National Security' and D notices, you'll see.'

The marine came over to her, his bulk briefly coming between her and the sunshine.

'Glad you're OK ma'am. We don't miss, you know,' he said jerking his head backwards at the policeman whose voice could still be heard.

'Thank you,' she said simply. In her years in Devon she had learnt respect for these large, usually inarticulate military men. In a crisis they could be depended on. They didn't make a fuss.

And, she continued the thought to herself. They did a good line in the emergency delivery of their own babies, the last one she recalled, a few years ago was delivered under its own Christmas tree.

'I know you didn't have any choice,' she said to the soldier. She took another deep breathe of good fresh Devon air and tried out her voice again. 'Mr Coniston Brown. Him?'

The marine answered.

'No possibility of just wounding. He had the switch,' he said, still towering over her as she lay on the stretcher.

'It was what he intended you to do you know. Except that you didn't get me. Really, thank you for that,' said Annie.

Still wrapped in the red blanket, she sat up and stretched out her hand to shake his. He looked a little alarmed, but took the hand and shook it.

'Glad we could help,' he said and rapidly retreated no doubt to continue his jurisdictional discussion with the policeman.

The porter who had given her the incomprehensible directions earlier, had been hovering and was determined to have his say.

'Everyone knows you Sister Larriot. We knew you couldn't be one of them. They have coloured CCTV now.' He looked momentarily uncomfortable as he realised what he had said. 'I meant that yellow dress.'

She understood. The man was saying that it was the colour of her skin that made her so memorable and had saved her life. She had worked in and around this hospital for nearly twenty years but she and three others were still the only nursing staff of colour.

She had many years ago as a child discovered and forgotten that if you are the only black face in a white crowd you show up, you are noticed, recognised and remembered. In the polite professional world of work, the phenomenon still applied.

It meant that people always greeted you by name but nevertheless treated you with that courteous English reserve that keeps the barriers up and strangers out, until true friendships are formed. Annie, English to her core, practiced the same techniques herself, on the new brand of oddities from Eastern Europe and Zimbabwe who were appearing as staff in the NHS. One offered a friendly greeting to an incomprehensible newcomer with an unpronounceable name but, safely from behind a firm barrier of personal privacy.

Annie was still sitting up. The paramedic began to rewrap her shoulders in the blanket. There was something in the touch of the hands, a kindness perhaps.

She started sobbing and found she couldn't stop. As she cried she felt her throat tighten and her breath begin to come in gasps. The paramedic rather firmly laid her back down again, turned her on her side and reapplied the oxygen mask. She looked around at the assembled company.

'That's it. We need to go now,' she said. 'Look at her. Her throat is swelling from the strangulation. She may obstruct. She may need intubation. We'll be in Casualty. You can find us there.'

Annie woke to find Max watching her. It gave her a sense of déjà vu. Three days ago she had also opened her eyes to see Max sitting by her hospital bed. She raised her eyebrows at him questioningly.

'No Aunty. It's not on,' he said. 'If Mum was going to kill me last time you ended up in hospital, now she'll feed my body to the sharks.'

'I am sorry, really sorry,' said Annie, trying out her voice. It seemed to work, but sounded a little rusty to her ears. 'I know I caused all that. I should have backed off. Somehow I pushed him over the top and I shouldn't have done it. He should be alive now.'

'Trigger happy sniper,' said Max.

'Don't you dare blame them,' said Annie. 'They did their job. They had no choice. He tricked them into it. And they didn't shoot me. It was all my fault.'

She reached out for a drink of water with her good arm and looked around her.

'Where am I? Why aren't I in a proper ward? Where is everybody?'

'You're in the isolation unit, under guard,' he said. 'But only from the press or anyone who might show an interest in what went on. I've had to sign the official secrets act to get in here. Military gunmen shooting an unarmed civilian in a public hospital is not a circumstance anyone wants made public. There has been nothing in the papers or on TV. There's a grand policeman wants to talk to you. So does the Brig. He's been great. Seems to know everyone.'

Annie sat silent, sipping her water and digesting all this.

'I suppose it really is all over now,' she said. 'But it shouldn't ever have happened. I'll never, ever do that again. I was being so self-righteous and, I forgot to watch and see what effect my words had. Not like me.'

Max looked at her, not really following her train of thought.

'Look now you're with us again, I'll go. I'll tell Rosina and the Brig you'll be able to see them this afternoon. They are the only ordinary people who can get in.'

He went and as he left a nurse and a doctor came in. They were both in Naval uniform, the nurse in her full collar, cuffs and cap. Annie grinned at her and she in return, acknowledged the unspoken comment from one professional to another.

The doctor and nurse then proceeded to tell her exactly what had happened.

She was shocked to discover she'd been sedated and put on a ventilator while the swelling in her throat subsided. In addition they had reset and replastered her arm.

Her own last memory had been being lifted into the ambulance, but apparently that was two days ago. They reassured her that there was no permanent damage and that all would be well.

'But,' added the doctor, eyeing her keenly. 'You may find you need to talk to someone about all this.   Ignore all that official secrets stuff. If you need counselling then we'll find you someone. OK? They tell me you are off to Australia soon, but here is the number and my name.' He gave her a card. 'If you need to, ring us.'

The next visitor was the policeman whose voice Annie recalled the moment he introduced himself.

'You were there weren't you?' she said. He agreed

'I didn't mean it to happen like that you know,' she said.

'It was all very unfortunate,' he said. 'We should have been called earlier. But you madam, should learn not to play with fire, if you don't want to get burnt.'

She felt bad enough without him piling it on and said so. He seemed pleased to accept her acknowledgement of guilt, but rather to her surprise had no further questions for her.

'I came to remind you that these events are all covered by the official secrets act so this affair can be discussed with nobody. Do you understand?'

A little startled by his firmness, Annie agreed she did understand. He continued.

'No inquest on Mr Coniston-Brown's death is scheduled. I'm told you are off to Australia. If we want any more detail we'll get the Australian police to take a statement.'

With that he got up and left the room.

I get the impression, thought Annie to herself, that the idea of 'Annie in Australia' appeals to everyone. They just want me out of the way while they tidy up. No one seemed interested in any explanations I may have to offer.

The interviews had tired her and her arm was still aching. She turned over and went to sleep. She did dream though, of big and small furry animals and sandy beaches.

In the afternoon Max came back with Rosina and the Brigadier. 'You look better he said.'

'How are you, really,' said Rosina. 'That bloody psychopath, and he was so charming too.'

'I feel awful,' said Annie, who had spent the time since she'd woken up recalling the policeman's words of the morning. 'I keep asking myself. Could I have stopped him? Maybe I drove him to it. That's a human life gone. Perhaps he just needed support.'

'Don't be ridiculous. He was trying to kill you,' said Max.

'I know but one should be able to save people from themselves. No one is bad, just trapped, manoeuvred or disillusioned. He felt he couldn't bear the disgrace. His status was everything to him. If only I could have talked to him maybe I could have persuaded him back.'

'You couldn't have. He was a psychopath,' said Rosina. 'I want, I need, I'm going to have. His life was about getting what he wanted. You thwarted him. You had to be dealt with.'

'It was extraordinary at the end though,' said Annie remembering her view of the two of them in the mirror. 'He wasn't afraid. He was treating the whole thing as a game. He seemed to think we were going to a fancy dress party. He taped my mouth so I couldn't argue with him.'

'He was an old fashioned misogynist, and it was just me, me, me,' said Rosina.

'But I could have talked him down, especially as I still think I tipped him over in the first place.'

'Don't you think he knew that?' responded Rosina. 'I think he just hated women, especially those with opinions who spoke up. That's what the tape was about. He'd made his decision and didn't want to back down. Don't you forget he wanted you dead as well. If it hadn't been for the Brig. you would have been. He was here that day to get some award or other.'

'So it was just coincidence I didn't get shot too?' said Annie. 'Just like it was only coincidence I bumped into him. I'd got lost in the building renovations.'

'Except that I didn't think you really believe in coincidence do you?' said Max.

'I don't,' said Annie.

The Brigadier, who had been listening, standing in the back ground, came forward and spoke.

'Sister Larriot, Miss Larriot,' he began.

'Annie,' said Annie interrupting him.

'Annie,' he went on, 'It wasn't just me that day, you know. You were recognised by many people on those monitors. They never for one minute believed you were a genuine bomber. You do have the respect of your colleagues.'

Annie looked at him, a little startled. He seemed to be the only person who really understood where she was coming from. She turned to Max.

'The CCTV was in colour,' she said. So they knew me and… So they shot him and left me. But I still nearly got strangled by that noose.'

The Brigadier went on.

'It's never easy to tread the fine line between sticking to your principles and speaking out. You must remember you weren't the professional in charge. You were off duty. You thought you were having a sensible conversation with another adult. You could not know he was a madman. You simply must not take responsibility for his death any more than the marine who shot him should. That sailor did his duty. Coniston-Brown did what he did to himself. It would be a maudlin indulgence on your part to think anything else. I don't think you're that sort of woman.'

'Listen to the man,' said Max.

E mail :Max McClaren to Mrs Julia McClaren

Mum

Aunty Annie is finally on the plane. She has 6 weeks sick leave. She's well now, arm in plaster though. Don't worry. She'll tell you all about it. She lands Sydney tomorrow, but please, please keep her out of trouble and in Oz. for at least a month. And she wants to go panning for gold at Gulgong, though how with that arm, I don't know. Expect she'll find a way. I did do my best.

Max

THE END

You have just read '**A Midwife Abroad**' by **Avalon Weston**
If you enjoyed it, I have written other things, but perhaps for different audiences.

Sian and the Winterwife is a fairytale for younger children, written originally for my daughter, about a young Welsh girl who saves her village.

*

The Disappearing Snake, a Journey, is a novel for adults and deals with adult themes.

The Night Visitor and other stories are short stories about happenings in the lives of women.

If you would like to contact me, or have your name on a mailing list for further stories, avalon.weston@gmail.com
Or visit my website
avalonweston@wordpress.com

My next book, soon to be available via Amazon
ALL THE SKY
A short novel for young adults about six foxes forced to leave London for Devon. due to over population. It would like to be a new 'Watership Down' or 'Wind in the Willows'

All my work will eventually be available in both ebook and print book format.